SPELLBINDING READS

How to enjoy your bewitched book journal!

***The Great TBR List:** 13 pages allow you to easily list 546 books 'To Be Read.'

***'Spooky Good Books'** and **'Magical & Memorable'** pages invite you to challenge yourself to read different books and rank your reads!

***The Bewitched Bookshelf:** Decorate with the top 50 books you read & journaled about.

***Journal Pages:** 250 pages have been included to rate & review each book you read. Print off a picture of the cover & attach it in the designated spot, or lean on your artistic skills to recreate it!

***The Dusty DNFs (Did Not Finish):** Not every book is for every reader. 6 pages are included (72 entries) for you to list the title and your progress before you decided to put the book down (e.g. 100/200 pages read, or 50%). A space is included for commentary.

***Extra Pages:** 18 extra lined pages have been added in case those included for other topics didn't happen to be enough for your particular reading habits!

*For best results: use pens, pencils, or markers that are non-bleeding.

**For merch, extra tips, and free templates related to this book journal, go to JHouserWrites.com

* THE GREAT TBR LIST *

# * THE GREAT TBR LIST * 

* The Great TBR List *

* THE GREAT TBR LIST *

* The Great TBR List *

* THE GREAT TBR List *

* The Great TBR List *

* THE GREAT TBR LIST *

* The Great TBR List *

* THE GREAT TBR LIST *

* THE GREAT TBR LIST *

* The Great TBR List *

* The Great TBR List *

 Spooky Good Books 

A book with witches____

Review #__________

A book with vampires____

Review #__________

A book with creepy crawlies____

Review #__________

A book with gothic vibes____

Review #__________

A book with ghosts____

Review #__________

A book with undead____

Review #__________

A book with a familiar____

Review #__________

A book with sweet/cozy vibes_______________________________

    Review #________

A book with fairies/elves__________________________________

Review #________

A book with elemental magic_______________________________

    Review #________

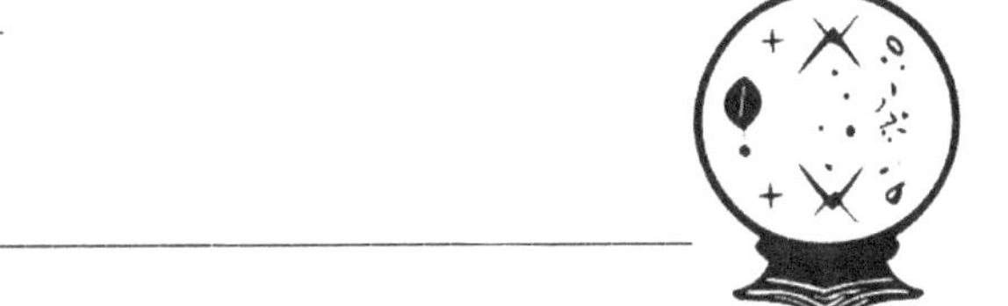

A book with prophesies____________________________________

Review #________

A book with spells/potions________________________________

    Review #________

A book with winged people/beasts__________________________

Review #________

A book with
shifters/werewolves_______________________________________

    Review #________

A book with monsters______________________________________

Review #________

 # Magical & Memorable 

Most unique magic system_______________________

Review #_________

Creepiest villain/antagonist_______________________

Review #_________

Most bone-chilling read_______________________

Review #_________

Best cozy story_______________________

Review #_________

My most surprising read:_______________________

Review #_________

A series worth binging_______________________

Review #s_______________________

A book/series worth rereading_______________________

Review #s_______________________

New-to-me authors I'll be reading more from_______________________

____

____

Review #s_______________________

Favorite tropes & best books for them_______________________

____

____

____

Review #s_______________________

THE BEWITCHED BOOKSHELF

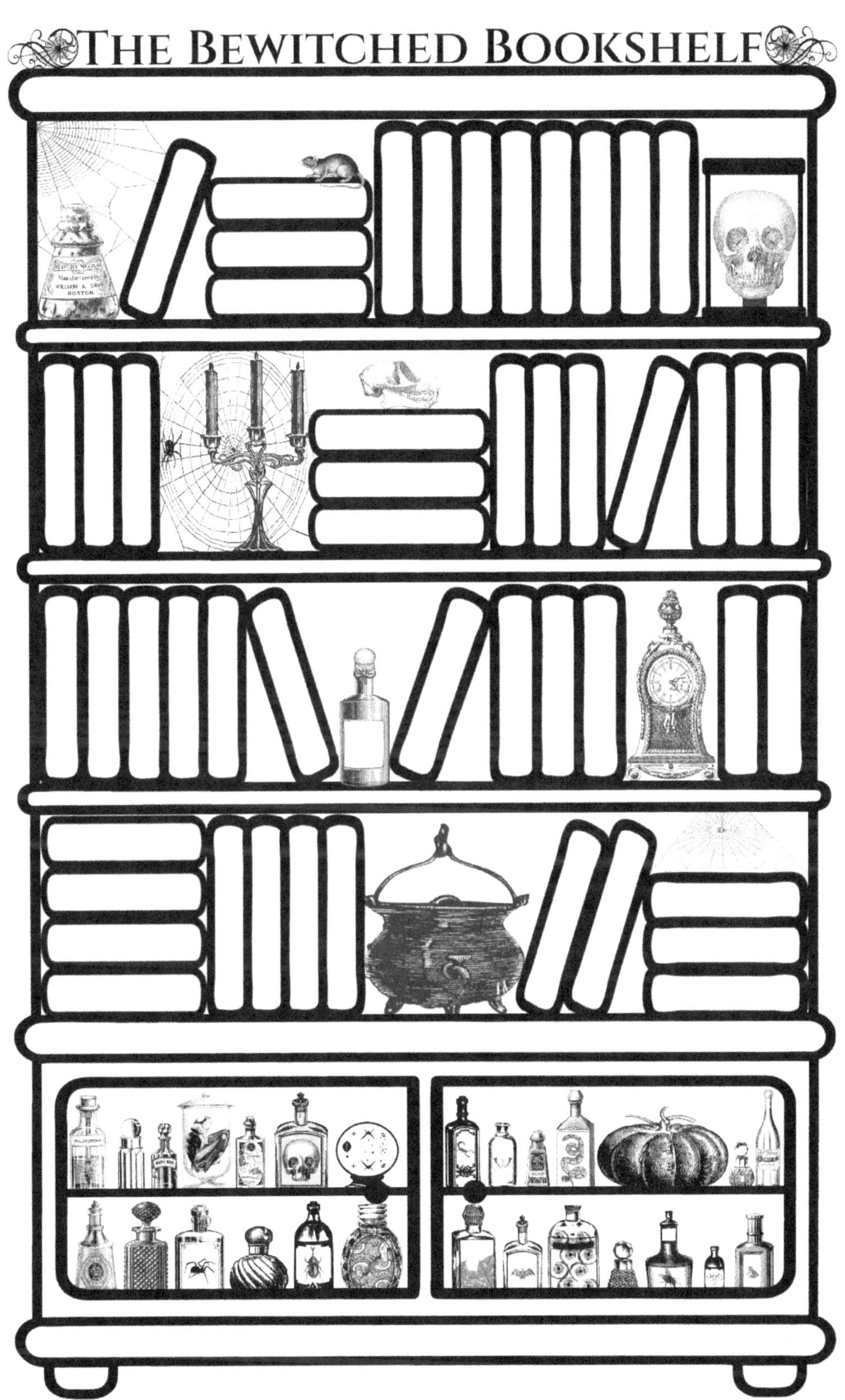

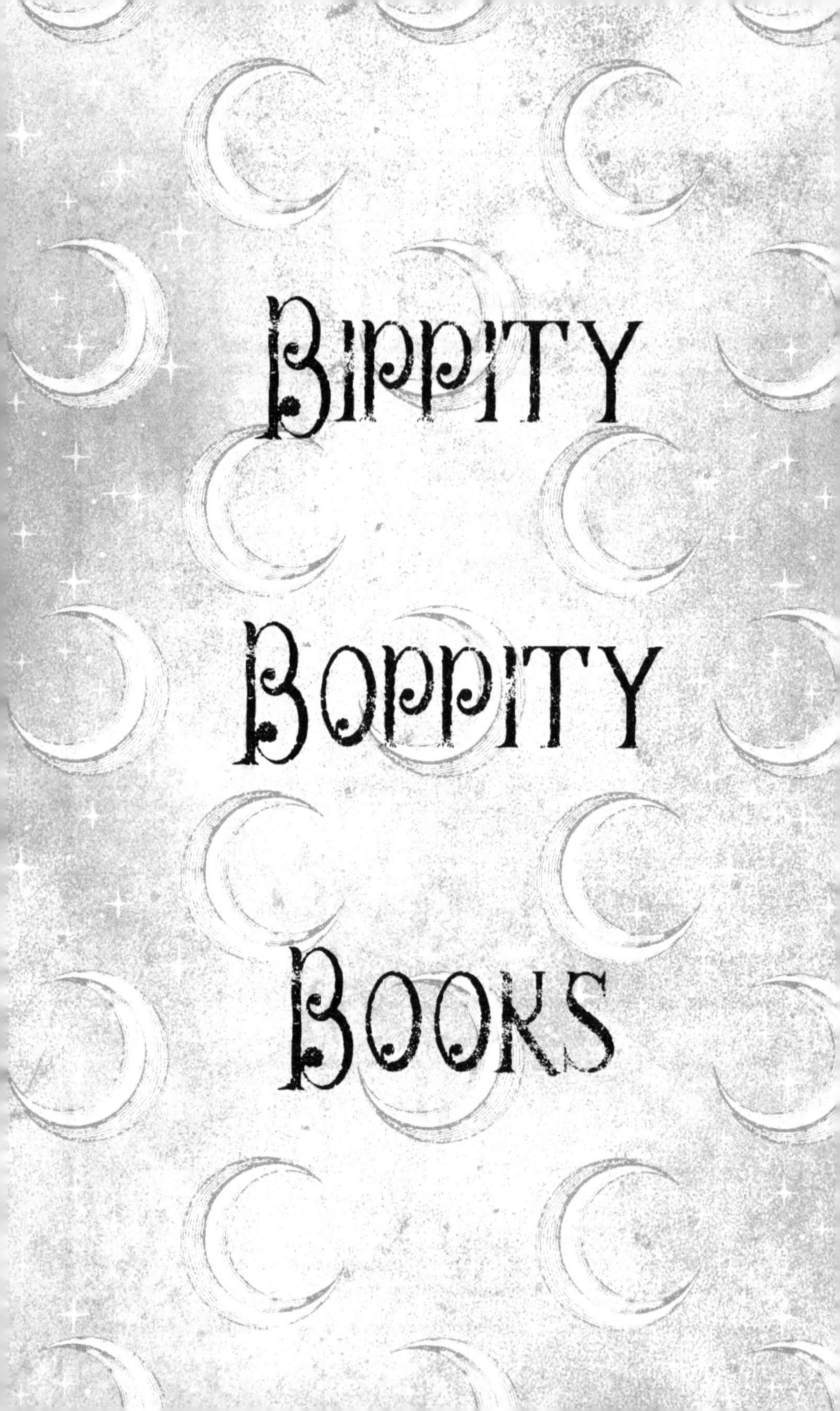
Bippity
Boppity
Books

TITLE: _______________________

GENRE: _______________________

SERIES: _______________________

AUTHOR: _______________________

PAGES: _______________________

STARTED: _______________________

FINISHED: _______________________

☆ ☆ ☆ ☆ ☆

FORMAT READ: EBOOK / PRINT / AUDIOBOOK

✔ SYNOPSIS/THINGS I LIKED:

____

____

____

____

🚫 THINGS I DIDN'T LIKE:

____

____

____

____

✎ FAVORITE QUOTE(S):

____

____

____

____

____

____

____

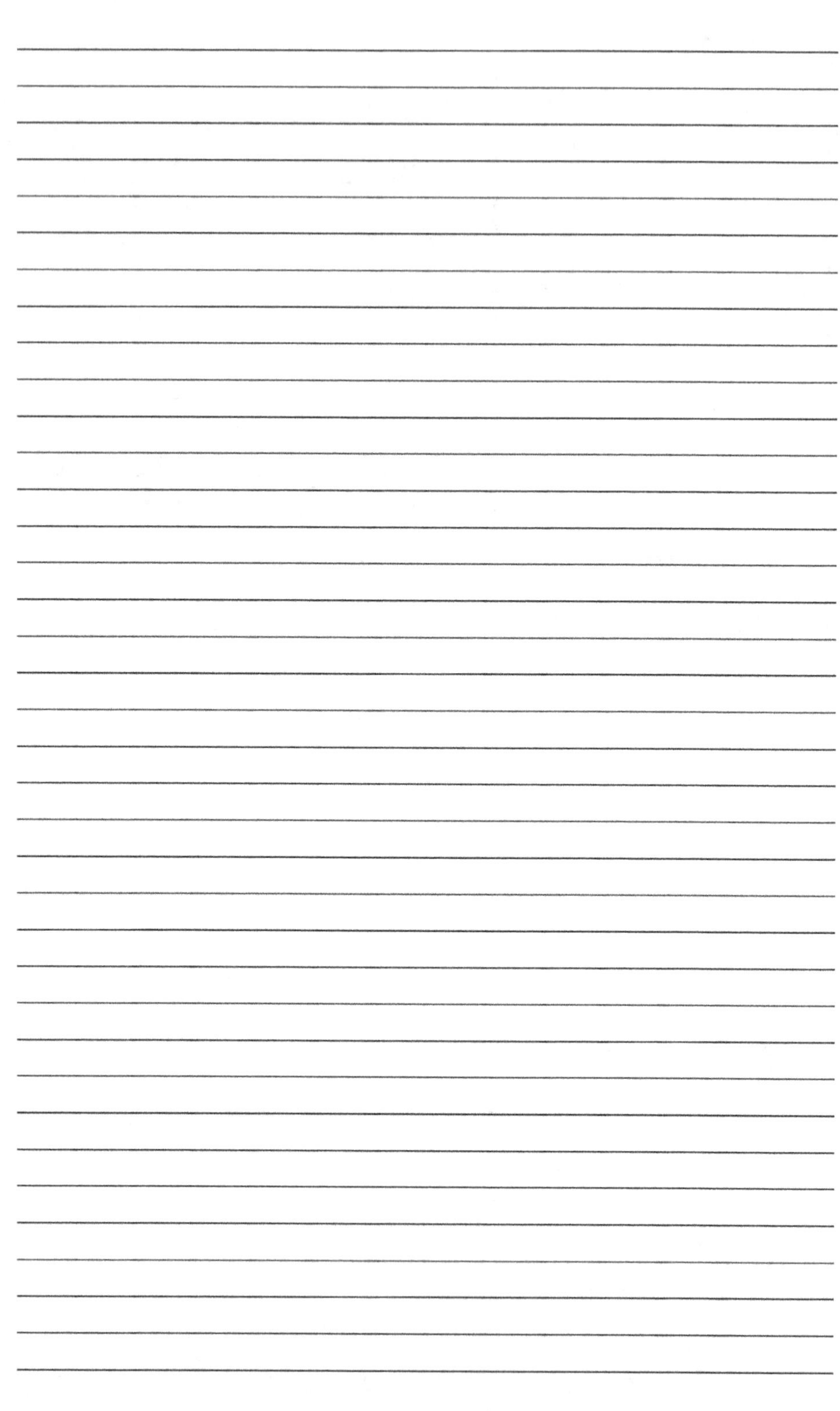

TITLE: ____________________

GENRE: ____________________

SERIES: ____________________

AUTHOR: ____________________

PAGES: ____________________

STARTED: ____________________

FINISHED: ____________________

☆☆☆☆☆

FORMAT READ: EBOOK / PRINT / AUDIOBOOK

✓ SYNOPSIS/THINGS I LIKED:

____

____

____

____

🚫 THINGS I DIDN'T LIKE:

____

____

____

____

✐ FAVORITE QUOTE(S):

____

____

____

____

____

____

____

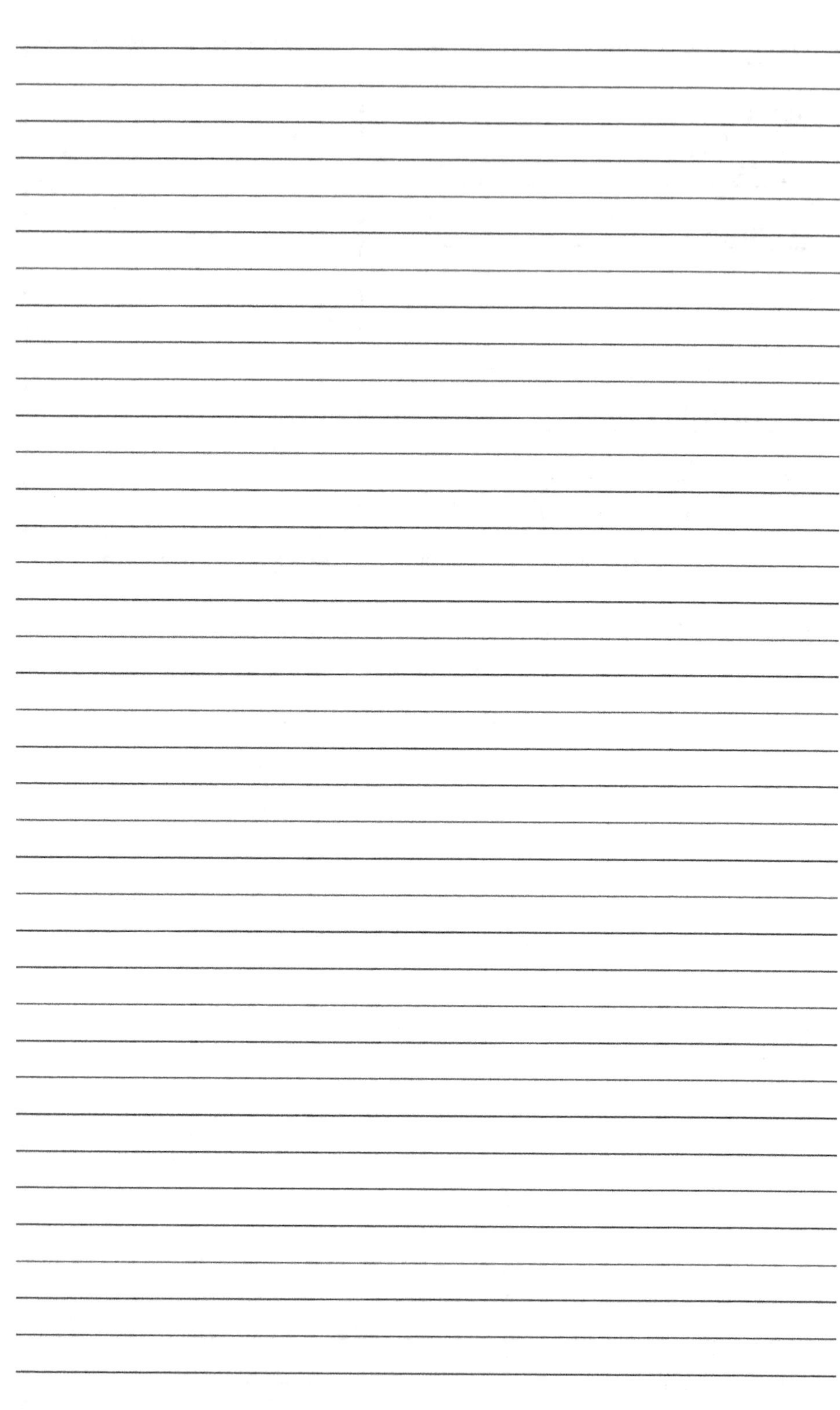

☑ SYNOPSIS/THINGS I LIKED:
🚫 THINGS I DIDN'T LIKE:
✎ FAVORITE QUOTE(S):
TITLE:
GENRE:
SERIES:
AUTHOR:
PAGES:
STARTED:
FINISHED:
FORMAT READ: EBOOK / PRINT / AUDIOBOOK

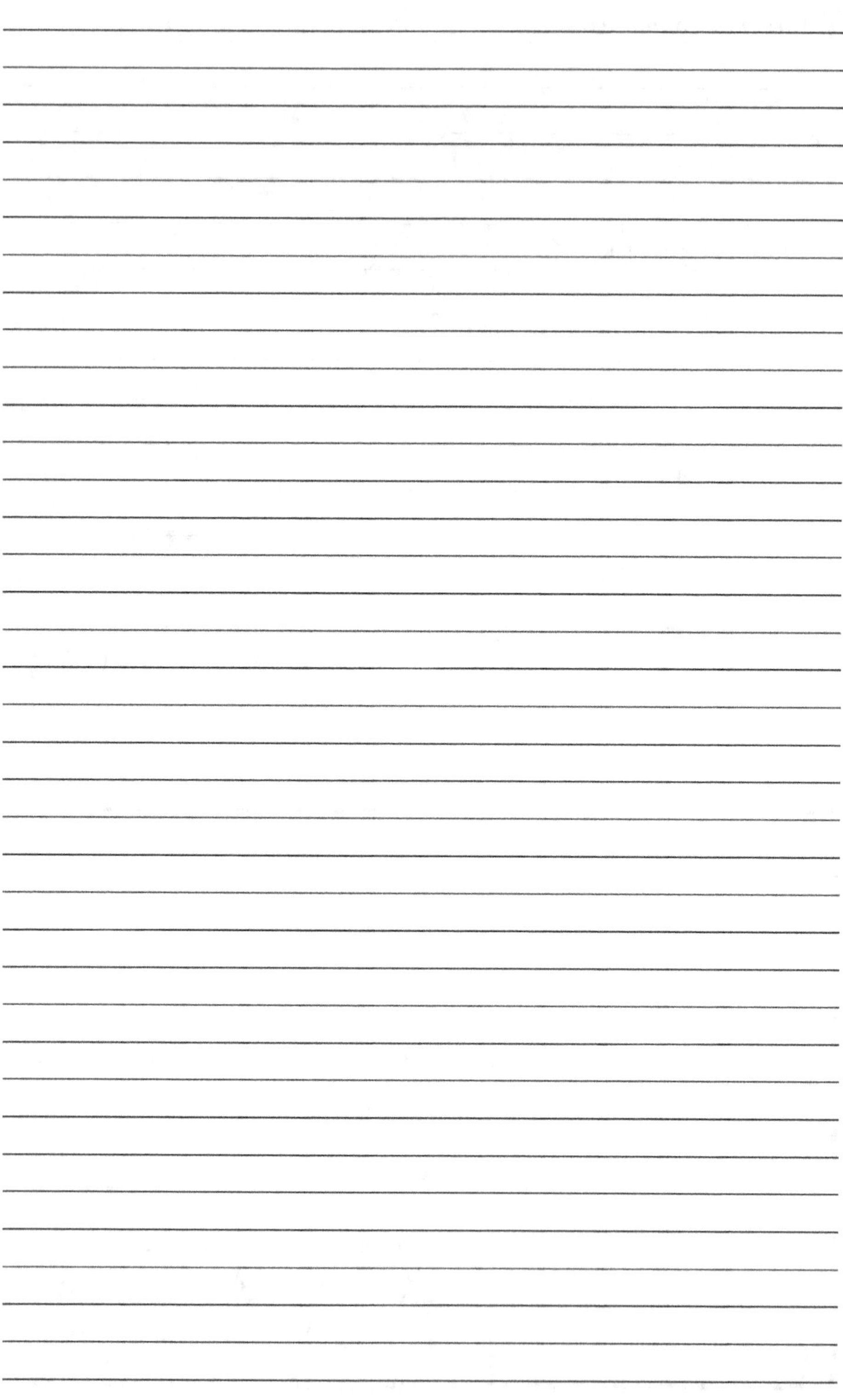

☑ **Synopsis/Things I liked:**

____

____

____

____

🚫 **Things I didn't like:**

____

____

____

____

✎ **Favorite quote(s):**

____

____

____

____

____

____

____

____

Title: _______________________

Genre: _______________________

Series: _______________________

Author: _______________________

Pages: _______________________

Started: _______________________

Finished: _______________________

☆ ☆ ☆ ☆ ☆

Format read: Ebook / Print / Audiobook

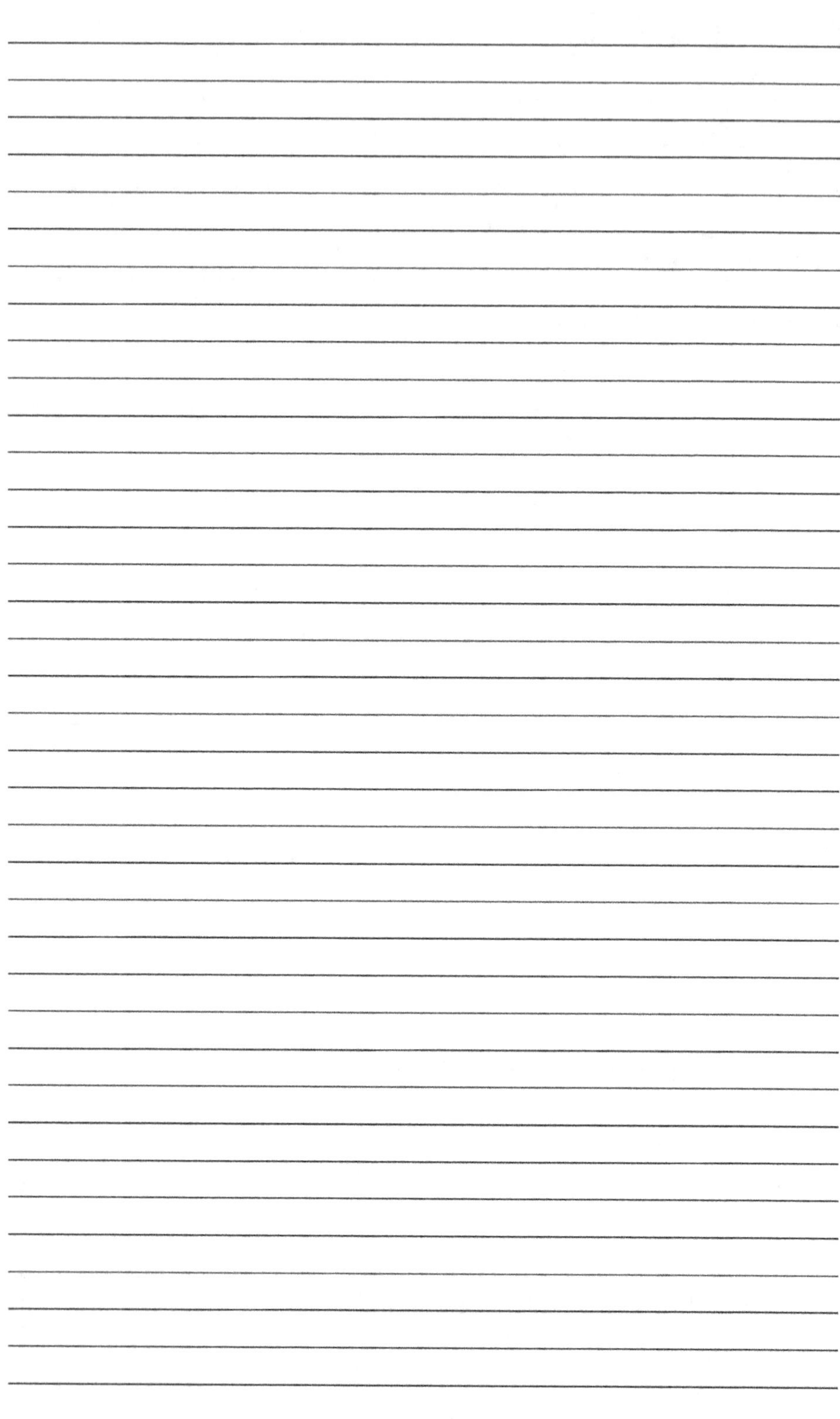

TITLE:

GENRE:

SERIES:

AUTHOR:

PAGES:

STARTED:

FINISHED:

FORMAT READ: EBOOK / PRINT / AUDIOBOOK

✓ SYNOPSIS/THINGS I LIKED:

🚫 THINGS I DIDN'T LIKE:

✏️ FAVORITE QUOTE(S):

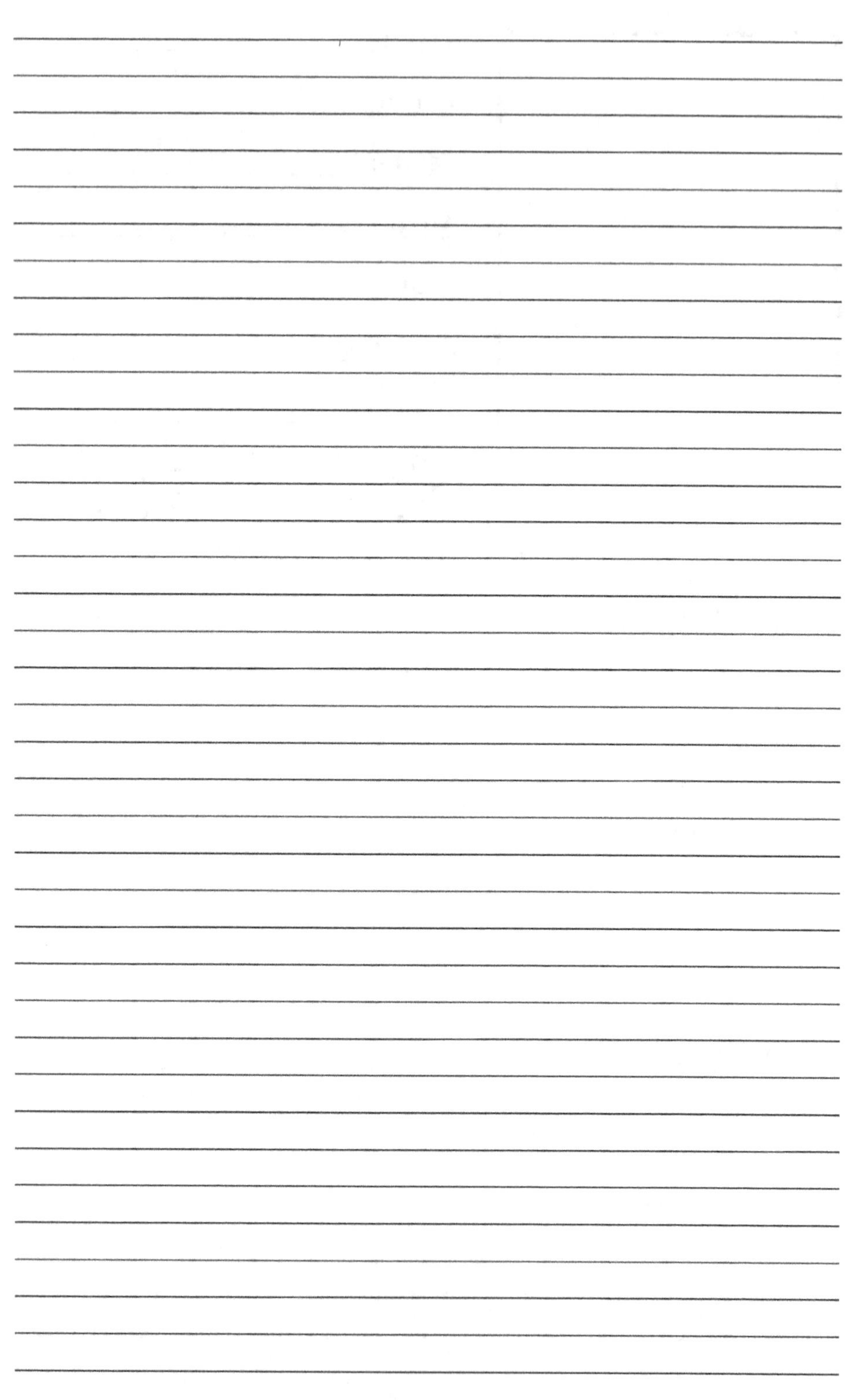

TITLE: _______________

GENRE: _______________

SERIES: _______________

AUTHOR: _______________

PAGES: _______________

STARTED: _______________

FINISHED: _______________

☆ ☆ ☆ ☆ ☆

FORMAT READ: EBOOK / PRINT / AUDIOBOOK

✔ **SYNOPSIS/THINGS I LIKED:**

____

____

____

____

🚫 **THINGS I DIDN'T LIKE:**

____

____

____

____

✏ **FAVORITE QUOTE(S):**

____

____

____

____

____

____

____

____

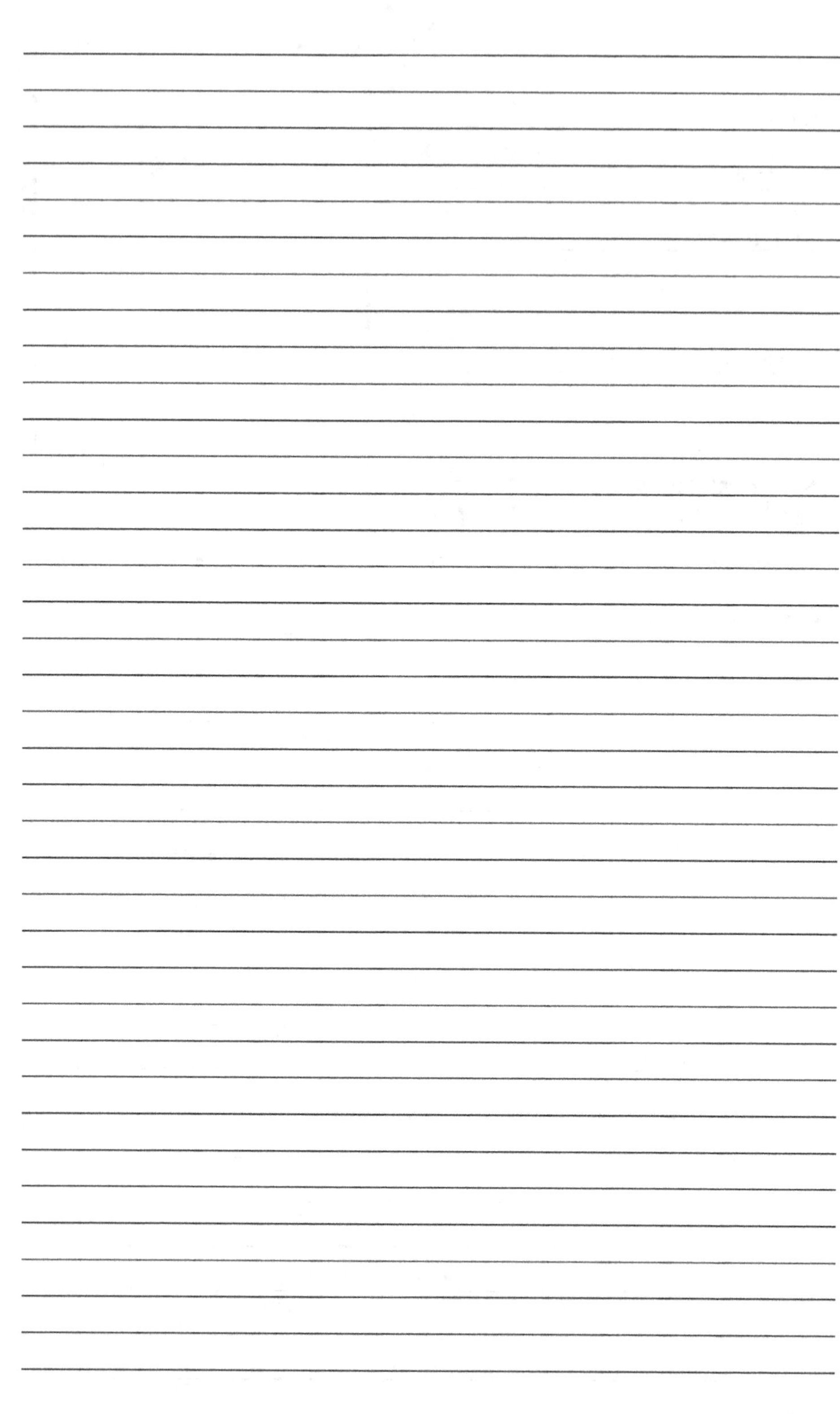

TITLE:

GENRE:

SERIES:

AUTHOR:

PAGES:

STARTED:

FINISHED:

FORMAT READ: EBOOK / PRINT / AUDIOBOOK

7

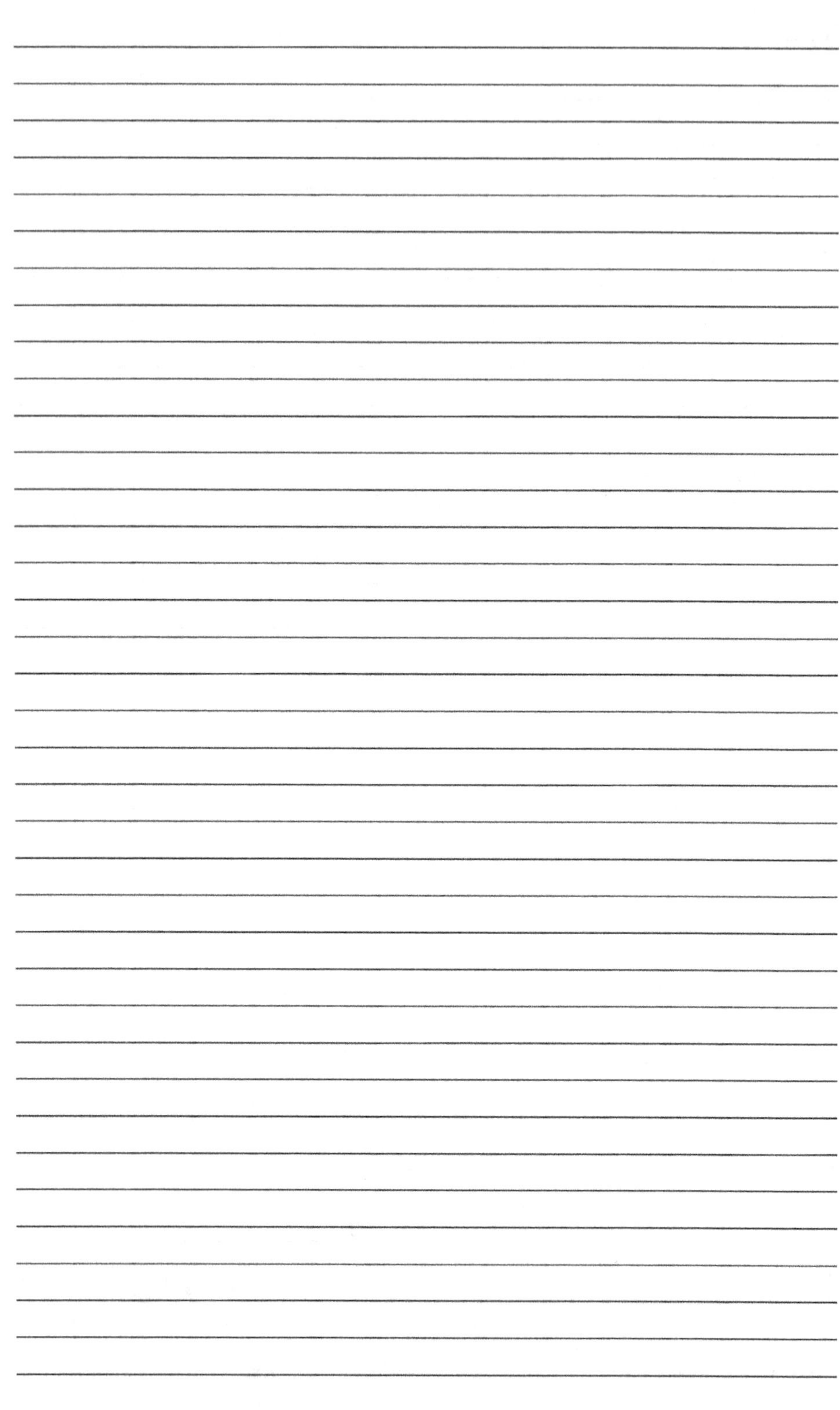

TITLE:

GENRE:

SERIES:

AUTHOR:

PAGES:

STARTED:

FINISHED:

FORMAT READ: EBOOK / PRINT / AUDIOBOOK

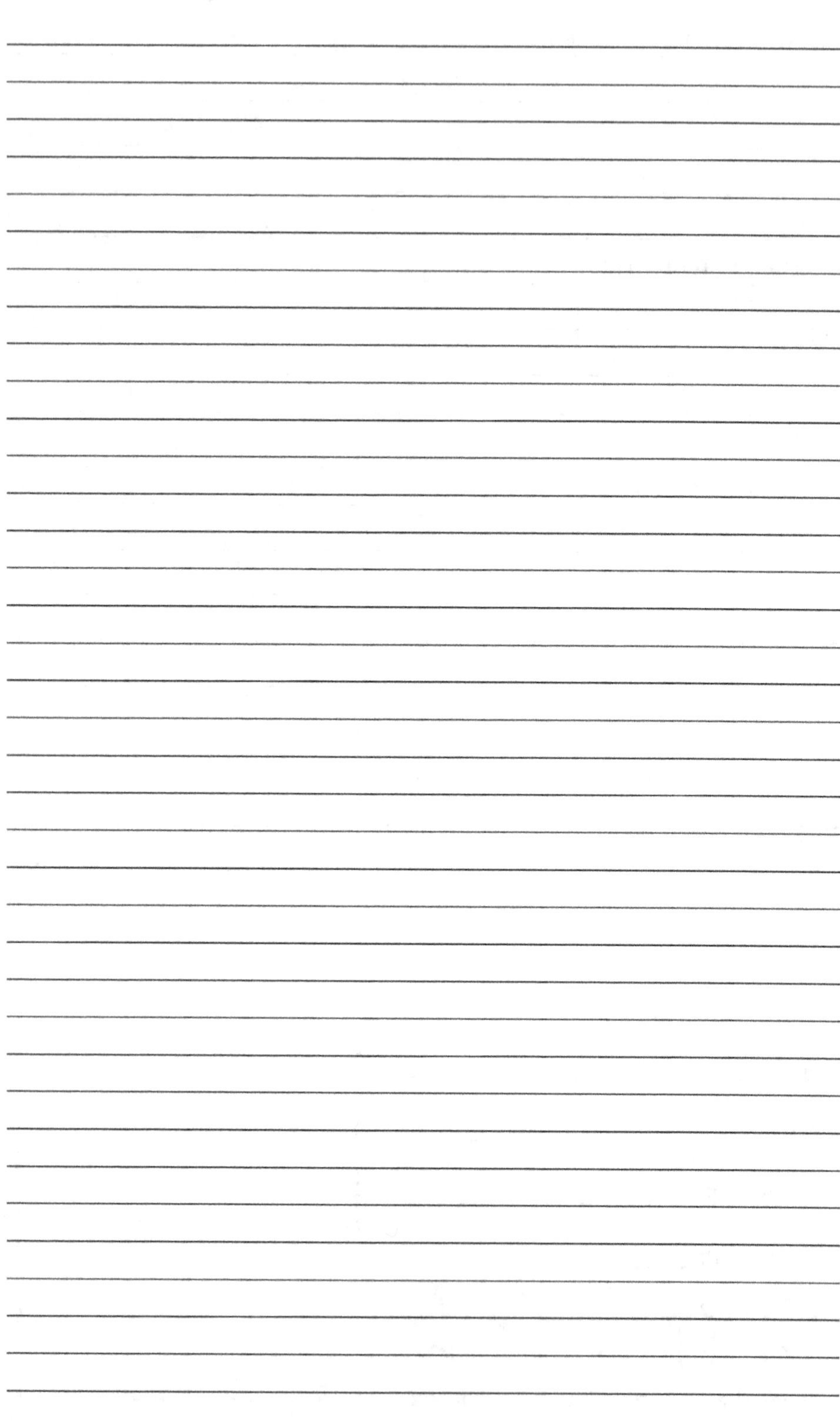

TITLE: ___________________________

GENRE: ___________________________

SERIES: ___________________________

AUTHOR: ___________________________

PAGES: ___________________________

STARTED: ___________________________

FINISHED: ___________________________

☆ ☆ ☆ ☆ ☆

FORMAT READ: EBOOK / PRINT / AUDIOBOOK

✔ SYNOPSIS/THINGS I LIKED:

____

____

____

____

🚫 THINGS I DIDN'T LIKE:

____

____

____

____

✎ FAVORITE QUOTE(S):

____

____

____

____

____

____

____

____

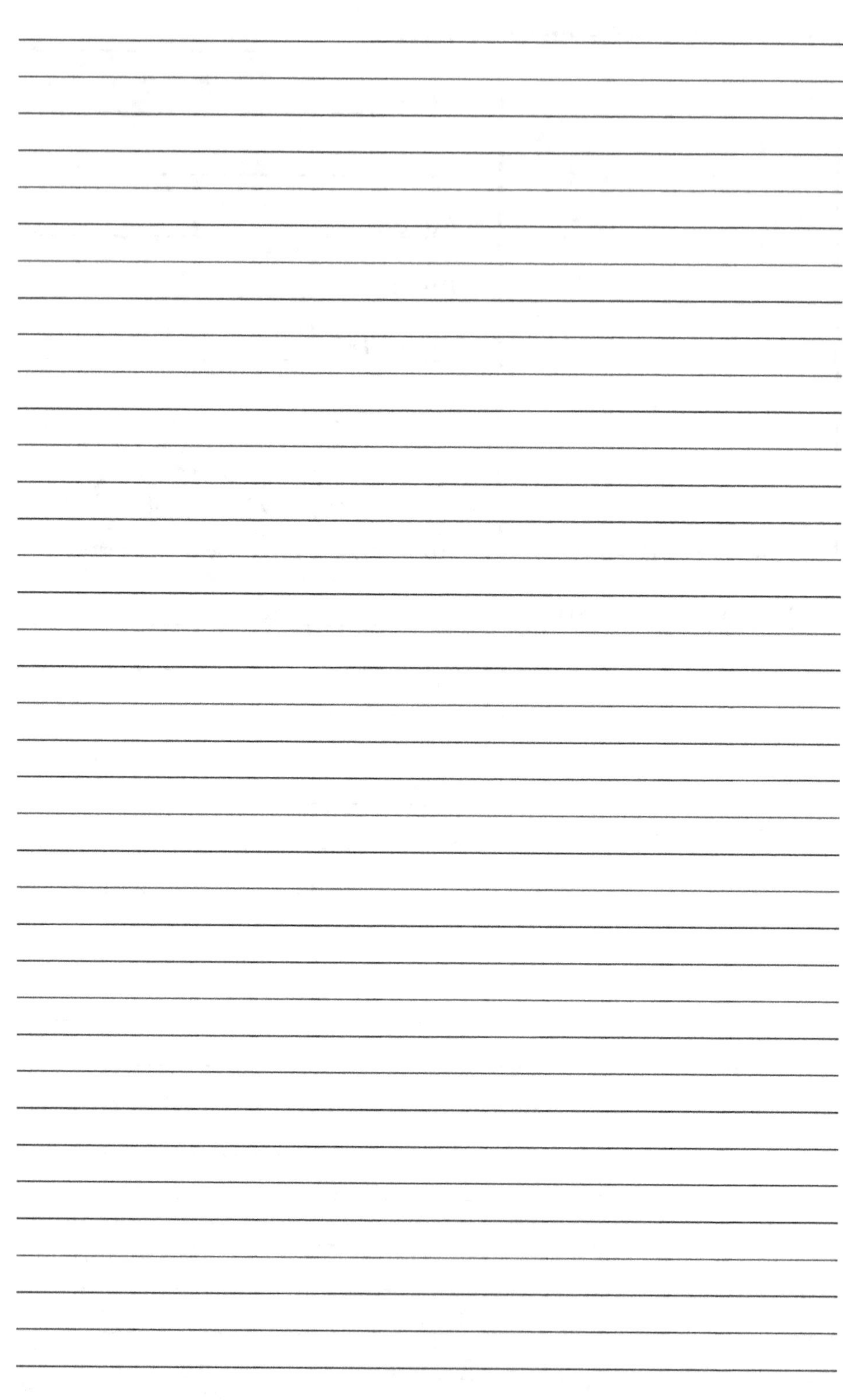

TITLE: _______________________

GENRE: _______________________

SERIES: _______________________

AUTHOR: _______________________

PAGES: _______________________

STARTED: _______________________

FINISHED: _______________________

★ ★ ★ ★ ☆

FORMAT READ: EBOOK / PRINT / AUDIOBOOK

✓ SYNOPSIS/THINGS I LIKED:

____

____

____

____

⊘ THINGS I DIDN'T LIKE:

____

____

____

____

✎ FAVORITE QUOTE(S):

____

____

____

____

____

____

____

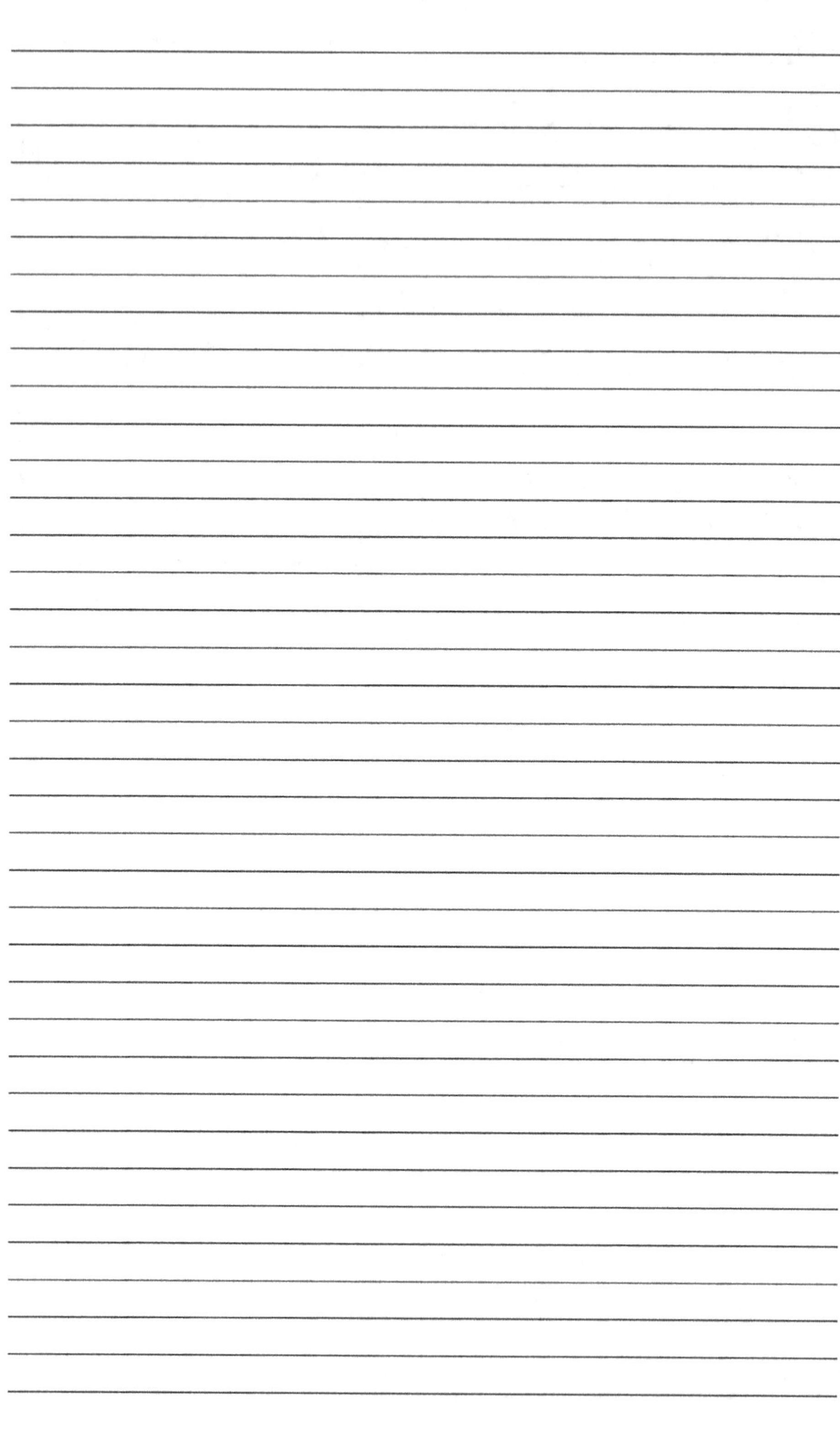

TITLE:

GENRE:

SERIES:

AUTHOR:

PAGES:

STARTED:

FINISHED:

FORMAT READ: EBOOK / PRINT / AUDIOBOOK

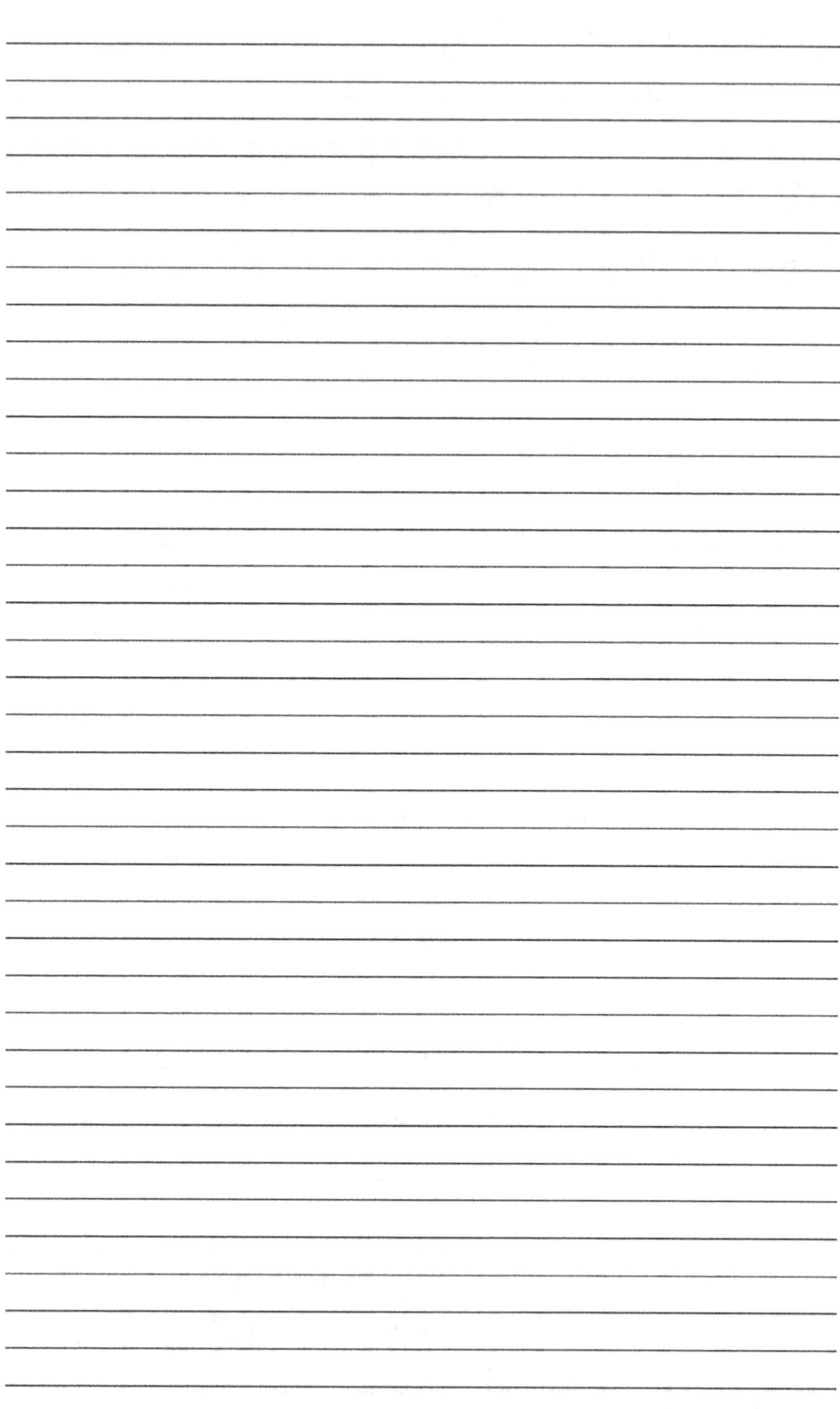

SYNOPSIS/THINGS I LIKED:

THINGS I DIDN'T LIKE:

FAVORITE QUOTE(S):

TITLE:

GENRE:

SERIES:

AUTHOR:

PAGES:

STARTED:

FINISHED:

☆☆☆☆☆

FORMAT READ: EBOOK / PRINT / AUDIOBOOK

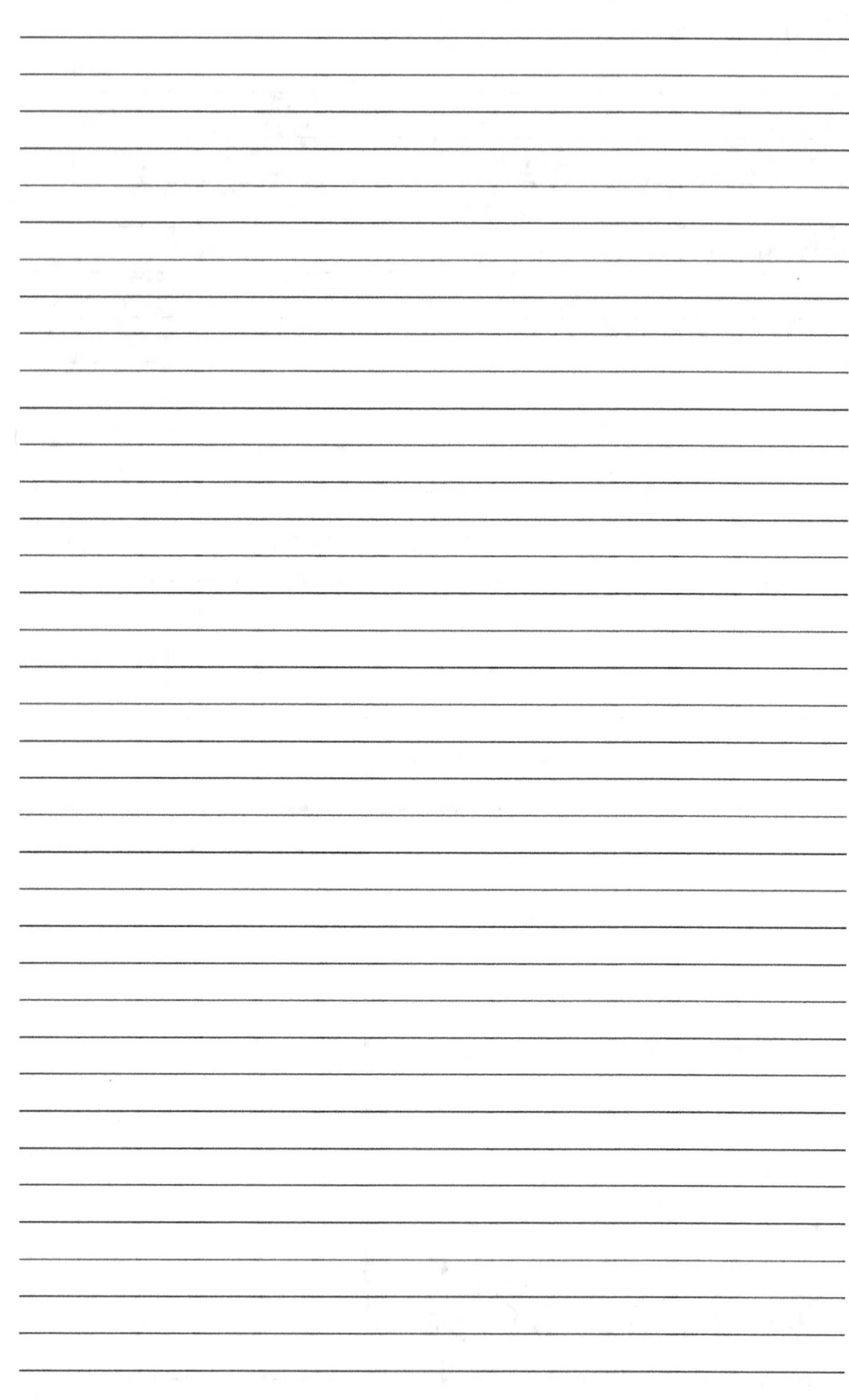

<table><tr><td style="border:2px dashed #000; width:40%; height:400px;"></td><td>

TITLE: _______________________

GENRE: _______________________

SERIES: _______________________

AUTHOR: _______________________

PAGES: _______________________

STARTED: _______________________

FINISHED: _______________________

☆ ☆ ☆ ☆ ☆

FORMAT READ: EBOOK / PRINT / AUDIOBOOK

</td></tr></table>

✔ **SYNOPSIS/THINGS I LIKED:**

____

____

____

____

🚫 **THINGS I DIDN'T LIKE:**

____

____

____

____

✎ **FAVORITE QUOTE(S):**

____

____

____

____

____

____

____

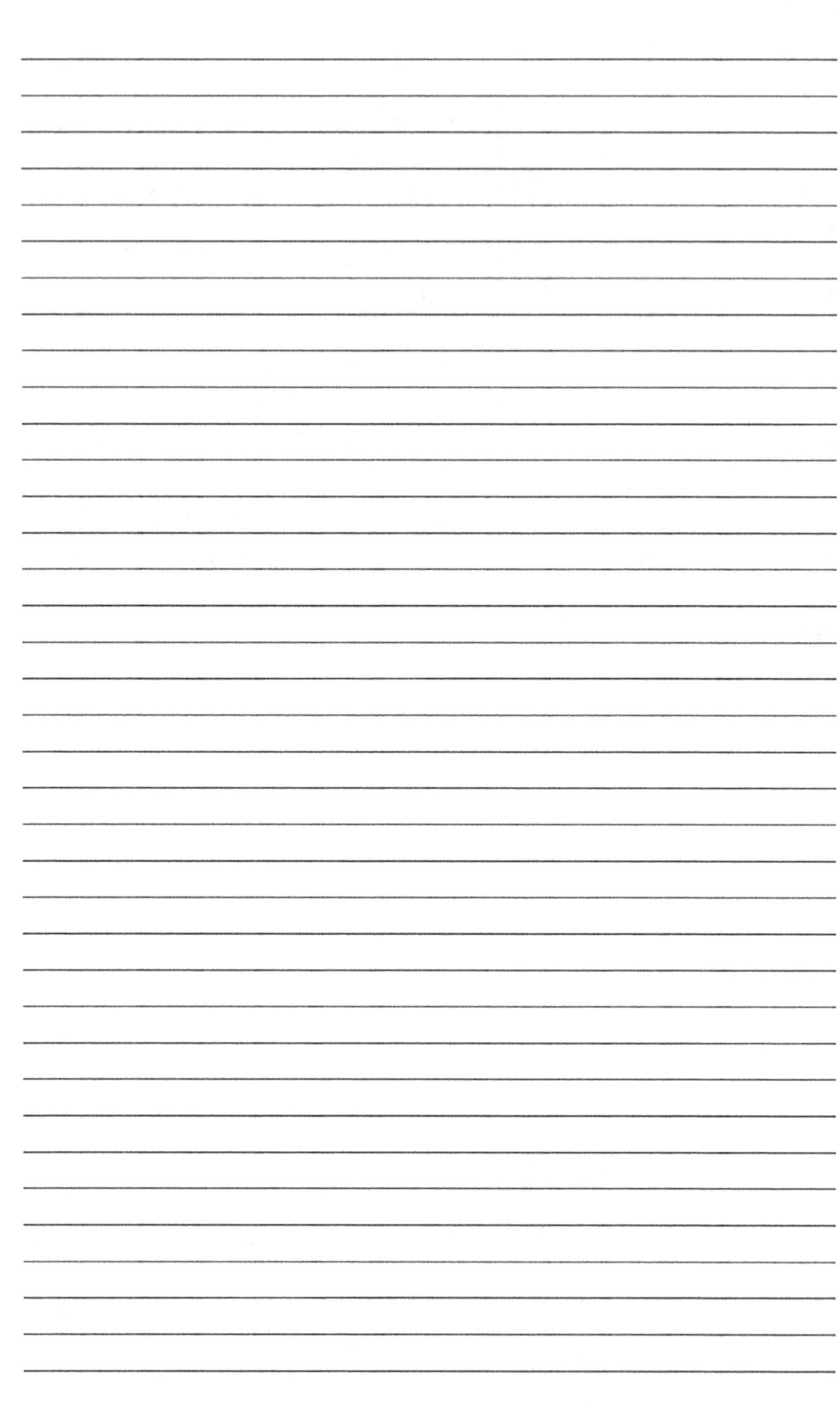

TITLE:

GENRE:

SERIES:

AUTHOR:

PAGES:

STARTED:

FINISHED:

☆☆☆☆☆

FORMAT READ: EBOOK / PRINT / AUDIOBOOK

SYNOPSIS/THINGS I LIKED:

THINGS I DIDN'T LIKE:

FAVORITE QUOTE(S):

TITLE:

GENRE:

SERIES:

AUTHOR:

PAGES:

STARTED:

FINISHED:

FORMAT READ: EBOOK / PRINT / AUDIOBOOK

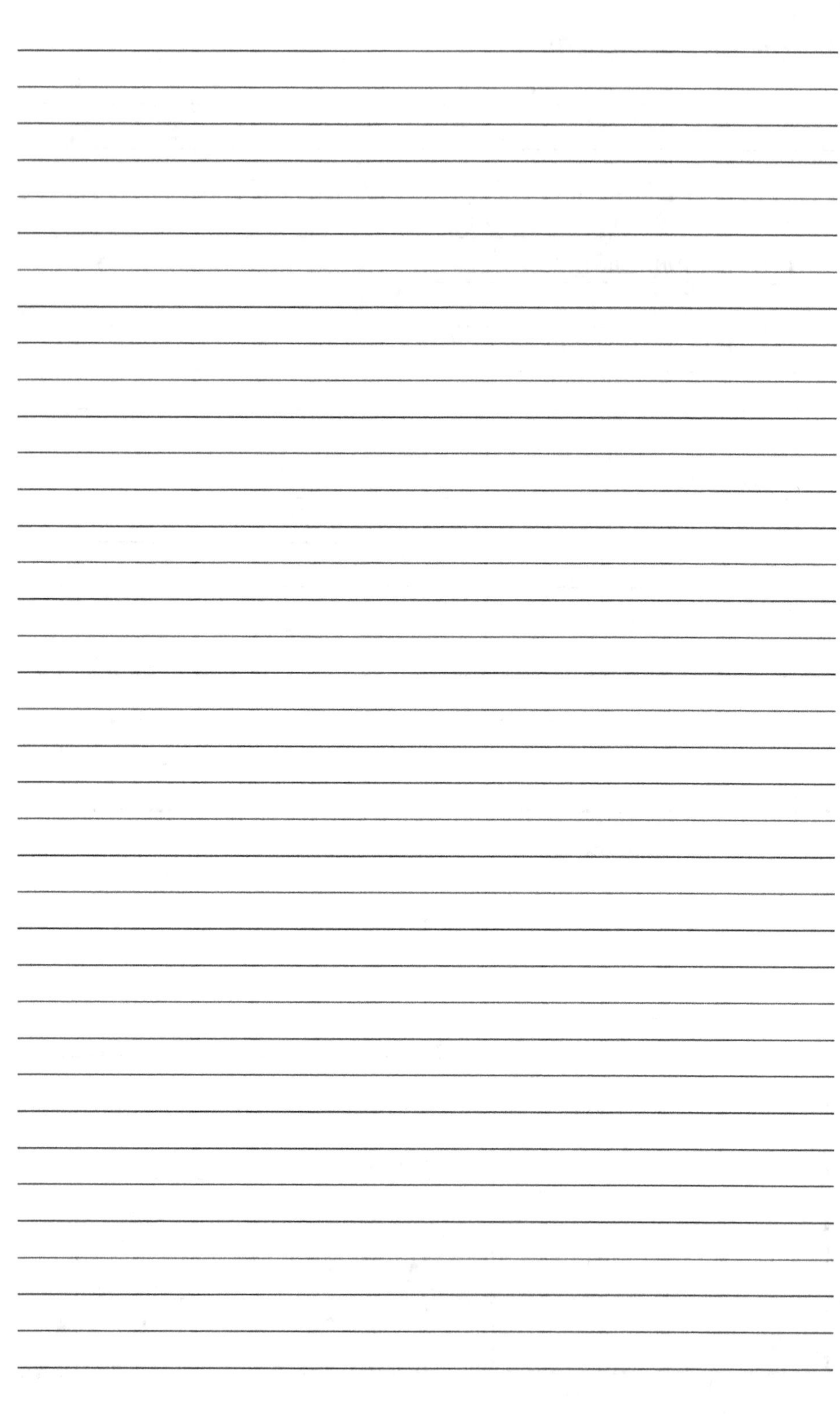

TITLE:

GENRE:

SERIES:

AUTHOR:

PAGES:

STARTED:

FINISHED:

FORMAT READ: EBOOK / PRINT / AUDIOBOOK

TITLE:

GENRE:

SERIES:

AUTHOR:

PAGES:

STARTED:

FINISHED:

FORMAT READ: EBOOK / PRINT / AUDIOBOOK

SYNOPSIS/THINGS I LIKED:

THINGS I DIDN'T LIKE:

FAVORITE QUOTE(S):

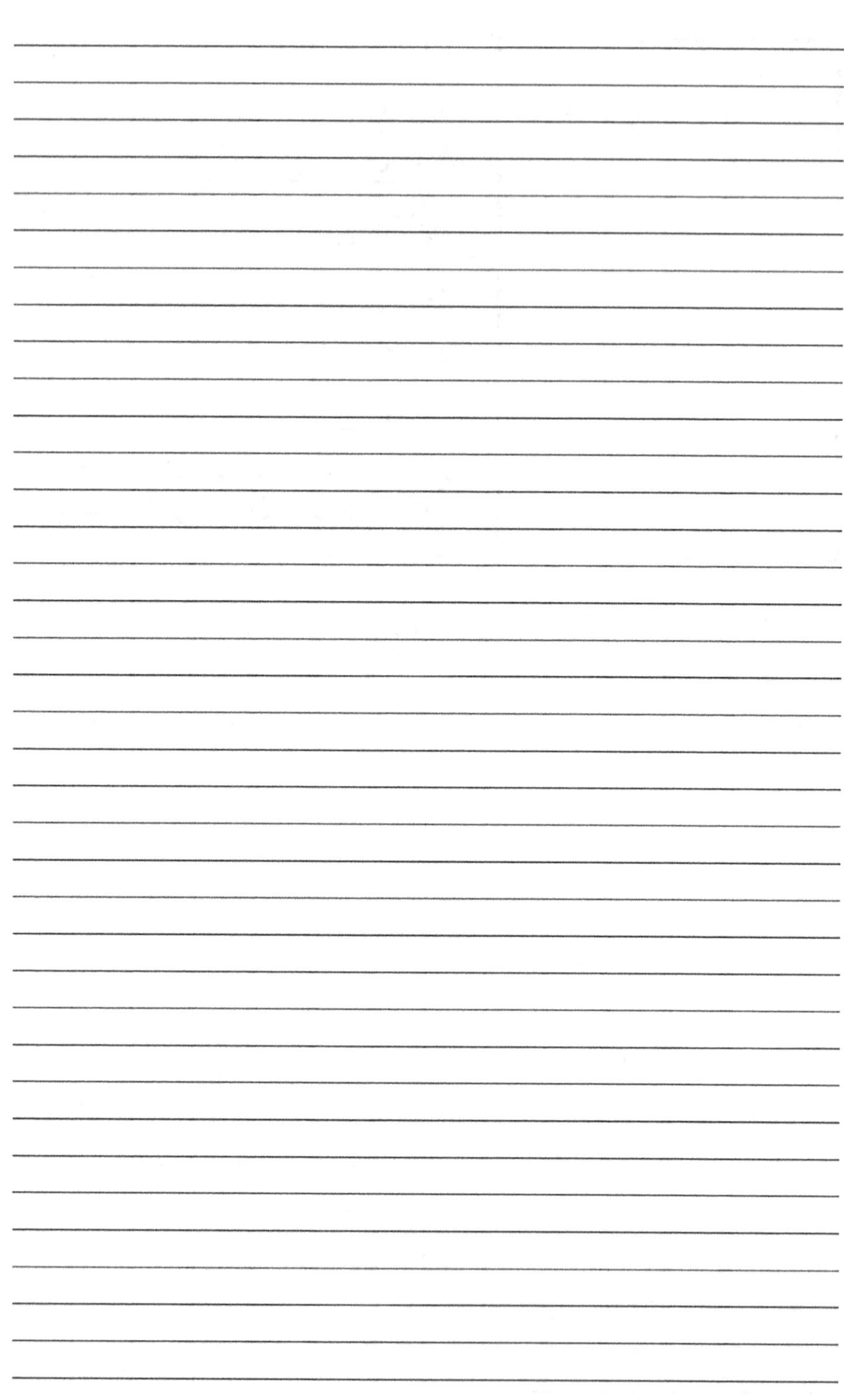

TITLE: _______________

GENRE: _______________

SERIES: _______________

AUTHOR: _______________

PAGES: _______________

STARTED: _______________

FINISHED: _______________

☆ ☆ ☆ ☆ ☆

FORMAT READ: EBOOK / PRINT / AUDIOBOOK

✓ **SYNOPSIS/THINGS I LIKED:**

____
____
____
____

🚫 **THINGS I DIDN'T LIKE:**

____
____
____
____

✏ **FAVORITE QUOTE(S):**

____
____
____
____
____
____
____

SYNOPSIS/THINGS I LIKED:

THINGS I DIDN'T LIKE:

FAVORITE QUOTE(S):

TITLE:

GENRE:

SERIES:

AUTHOR:

PAGES:

STARTED:

FINISHED:

FORMAT READ: EBOOK / PRINT / AUDIOBOOK 19

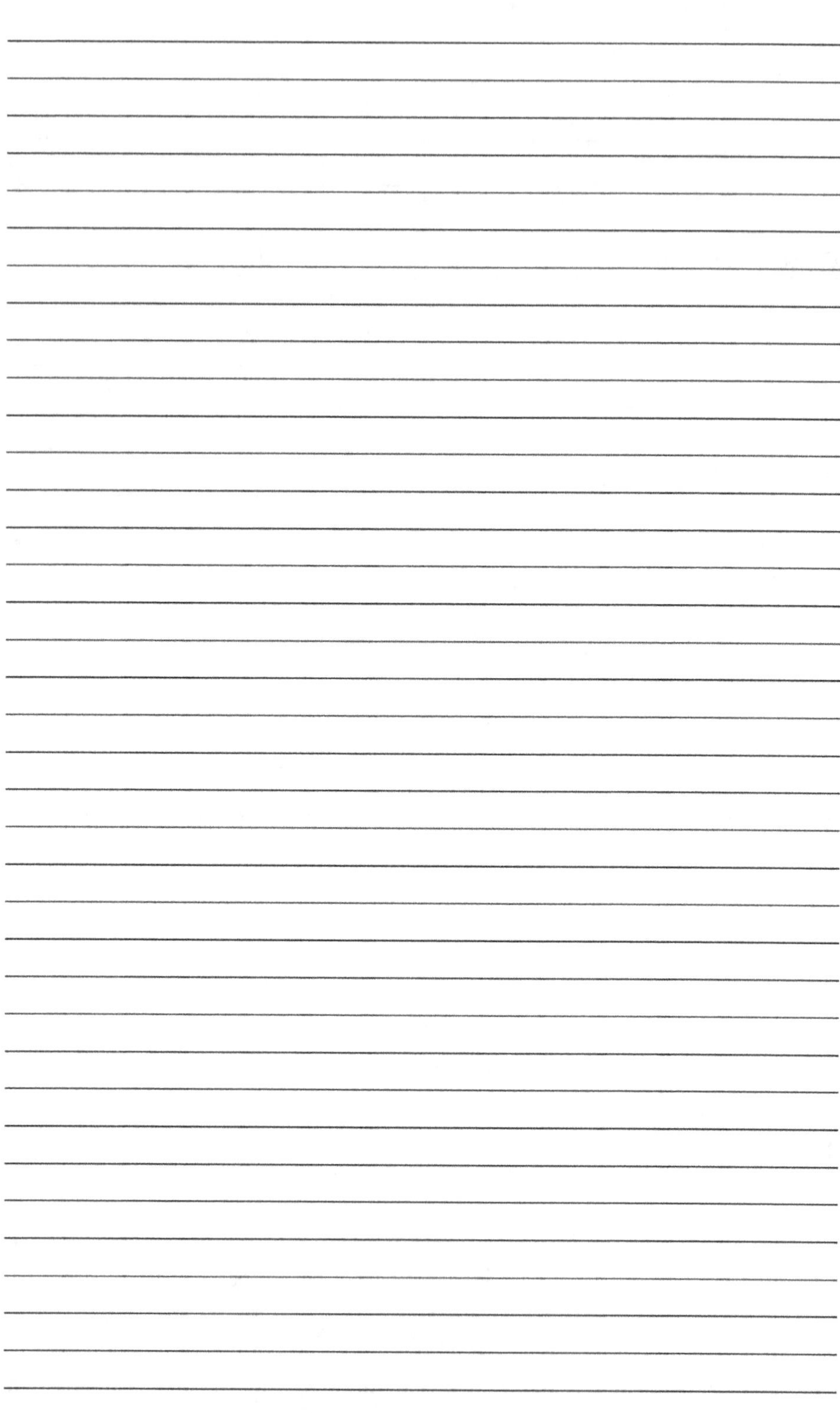

TITLE:

GENRE:

SERIES:

AUTHOR:

PAGES:

STARTED:

FINISHED:

FORMAT READ: EBOOK / PRINT / AUDIOBOOK

20

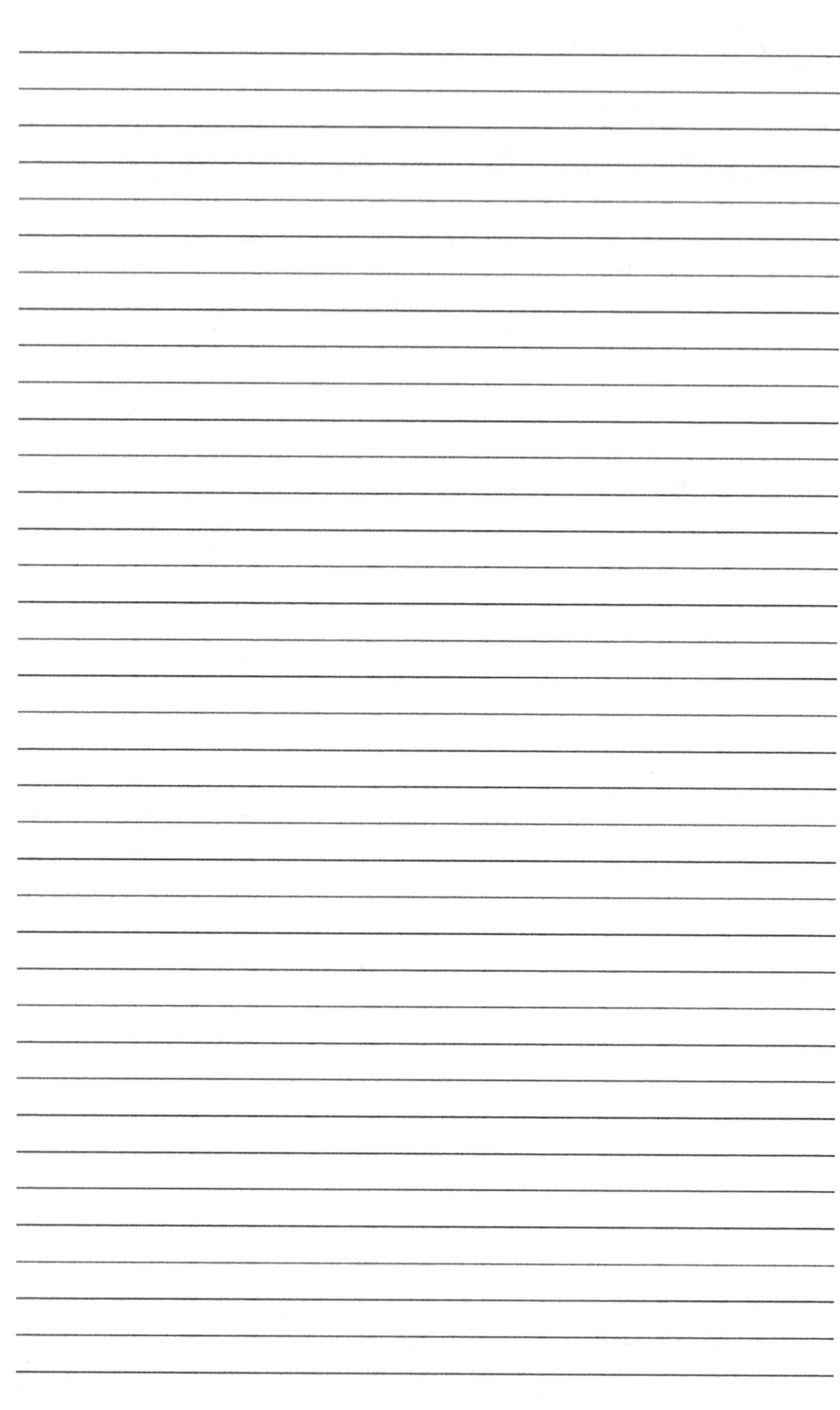

TITLE:

GENRE:

SERIES:

AUTHOR:

PAGES:

STARTED:

FINISHED:

FORMAT READ: EBOOK / PRINT / AUDIOBOOK

✔ **SYNOPSIS/THINGS I LIKED:**

🚫 **THINGS I DIDN'T LIKE:**

✏ **FAVORITE QUOTE(S):**

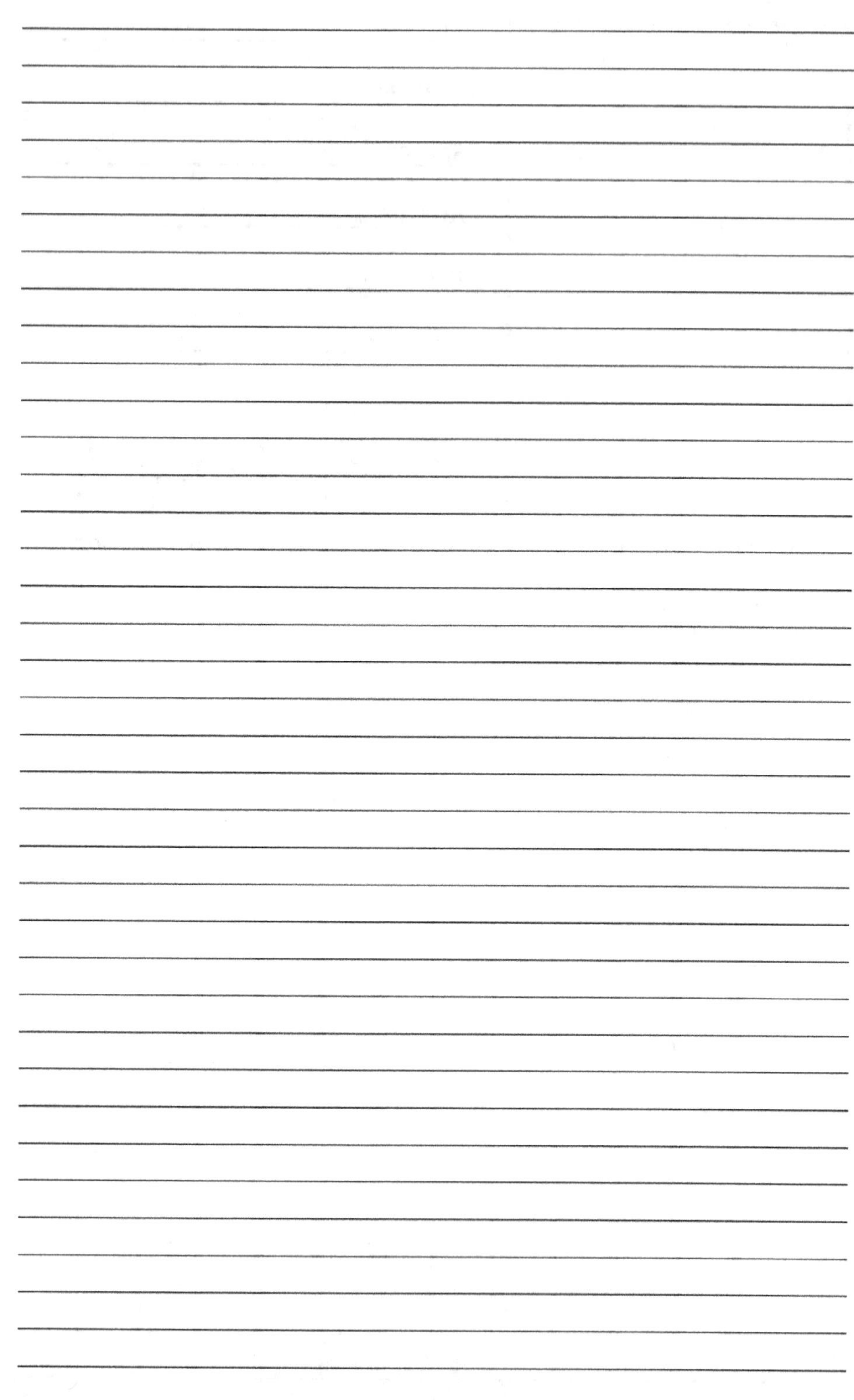

TITLE: _______________

GENRE: _______________

SERIES: _______________

AUTHOR: _______________

PAGES: _______________

STARTED: _______________

FINISHED: _______________

☆ ☆ ☆ ☆ ☆

FORMAT READ: EBOOK / PRINT / AUDIOBOOK

✔ **SYNOPSIS/THINGS I LIKED:**

____
____
____

🚫 **THINGS I DIDN'T LIKE:**

____
____
____

✏ **FAVORITE QUOTE(S):**

____
____
____
____
____
____

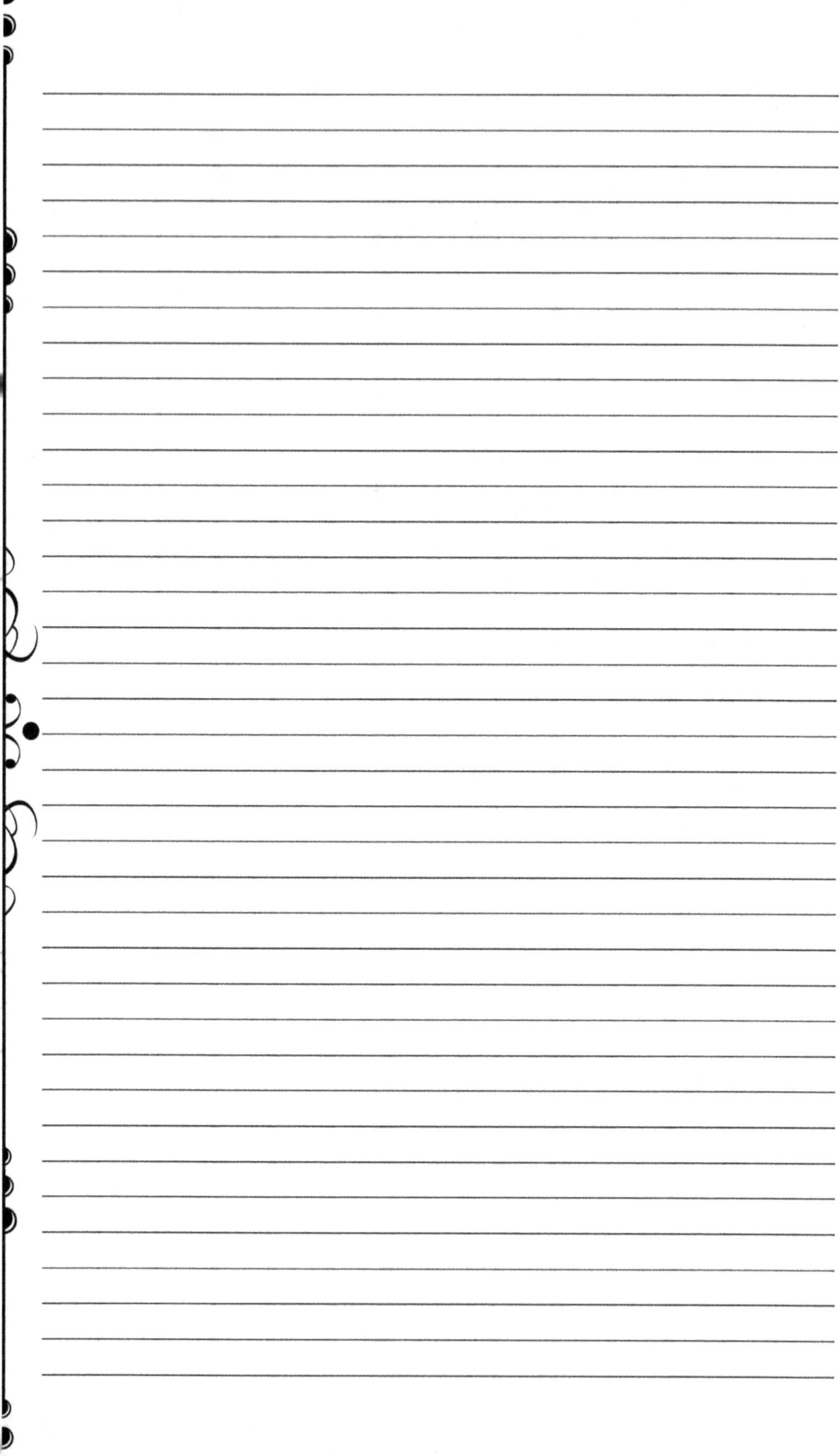

✔ **Synopsis/Things I liked:**

⊘ **Things I didn't like:**

✎ **Favorite quote(s):**

Title:

Genre:

Series:

Author:

Pages:

Started:

Finished:

☆ ☆ ☆ ☆ ☆

Format read: Ebook / Print / Audiobook 23

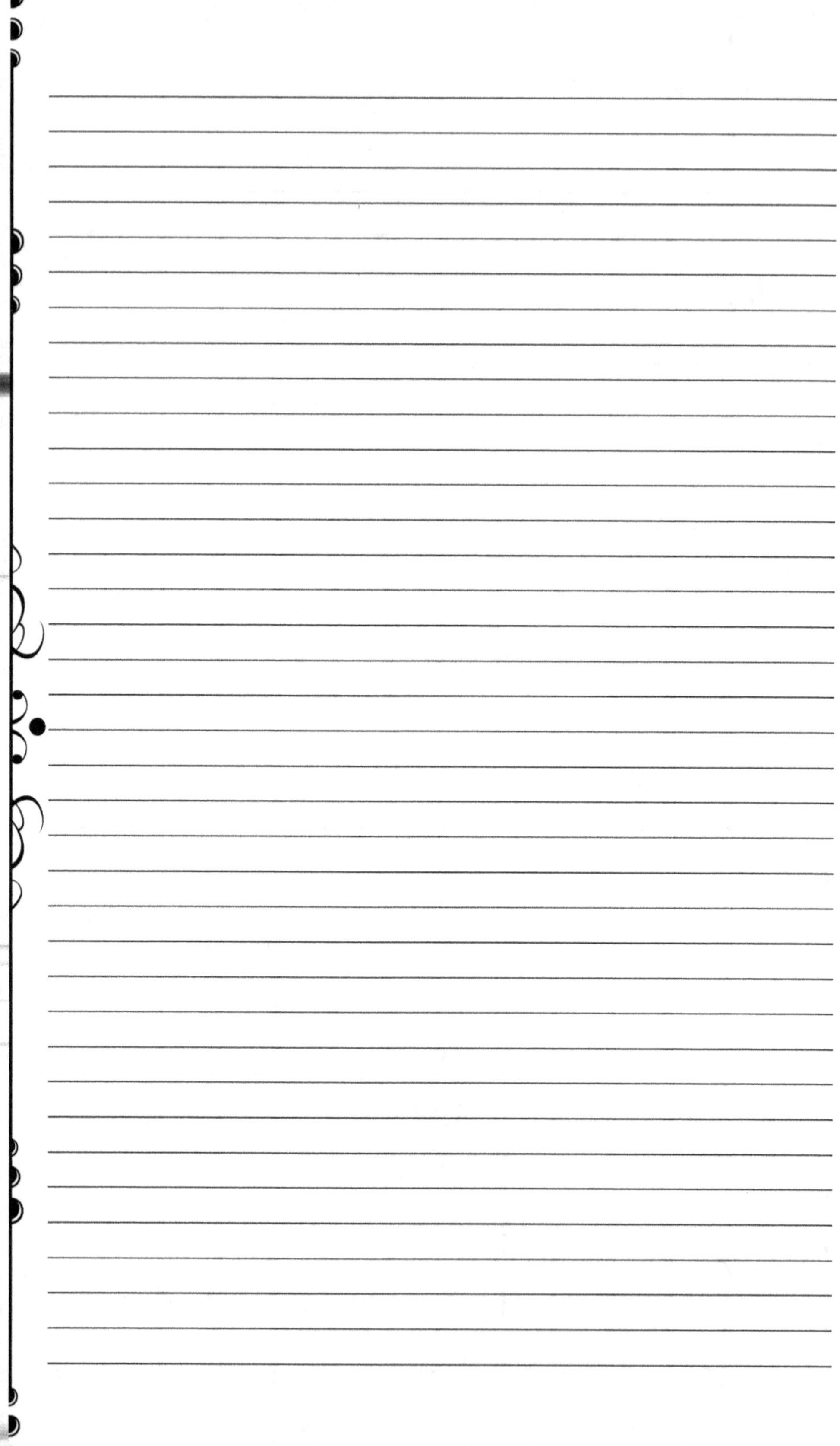

✅ **S**YNOPSIS/**T**HINGS **I** LIKED:

🚫 **T**HINGS **I** DIDN'T LIKE:

✏️ **F**AVORITE QUOTE(S):

TITLE:

GENRE:

SERIES:

AUTHOR:

PAGES:

STARTED:

FINISHED:

☆ ☆ ☆ ☆ ☆

FORMAT READ: **E**BOOK / **P**RINT / **A**UDIOBOOK

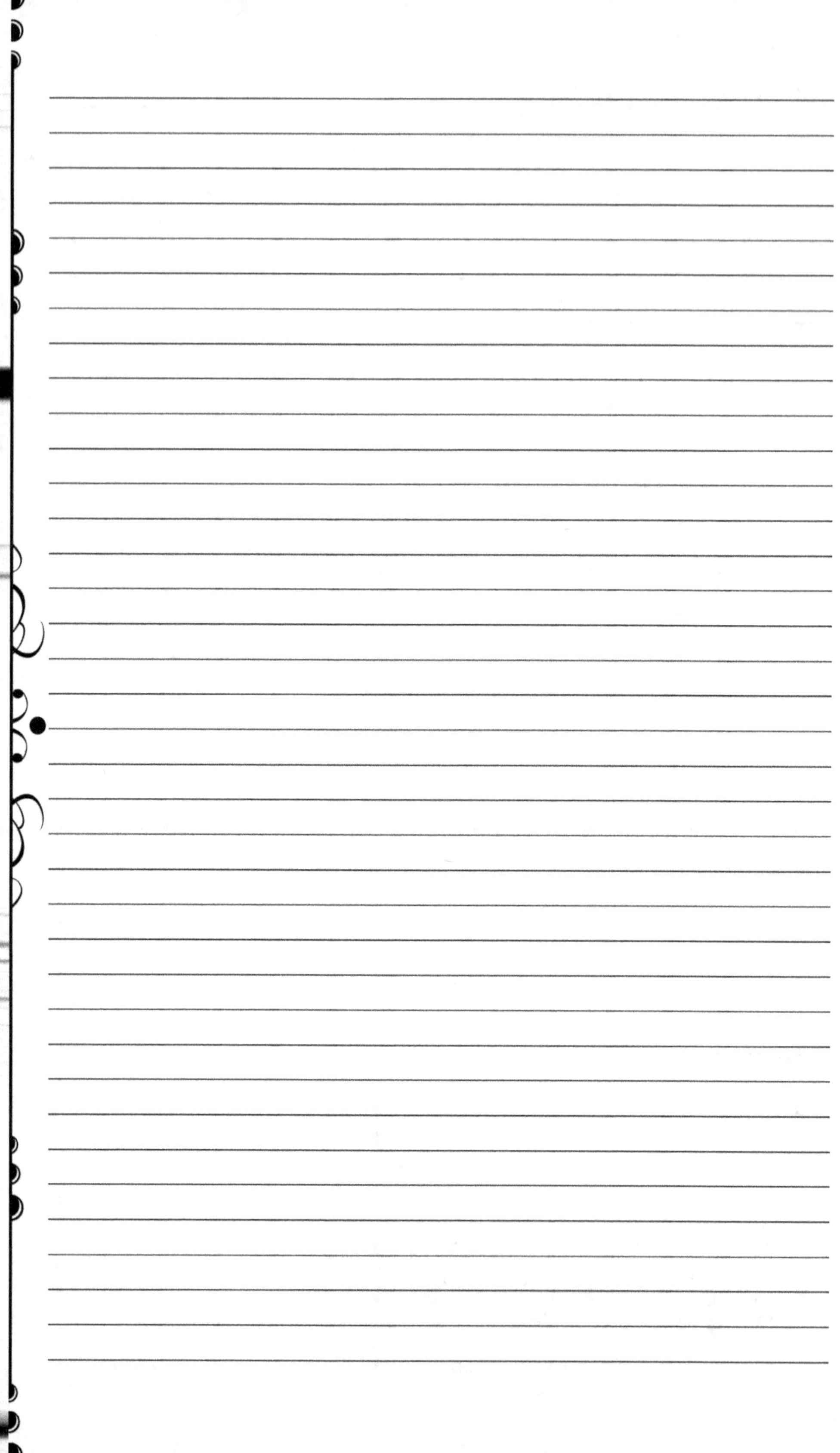

TITLE:

GENRE:

SERIES:

AUTHOR:

PAGES:

STARTED:

FINISHED:

FORMAT READ: EBOOK / PRINT / AUDIOBOOK

SYNOPSIS/THINGS I LIKED:

THINGS I DIDN'T LIKE:

FAVORITE QUOTE(S):

25

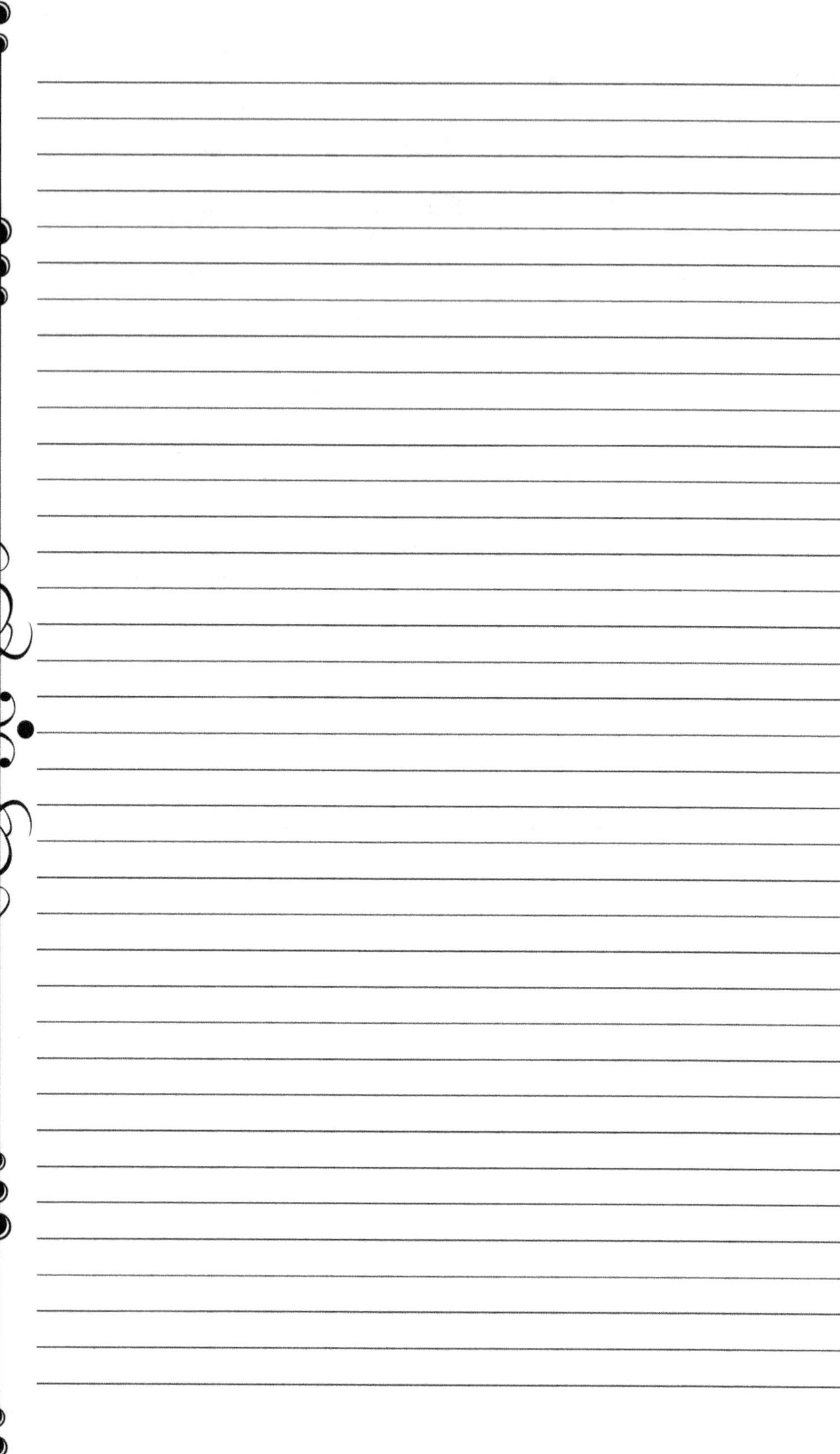

TITLE: ___________________________

GENRE: ___________________________

SERIES: ___________________________

AUTHOR: ___________________________

PAGES: ___________________________

STARTED: ___________________________

FINISHED: ___________________________

☆ ☆ ☆ ☆ ☆

FORMAT READ: EBOOK / PRINT / AUDIOBOOK

✓ **SYNOPSIS/THINGS I LIKED:**

____
____
____
____

🚫 **THINGS I DIDN'T LIKE:**

____
____
____
____

✎ **FAVORITE QUOTE(S):**

____
____
____
____
____
____
____

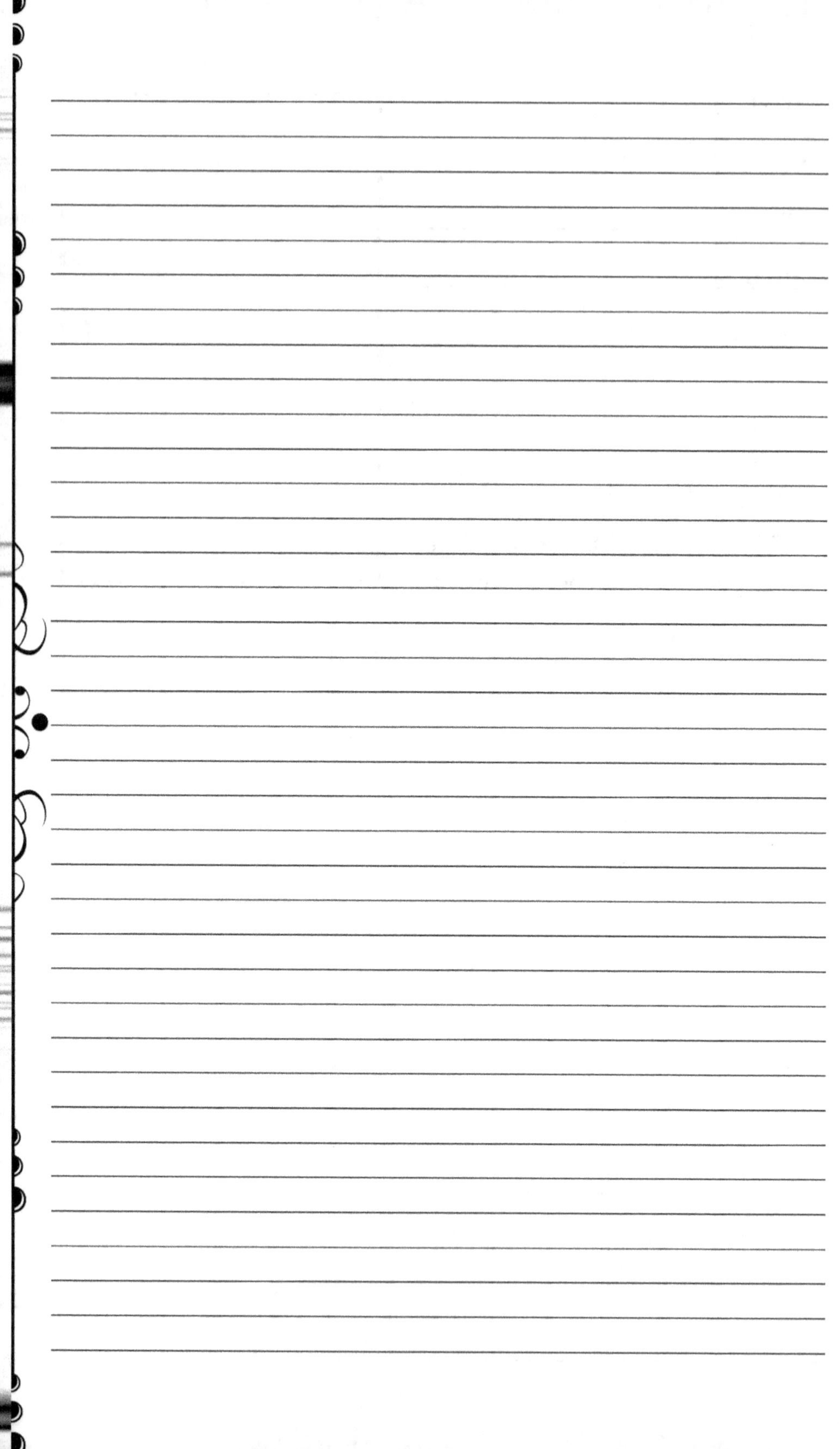

TITLE:

GENRE:

SERIES:

AUTHOR:

PAGES:

STARTED:

FINISHED:

FORMAT READ: EBOOK / PRINT / AUDIOBOOK 27

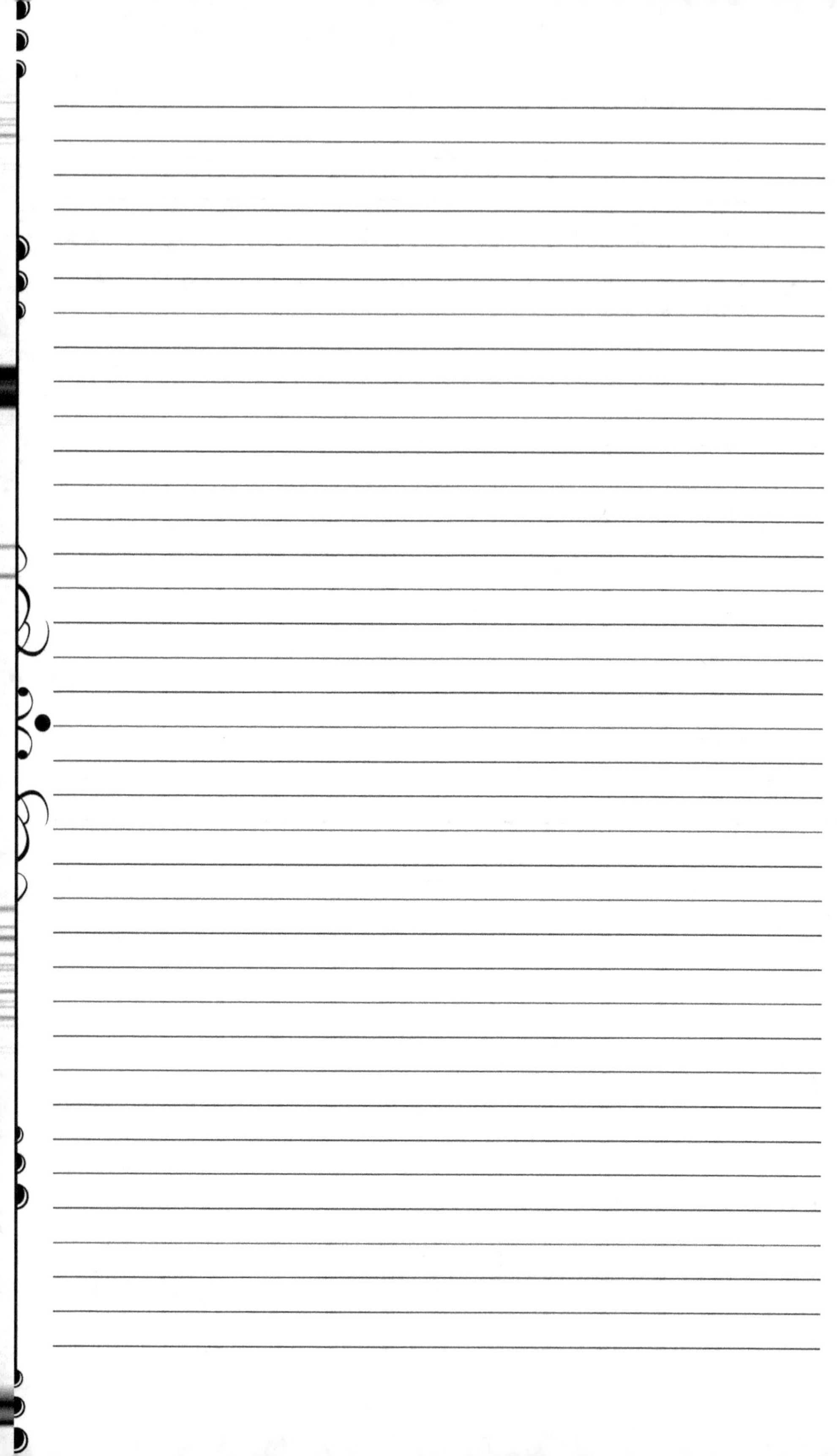

☑ **SYNOPSIS/THINGS I LIKED:**

🚫 **THINGS I DIDN'T LIKE:**

✎ **FAVORITE QUOTE(S):**

TITLE:

GENRE:

SERIES:

AUTHOR:

PAGES:

STARTED:

FINISHED:

☆ ☆ ☆ ☆ ☆

FORMAT READ: EBOOK / PRINT / AUDIOBOOK

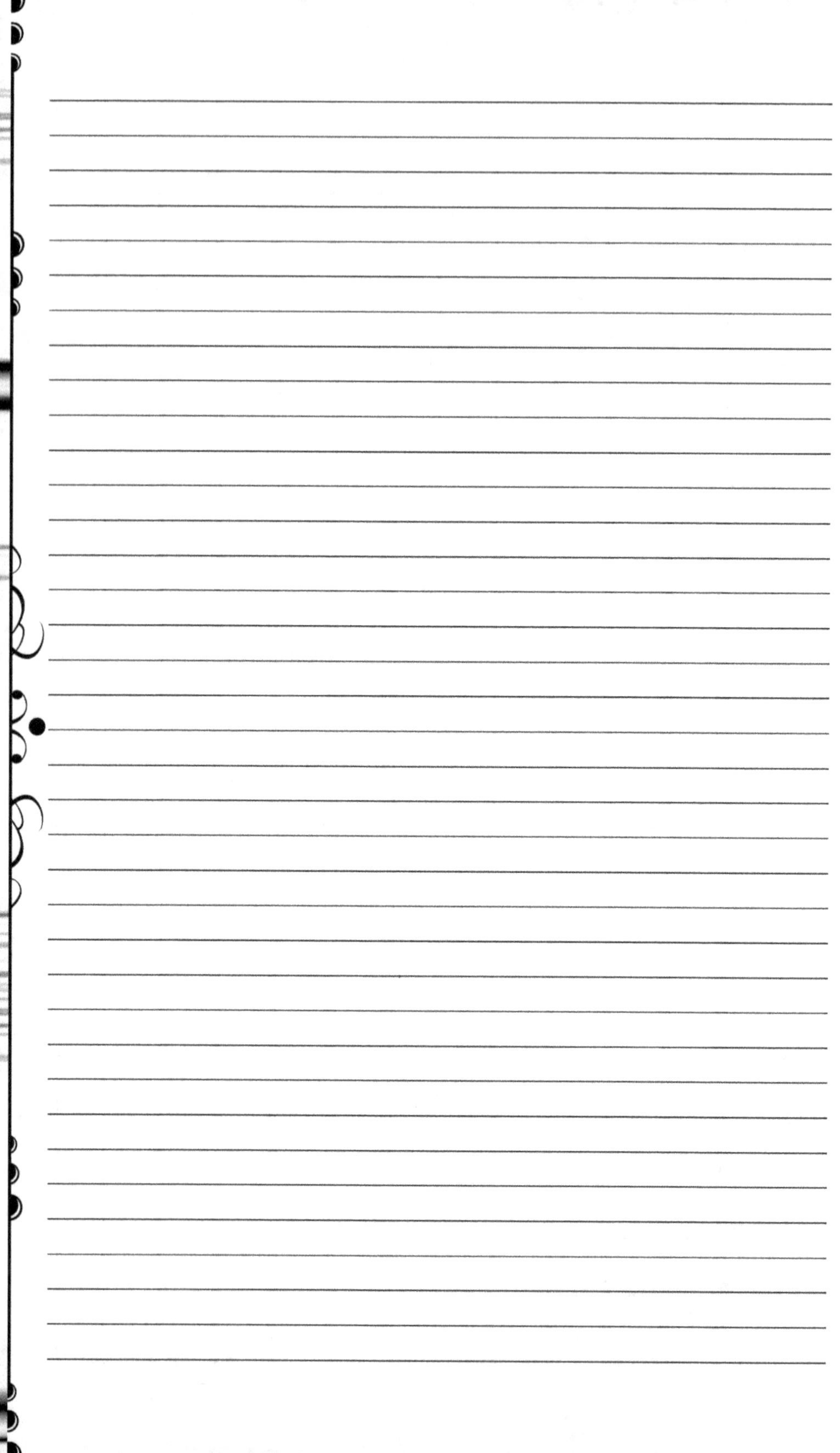

TITLE:

GENRE:

SERIES:

AUTHOR:

PAGES:

STARTED:

FINISHED:

FORMAT READ: EBOOK / PRINT / AUDIOBOOK

SYNOPSIS/THINGS I LIKED:

THINGS I DIDN'T LIKE:

FAVORITE QUOTE(S):

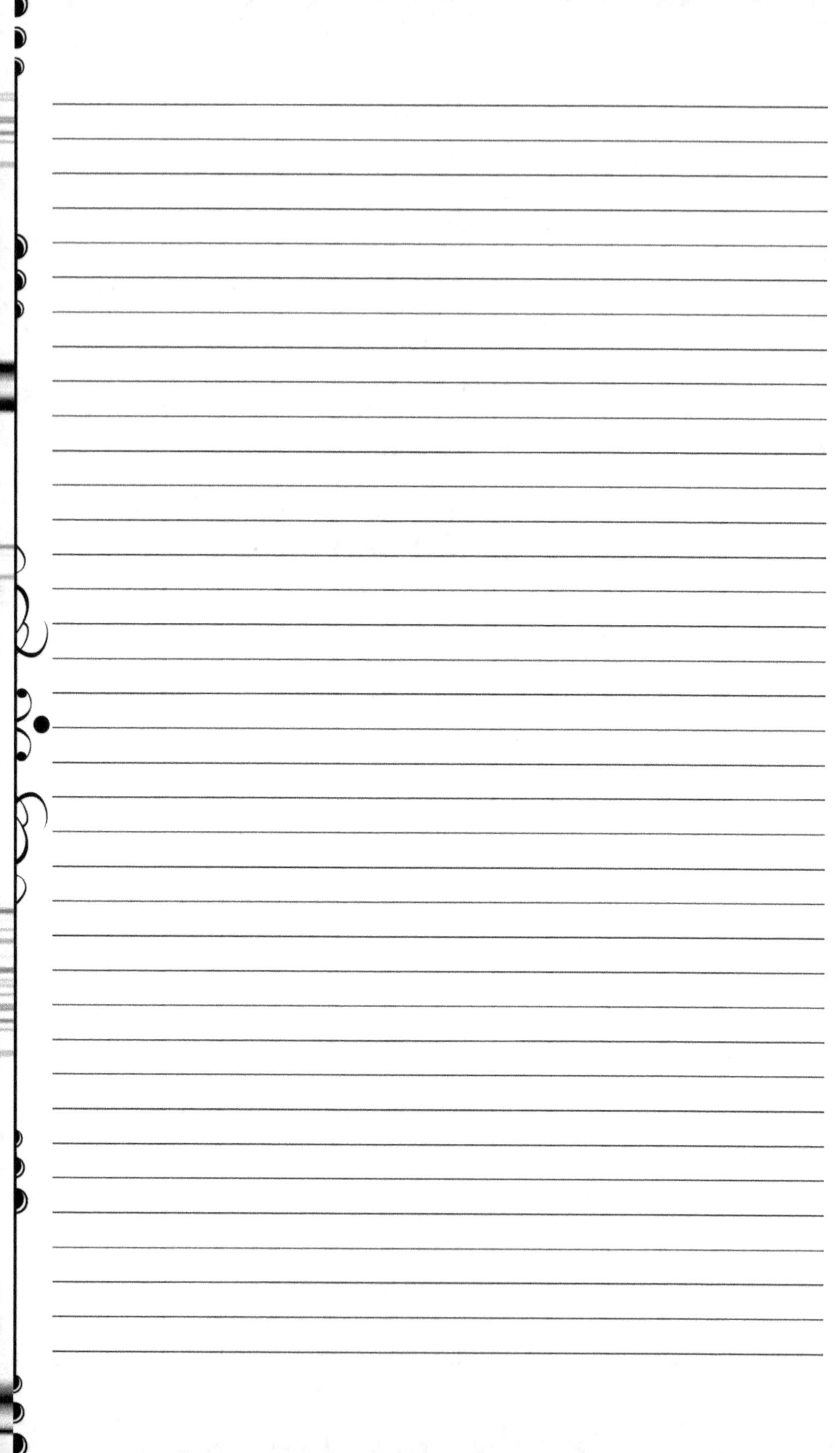

TITLE: ___________________________

GENRE: ___________________________

SERIES: ___________________________

AUTHOR: ___________________________

PAGES: ___________________________

STARTED: ___________________________

FINISHED: ___________________________

☆ ☆ ☆ ☆ ☆

FORMAT READ: EBOOK / PRINT / AUDIOBOOK

✓ SYNOPSIS/THINGS I LIKED:

🚫 THINGS I DIDN'T LIKE:

✎ FAVORITE QUOTE(S):

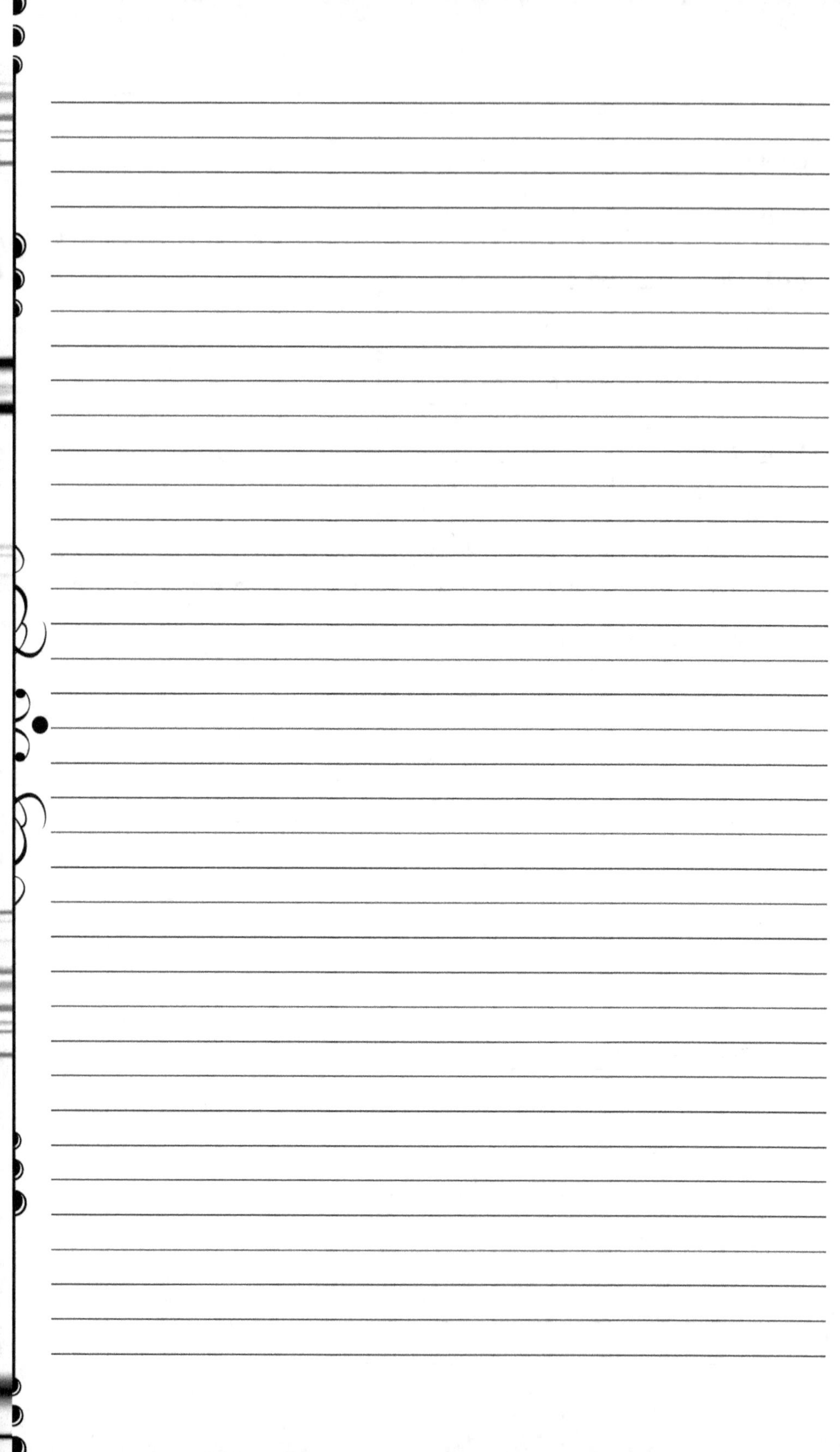

✓ **SYNOPSIS/THINGS I LIKED:**

🚫 **THINGS I DIDN'T LIKE:**

✎ **FAVORITE QUOTE(S):**

TITLE:

GENRE:

SERIES:

AUTHOR:

PAGES:

STARTED:

FINISHED:

☆ ☆ ☆ ☆ ☆

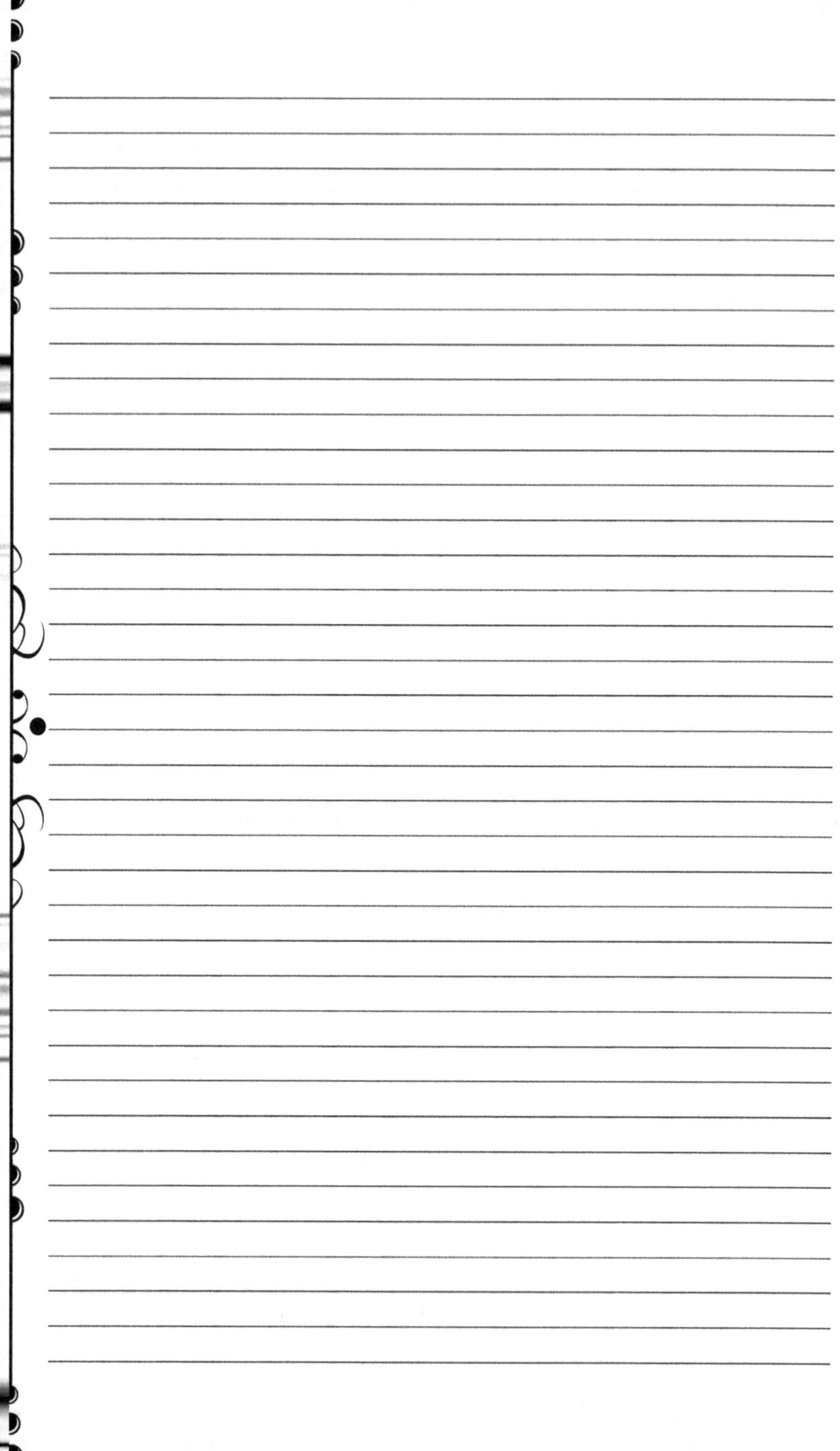

TITLE:

GENRE:

SERIES:

AUTHOR:

PAGES:

STARTED:

FINISHED:

☆ ☆ ☆ ☆ ☆

FORMAT READ: EBOOK / PRINT / AUDIOBOOK

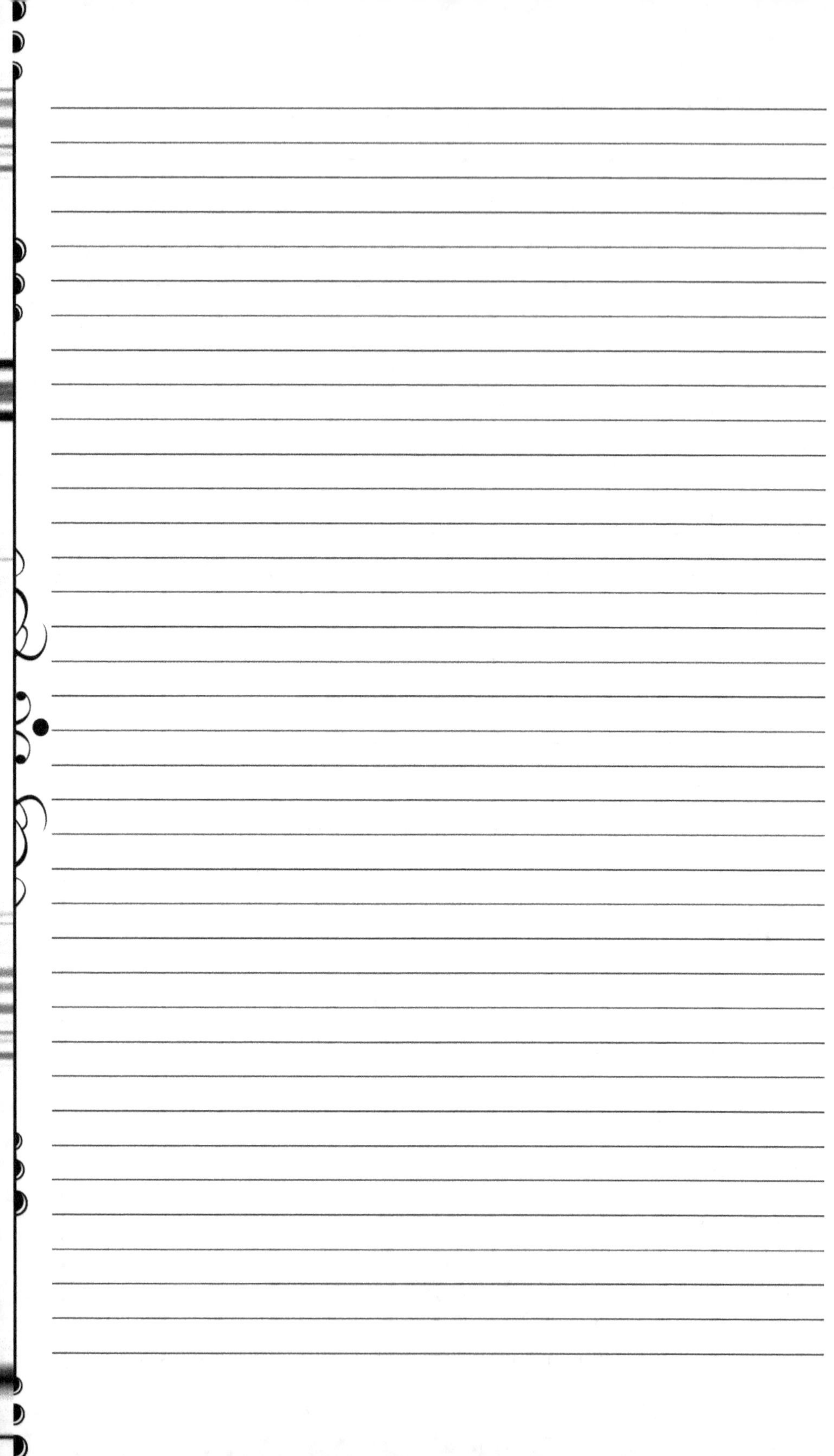

TITLE: ___________________________

GENRE: ___________________________

SERIES: ___________________________

AUTHOR: ___________________________

PAGES: ___________________________

STARTED: ___________________________

FINISHED: ___________________________

☆ ☆ ☆ ☆ ☆

FORMAT READ: EBOOK / PRINT / AUDIOBOOK

✓ **SYNOPSIS/THINGS I LIKED:**

____

____

____

____

🚫 **THINGS I DIDN'T LIKE:**

____

____

____

____

✏ **FAVORITE QUOTE(S):**

____

____

____

____

____

____

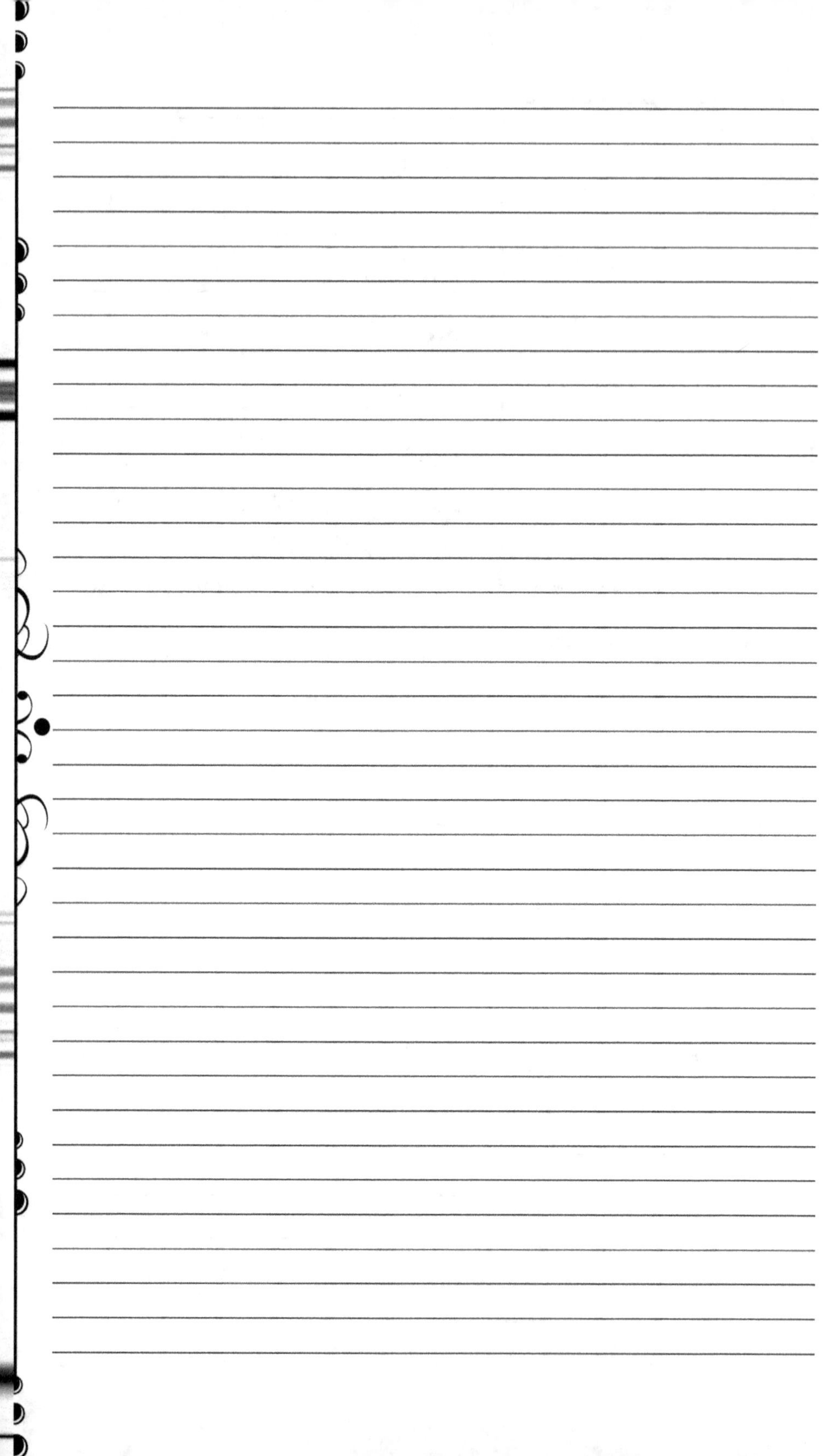

TITLE: _______________

GENRE: _______________

SERIES: _______________

AUTHOR: _______________

PAGES: _______________

STARTED: _______________

FINISHED: _______________

☆ ☆ ☆ ☆ ☆

FORMAT READ: EBOOK / PRINT / AUDIOBOOK

✔ **SYNOPSIS/THINGS I LIKED:**

____
____
____
____

🚫 **THINGS I DIDN'T LIKE:**

____
____
____
____

✎ **FAVORITE QUOTE(S):**

____
____
____
____
____
____
____

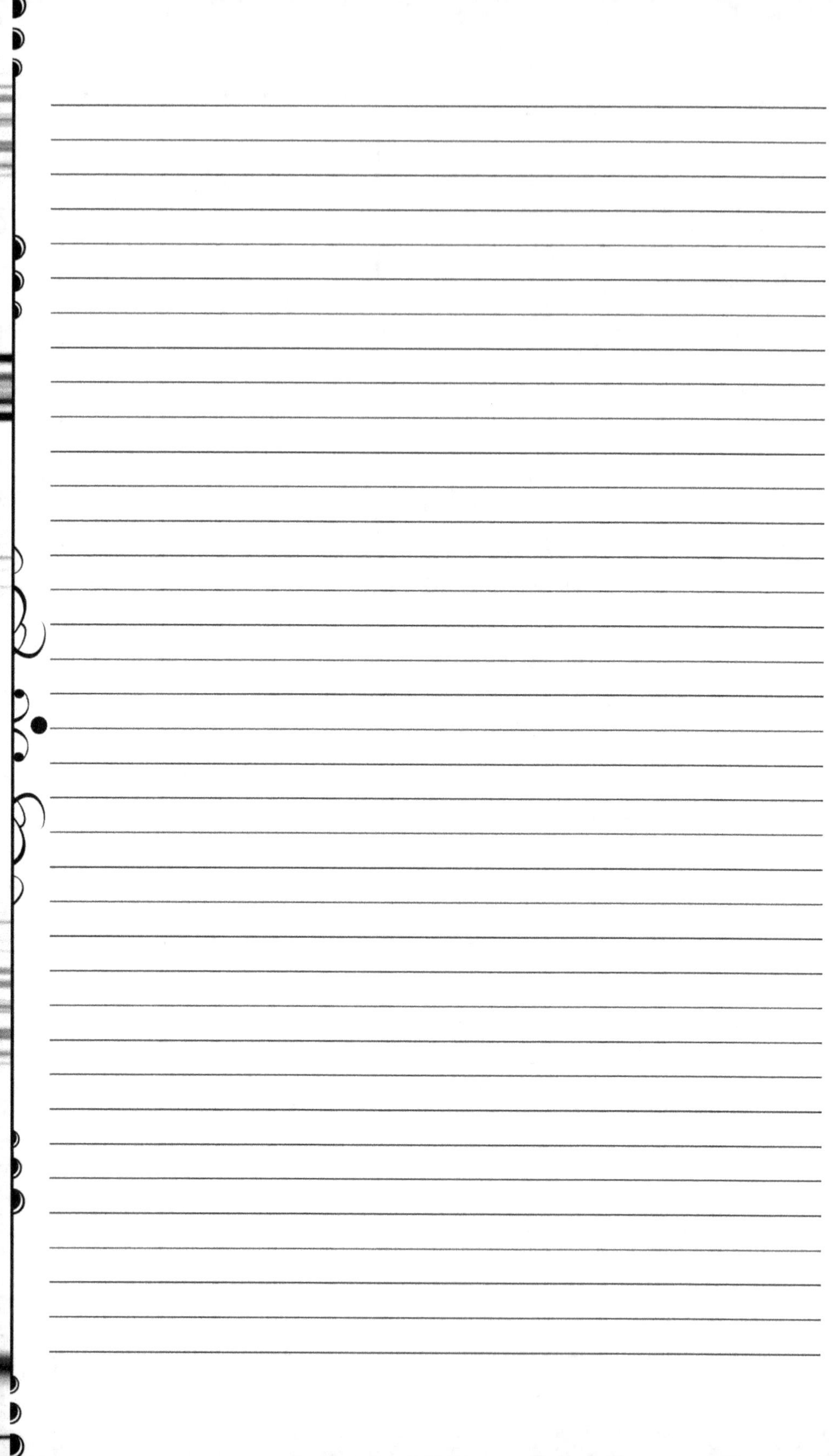

TITLE:

GENRE:

SERIES:

AUTHOR:

PAGES:

STARTED:

FINISHED:

FORMAT READ: EBOOK / PRINT / AUDIOBOOK 35

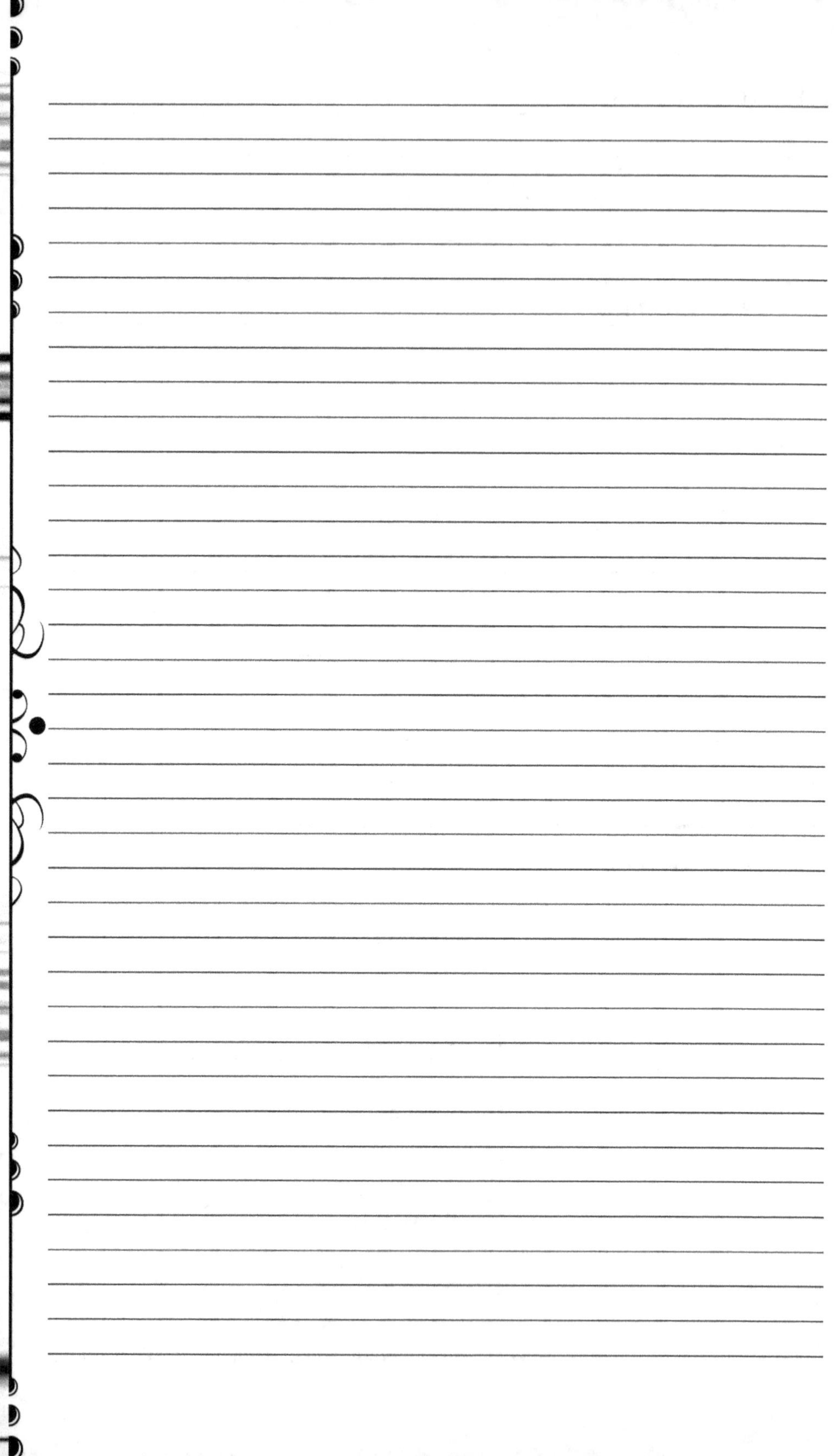

SYNOPSIS/THINGS I LIKED:

THINGS I DIDN'T LIKE:

FAVORITE QUOTE(S):

TITLE:

GENRE:

SERIES:

AUTHOR:

PAGES:

STARTED:

FINISHED:

FORMAT READ: EBOOK / PRINT / AUDIOBOOK

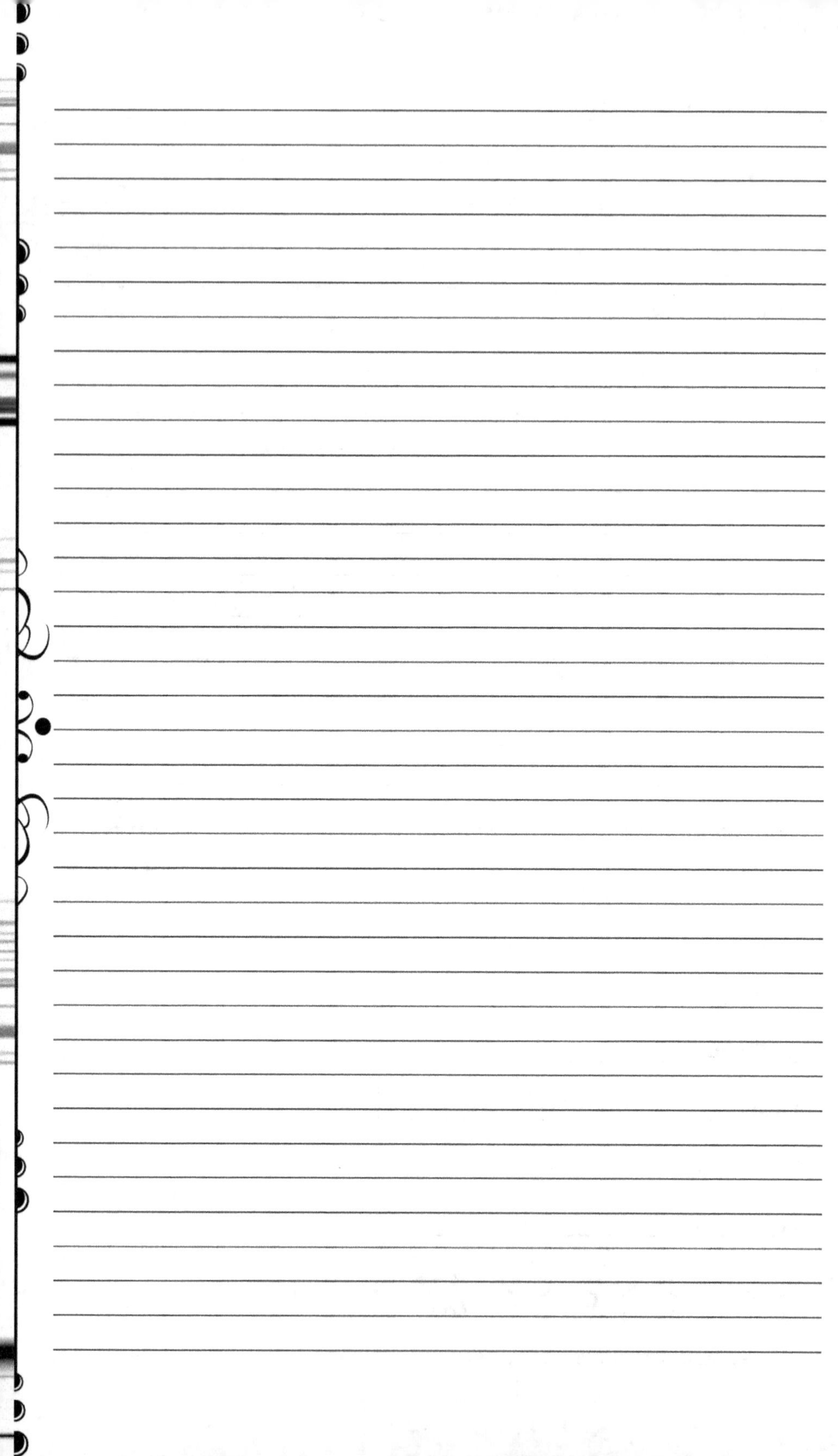

TITLE:

GENRE:

SERIES:

AUTHOR:

PAGES:

STARTED:

FINISHED:

FORMAT READ: EBOOK / PRINT / AUDIOBOOK

✅ SYNOPSIS/THINGS I LIKED:

🚫 THINGS I DIDN'T LIKE:

✏️ FAVORITE QUOTE(S):

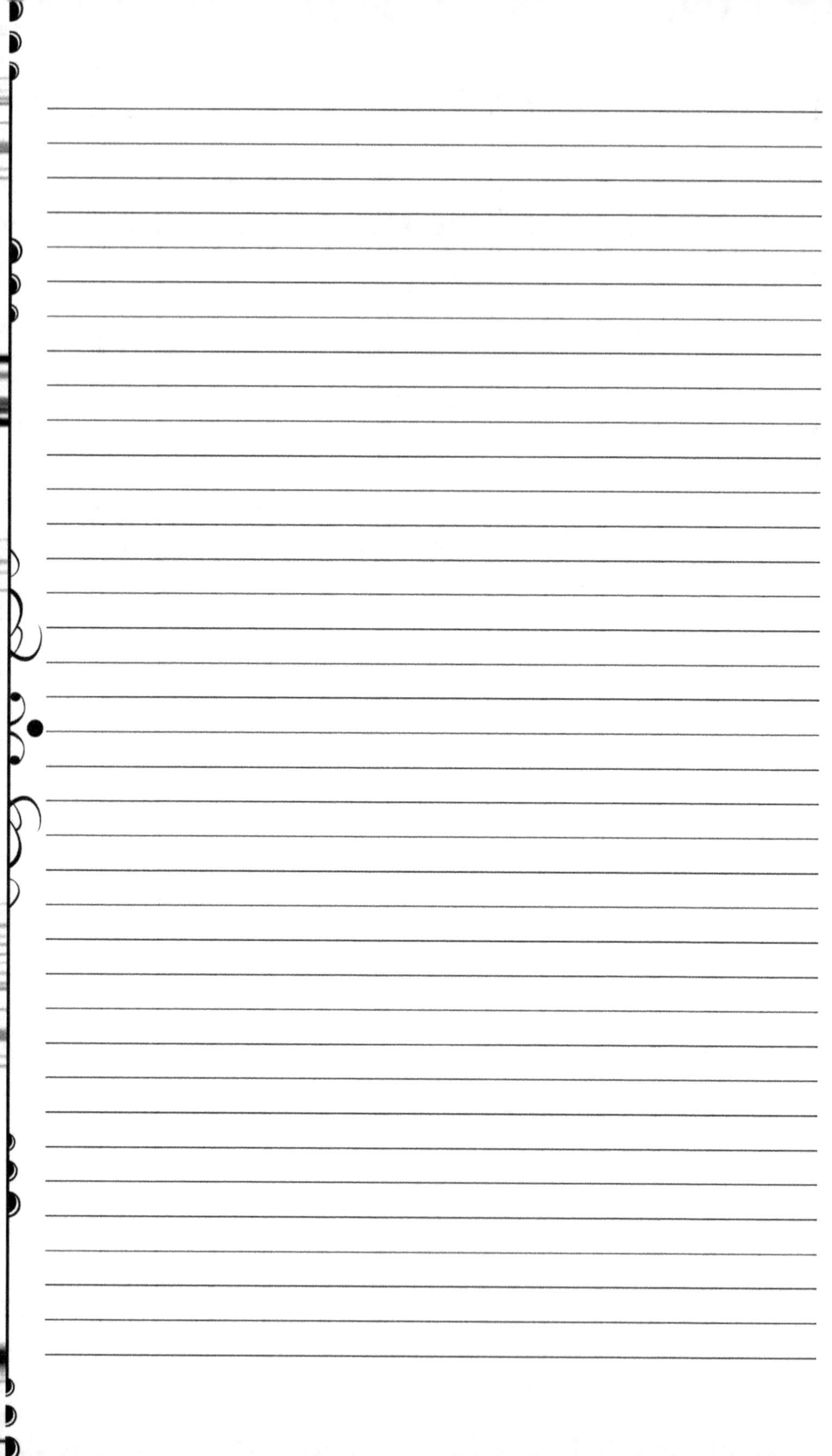

TITLE:

GENRE:

SERIES:

AUTHOR:

PAGES:

STARTED:

FINISHED:

FORMAT READ: EBOOK / PRINT / AUDIOBOOK

✔ SYNOPSIS/THINGS I LIKED:

🚫 THINGS I DIDN'T LIKE:

✎ FAVORITE QUOTE(S):

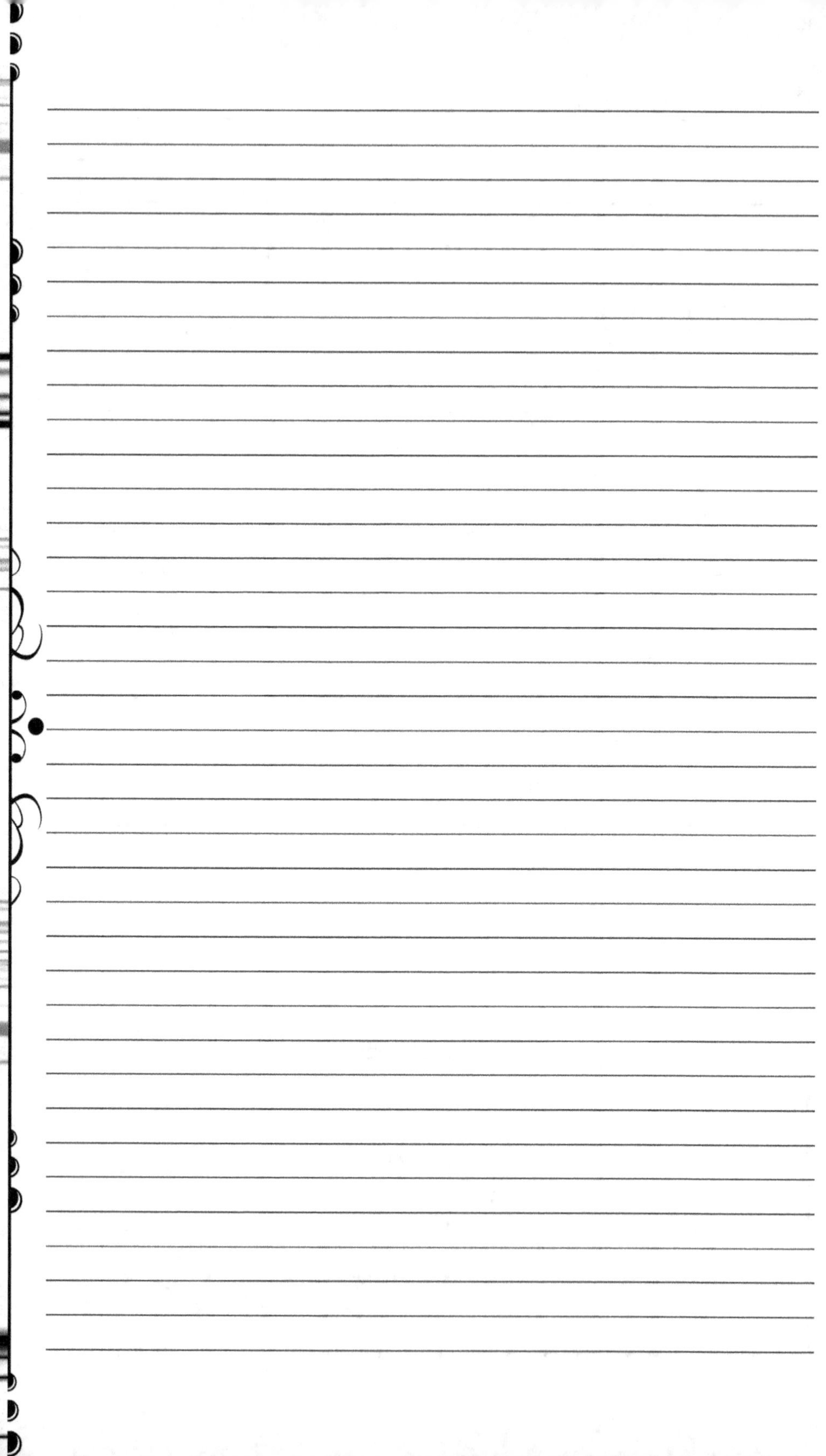

☑ **Synopsis/Things I liked:**

⊘ **Things I didn't like:**

🖌 **Favorite quote(s):**

Title:

Genre:

Series:

Author:

Pages:

Started:

Finished:

☆ ☆ ☆ ☆ ☆

Format read: Ebook / Print / Audiobook

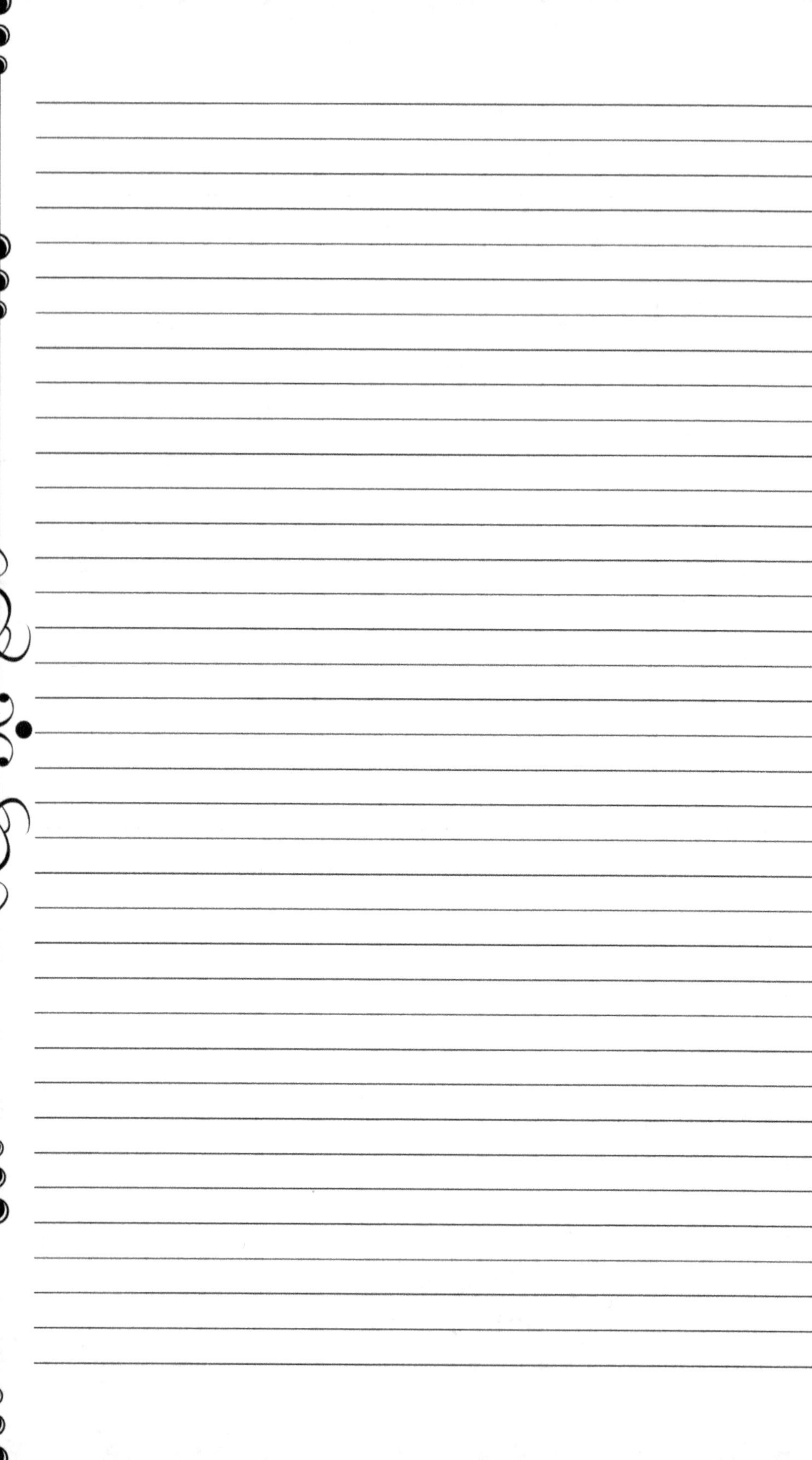

TITLE: _______________

GENRE: _______________

SERIES: _______________

AUTHOR: _______________

PAGES: _______________

STARTED: _______________

FINISHED: _______________

☆ ☆ ☆ ☆ ☆

FORMAT READ: EBOOK / PRINT / AUDIOBOOK

✓ **SYNOPSIS/THINGS I LIKED:**

____
____
____
____

🚫 **THINGS I DIDN'T LIKE:**

____
____
____

✏️ **FAVORITE QUOTE(S):**

____
____
____
____
____
____

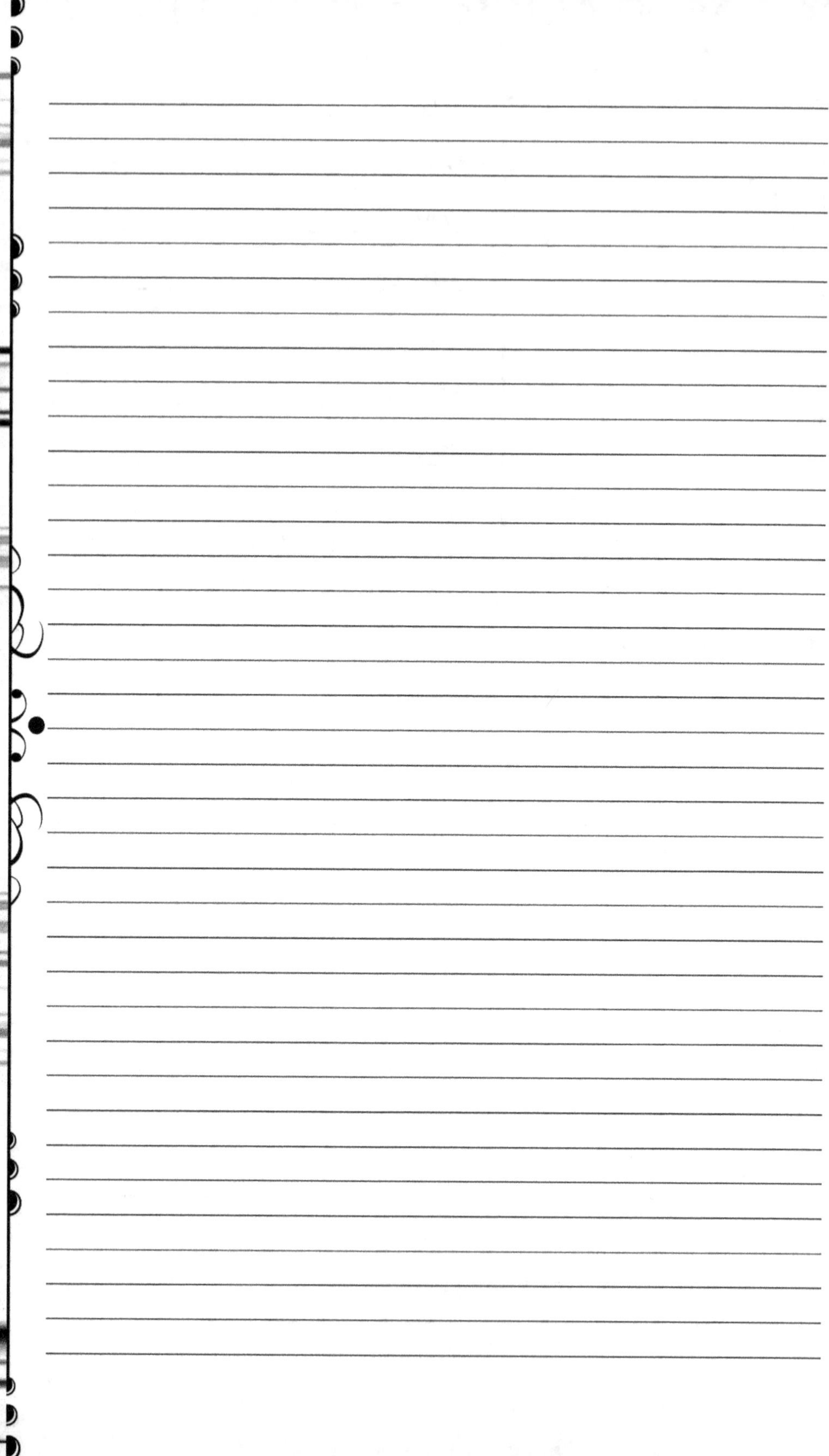

TITLE: _______________

GENRE: _______________

SERIES: _______________

AUTHOR: _______________

PAGES: _______________

STARTED: _______________

FINISHED: _______________

☆ ☆ ☆ ☆ ☆

FORMAT READ: EBOOK / PRINT / AUDIOBOOK

✅ **SYNOPSIS/THINGS I LIKED:**

____
____
____
____

🚫 **THINGS I DIDN'T LIKE:**

____
____
____
____

📝 **FAVORITE QUOTE(S):**

____
____
____
____
____
____
____

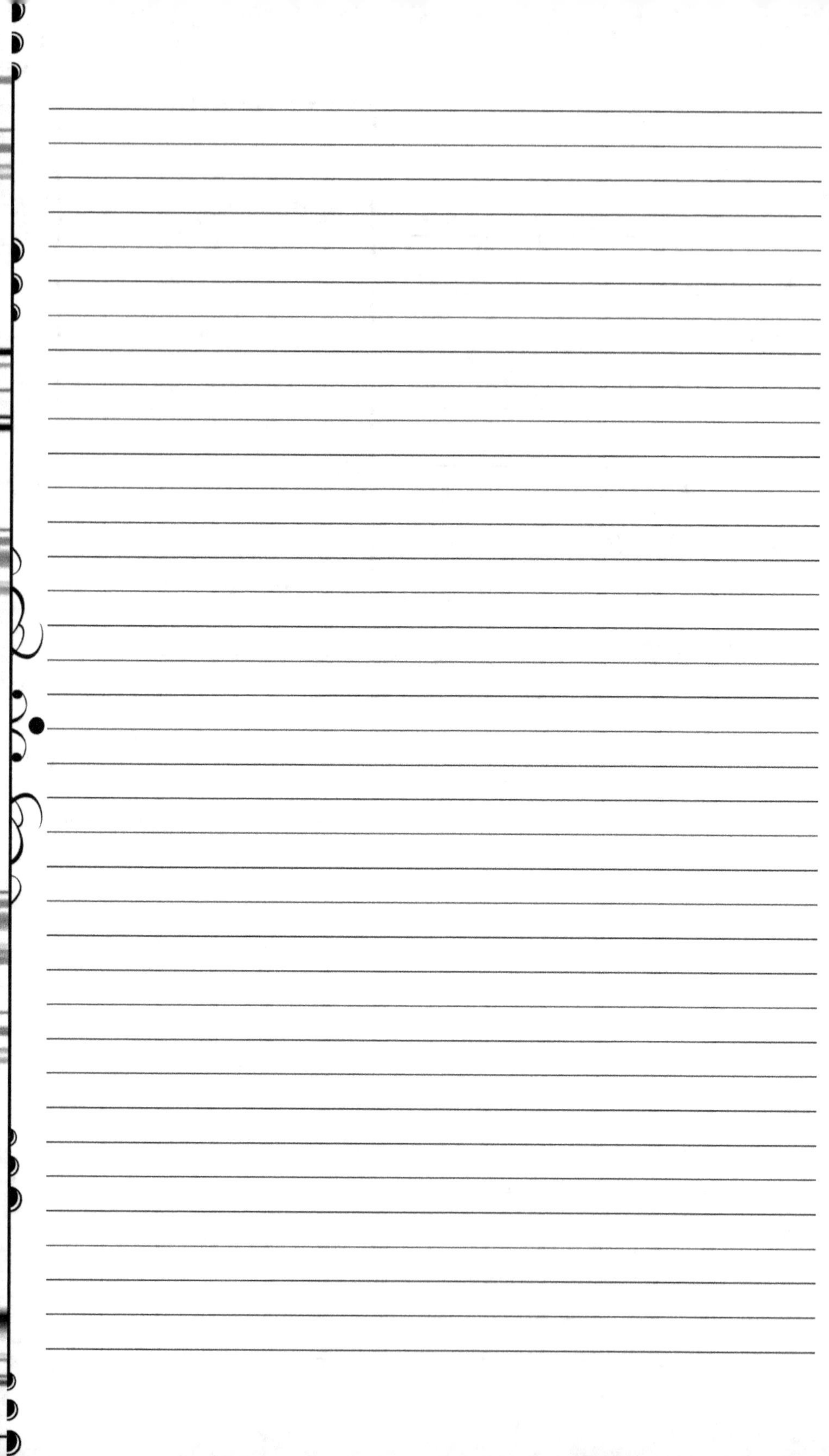

✓ **SYNOPSIS/THINGS I LIKED:**

⊘ **THINGS I DIDN'T LIKE:**

✎ **FAVORITE QUOTE(S):**

TITLE:

GENRE:

SERIES:

AUTHOR:

PAGES:

STARTED:

FINISHED:

☆☆☆☆☆

FORMAT READ: EBOOK / PRINT / AUDIOBOOK 43

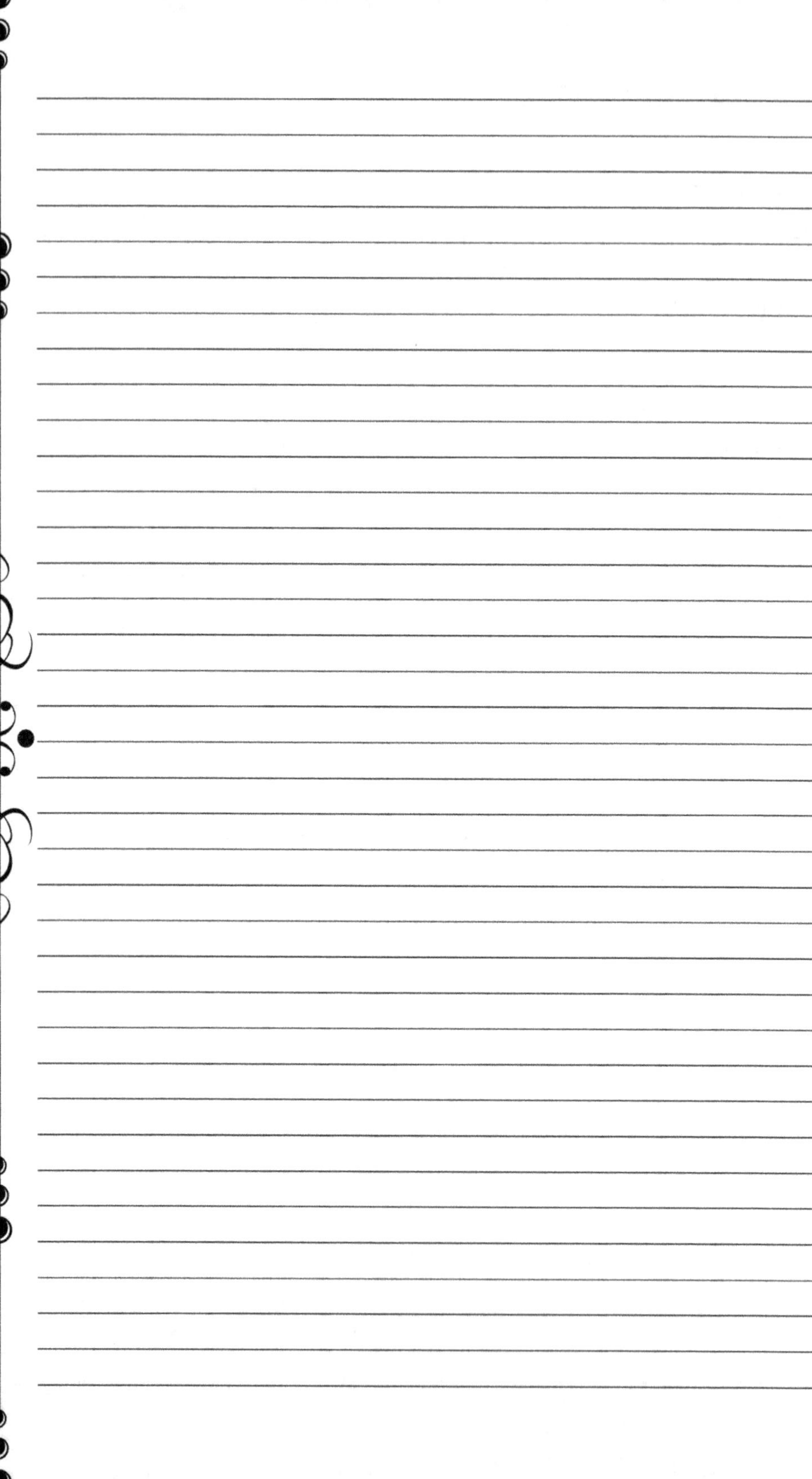

TITLE:

GENRE:

SERIES:

AUTHOR:

PAGES:

STARTED:

FINISHED:

FORMAT READ: EBOOK / PRINT / AUDIOBOOK

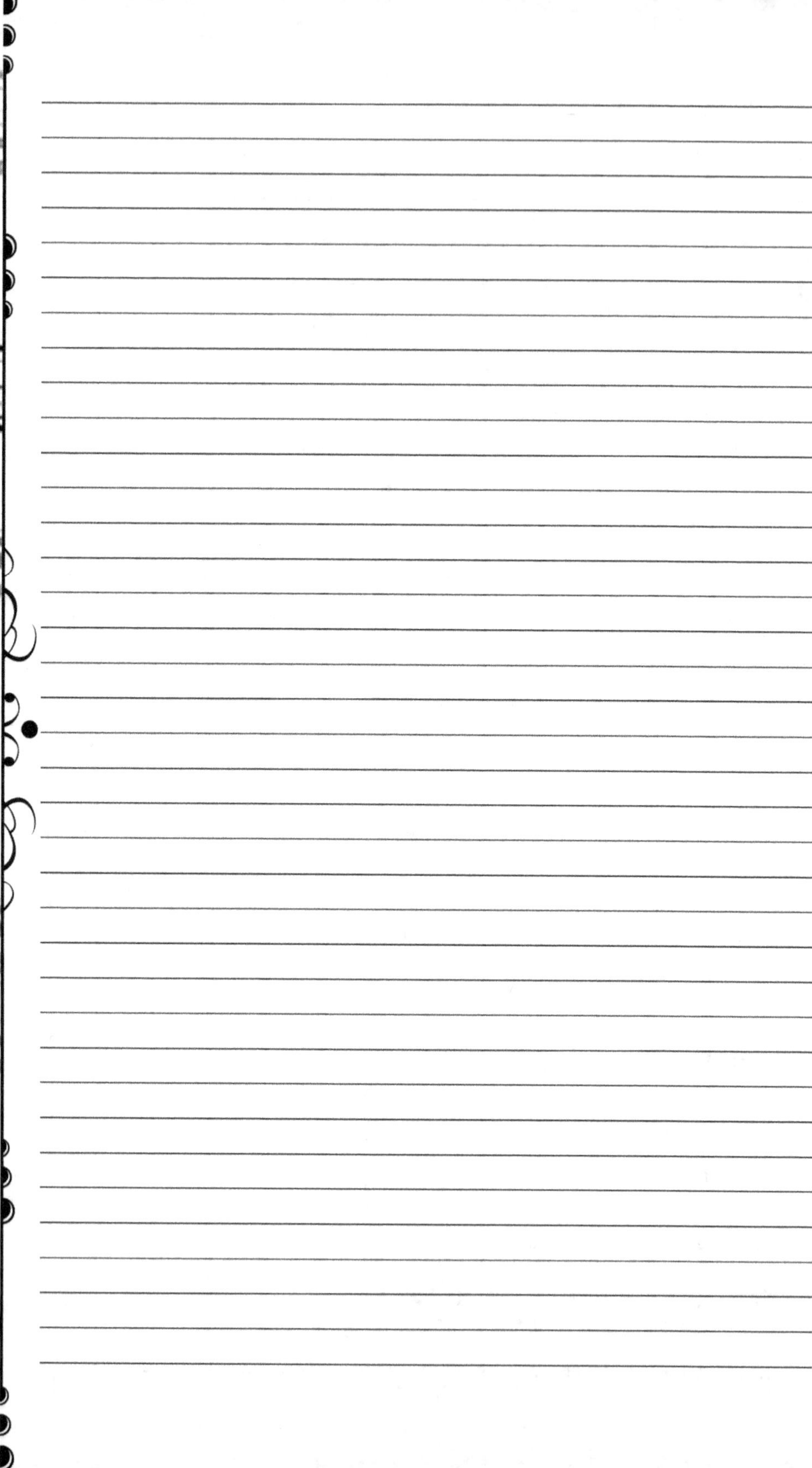

TITLE: ___________________________

GENRE: ___________________________

SERIES: ___________________________

AUTHOR: ___________________________

PAGES: ___________________________

STARTED: ___________________________

FINISHED: ___________________________

☆ ☆ ☆ ☆ ☆

FORMAT READ: EBOOK / PRINT / AUDIOBOOK

✅ **SYNOPSIS/THINGS I LIKED:**

____
____
____
____

🚫 **THINGS I DIDN'T LIKE:**

____
____
____
____

📝 **FAVORITE QUOTE(S):**

____
____
____
____
____
____
____

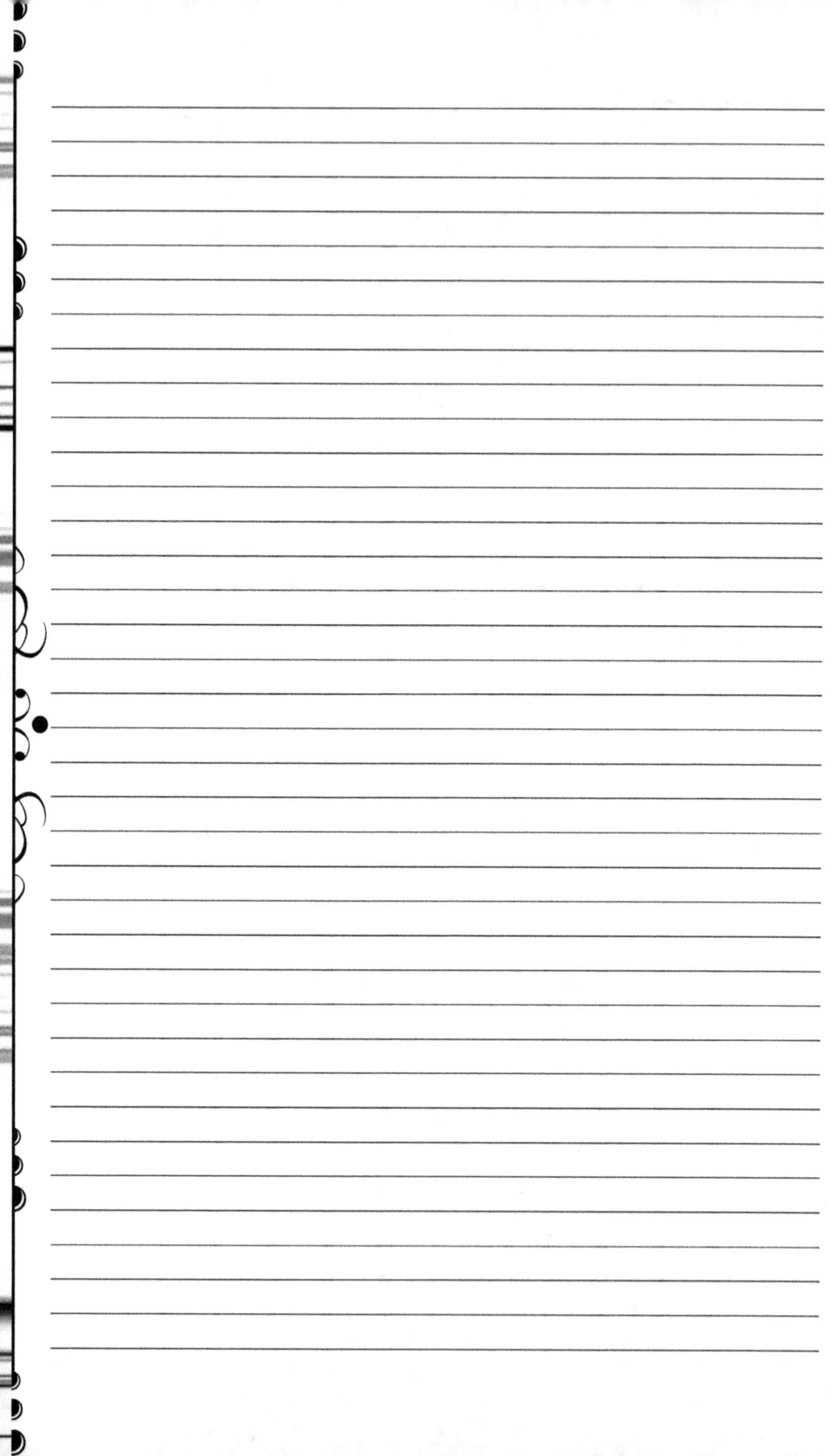

<u>**Title:**</u>

<u>**Genre:**</u>

<u>**Series:**</u>

<u>**Author:**</u>

<u>**Pages:**</u>

<u>**Started:**</u>

<u>**Finished:**</u>

☆ ☆ ☆ ☆ ☆

Format read: Ebook / Print / Audiobook

✅ **Synopsis/Things I liked:**

🚫 **Things I didn't like:**

✏️ **Favorite quote(s):**

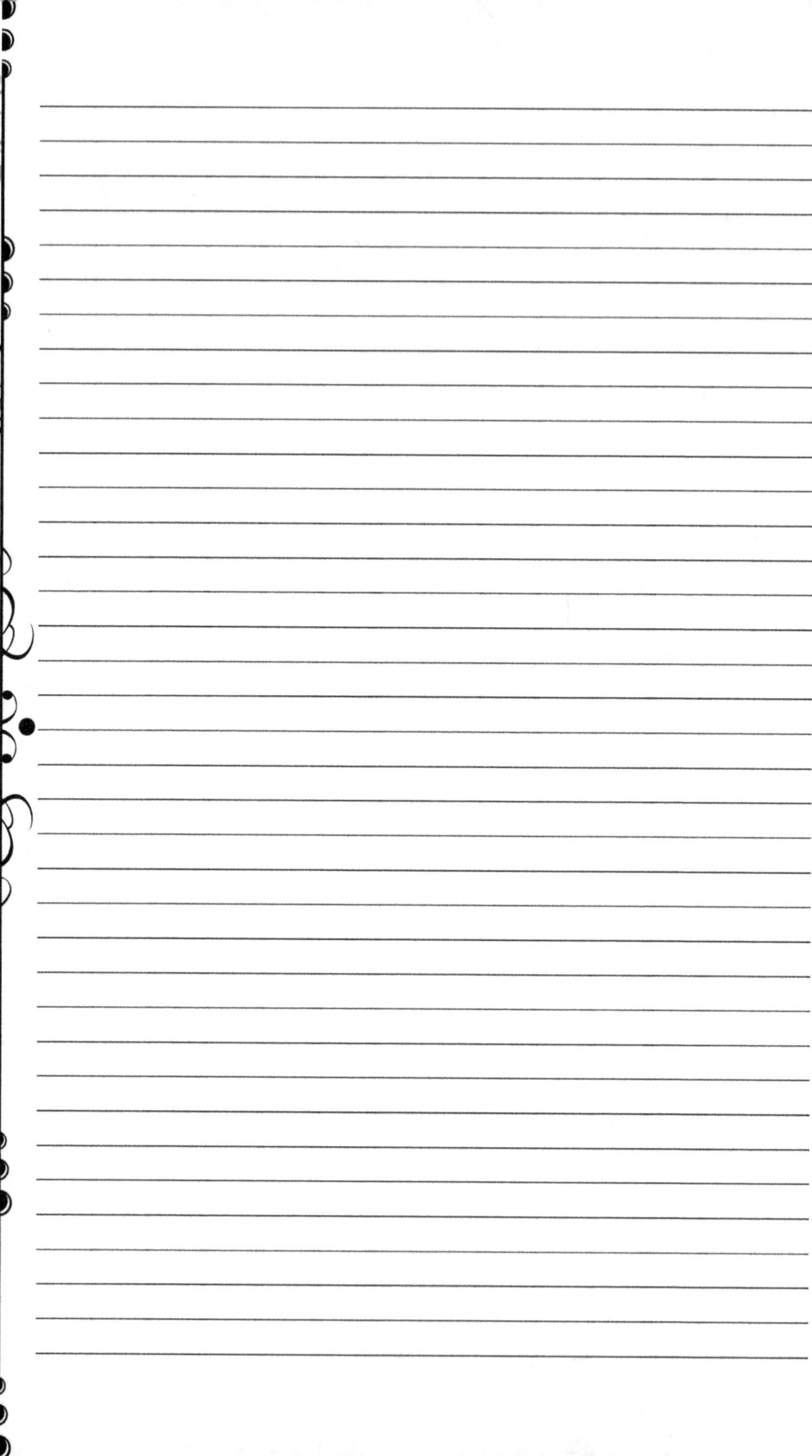

TITLE:

GENRE:

SERIES:

AUTHOR:

PAGES:

STARTED:

FINISHED:

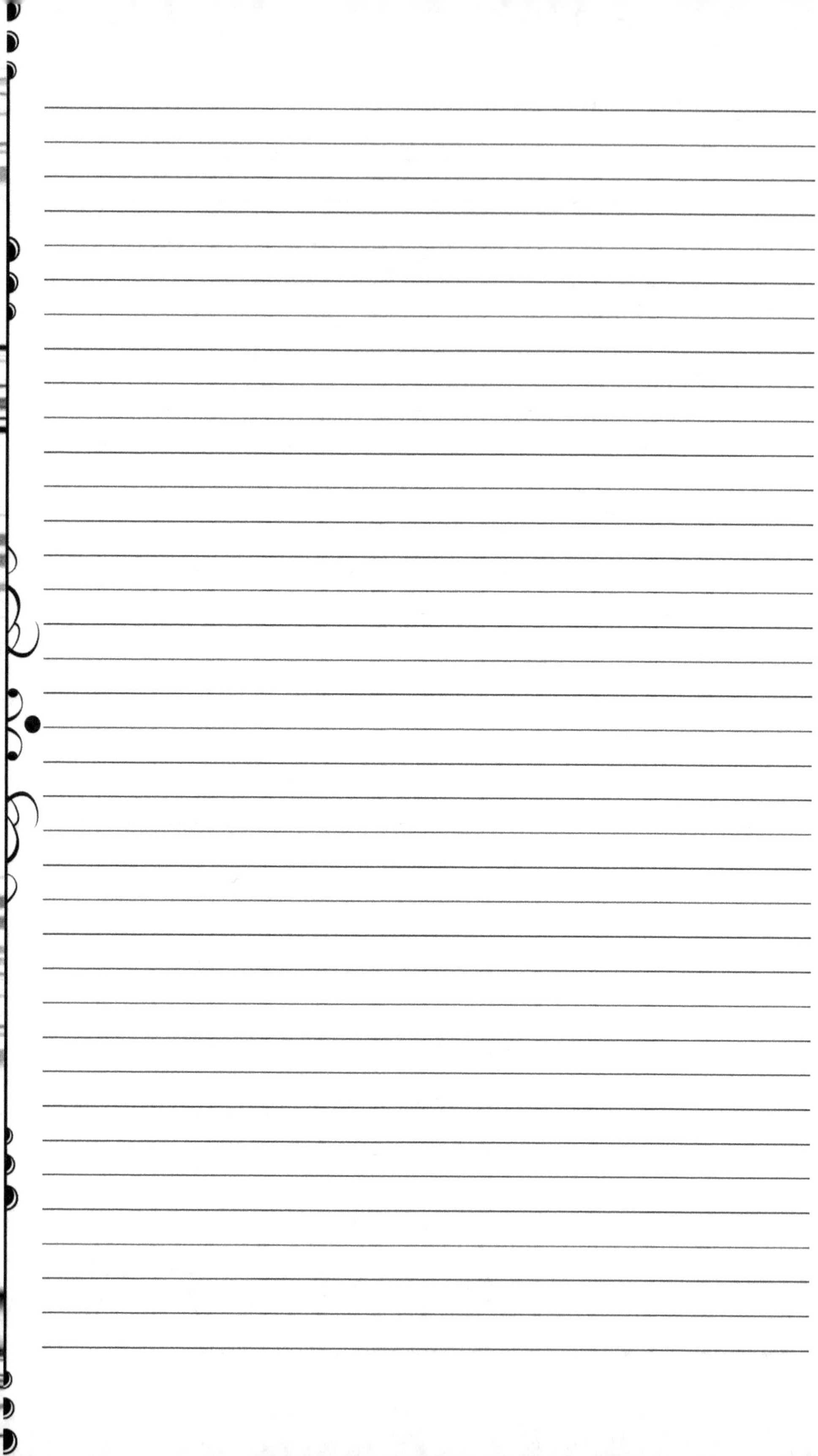

TITLE:

GENRE:

SERIES:

AUTHOR:

PAGES:

STARTED:

FINISHED:

☆ ☆ ☆ ☆ ☆

FORMAT READ: EBOOK / PRINT / AUDIOBOOK

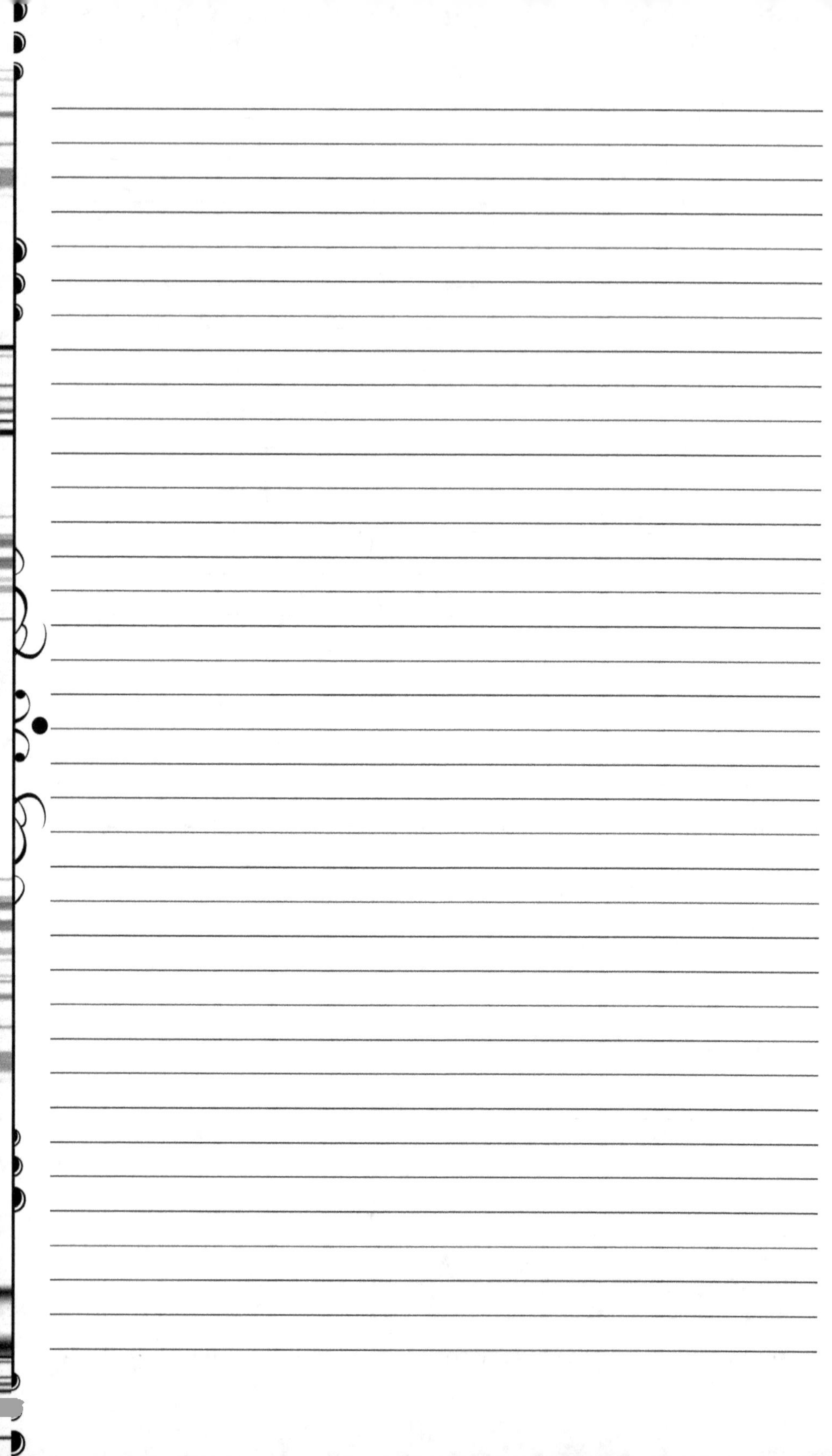

TITLE:

GENRE:

SERIES:

AUTHOR:

PAGES:

STARTED:

FINISHED:

FORMAT READ: EBOOK / PRINT / AUDIOBOOK

SYNOPSIS/THINGS I LIKED:

THINGS I DIDN'T LIKE:

FAVORITE QUOTE(S):

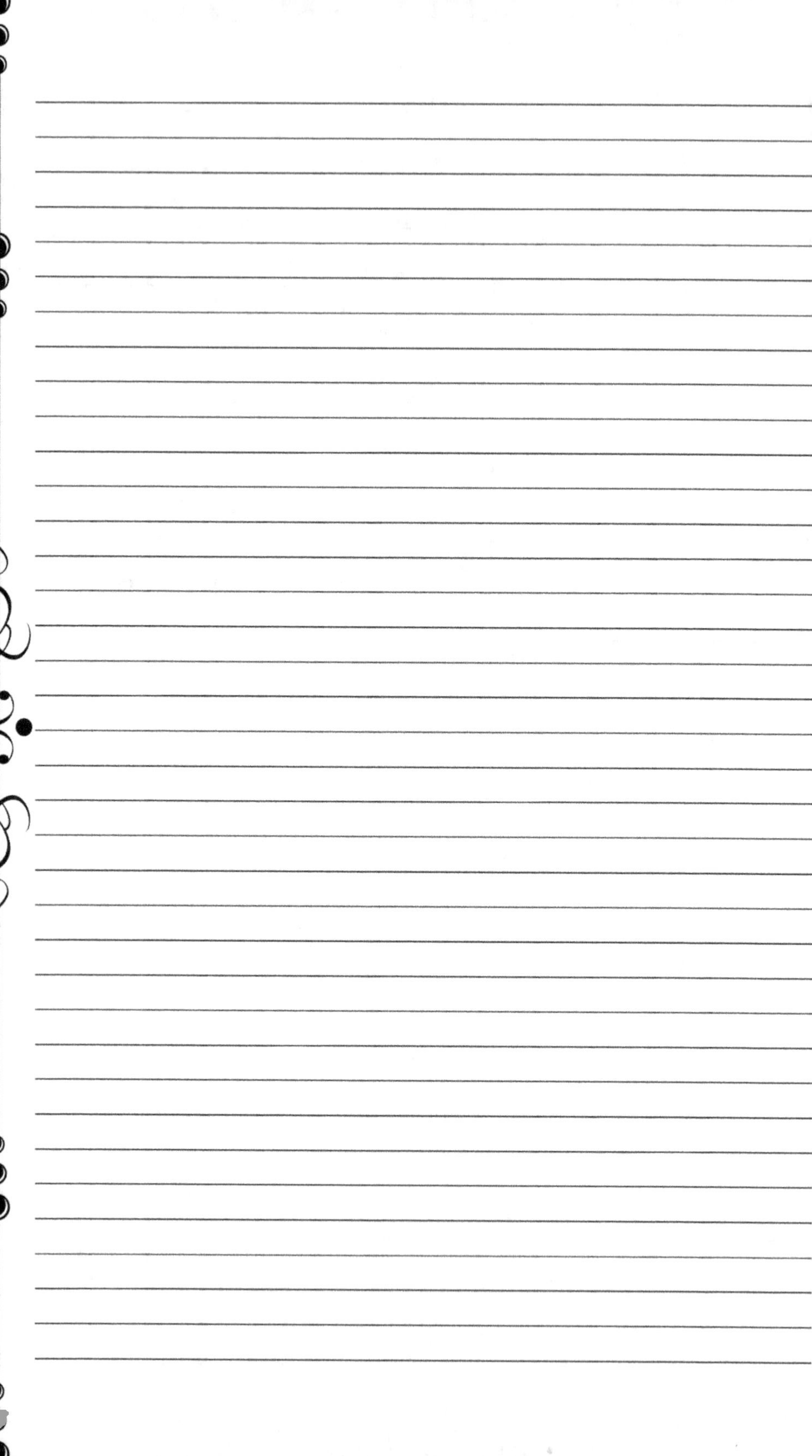

<u>**TITLE:**</u>

<u>**GENRE:**</u>

<u>**SERIES:**</u>

<u>**AUTHOR:**</u>

<u>**PAGES:**</u>

<u>**STARTED:**</u>

<u>**FINISHED:**</u>

☆ ☆ ☆ ☆ ☆

FORMAT READ: EBOOK / PRINT / AUDIOBOOK

✅ **SYNOPSIS/THINGS I LIKED:**

🚫 **THINGS I DIDN'T LIKE:**

✏️ **FAVORITE QUOTE(S):**

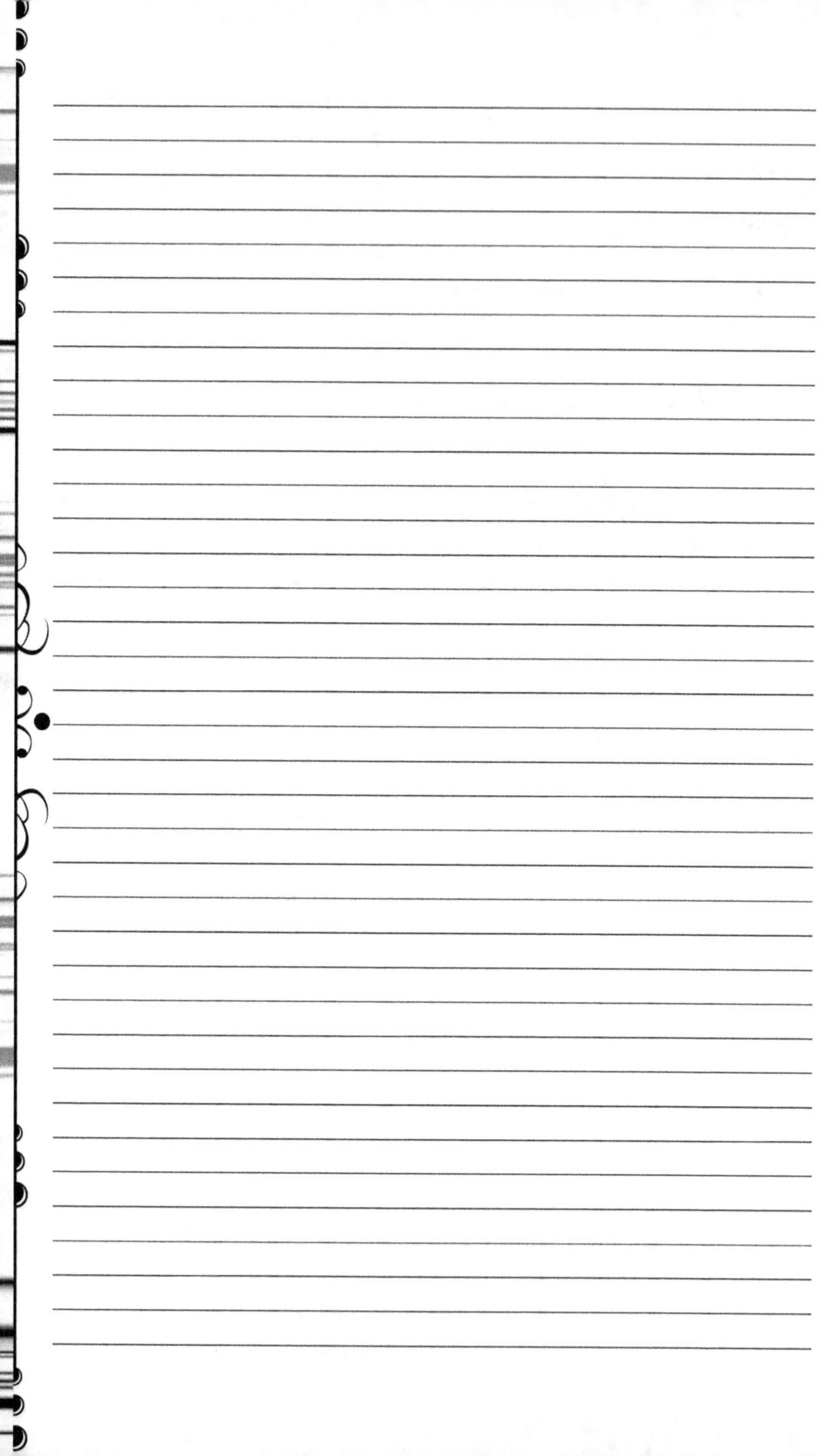

✅ **Synopsis/Things I liked:**

🚫 **Things I didn't like:**

✏️ **Favorite quote(s):**

Title:

Genre:

Series:

Author:

Pages:

Started:

Finished:

☆ ☆ ☆ ☆ ☆

Format read: Ebook / Print / Audiobook 51

TITLE:

GENRE:

SERIES:

AUTHOR:

PAGES:

STARTED:

FINISHED:

☆ ☆ ☆ ☆ ☆

FORMAT READ: EBOOK / PRINT / AUDIOBOOK

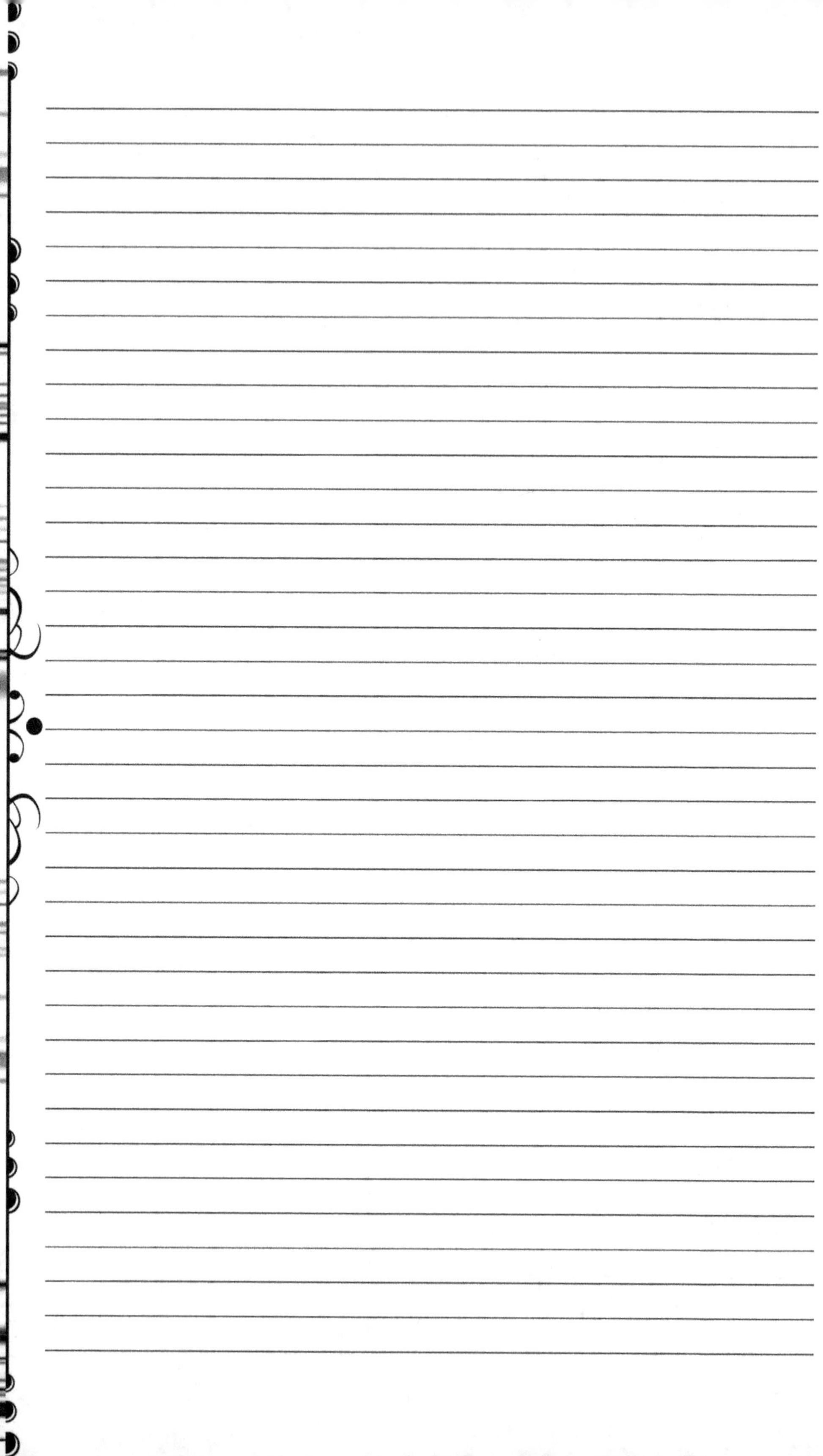

TITLE:

GENRE:

SERIES:

AUTHOR:

PAGES:

STARTED:

FINISHED:

☆☆☆☆☆

FORMAT READ: EBOOK / PRINT / AUDIOBOOK

SYNOPSIS/THINGS I LIKED:

THINGS I DIDN'T LIKE:

FAVORITE QUOTE(S):

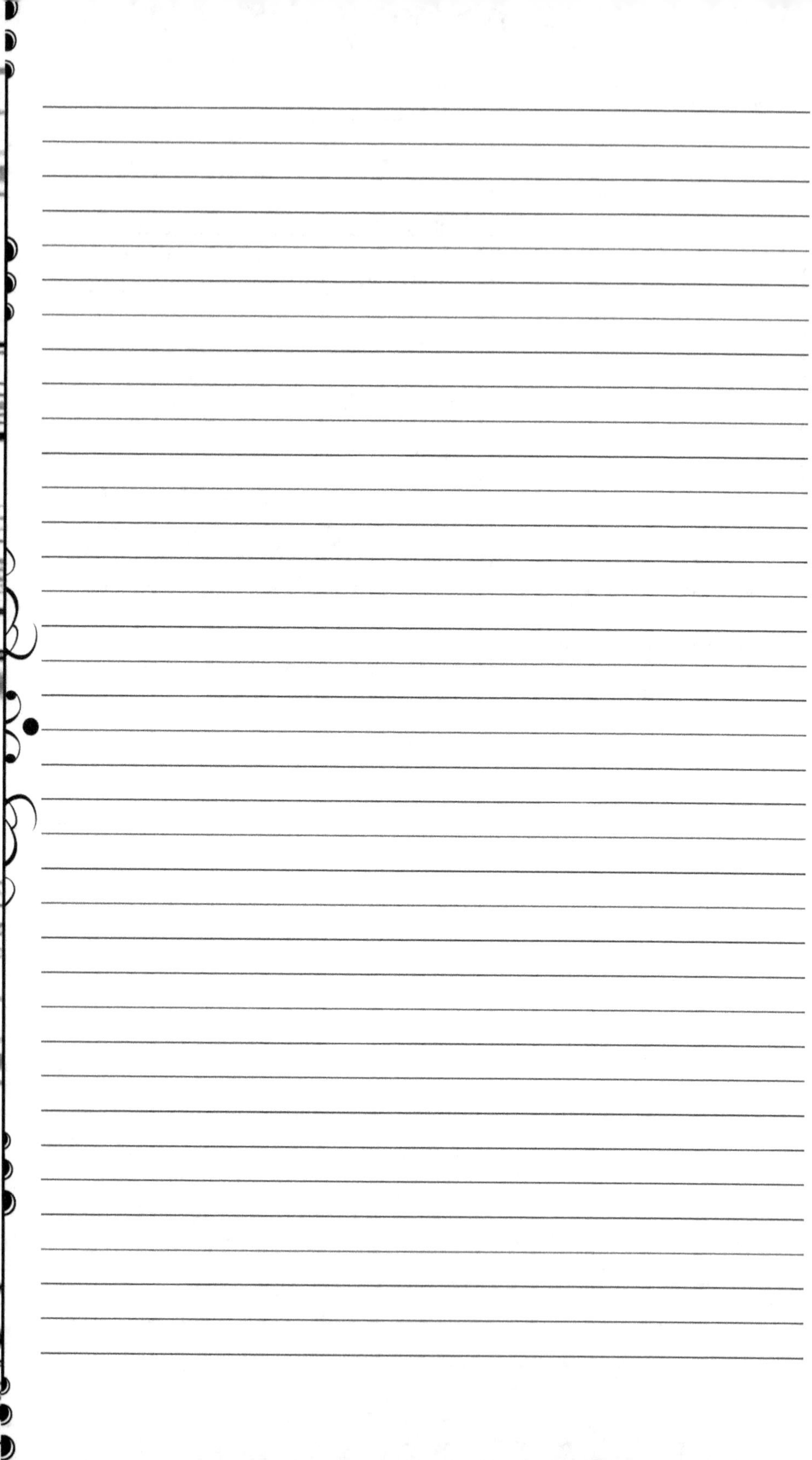

TITLE:

GENRE:

SERIES:

AUTHOR:

PAGES:

STARTED:

FINISHED:

☆ ☆ ☆ ☆ ☆

FORMAT READ: EBOOK / PRINT / AUDIOBOOK

✔ **SYNOPSIS/THINGS I LIKED:**

🚫 **THINGS I DIDN'T LIKE:**

✏ **FAVORITE QUOTE(S):**

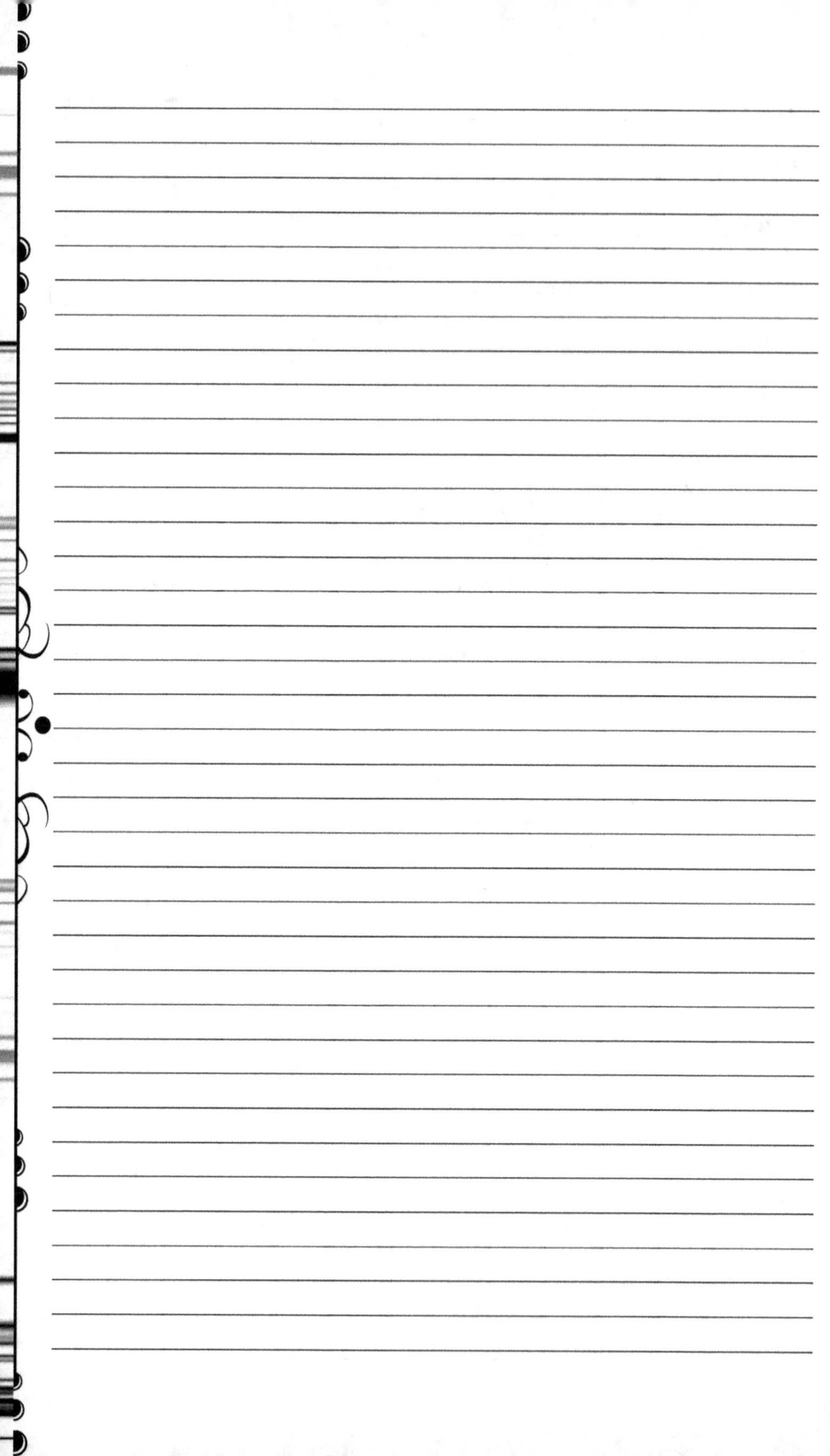

TITLE:

GENRE:

SERIES:

AUTHOR:

PAGES:

STARTED:

FINISHED:

FORMAT READ: EBOOK / PRINT / AUDIOBOOK 55

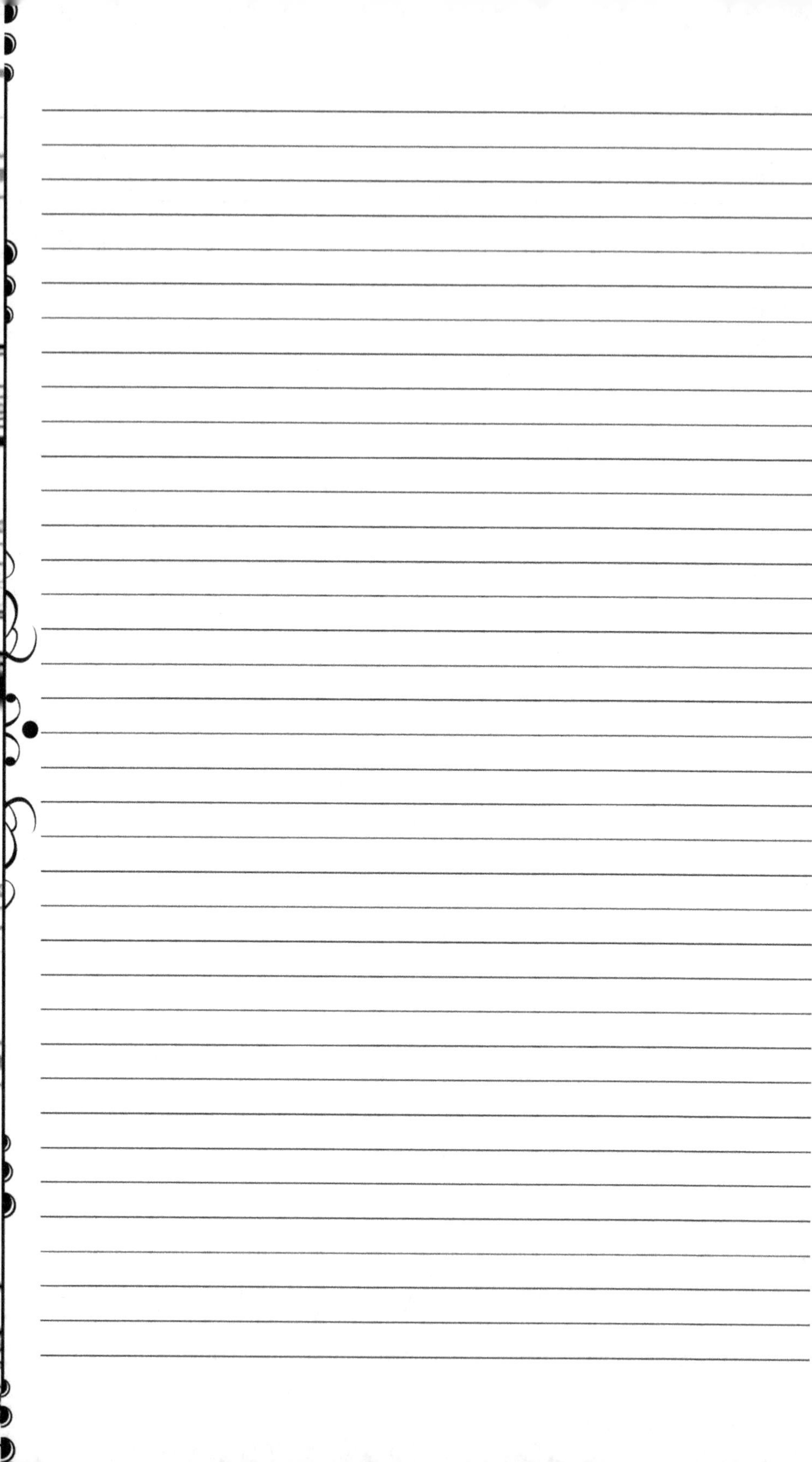

Title:

Genre:

Series:

Author:

Pages:

Started:

Finished:

☆ ☆ ☆ ☆ ☆

Format read: Ebook / Print / Audiobook

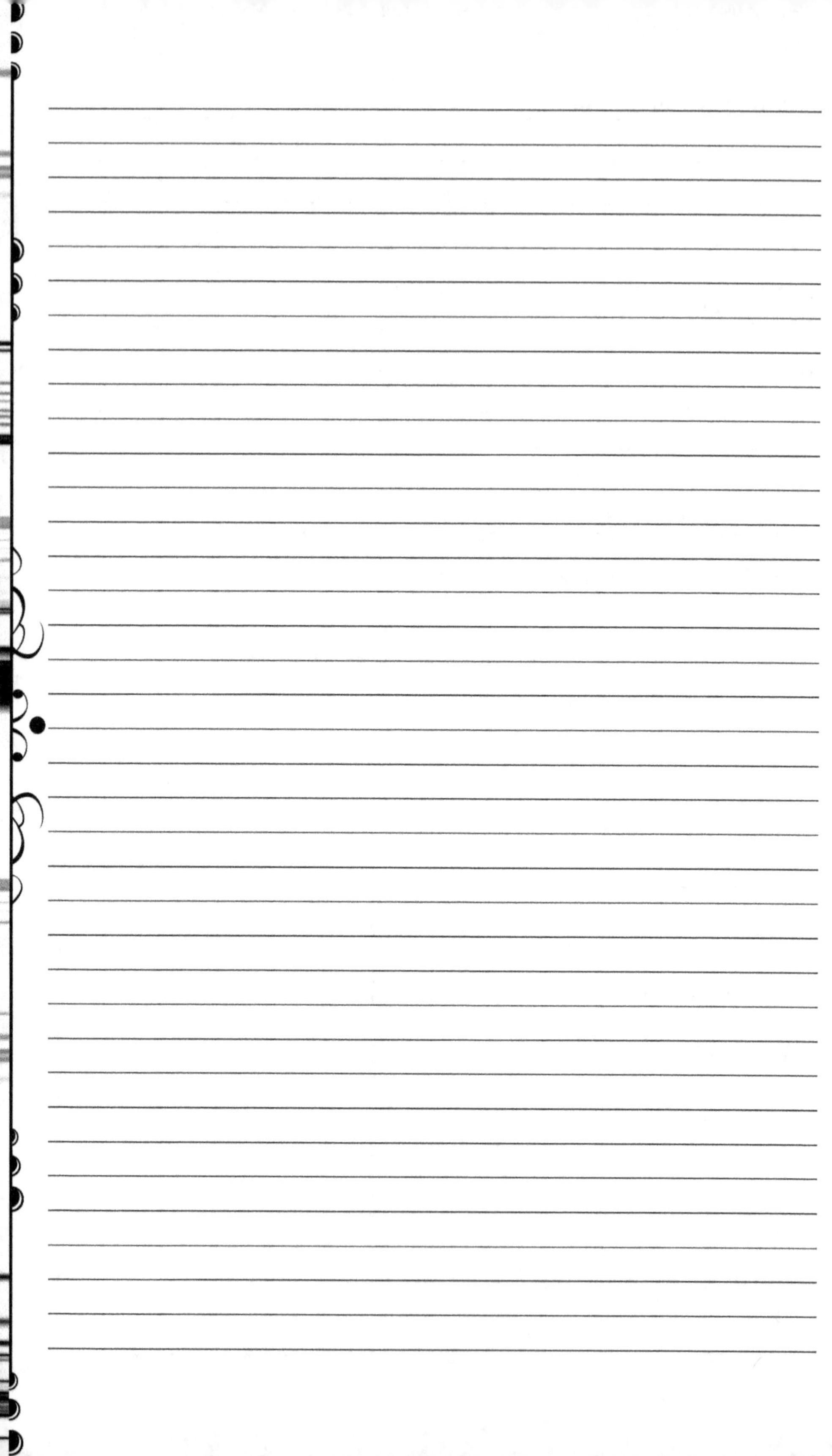

SYNOPSIS/THINGS I LIKED:

THINGS I DIDN'T LIKE:

FAVORITE QUOTE(S):

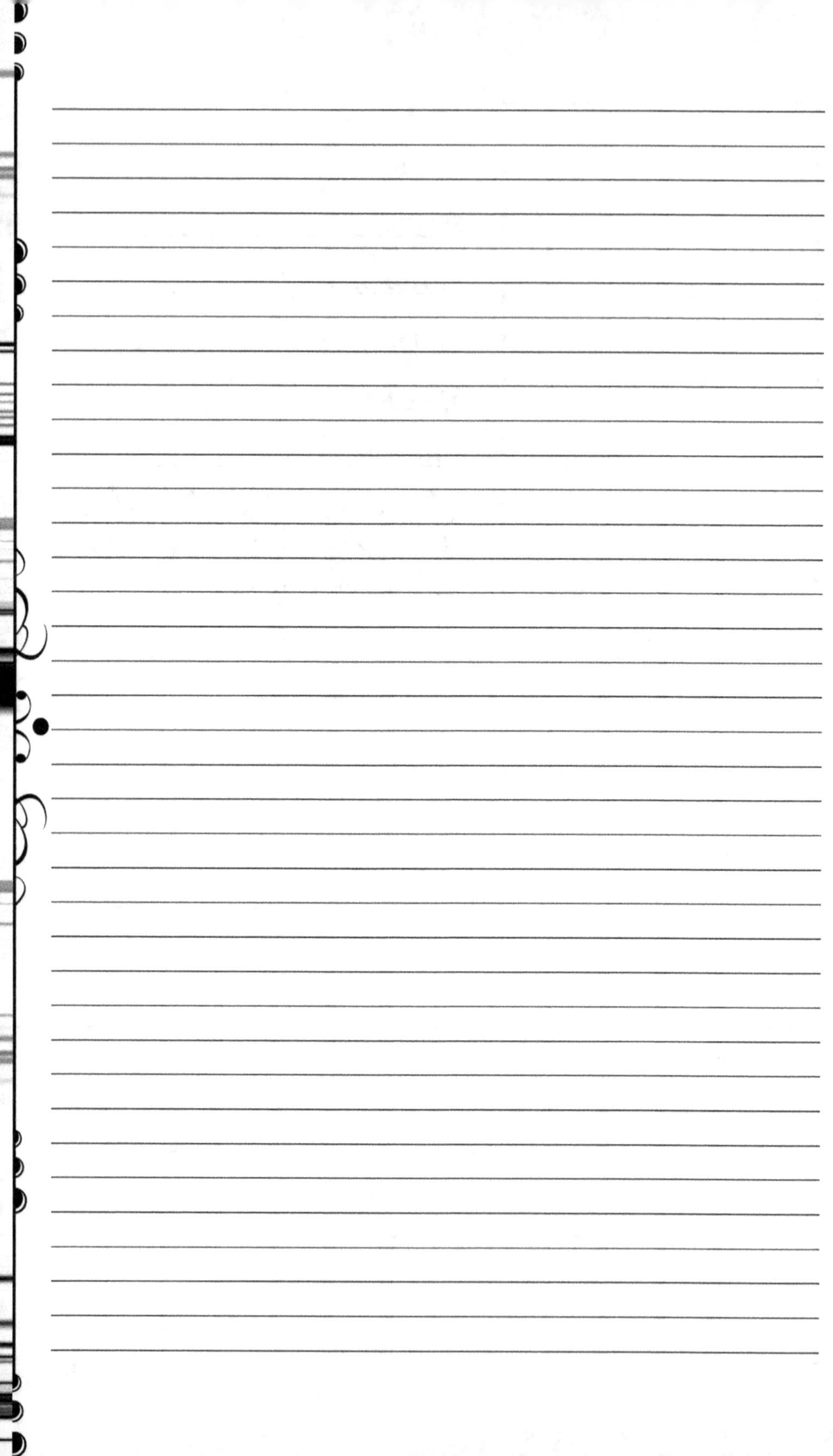

TITLE:

GENRE:

SERIES:

AUTHOR:

PAGES:

STARTED:

FINISHED:

FORMAT READ: EBOOK / PRINT / AUDIOBOOK

✓ SYNOPSIS/THINGS I LIKED:

🚫 THINGS I DIDN'T LIKE:

✏️ FAVORITE QUOTE(S):

TITLE:

GENRE:

SERIES:

AUTHOR:

PAGES:

STARTED:

FINISHED:

FORMAT READ: EBOOK / PRINT / AUDIOBOOK 59

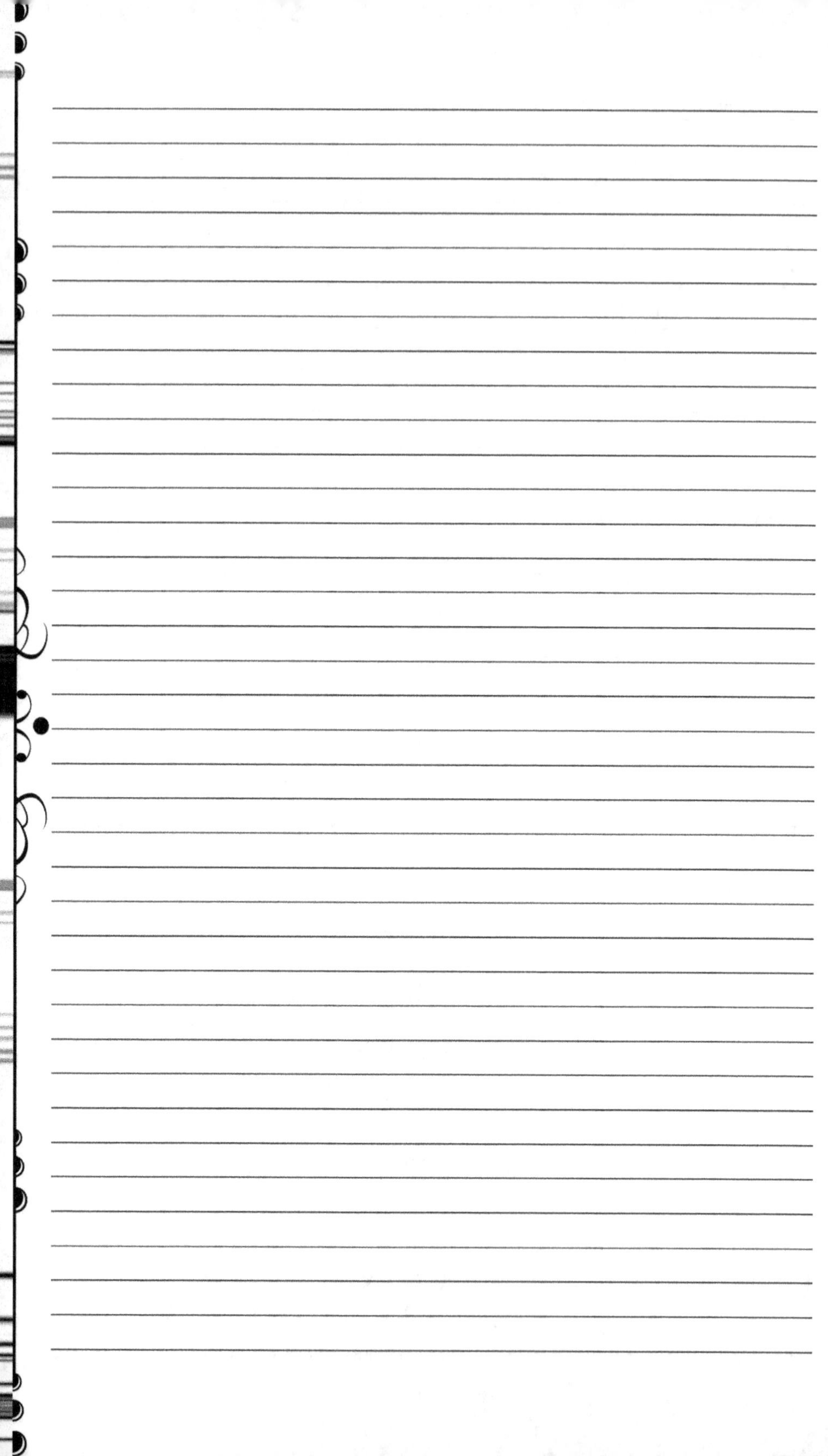

✅ **Synopsis/Things I liked:**

🚫 **Things I didn't like:**

✏️ **Favorite quote(s):**

Title:

Genre:

Series:

Author:

Pages:

Started:

Finished:

☆☆☆☆☆

Format read: Ebook / Print / Audiobook

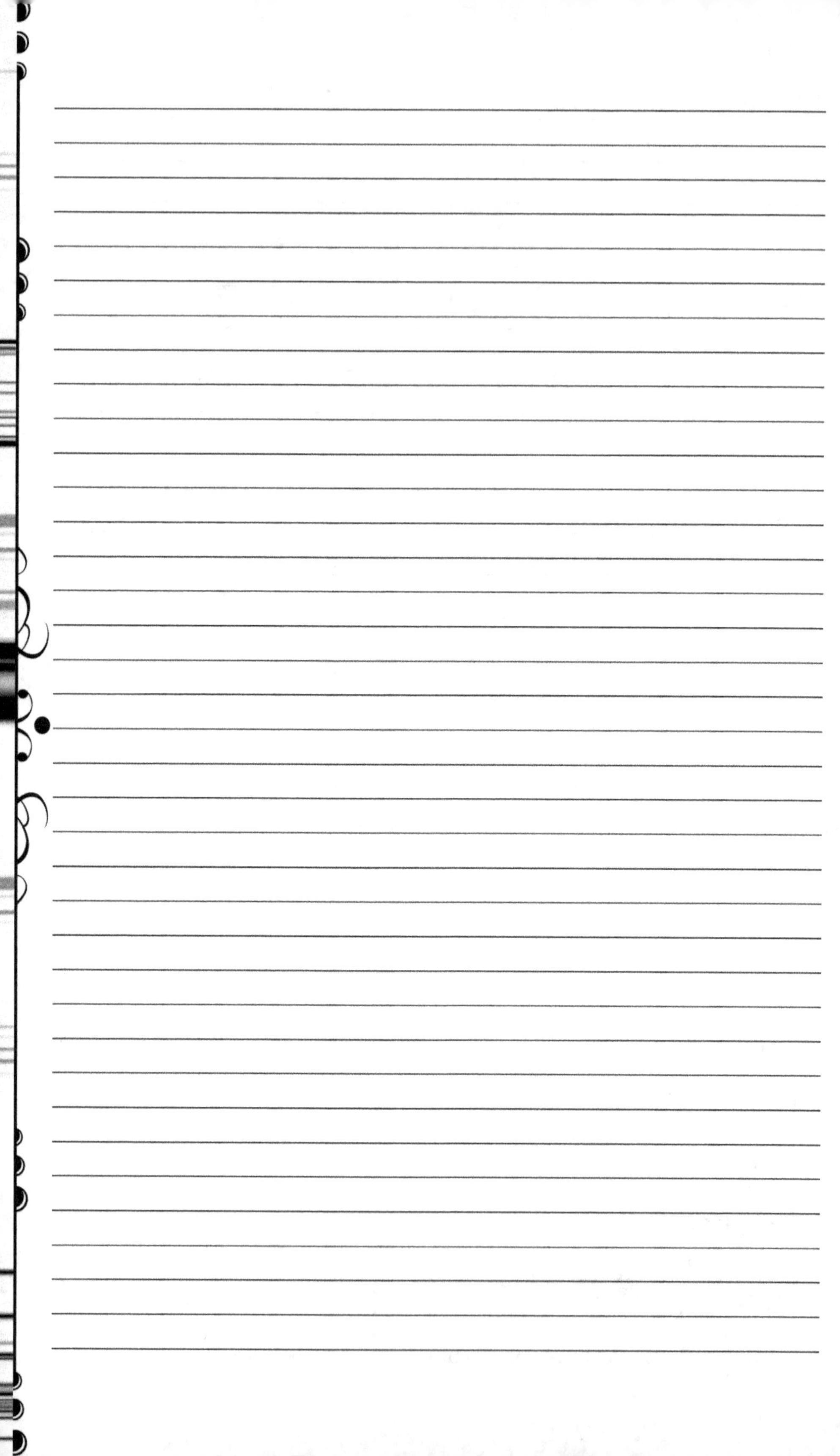

TITLE:

GENRE:

SERIES:

AUTHOR:

PAGES:

STARTED:

FINISHED:

FORMAT READ: EBOOK / PRINT / AUDIOBOOK

SYNOPSIS/THINGS I LIKED:

THINGS I DIDN'T LIKE:

FAVORITE QUOTE(S):

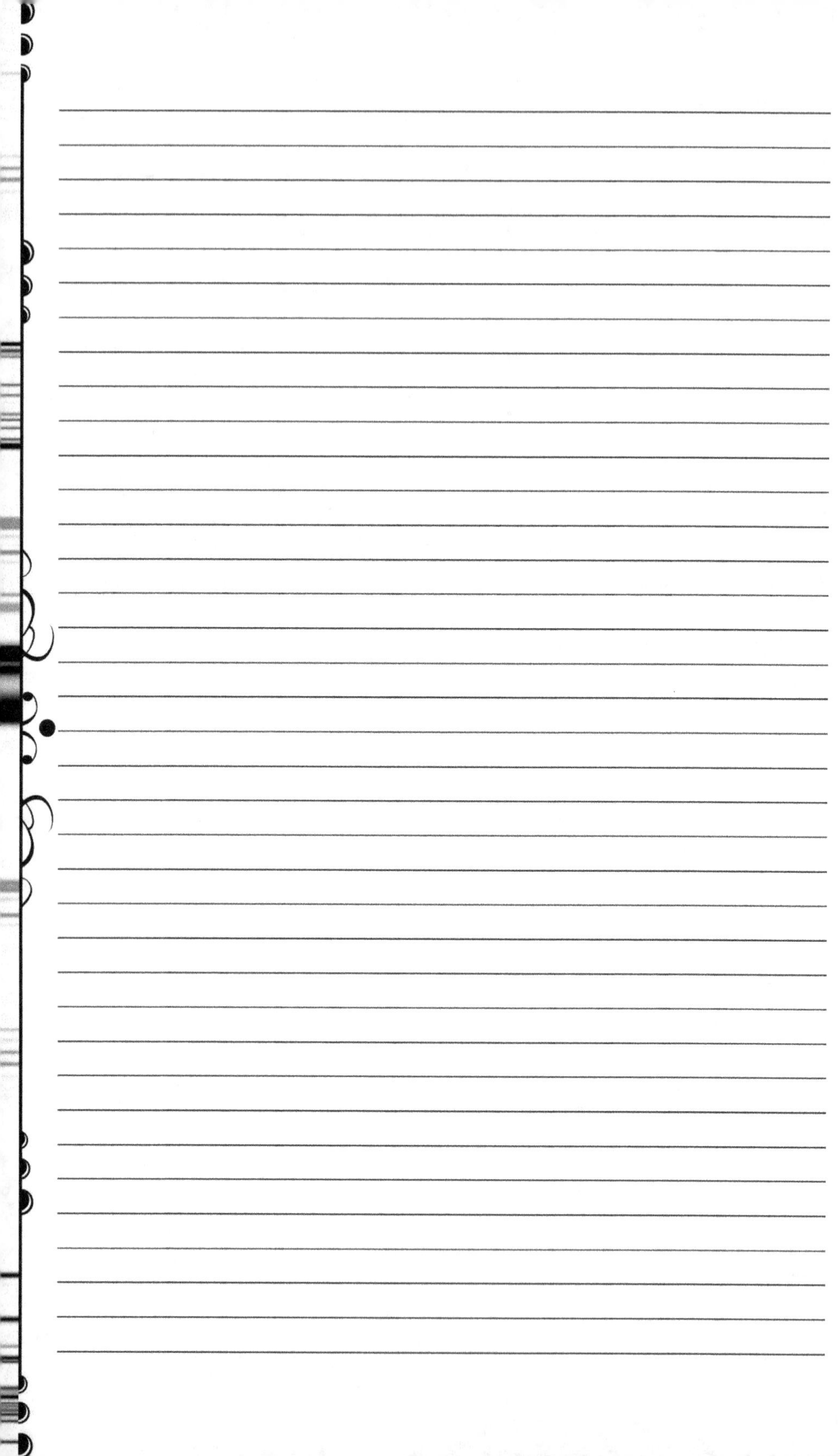

TITLE: _______________

GENRE: _______________

SERIES: _______________

AUTHOR: _______________

PAGES: _______________

STARTED: _______________

FINISHED: _______________

☆ ☆ ☆ ☆ ☆

FORMAT READ: EBOOK / PRINT / AUDIOBOOK

✔ **SYNOPSIS/THINGS I LIKED:**

____
____
____
____

🚫 **THINGS I DIDN'T LIKE:**

____
____
____
____

✎ **FAVORITE QUOTE(S):**

____
____
____
____
____
____
____

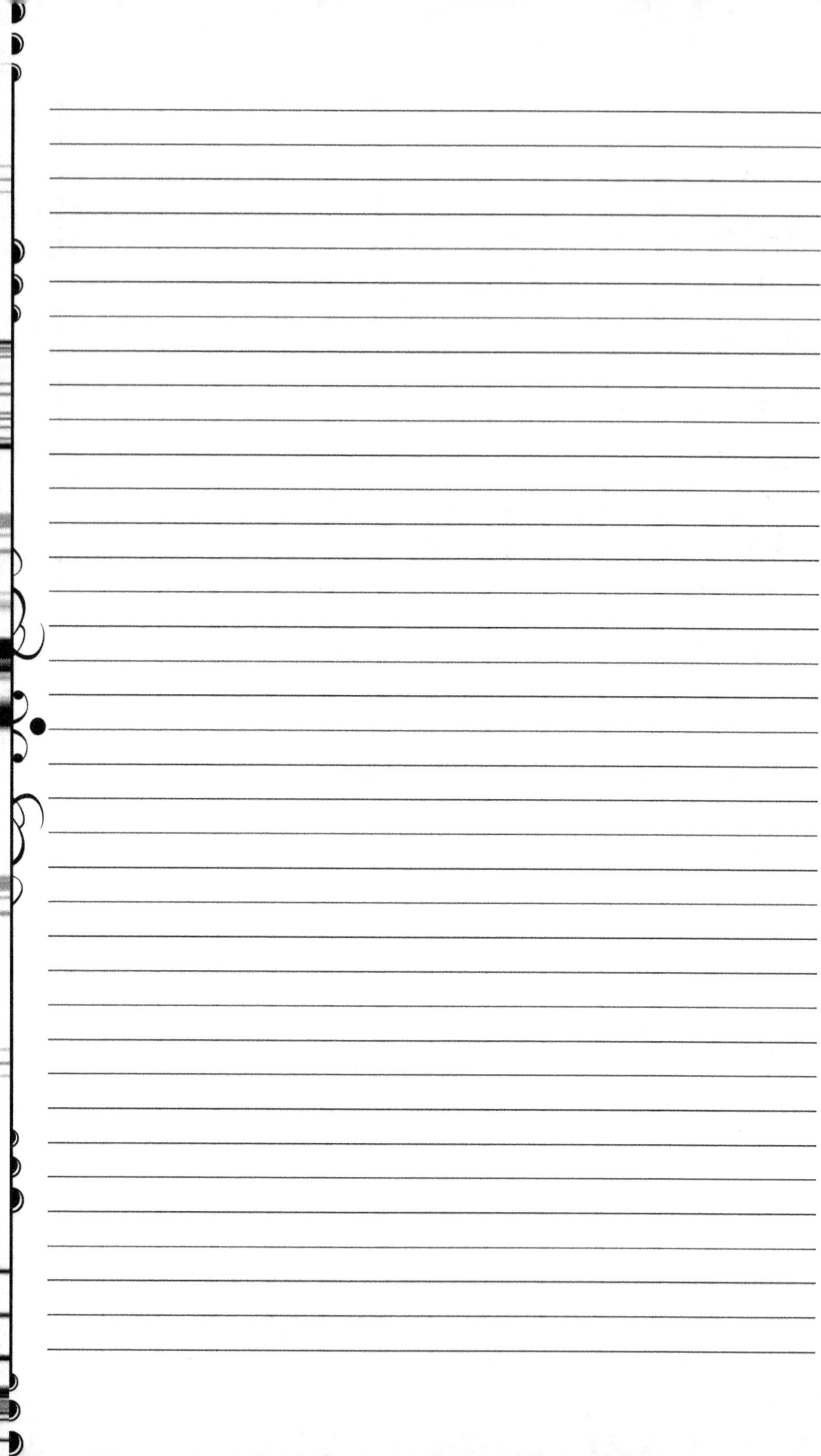

SYNOPSIS/THINGS I LIKED:

THINGS I DIDN'T LIKE:

FAVORITE QUOTE(S):

TITLE:
GENRE:
SERIES:
AUTHOR:
PAGES:
STARTED:
FINISHED:

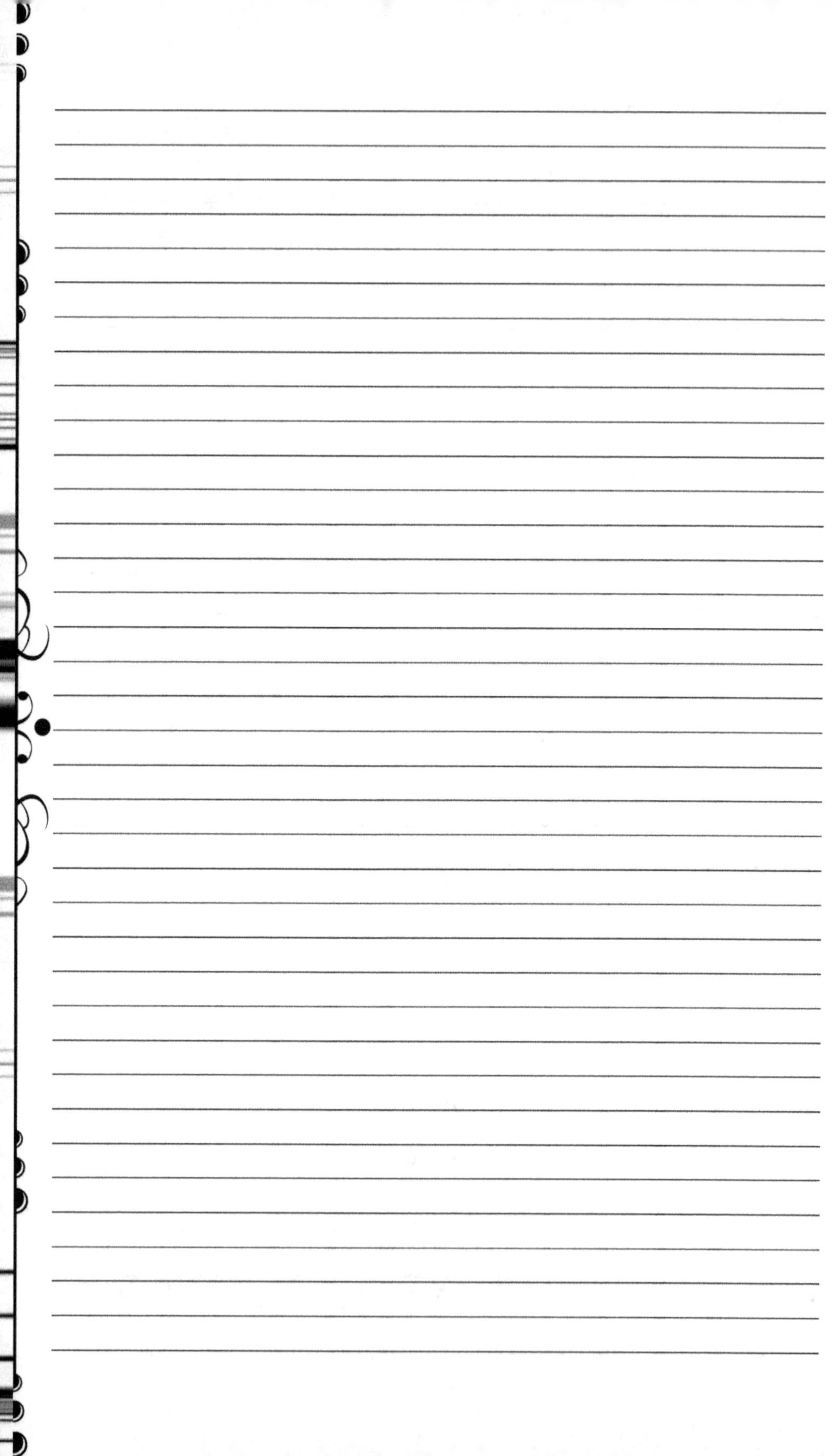

TITLE:

GENRE:

SERIES:

AUTHOR:

PAGES:

STARTED:

FINISHED:

FORMAT READ: EBOOK / PRINT / AUDIOBOOK

TITLE:

GENRE:

SERIES:

AUTHOR:

PAGES:

STARTED:

FINISHED:

FORMAT READ: EBOOK / PRINT / AUDIOBOOK

✓ SYNOPSIS/THINGS I LIKED:

⊘ THINGS I DIDN'T LIKE:

✎ FAVORITE QUOTE(S):

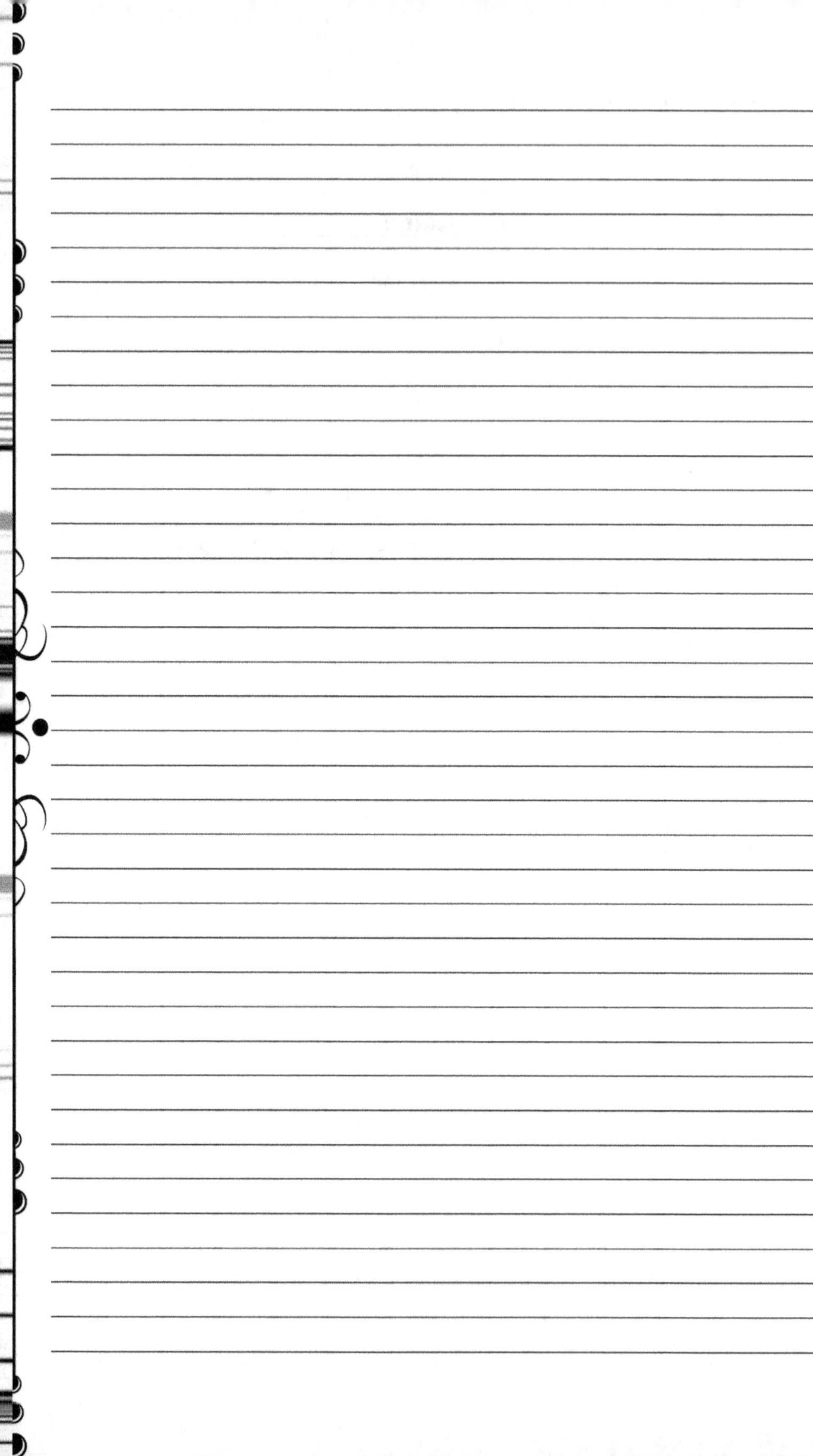

TITLE: ___________________________

GENRE: ___________________________

SERIES: ___________________________

AUTHOR: ___________________________

PAGES: ___________________________

STARTED: ___________________________

FINISHED: ___________________________

☆ ☆ ☆ ☆ ☆

FORMAT READ: EBOOK / PRINT / AUDIOBOOK

✔ SYNOPSIS/THINGS I LIKED:

____
____
____
____

🚫 THINGS I DIDN'T LIKE:

____
____
____
____

✎ FAVORITE QUOTE(S):

____
____
____
____
____
____
____

TITLE:

GENRE:

SERIES:

AUTHOR:

PAGES:

STARTED:

FINISHED:

FORMAT READ: EBOOK / PRINT / AUDIOBOOK

TITLE:

GENRE:

SERIES:

AUTHOR:

PAGES:

STARTED:

FINISHED:

FORMAT READ: EBOOK / PRINT / AUDIOBOOK

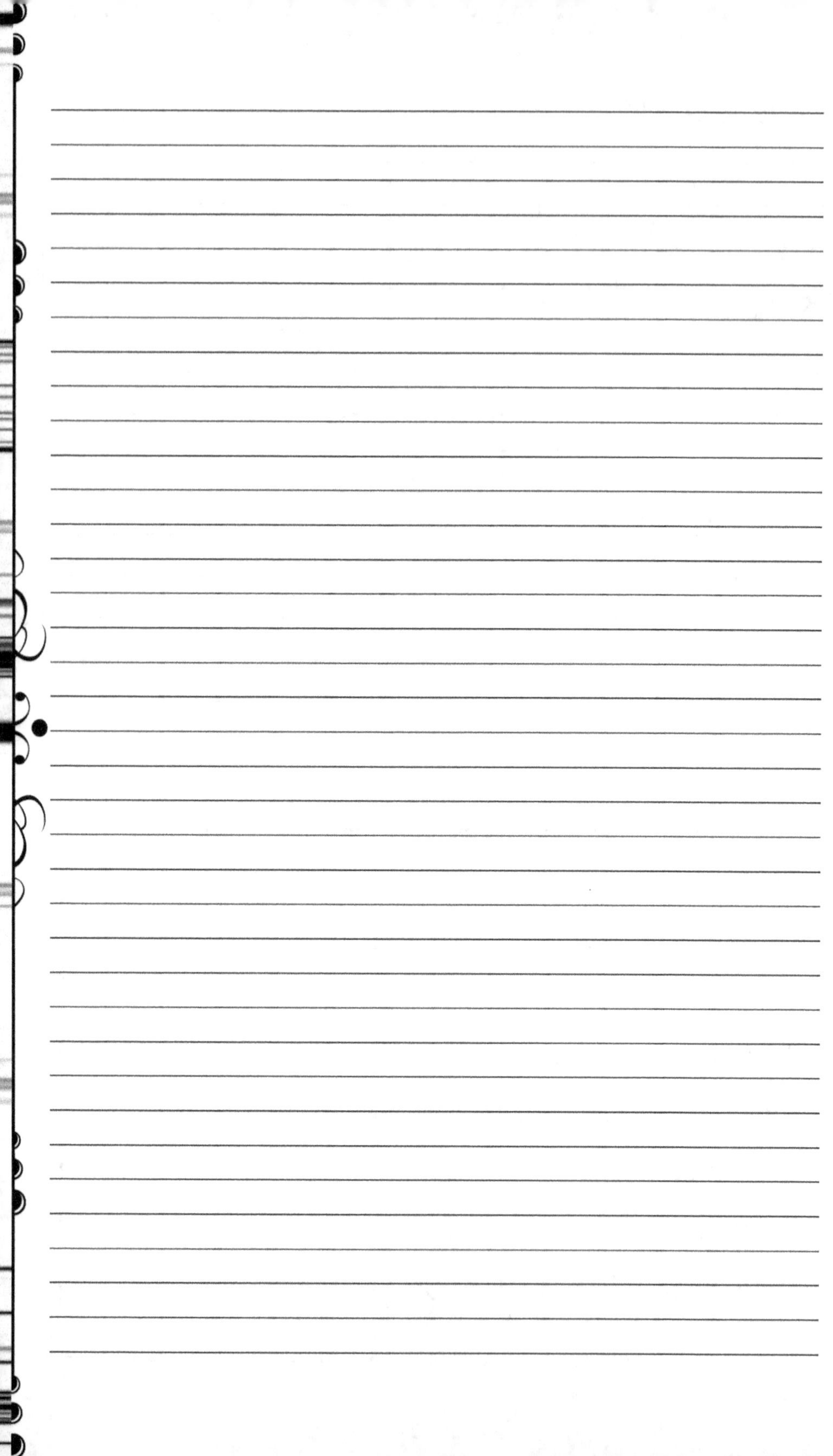

TITLE: _______________________

GENRE: _______________________

SERIES: _______________________

AUTHOR: _______________________

PAGES: _______________________

STARTED: _______________________

FINISHED: _______________________

☆ ☆ ☆ ☆ ☆

FORMAT READ: EBOOK / PRINT / AUDIOBOOK

✅ **SYNOPSIS/THINGS I LIKED:**

____
____
____
____

🚫 **THINGS I DIDN'T LIKE:**

____
____
____

✏️ **FAVORITE QUOTE(S):**

____
____
____
____
____
____
____

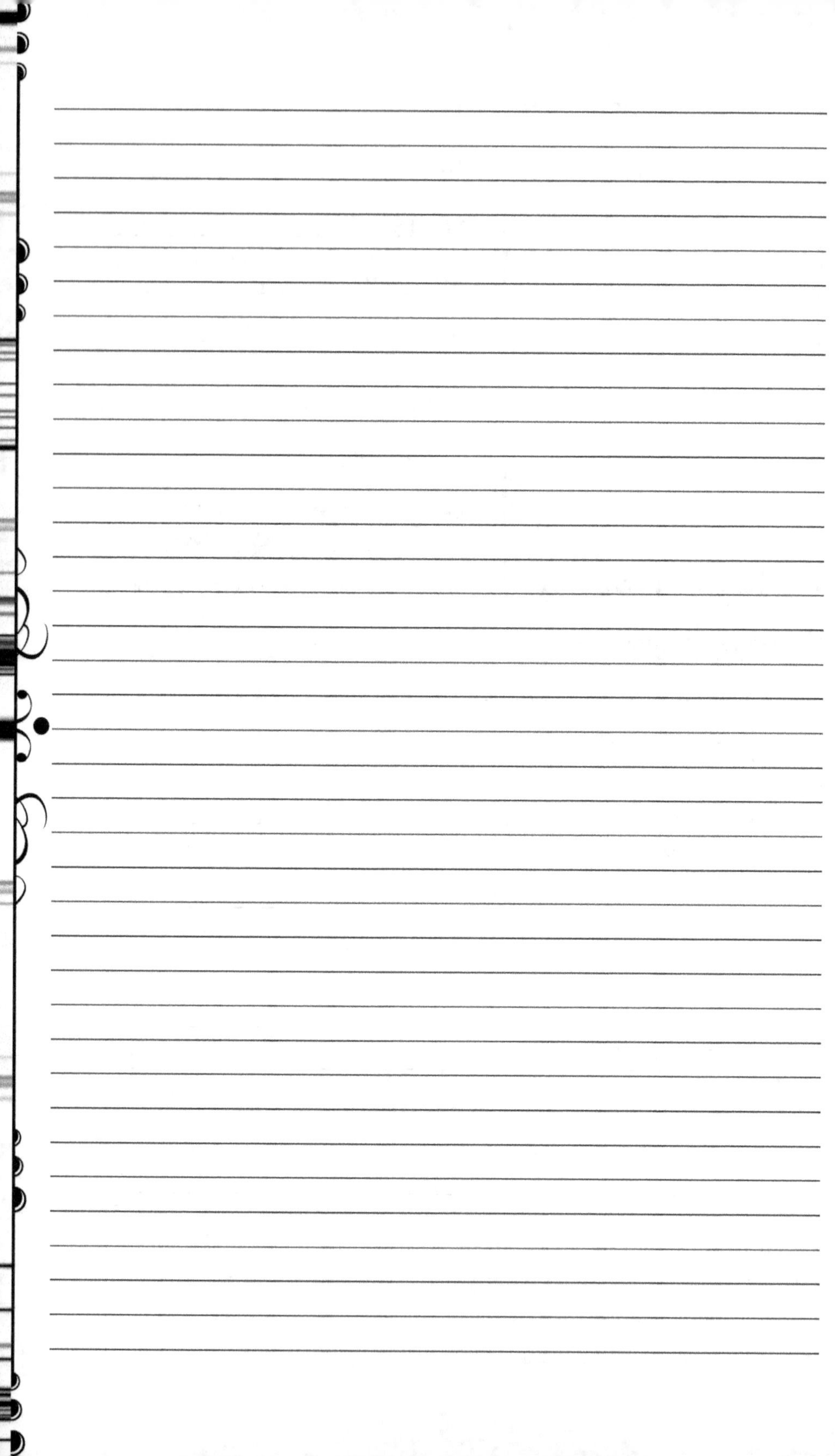

TITLE: ___________________________

GENRE: ___________________________

SERIES: ___________________________

AUTHOR: ___________________________

PAGES: ___________________________

STARTED: ___________________________

FINISHED: ___________________________

☆ ☆ ☆ ☆ ☆

FORMAT READ: EBOOK / PRINT / AUDIOBOOK

☑ **SYNOPSIS/THINGS I LIKED:**

____
____
____
____

🚫 **THINGS I DIDN'T LIKE:**

____
____
____
____

✎ **FAVORITE QUOTE(S):**

____
____
____
____
____
____
____

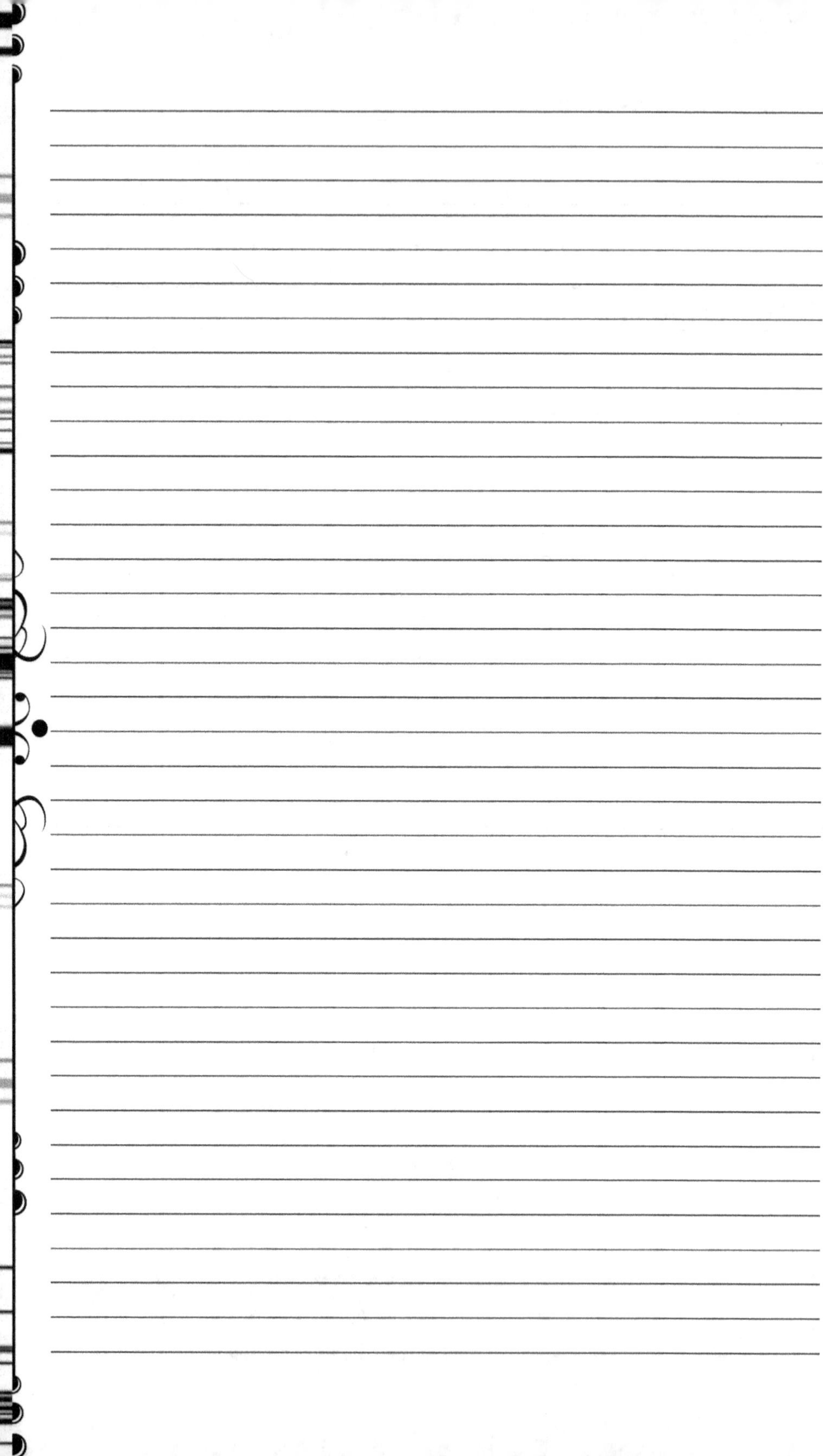

TITLE:

GENRE:

SERIES:

AUTHOR:

PAGES:

STARTED:

FINISHED:

FORMAT READ: EBOOK / PRINT / AUDIOBOOK

TITLE:

GENRE:

SERIES:

AUTHOR:

PAGES:

STARTED:

FINISHED:

FORMAT READ: EBOOK / PRINT / AUDIOBOOK

✔ SYNOPSIS/THINGS I LIKED:

🚫 THINGS I DIDN'T LIKE:

✎ FAVORITE QUOTE(S):

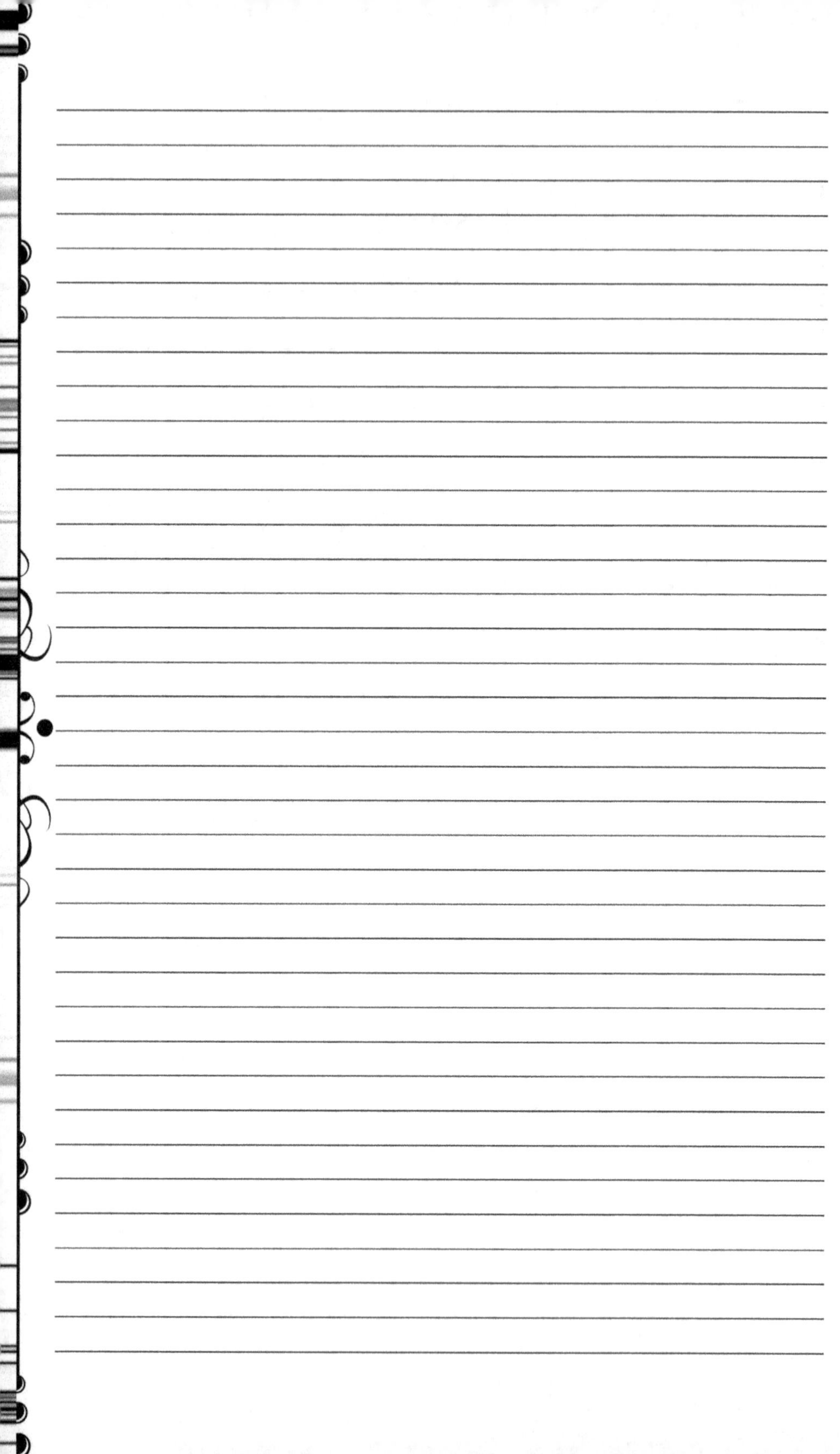

TITLE:

GENRE:

SERIES:

AUTHOR:

PAGES:

STARTED:

FINISHED:

☆☆☆☆☆

FORMAT READ: EBOOK / PRINT / AUDIOBOOK

✓ **SYNOPSIS/THINGS I LIKED:**

🚫 **THINGS I DIDN'T LIKE:**

✎ **FAVORITE QUOTE(S):**

TITLE:

GENRE:

SERIES:

AUTHOR:

PAGES:

STARTED:

FINISHED:

☆ ☆ ☆ ☆ ☆

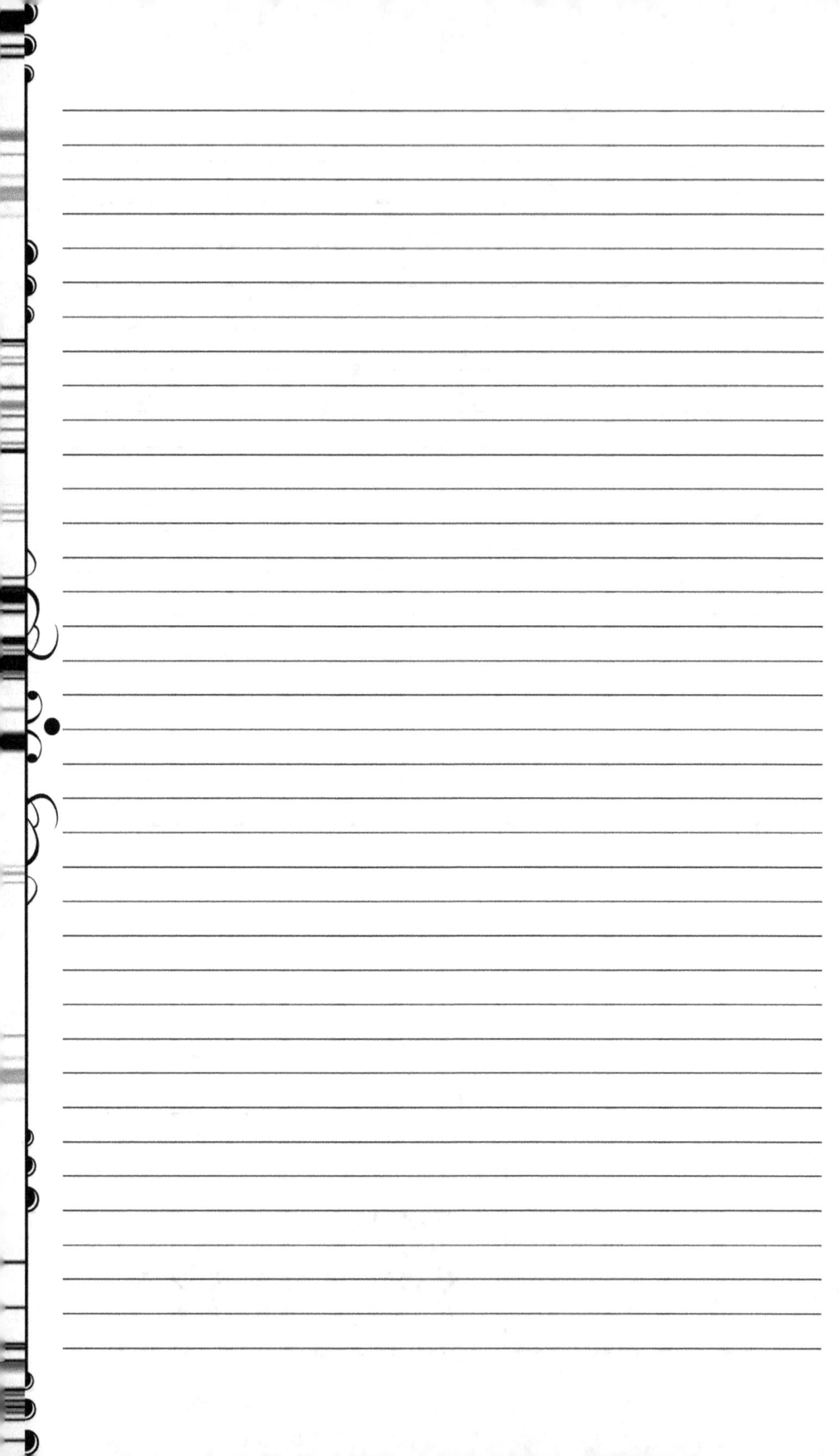

✓ **SYNOPSIS/THINGS I LIKED:**

🚫 **THINGS I DIDN'T LIKE:**

✎ **FAVORITE QUOTE(S):**

TITLE:

GENRE:

SERIES:

AUTHOR:

PAGES:

STARTED:

FINISHED:

☆☆☆☆☆

FORMAT READ: EBOOK / PRINT / AUDIOBOOK

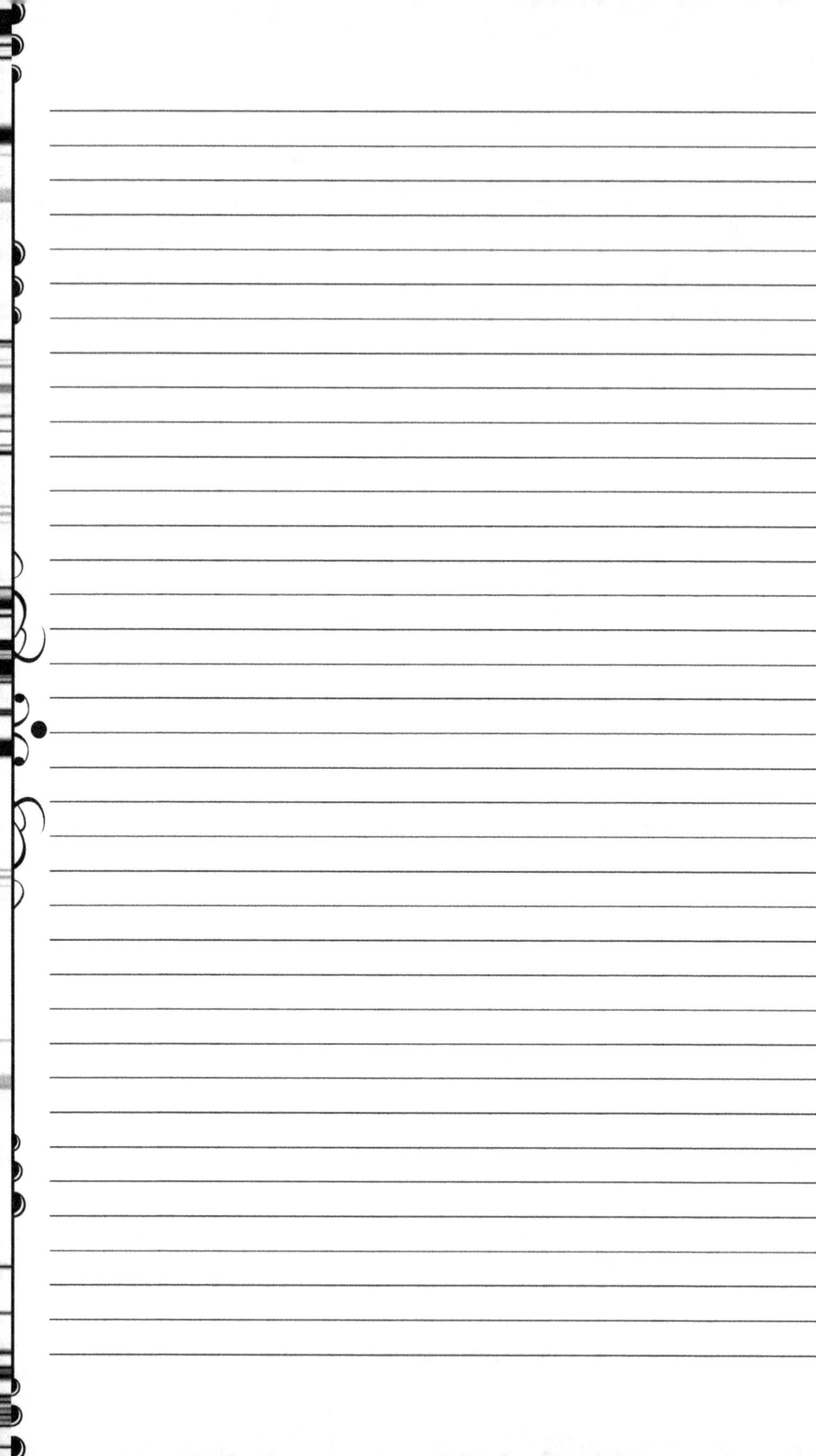

TITLE:

GENRE:

SERIES:

AUTHOR:

PAGES:

STARTED:

FINISHED:

FORMAT READ: EBOOK / PRINT / AUDIOBOOK

✔ SYNOPSIS/THINGS I LIKED:

🚫 THINGS I DIDN'T LIKE:

✎ FAVORITE QUOTE(S):

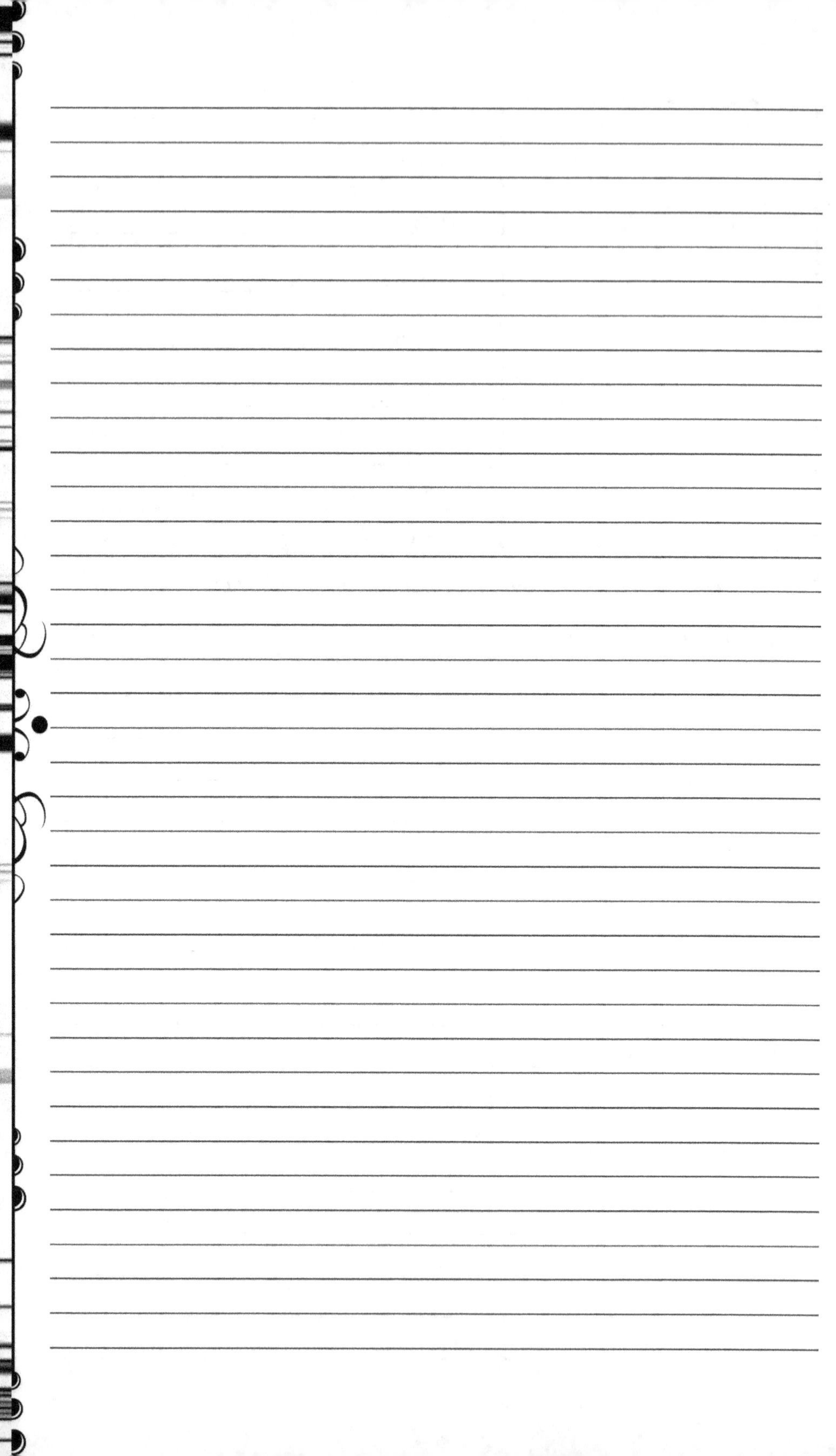

TITLE: ___________________

GENRE: ___________________

SERIES: ___________________

AUTHOR: ___________________

PAGES: ___________________

STARTED: ___________________

FINISHED: ___________________

☆ ☆ ☆ ☆ ☆

FORMAT READ: EBOOK / PRINT / AUDIOBOOK

✓ **SYNOPSIS/THINGS I LIKED:**

____
____
____
____

🚫 **THINGS I DIDN'T LIKE:**

____
____
____
____

✎ **FAVORITE QUOTE(S):**

____
____
____
____
____
____
____

SYNOPSIS/THINGS I LIKED:

THINGS I DIDN'T LIKE:

FAVORITE QUOTE(S):

TITLE:
GENRE:
SERIES:
AUTHOR:
PAGES:
STARTED:
FINISHED:

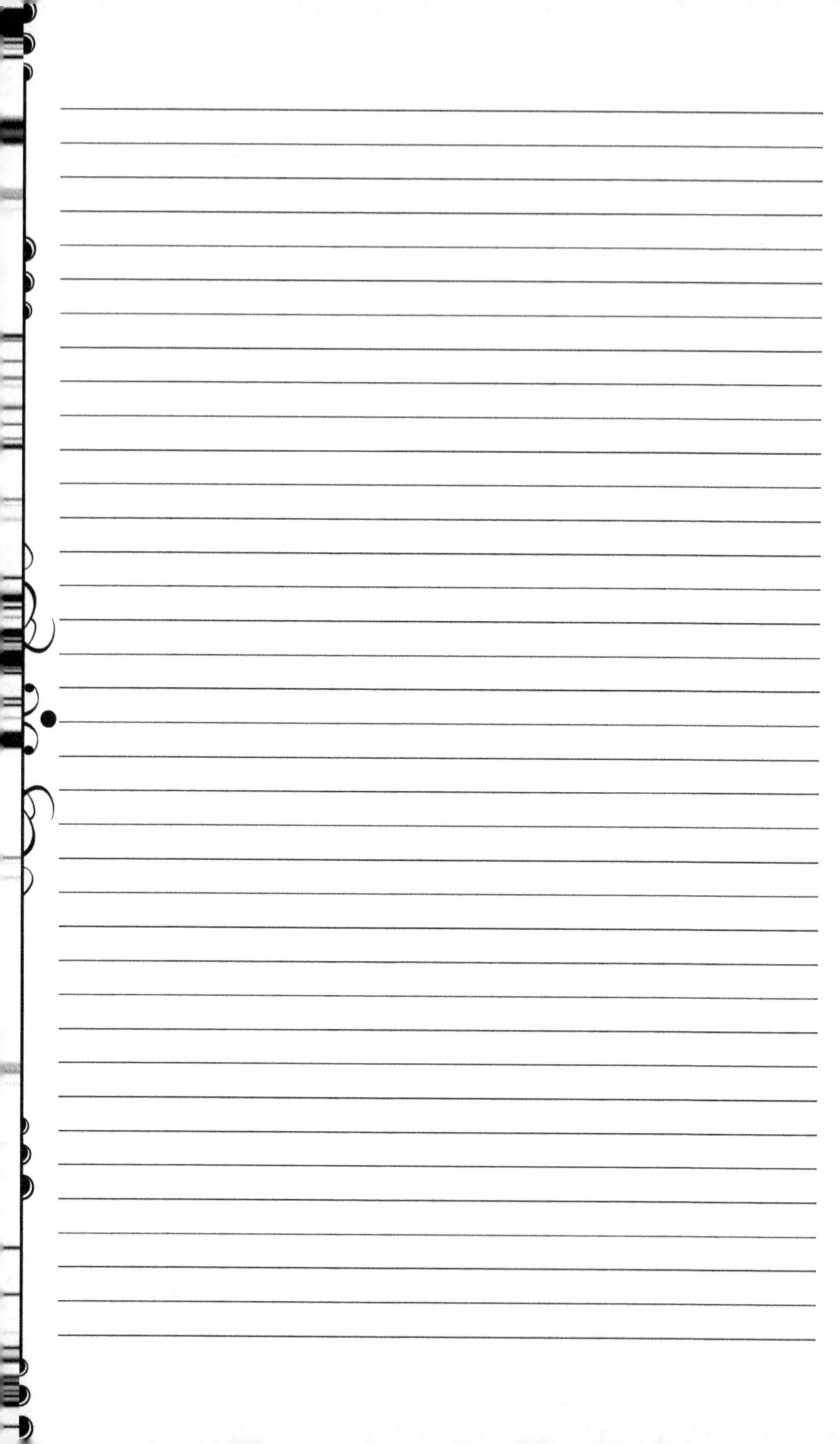

TITLE:

GENRE:

SERIES:

AUTHOR:

PAGES:

STARTED:

FINISHED:

FORMAT READ: EBOOK / PRINT / AUDIOBOOK

80

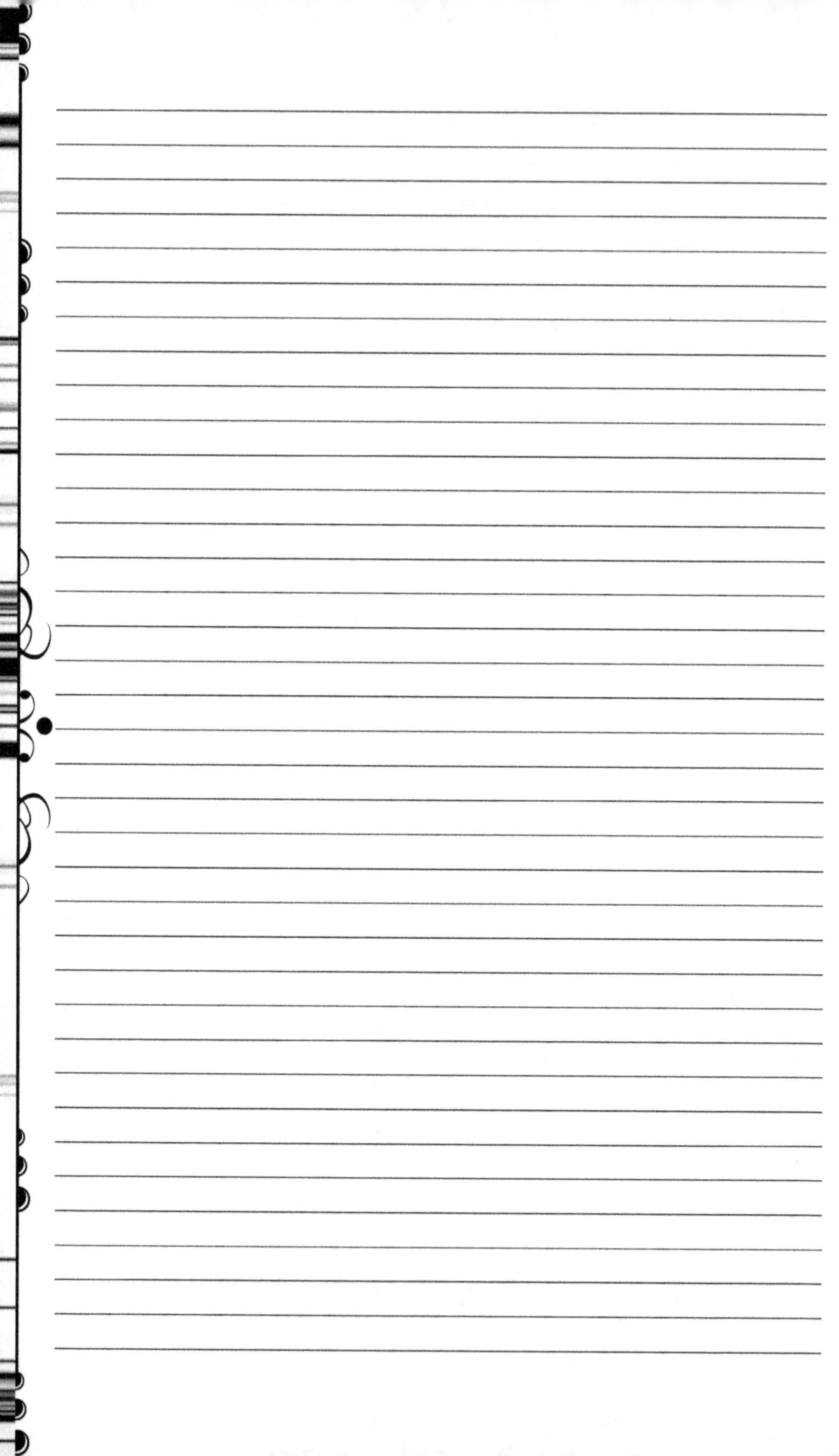

TITLE:

GENRE:

SERIES:

AUTHOR:

PAGES:

STARTED:

FINISHED:

☆☆☆☆☆

FORMAT READ: EBOOK / PRINT / AUDIOBOOK

✓ **SYNOPSIS/THINGS I LIKED:**

🚫 **THINGS I DIDN'T LIKE:**

✏️ **FAVORITE QUOTE(S):**

TITLE: _______________________

GENRE: _______________________

SERIES: _______________________

AUTHOR: _______________________

PAGES: _______________________

STARTED: _______________________

FINISHED: _______________________

☆☆☆☆☆

FORMAT READ: EBOOK / PRINT / AUDIOBOOK

✓ **SYNOPSIS/THINGS I LIKED:**

____

____

____

____

🚫 **THINGS I DIDN'T LIKE:**

____

____

____

____

✎ **FAVORITE QUOTE(S):**

____

____

____

____

____

____

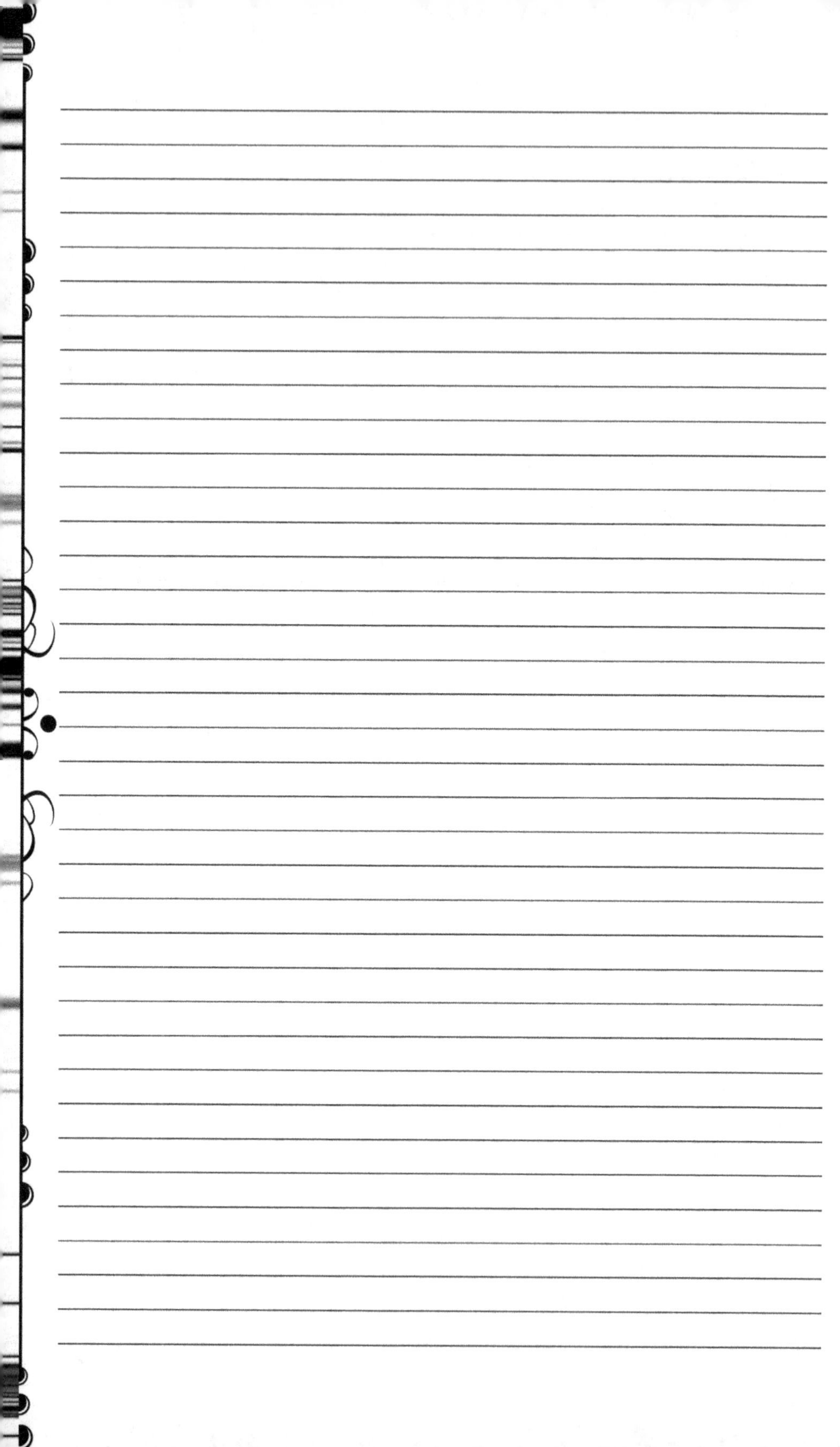

🚫 THINGS I DIDN'T LIKE:

✎ FAVORITE QUOTE(S):

TITLE:

GENRE:

SERIES:

AUTHOR:

PAGES:

STARTED:

FINISHED:

☆ ☆ ☆ ☆ ☆

FORMAT READ: EBOOK / PRINT / AUDIOBOOK **83**

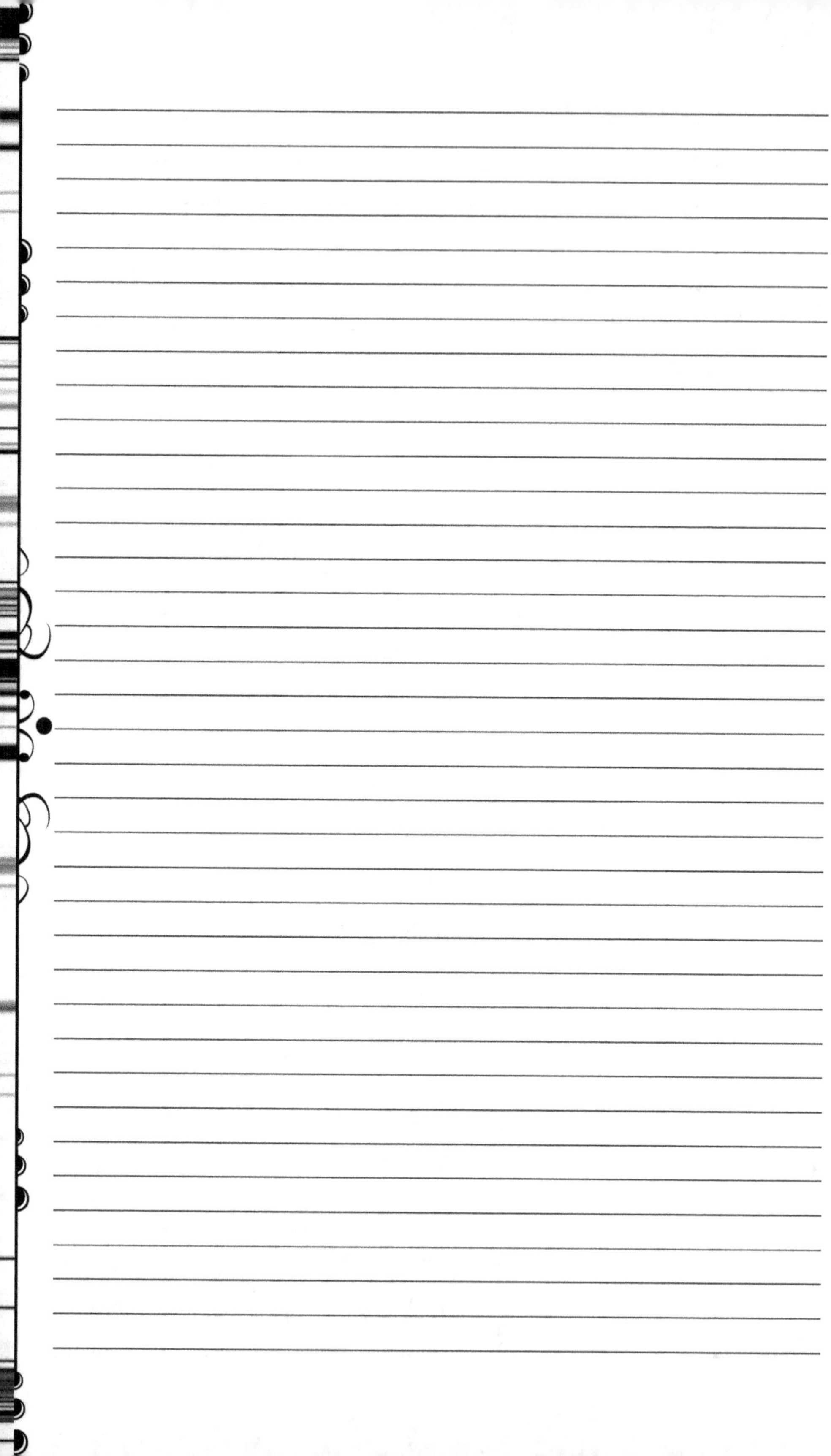

TITLE:

GENRE:

SERIES:

AUTHOR:

PAGES:

STARTED:

FINISHED:

FORMAT READ: EBOOK / PRINT / AUDIOBOOK

TITLE:

GENRE:

SERIES:

AUTHOR:

PAGES:

STARTED:

FINISHED:

FORMAT READ: EBOOK / PRINT / AUDIOBOOK

☑ SYNOPSIS/THINGS I LIKED:

🚫 THINGS I DIDN'T LIKE:

✎ FAVORITE QUOTE(S):

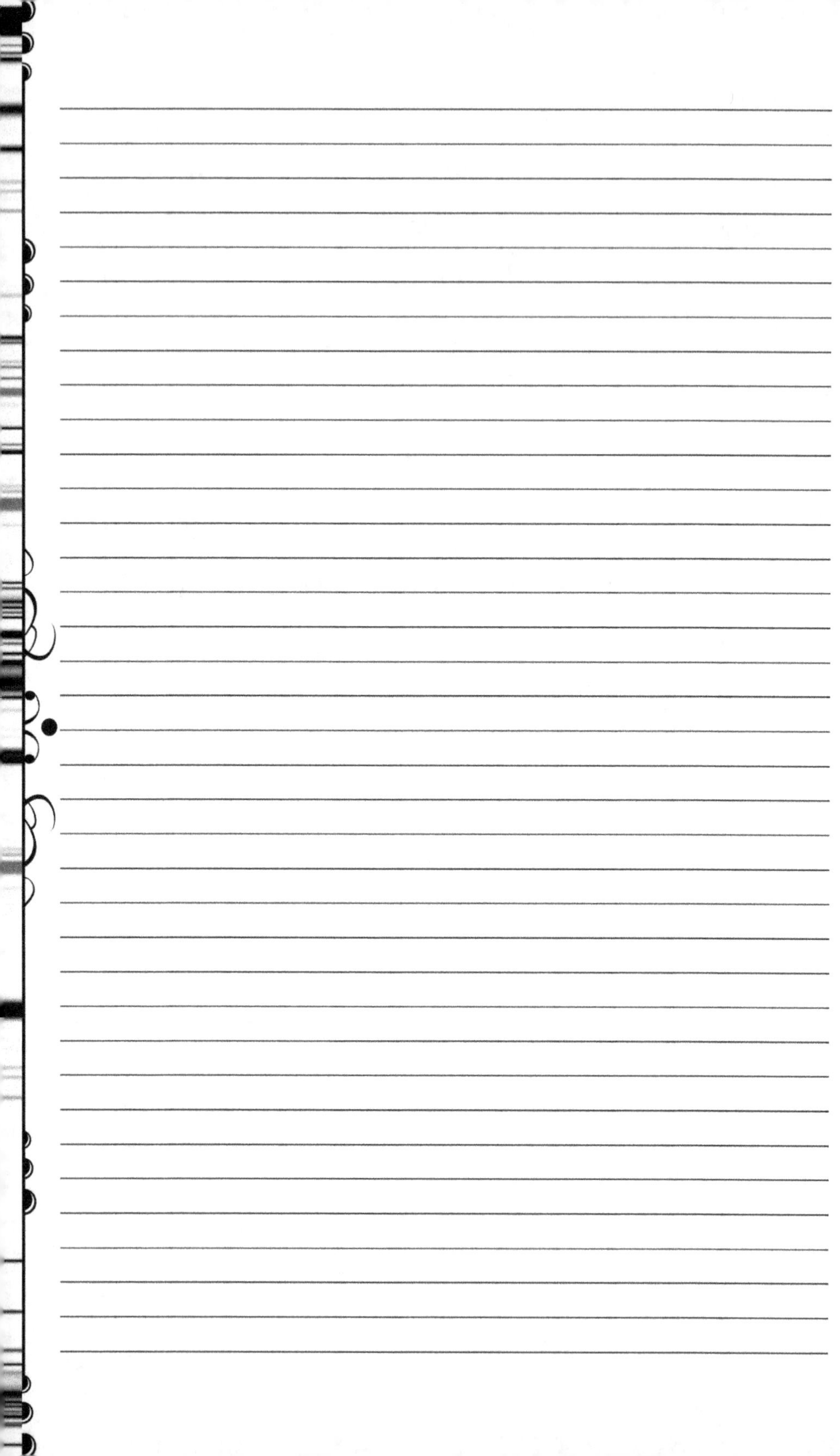

TITLE: ______________________

GENRE: ______________________

SERIES: ______________________

AUTHOR: ______________________

PAGES: ______________________

STARTED: ______________________

FINISHED: ______________________

☆ ☆ ☆ ☆ ☆

FORMAT READ: EBOOK / PRINT / AUDIOBOOK

✓ **SYNOPSIS/THINGS I LIKED:**

____
____
____

🚫 **THINGS I DIDN'T LIKE:**

____
____
____

✏️ **FAVORITE QUOTE(S):**

____
____
____
____
____

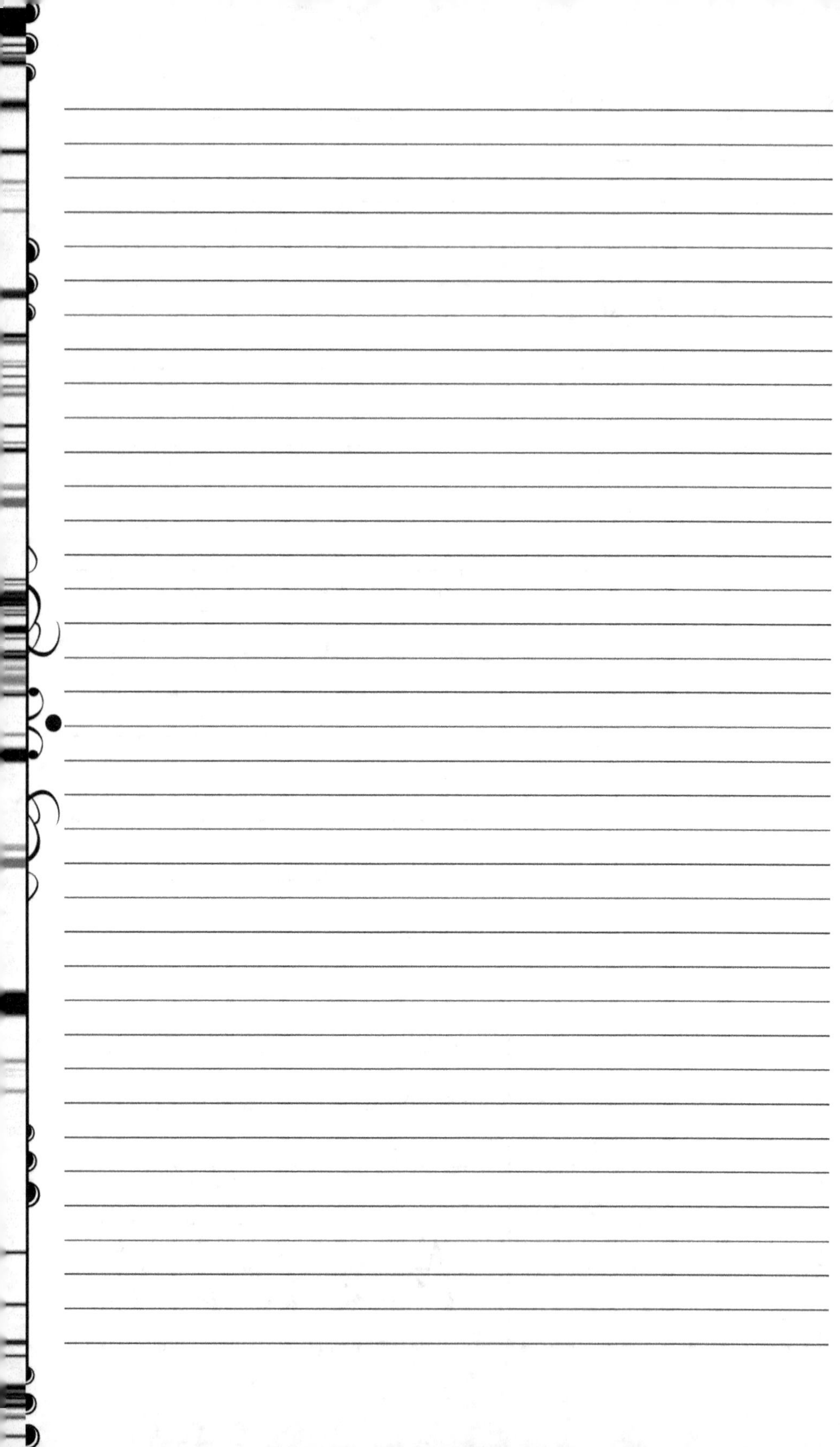

SYNOPSIS/THINGS I LIKED:

THINGS I DIDN'T LIKE:

FAVORITE QUOTE(S):

TITLE:

GENRE:

SERIES:

AUTHOR:

PAGES:

STARTED:

FINISHED:

FORMAT READ: EBOOK / PRINT / AUDIOBOOK

TITLE:

GENRE:

SERIES:

AUTHOR:

PAGES:

STARTED:

FINISHED:

☆☆☆☆☆

FORMAT READ: EBOOK / PRINT / AUDIOBOOK

✓ SYNOPSIS/THINGS I LIKED:

🚫 THINGS I DIDN'T LIKE:

✎ FAVORITE QUOTE(S):

TITLE: _________________

GENRE: _________________

SERIES: _________________

AUTHOR: _________________

PAGES: _________________

STARTED: _________________

FINISHED: _________________

☆ ☆ ☆ ☆ ☆

FORMAT READ: EBOOK / PRINT / AUDIOBOOK

✔ **SYNOPSIS/THINGS I LIKED:**

____
____
____
____

🚫 **THINGS I DIDN'T LIKE:**

____
____
____
____

✏ **FAVORITE QUOTE(S):**

____
____
____
____
____
____

TITLE:

GENRE:

SERIES:

AUTHOR:

PAGES:

STARTED:

FINISHED:

FORMAT READ: EBOOK / PRINT / AUDIOBOOK 91

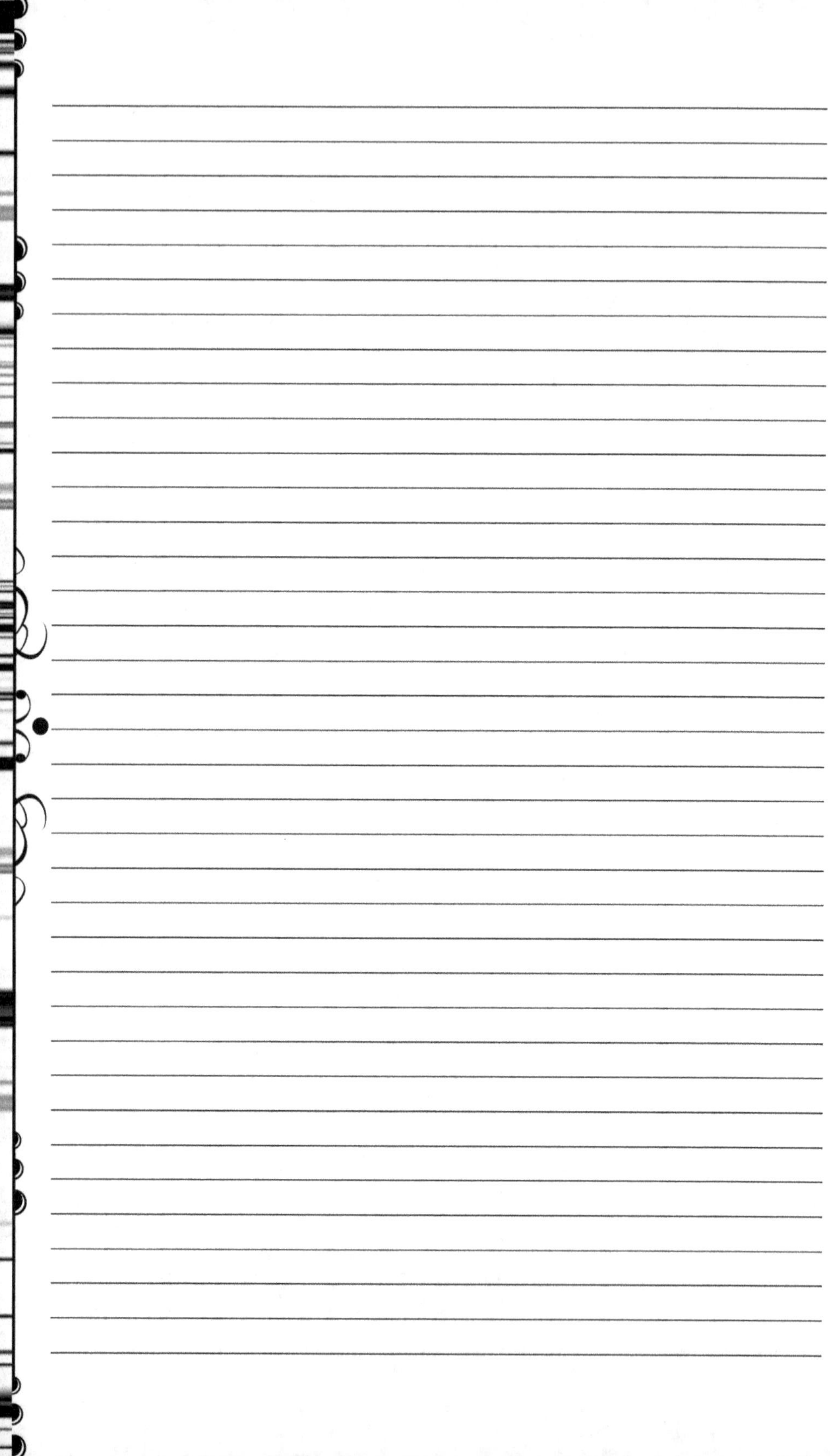

TITLE:

GENRE:

SERIES:

AUTHOR:

PAGES:

STARTED:

FINISHED:

FORMAT READ: EBOOK / PRINT / AUDIOBOOK

TITLE: ______________________

GENRE: ______________________

SERIES: ______________________

AUTHOR: ______________________

PAGES: ______________________

STARTED: ______________________

FINISHED: ______________________

☆☆☆☆☆

FORMAT READ: EBOOK / PRINT / AUDIOBOOK

✔ **SYNOPSIS/THINGS I LIKED:**

____
____
____
____

🚫 **THINGS I DIDN'T LIKE:**

____
____
____
____

✎ **FAVORITE QUOTE(S):**

____
____
____
____
____
____
____
____

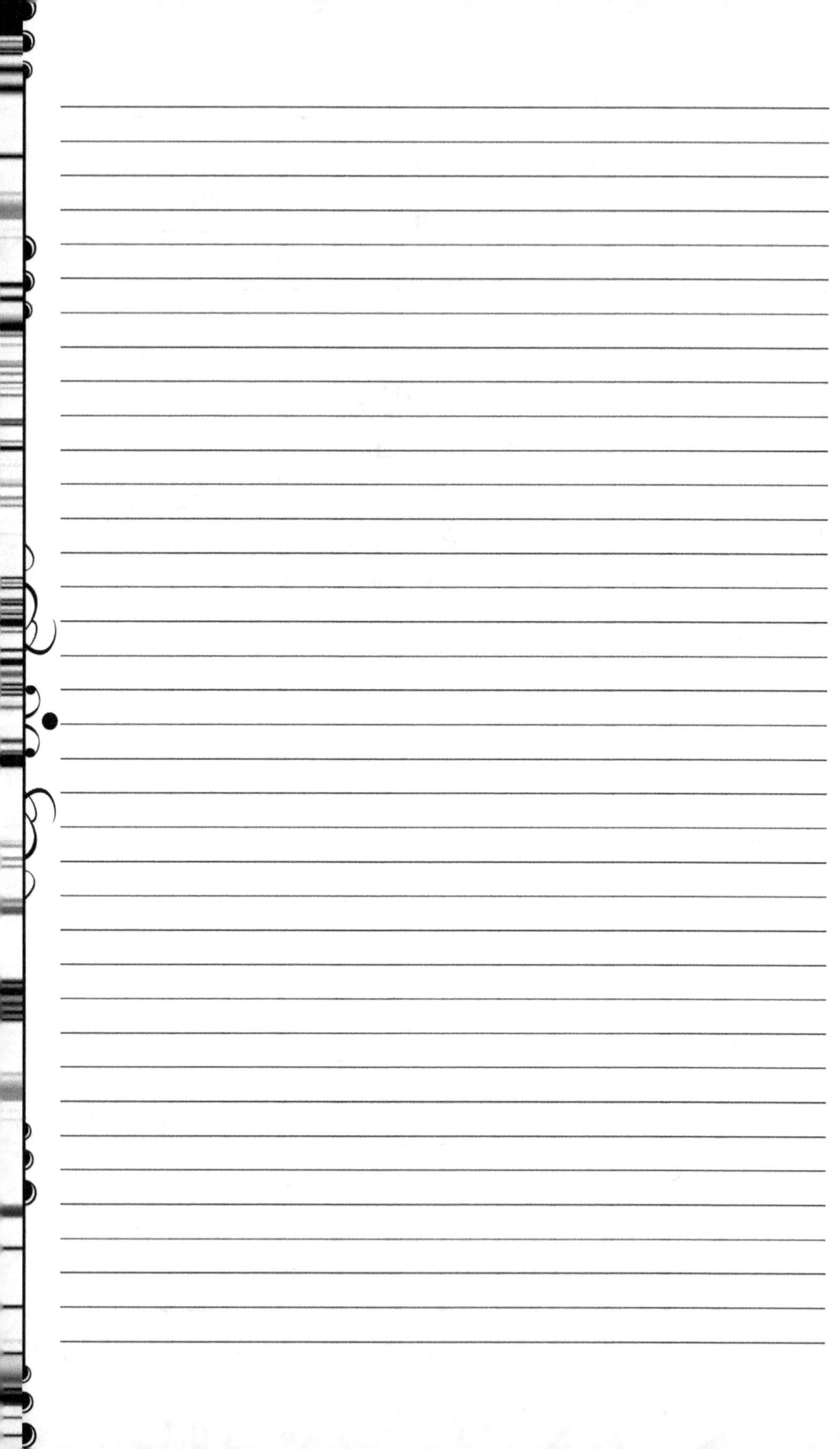

TITLE:

GENRE:

SERIES:

AUTHOR:

PAGES:

STARTED:

FINISHED:

☆ ☆ ☆ ☆ ☆

FORMAT READ: EBOOK / PRINT / AUDIOBOOK

SYNOPSIS/THINGS I LIKED:

THINGS I DIDN'T LIKE:

FAVORITE QUOTE(S):

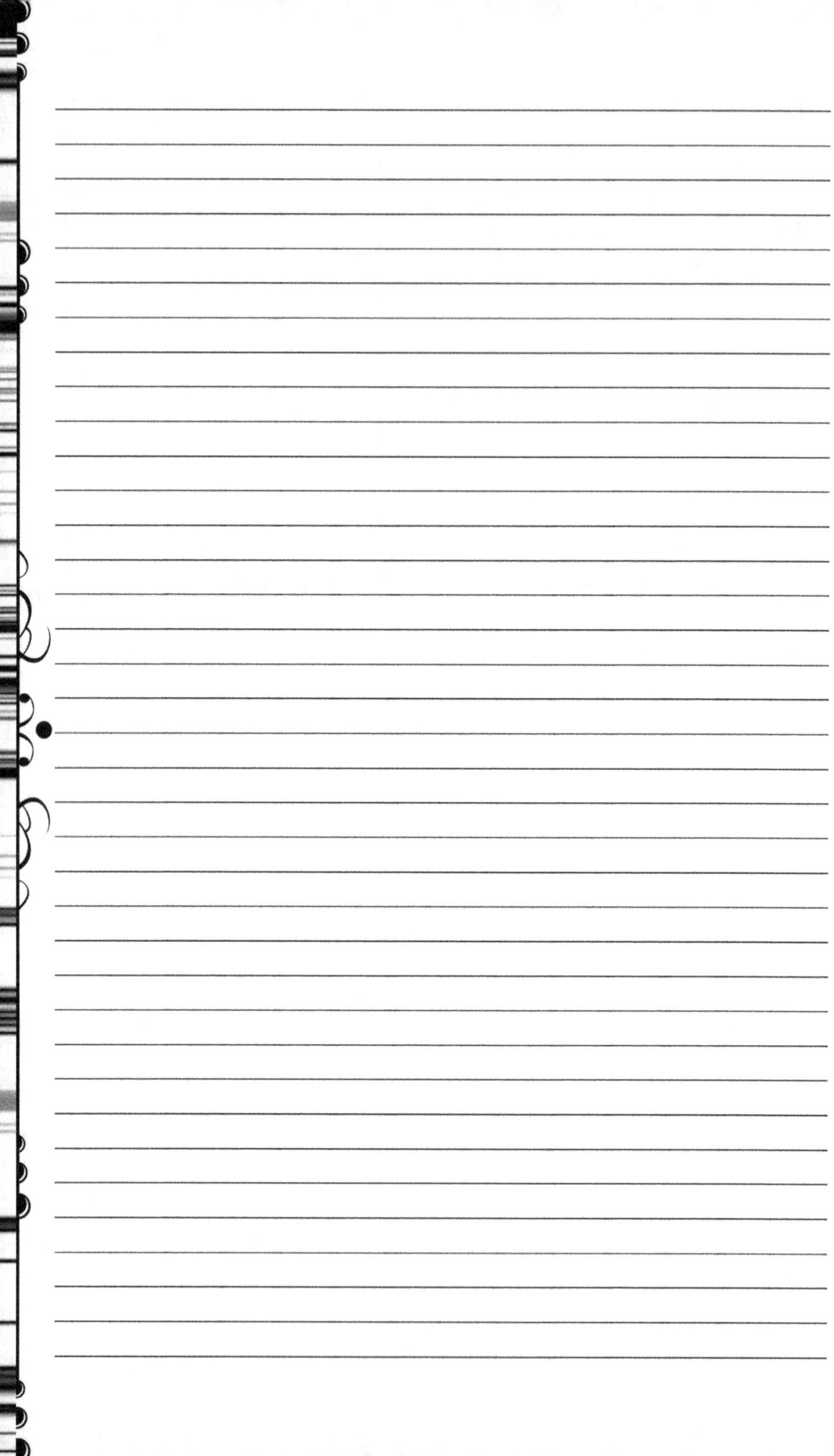

TITLE:

GENRE:

SERIES:

AUTHOR:

PAGES:

STARTED:

FINISHED:

FORMAT READ: EBOOK / PRINT / AUDIOBOOK 95

TITLE:

GENRE:

SERIES:

AUTHOR:

PAGES:

STARTED:

FINISHED:

FORMAT READ: EBOOK / PRINT / AUDIOBOOK

96

TITLE:

GENRE:

SERIES:

AUTHOR:

PAGES:

STARTED:

FINISHED:

☆ ☆ ☆ ☆ ☆

FORMAT READ: EBOOK / PRINT / AUDIOBOOK

✓ SYNOPSIS/THINGS I LIKED:

🚫 THINGS I DIDN'T LIKE:

✎ FAVORITE QUOTE(S):

TITLE: ___________________

GENRE: ___________________

SERIES: ___________________

AUTHOR: ___________________

PAGES: ___________________

STARTED: ___________________

FINISHED: ___________________

☆ ☆ ☆ ☆ ☆

FORMAT READ: EBOOK / PRINT / AUDIOBOOK

✔ **SYNOPSIS/THINGS I LIKED:**

____
____
____
____

🚫 **THINGS I DIDN'T LIKE:**

____
____
____
____

📝 **FAVORITE QUOTE(S):**

____
____
____
____
____
____
____

TITLE:

GENRE:

SERIES:

AUTHOR:

PAGES:

STARTED:

FINISHED:

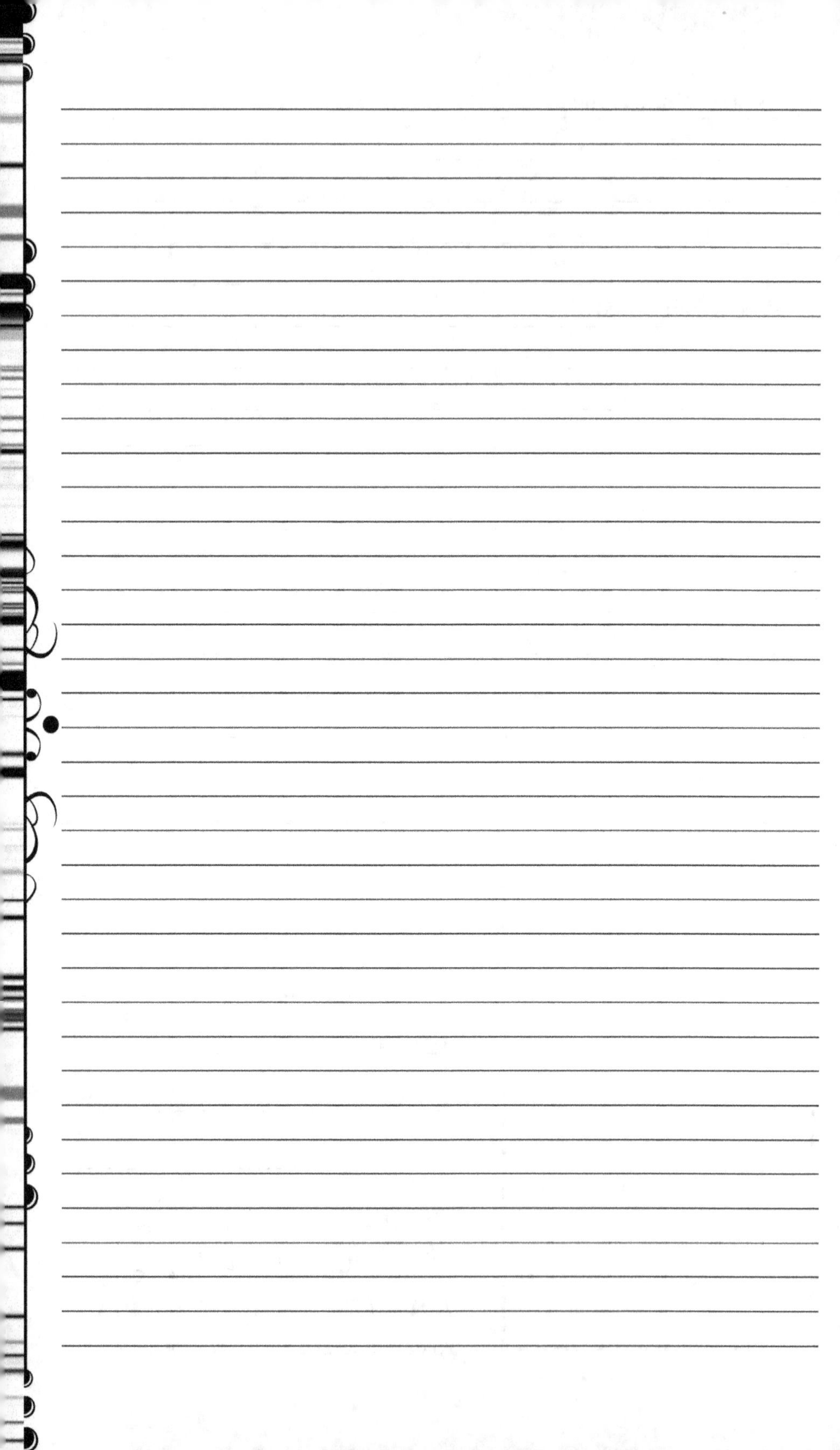

✓ **Synopsis/Things I liked:**

⊘ **Things I didn't like:**

✎ **Favorite quote(s):**

Title:

Genre:

Series:

Author:

Pages:

Started:

Finished:

☆ ☆ ☆ ☆ ☆

Format read: Ebook / Print / Audiobook

TITLE:

<u>GENRE:</u>

<u>SERIES:</u>

<u>AUTHOR:</u>

<u>PAGES:</u>

<u>STARTED:</u>

<u>FINISHED:</u>

☆☆☆☆☆

FORMAT READ: Ebook / Print / Audiobook

✓ **SYNOPSIS/THINGS I LIKED:**

🚫 **THINGS I DIDN'T LIKE:**

✏️ **FAVORITE QUOTE(S):**

TITLE: _______________

GENRE: _______________

SERIES: _______________

AUTHOR: _______________

PAGES: _______________

STARTED: _______________

FINISHED: _______________

☆ ☆ ☆ ☆ ☆

FORMAT READ: EBOOK / PRINT / AUDIOBOOK

✓ **SYNOPSIS/THINGS I LIKED:**

____

____

____

____

🚫 **THINGS I DIDN'T LIKE:**

____

____

____

____

✎ **FAVORITE QUOTE(S):**

____

____

____

____

____

____

✓ **SYNOPSIS/THINGS I LIKED:**

🚫 **THINGS I DIDN'T LIKE:**

FAVORITE QUOTE(S):

TITLE:

GENRE:

SERIES:

AUTHOR:

PAGES:

STARTED:

FINISHED:

FORMAT READ: EBOOK / PRINT / AUDIOBOOK

TITLE:

GENRE:

SERIES:

AUTHOR:

PAGES:

STARTED:

FINISHED:

FORMAT READ: EBOOK / PRINT / AUDIOBOOK

TITLE:

GENRE:

SERIES:

AUTHOR:

PAGES:

STARTED:

FINISHED:

☆ ☆ ☆ ☆ ☆

FORMAT READ: EBOOK / PRINT / AUDIOBOOK

☑ SYNOPSIS/THINGS I LIKED:

🚫 THINGS I DIDN'T LIKE:

✎ FAVORITE QUOTE(S):

TITLE: _______________

GENRE: _______________

SERIES: _______________

AUTHOR: _______________

PAGES: _______________

STARTED: _______________

FINISHED: _______________

☆ ☆ ☆ ☆ ☆

FORMAT READ: EBOOK / PRINT / AUDIOBOOK

✔ **SYNOPSIS/THINGS I LIKED:**

____
____
____

🚫 **THINGS I DIDN'T LIKE:**

____
____
____

✎ **FAVORITE QUOTE(S):**

____
____
____
____
____
____

107

TITLE:

GENRE:

SERIES:

AUTHOR:

PAGES:

STARTED:

FINISHED:

FORMAT READ: EBOOK / PRINT / AUDIOBOOK

TITLE: _______________________

GENRE: _______________________

SERIES: _______________________

AUTHOR: _______________________

PAGES: _______________________

STARTED: _______________________

FINISHED: _______________________

☆ ☆ ☆ ☆ ☆

FORMAT READ: EBOOK / PRINT / AUDIOBOOK

✓ **SYNOPSIS/THINGS I LIKED:**

____

____

____

____

🚫 **THINGS I DIDN'T LIKE:**

____

____

____

____

✎ **FAVORITE QUOTE(S):**

____

____

____

____

____

____

____

TITLE: _______________________

GENRE: _______________________

SERIES: _______________________

AUTHOR: _______________________

PAGES: _______________________

STARTED: _______________________

FINISHED: _______________________

☆ ☆ ☆ ☆ ☆

FORMAT READ: EBOOK / PRINT / AUDIOBOOK

☑ **SYNOPSIS/THINGS I LIKED:**

____
____
____
____

🚫 **THINGS I DIDN'T LIKE:**

____
____
____
____

📝 **FAVORITE QUOTE(S):**

____
____
____
____
____
____

✓ **SYNOPSIS/THINGS I LIKED:**

🚫 **THINGS I DIDN'T LIKE:**

✎ **FAVORITE QUOTE(S):**

TITLE:

GENRE:

SERIES:

AUTHOR:

PAGES:

STARTED:

FINISHED:

☆ ☆ ☆ ☆ ☆

FORMAT READ: EBOOK / PRINT / AUDIOBOOK

☑ **Synopsis/Things I liked:**

⊘ **Things I didn't like:**

✎ **Favorite quote(s):**

Title:

Genre:

Series:

Author:

Pages:

Started:

Finished:

☆☆☆☆☆

Format read: Ebook / Print / Audiobook

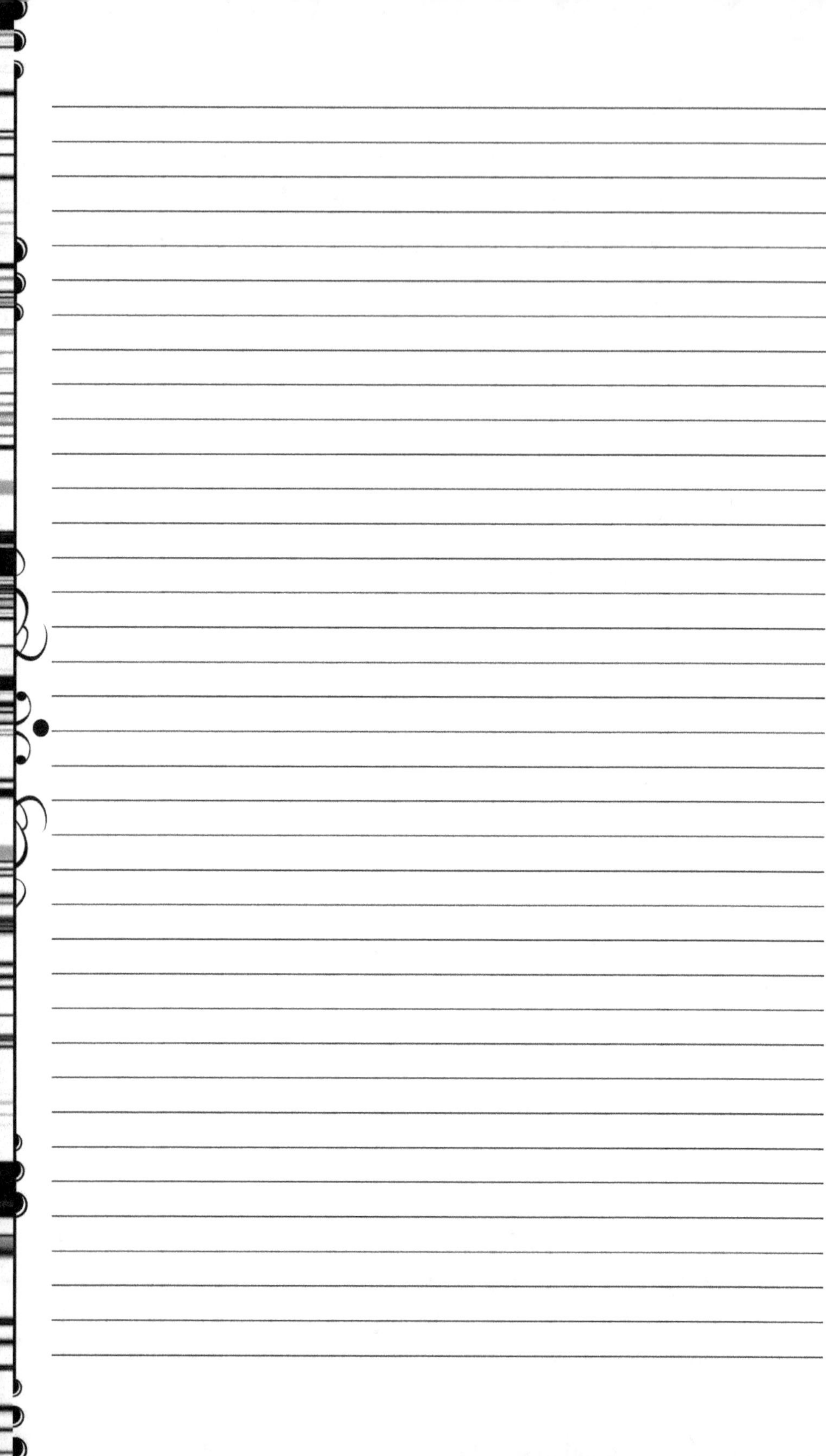

TITLE: _______________________

GENRE: _______________________

SERIES: _______________________

AUTHOR: _______________________

PAGES: _______________________

STARTED: _______________________

FINISHED: _______________________

☆ ☆ ☆ ☆ ☆

FORMAT READ: EBOOK / PRINT / AUDIOBOOK

✔ **SYNOPSIS/THINGS I LIKED:**

____

____

____

____

🚫 **THINGS I DIDN'T LIKE:**

____

____

____

____

✏ **FAVORITE QUOTE(S):**

____

____

____

____

____

____

Title:

Genre:

Series:

Author:

Pages:

Started:

Finished:

☆☆☆☆☆

Format read: Ebook / Print / Audiobook

✔ **Synopsis/Things I liked:**

🚫 **Things I didn't like:**

✎ **Favorite quote(s):**

TITLE:

GENRE:

SERIES:

AUTHOR:

PAGES:

STARTED:

FINISHED:

FORMAT READ: EBOOK / PRINT / AUDIOBOOK

☑ **SYNOPSIS/THINGS I LIKED:**

⊘ **THINGS I DIDN'T LIKE:**

✎ **FAVORITE QUOTE(S):**

TITLE:

GENRE:

SERIES:

AUTHOR:

PAGES:

STARTED:

FINISHED:

☆ ☆ ☆ ☆ ☆

FORMAT READ: EBOOK / PRINT / AUDIOBOOK

TITLE:

GENRE:

SERIES:

AUTHOR:

PAGES:

STARTED:

FINISHED:

☆ ☆ ☆ ☆ ☆

FORMAT READ: EBOOK / PRINT / AUDIOBOOK

☑ **SYNOPSIS/THINGS I LIKED:**

🚫 **THINGS I DIDN'T LIKE:**

✎ **FAVORITE QUOTE(S):**

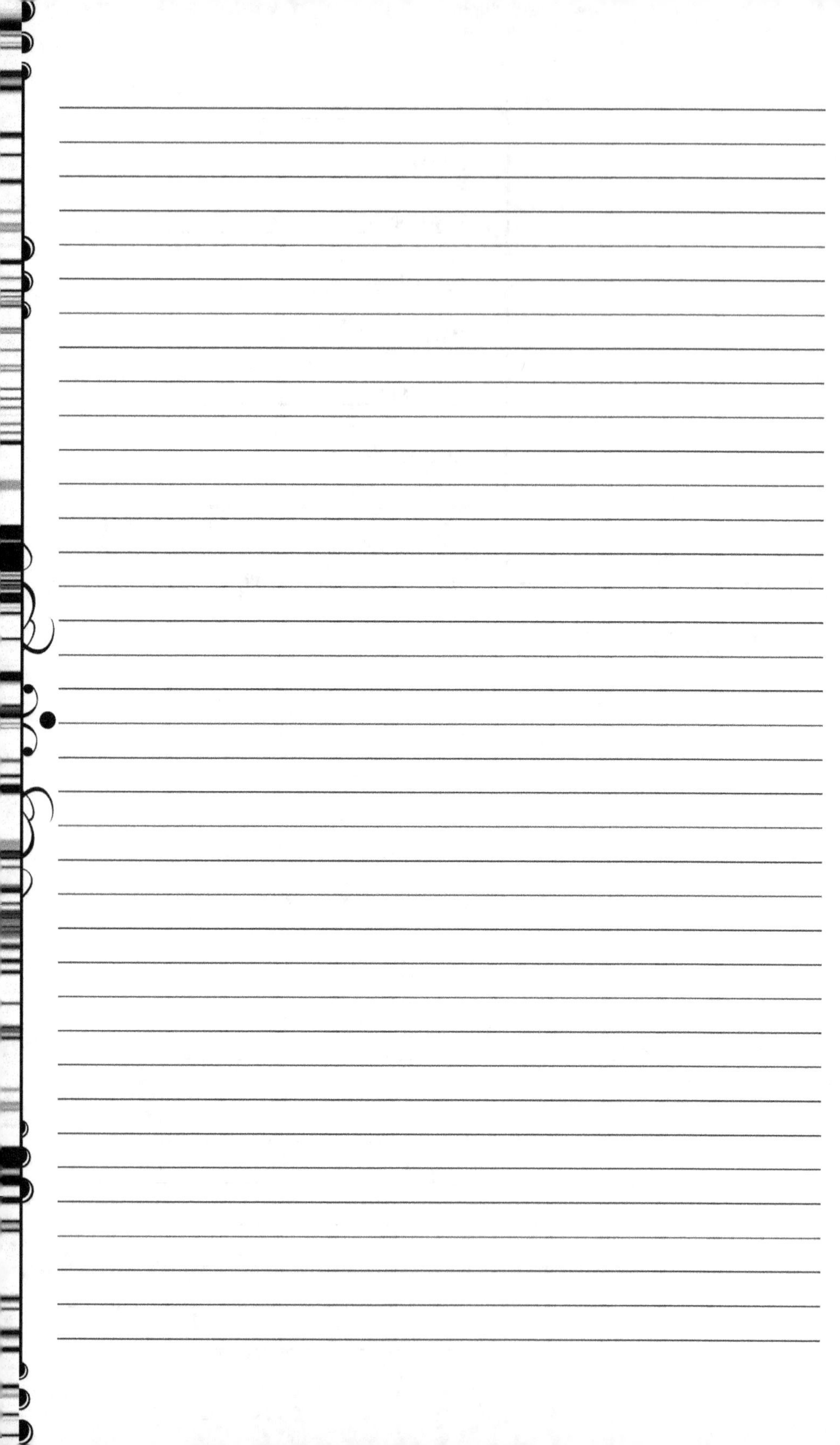

Title: _______________

Genre: _______________

Series: _______________

Author: _______________

Pages: _______________

Started: _______________

Finished: _______________

☆ ☆ ☆ ☆ ☆

Format read: Ebook / Print / Audiobook

✓ **Synopsis/Things I liked:**

____
____
____
____

🚫 **Things I didn't like:**

____
____
____
____

✏️ **Favorite quote(s):**

____
____
____
____
____
____
____

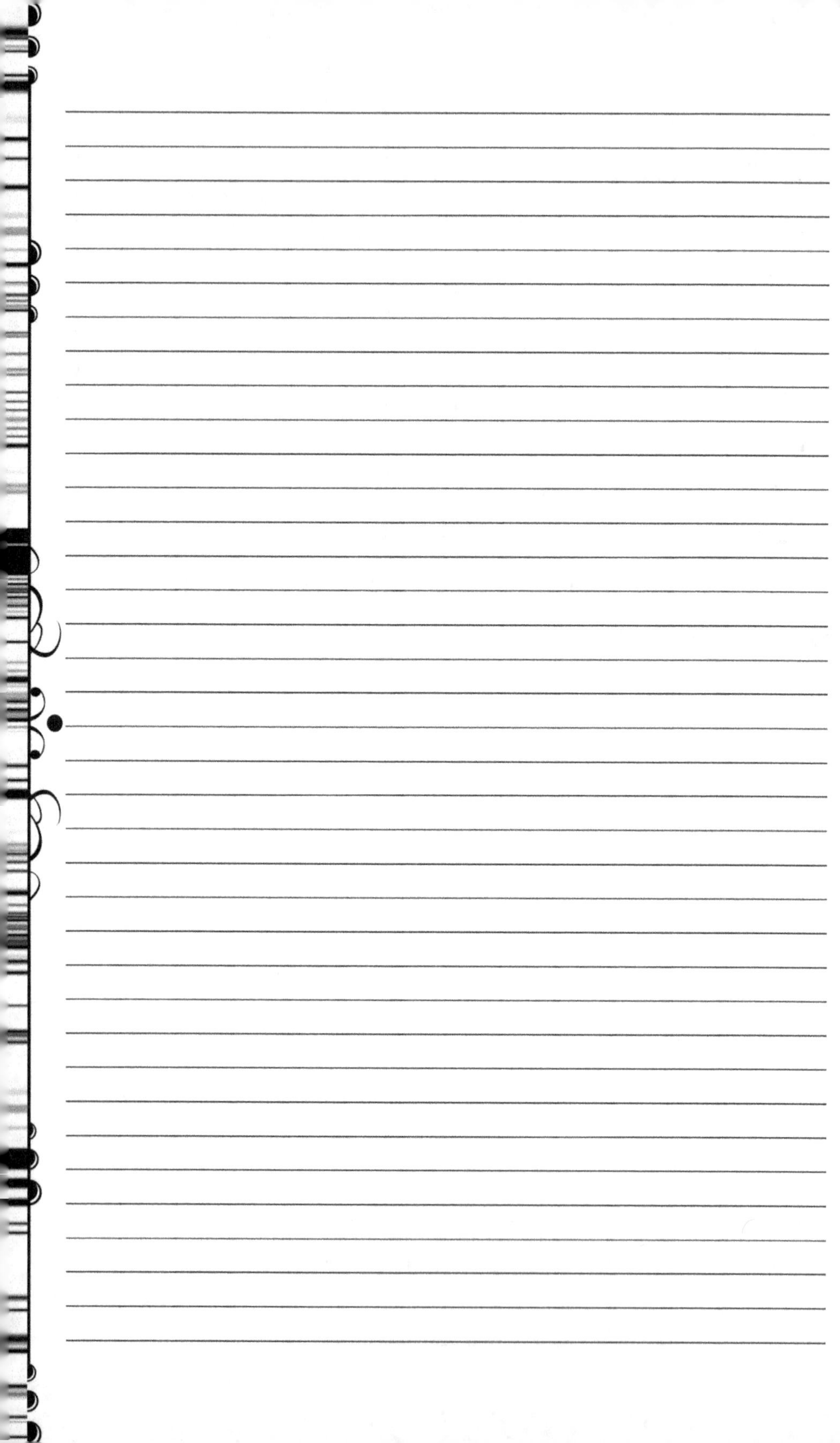

TITLE:

GENRE:

SERIES:

AUTHOR:

PAGES:

STARTED:

FINISHED:

FORMAT READ: EBOOK / PRINT / AUDIOBOOK

119

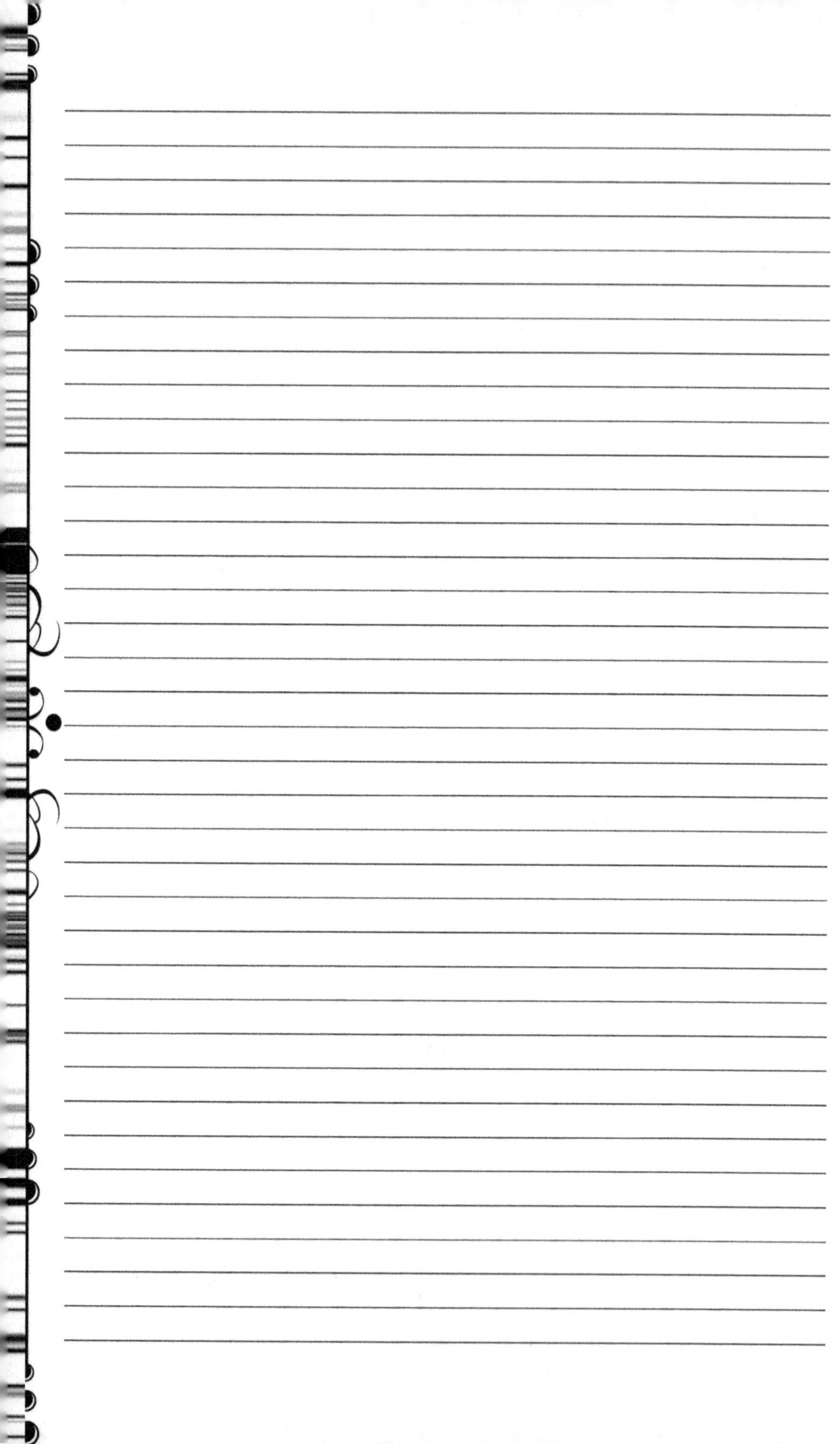

✓ **SYNOPSIS/THINGS I LIKED:**

⊘ **THINGS I DIDN'T LIKE:**

✎ **FAVORITE QUOTE(S):**

TITLE:

GENRE:

SERIES:

AUTHOR:

PAGES:

STARTED:

FINISHED:

☆ ☆ ☆ ☆ ☆

FORMAT READ: EBOOK / PRINT / AUDIOBOOK

✔ **SYNOPSIS/THINGS I LIKED:**

🚫 **THINGS I DIDN'T LIKE:**

✎ **FAVORITE QUOTE(S):**

TITLE:

GENRE:

SERIES:

AUTHOR:

PAGES:

STARTED:

FINISHED:

☆ ☆ ☆ ☆ ☆

FORMAT READ: EBOOK / PRINT / AUDIOBOOK

✔ **SYNOPSIS/THINGS I LIKED:**

🚫 **THINGS I DIDN'T LIKE:**

✏ **FAVORITE QUOTE(S):**

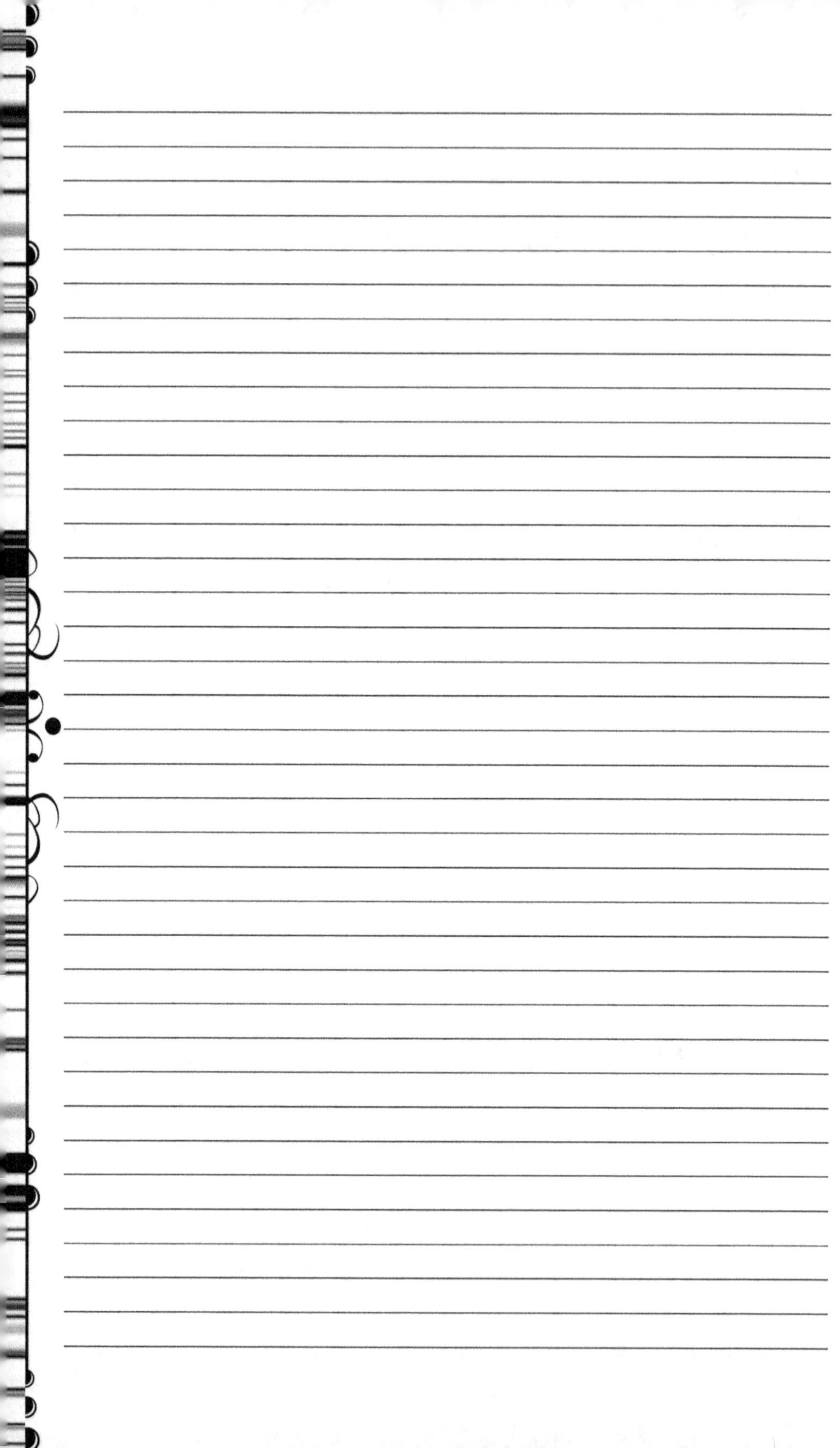

✓ **SYNOPSIS/THINGS I LIKED:**

🚫 **THINGS I DIDN'T LIKE:**

✎ **FAVORITE QUOTE(S):**

TITLE:

GENRE:

SERIES:

AUTHOR:

PAGES:

STARTED:

FINISHED:

☆ ☆ ☆ ☆ ☆

FORMAT READ: EBOOK / PRINT / AUDIOBOOK

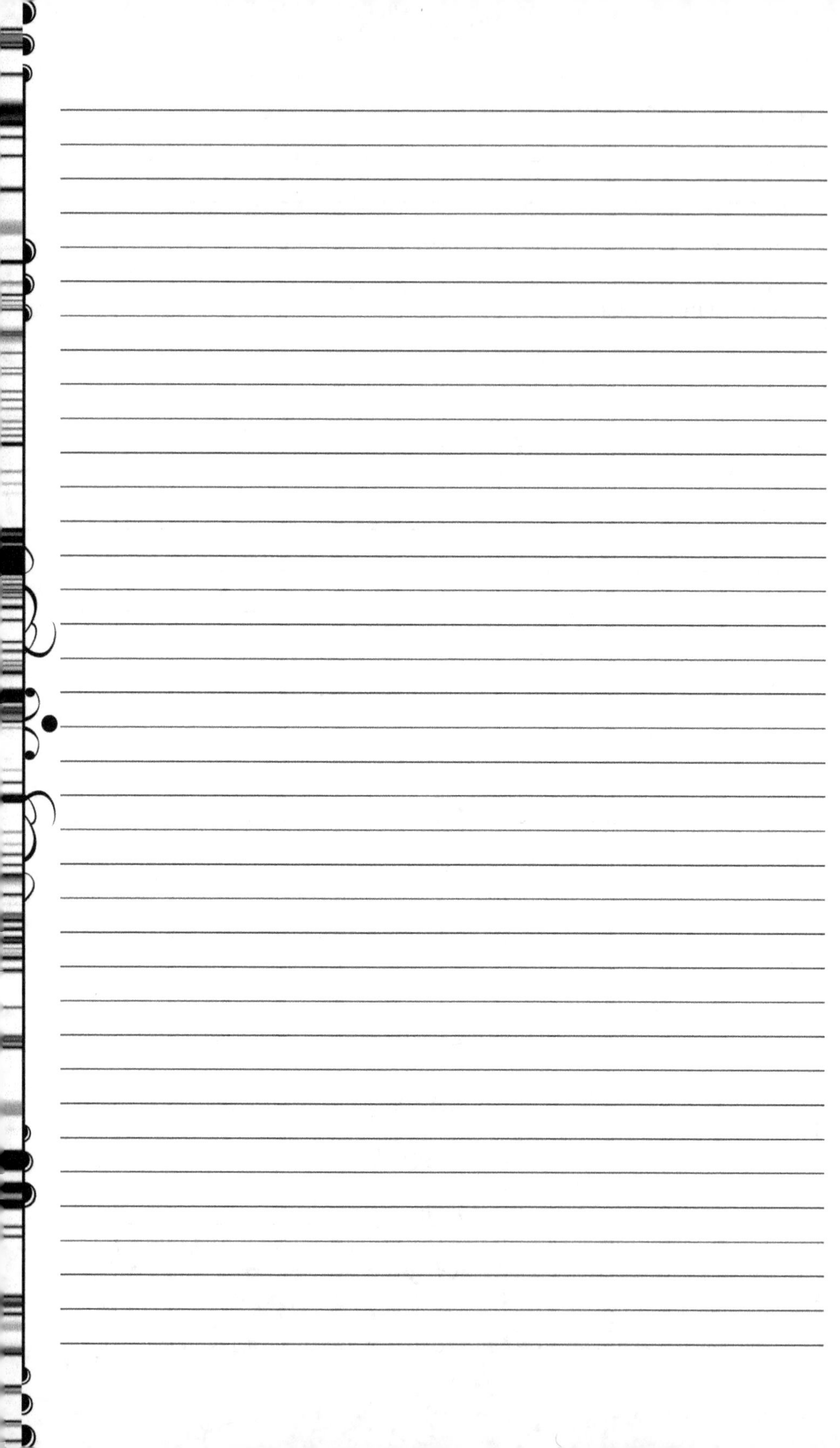

☑ **SYNOPSIS/THINGS I LIKED:**

🚫 **THINGS I DIDN'T LIKE:**

✎ **FAVORITE QUOTE(S):**

TITLE:

GENRE:

SERIES:

AUTHOR:

PAGES:

STARTED:

FINISHED:

☆ ☆ ☆ ☆ ☆

FORMAT READ: EBOOK / PRINT / AUDIOBOOK

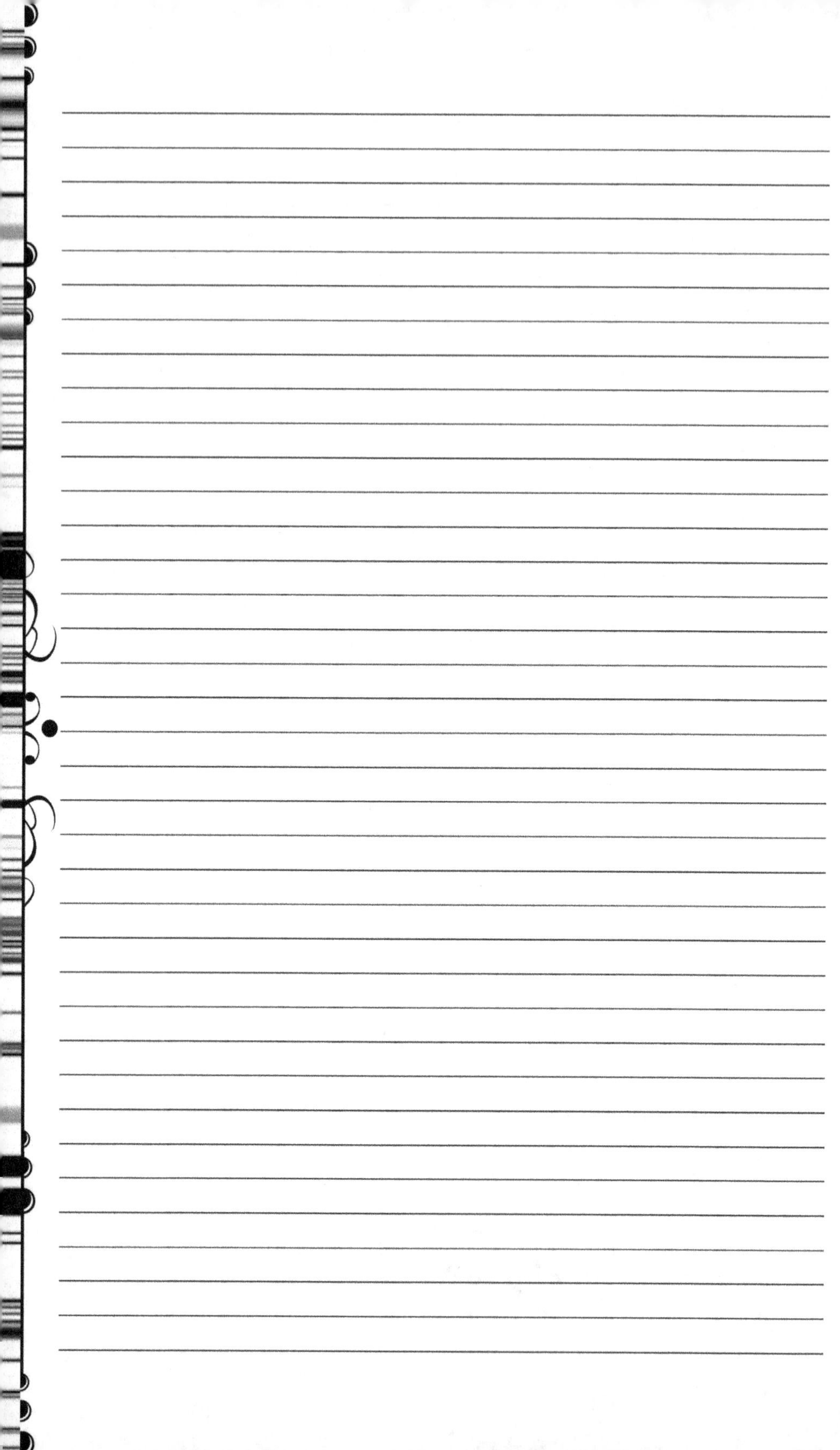

TITLE:

GENRE:

SERIES:

AUTHOR:

PAGES:

STARTED:

FINISHED:

FORMAT READ: EBOOK / PRINT / AUDIOBOOK

✔ SYNOPSIS/THINGS I LIKED:

🚫 THINGS I DIDN'T LIKE:

✎ FAVORITE QUOTE(S):

TITLE: _______________

GENRE: _______________

SERIES: _______________

AUTHOR: _______________

PAGES: _______________

STARTED: _______________

FINISHED: _______________

☆ ☆ ☆ ☆ ☆

FORMAT READ: EBOOK / PRINT / AUDIOBOOK

✔ **SYNOPSIS/THINGS I LIKED:**

____
____
____
____

🚫 **THINGS I DIDN'T LIKE:**

____
____
____
____

✎ **FAVORITE QUOTE(S):**

____
____
____
____
____
____

TITLE:

GENRE:

SERIES:

AUTHOR:

PAGES:

STARTED:

FINISHED:

FORMAT READ: EBOOK / PRINT / AUDIOBOOK

TITLE:

GENRE:

SERIES:

AUTHOR:

PAGES:

STARTED:

FINISHED:

☆ ☆ ☆ ☆ ☆

FORMAT READ: EBOOK / PRINT / AUDIOBOOK

TITLE:

GENRE:

SERIES:

AUTHOR:

PAGES:

STARTED:

FINISHED:

FORMAT READ: EBOOK / PRINT / AUDIOBOOK

SYNOPSIS/THINGS I LIKED:

THINGS I DIDN'T LIKE:

FAVORITE QUOTE(S):

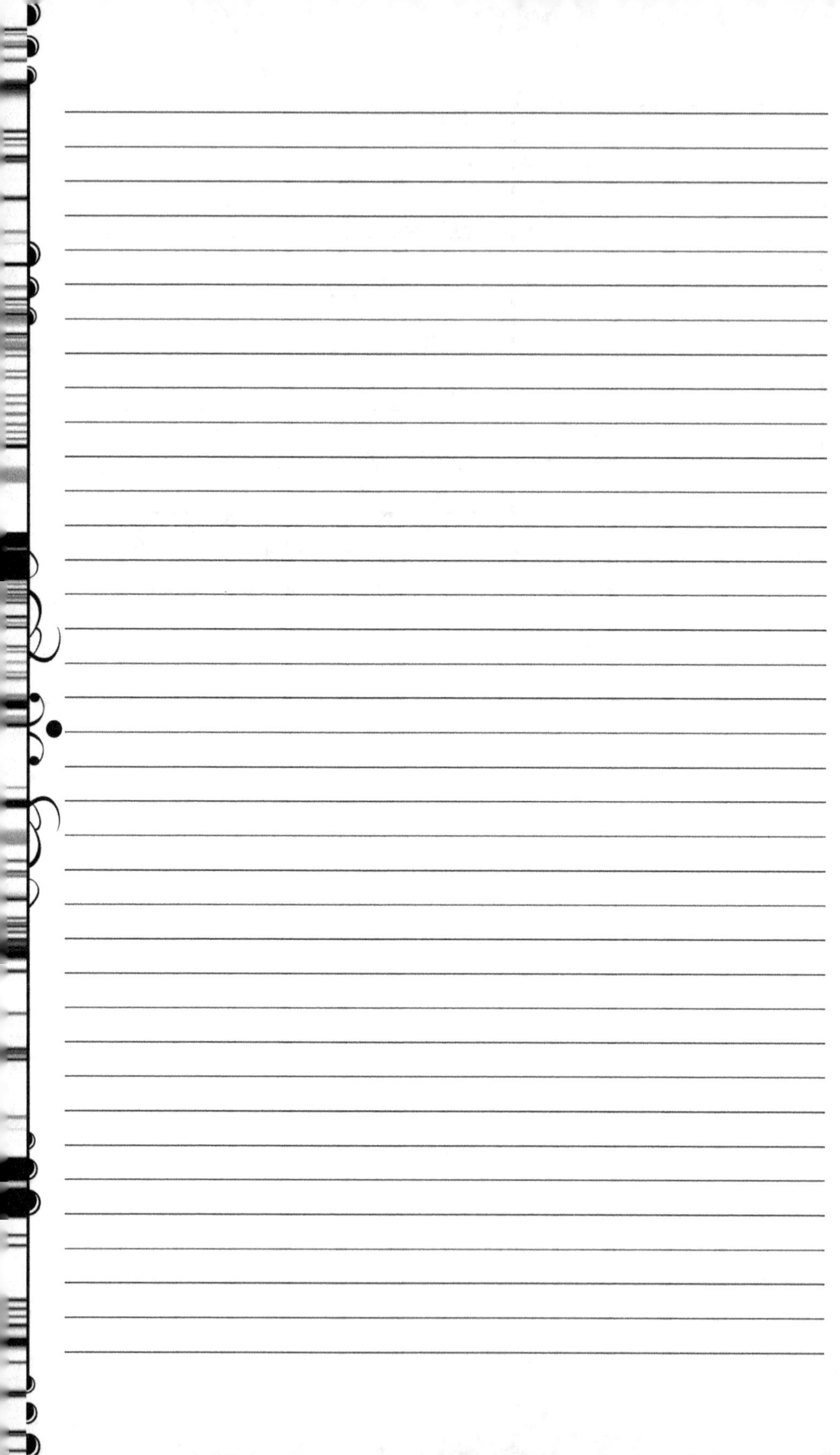

TITLE: _______________________

GENRE: _______________________

SERIES: _______________________

AUTHOR: _______________________

PAGES: _______________________

STARTED: _______________________

FINISHED: _______________________

☆ ☆ ☆ ☆ ☆

FORMAT READ: EBOOK / PRINT / AUDIOBOOK

✓ **SYNOPSIS/THINGS I LIKED:**

____
____
____
____

🚫 **THINGS I DIDN'T LIKE:**

____
____
____
____

✎ **FAVORITE QUOTE(S):**

____
____
____
____
____
____

SYNOPSIS/THINGS I LIKED:

THINGS I DIDN'T LIKE:

FAVORITE QUOTE(S):

TITLE:
GENRE:
SERIES:
AUTHOR:
PAGES:
STARTED:
FINISHED:
FORMAT READ: EBOOK / PRINT / AUDIOBOOK

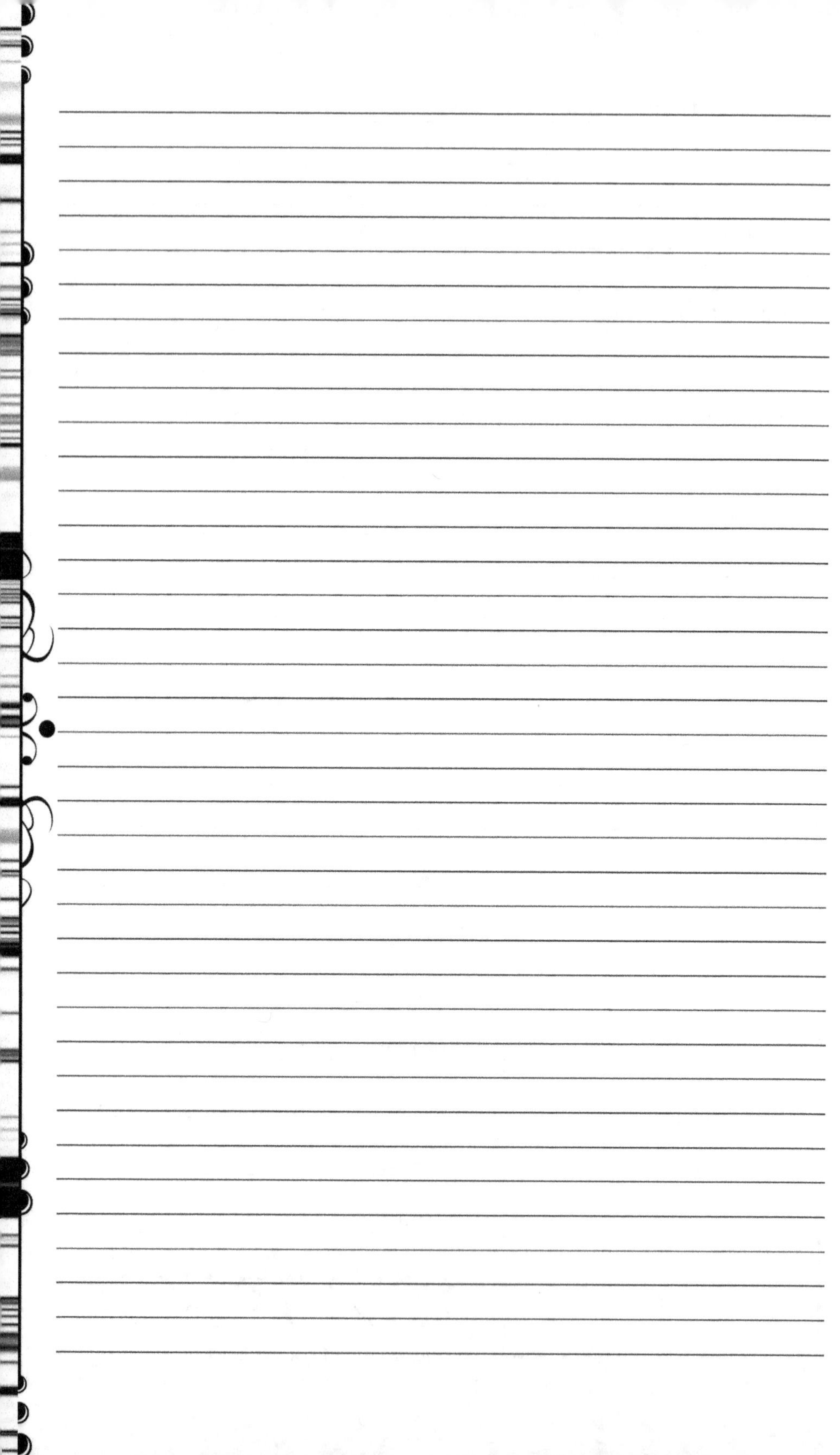

TITLE:

GENRE:

SERIES:

AUTHOR:

PAGES:

STARTED:

FINISHED:

FORMAT READ: EBOOK / PRINT / AUDIOBOOK

TITLE: ________________

GENRE: ________________

SERIES: ________________

AUTHOR: ________________

PAGES: ________________

STARTED: ________________

FINISHED: ________________

☆☆☆☆☆

FORMAT READ: EBOOK / PRINT / AUDIOBOOK

✔ SYNOPSIS/THINGS I LIKED:

____
____
____
____

🚫 THINGS I DIDN'T LIKE:

____
____
____

✏ FAVORITE QUOTE(S):

____
____
____
____
____
____

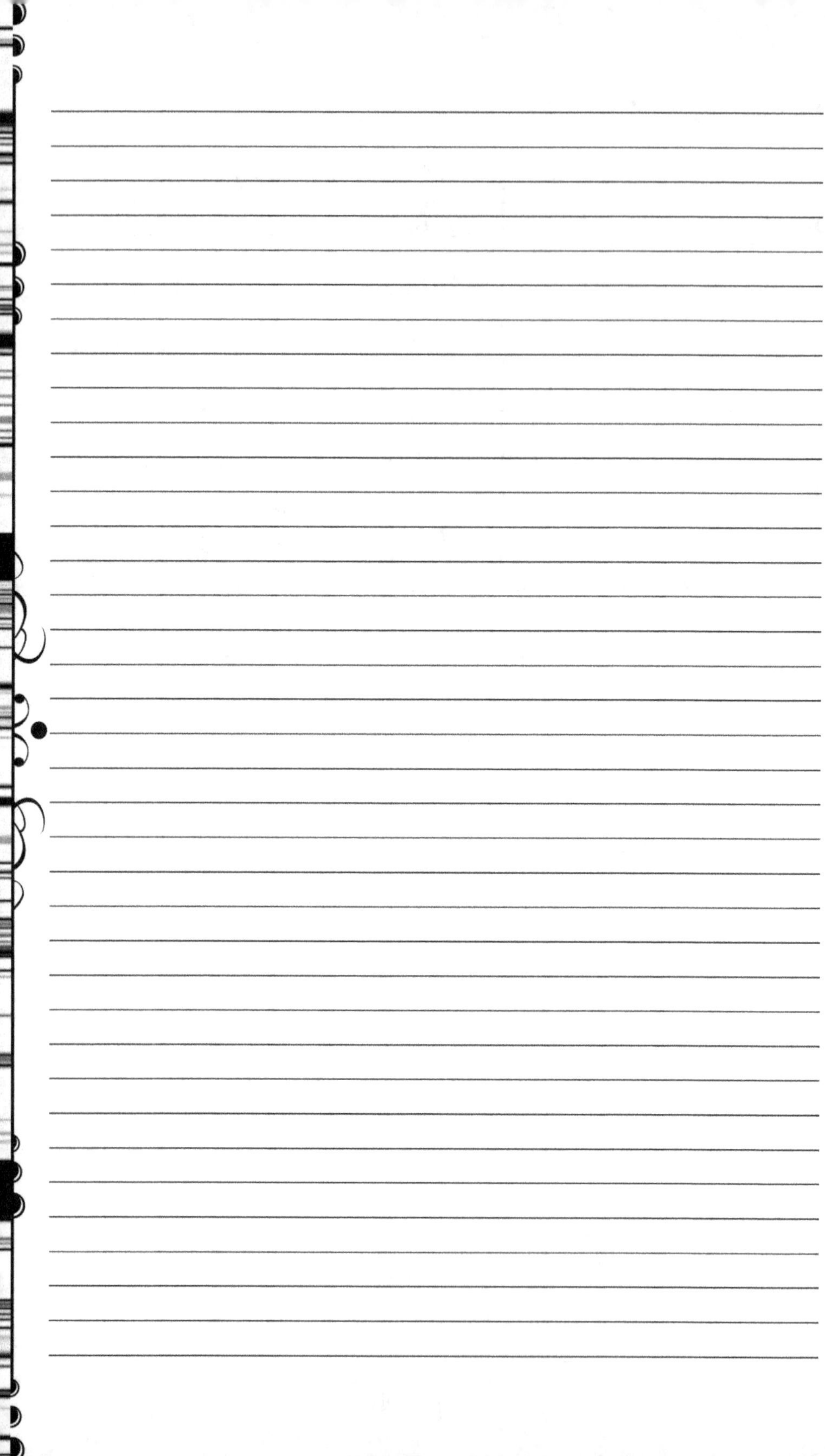

TITLE:

GENRE:

SERIES:

AUTHOR:

PAGES:

STARTED:

FINISHED:

FORMAT READ: EBOOK / PRINT / AUDIOBOOK

SYNOPSIS/THINGS I LIKED:

THINGS I DIDN'T LIKE:

FAVORITE QUOTE(S):

🚫 THINGS I DIDN'T LIKE:

🖌 FAVORITE QUOTE(S):

TITLE:

GENRE:

SERIES:

AUTHOR:

PAGES:

STARTED:

FINISHED:

☆ ☆ ☆ ☆ ☆

FORMAT READ: EBOOK / PRINT / AUDIOBOOK

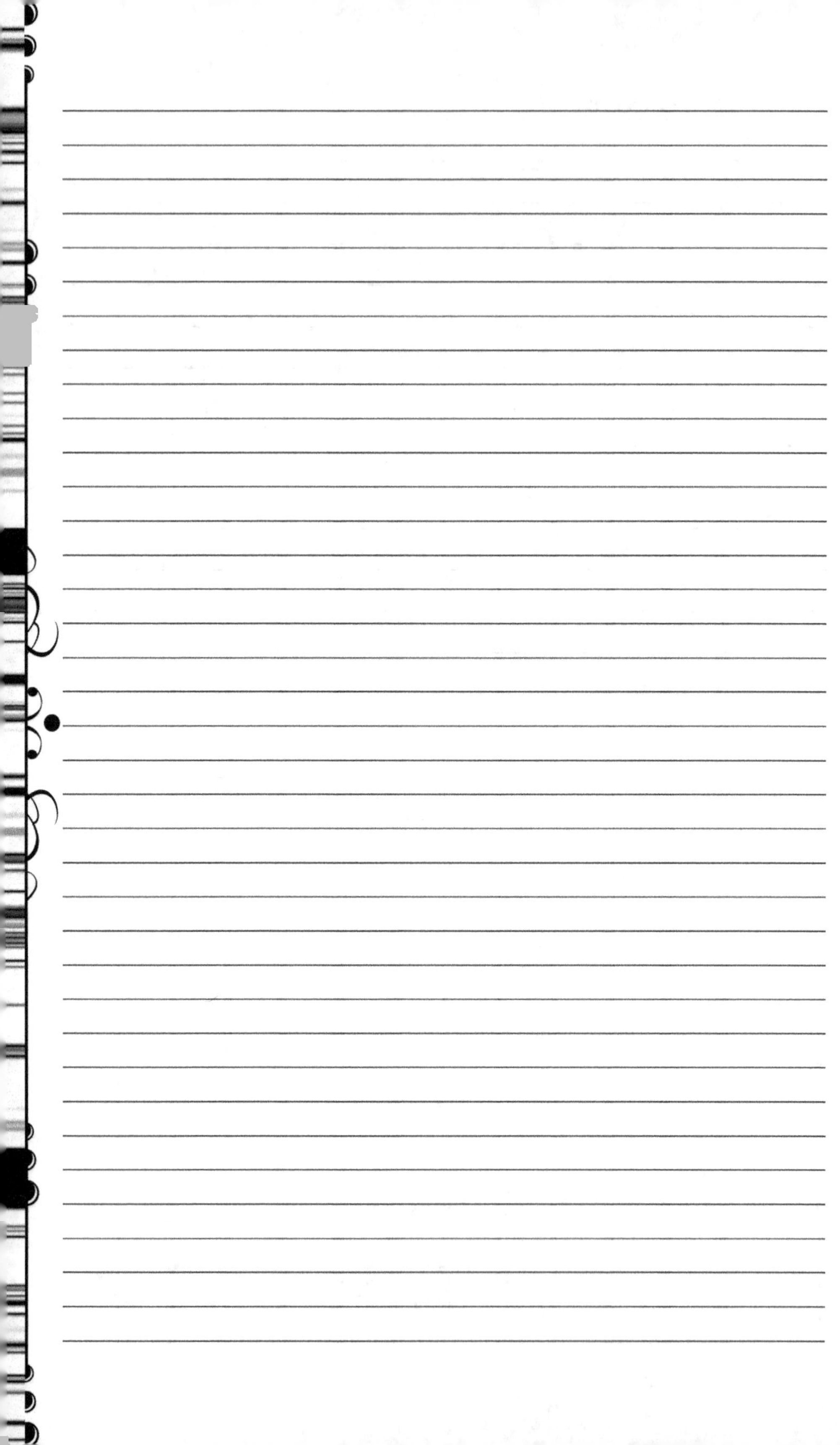

TITLE:

GENRE:

SERIES:

AUTHOR:

PAGES:

STARTED:

FINISHED:

FORMAT READ: EBOOK / PRINT / AUDIOBOOK

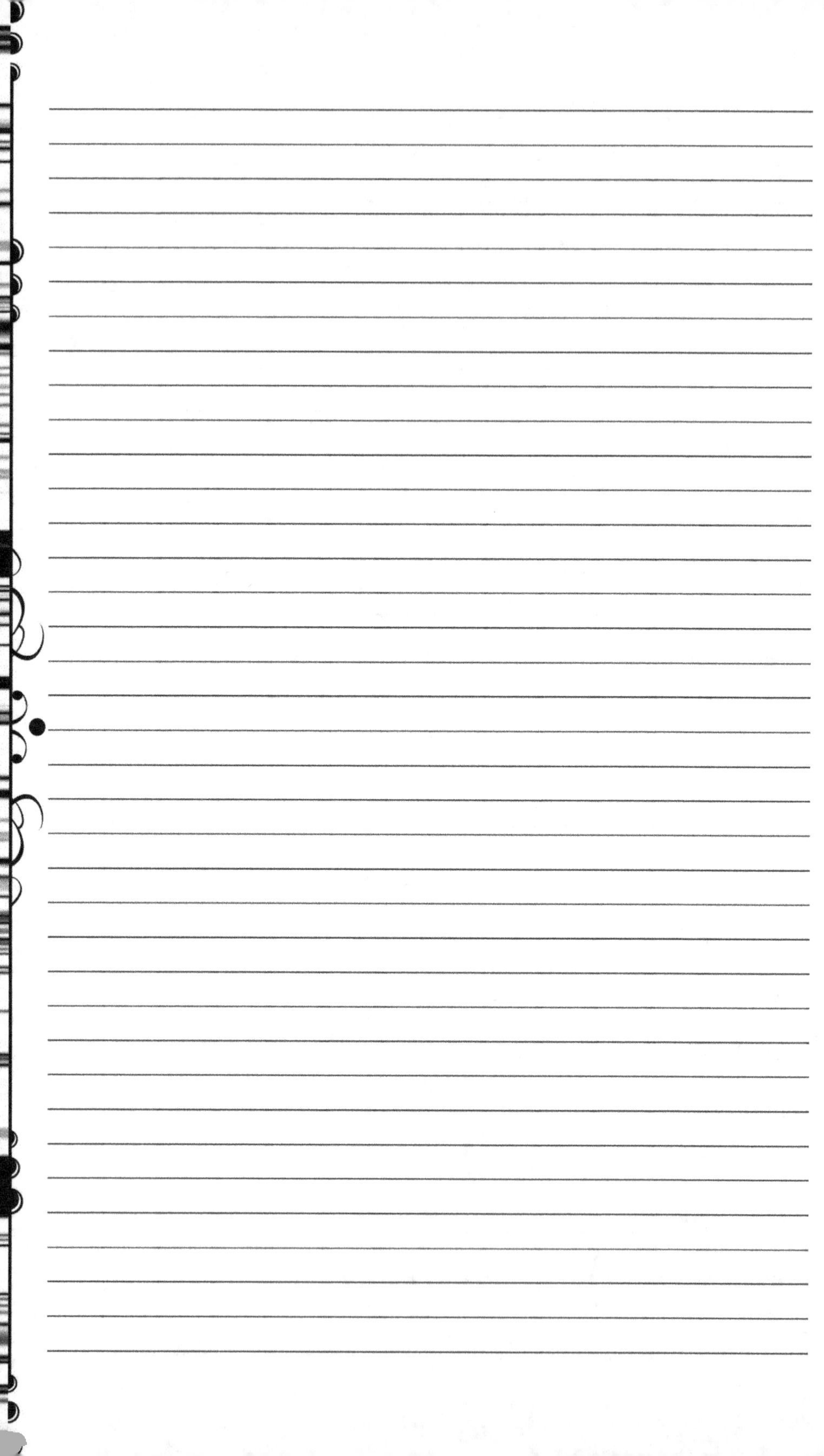

SYNOPSIS/THINGS I LIKED:

THINGS I DIDN'T LIKE:

FAVORITE QUOTE(S):

TITLE: _______________

GENRE: _______________

SERIES: _______________

AUTHOR: _______________

PAGES: _______________

STARTED: _______________

FINISHED: _______________

☆ ☆ ☆ ☆ ☆

FORMAT READ: EBOOK / PRINT / AUDIOBOOK

✓ **SYNOPSIS/THINGS I LIKED:**

____
____
____
____

🚫 **THINGS I DIDN'T LIKE:**

____
____
____
____

✎ **FAVORITE QUOTE(S):**

____
____
____
____
____
____

TITLE:

GENRE:

SERIES:

AUTHOR:

PAGES:

STARTED:

FINISHED:

FORMAT READ: EBOOK / PRINT / AUDIOBOOK

139

SYNOPSIS/THINGS I LIKED:

THINGS I DIDN'T LIKE:

FAVORITE QUOTE(S):

TITLE:

GENRE:

SERIES:

AUTHOR:

PAGES:

STARTED:

FINISHED:

FORMAT READ: EBOOK / PRINT / AUDIOBOOK

TITLE:

GENRE:

SERIES:

AUTHOR:

PAGES:

STARTED:

FINISHED:

☆ ☆ ☆ ☆ ☆

FORMAT READ: EBOOK / PRINT / AUDIOBOOK

SYNOPSIS/THINGS I LIKED:

THINGS I DIDN'T LIKE:

FAVORITE QUOTE(S):

TITLE:

GENRE:

SERIES:

AUTHOR:

PAGES:

STARTED:

FINISHED:

FORMAT READ: EBOOK / PRINT / AUDIOBOOK

SYNOPSIS/THINGS I LIKED:

THINGS I DIDN'T LIKE:

FAVORITE QUOTE(S):

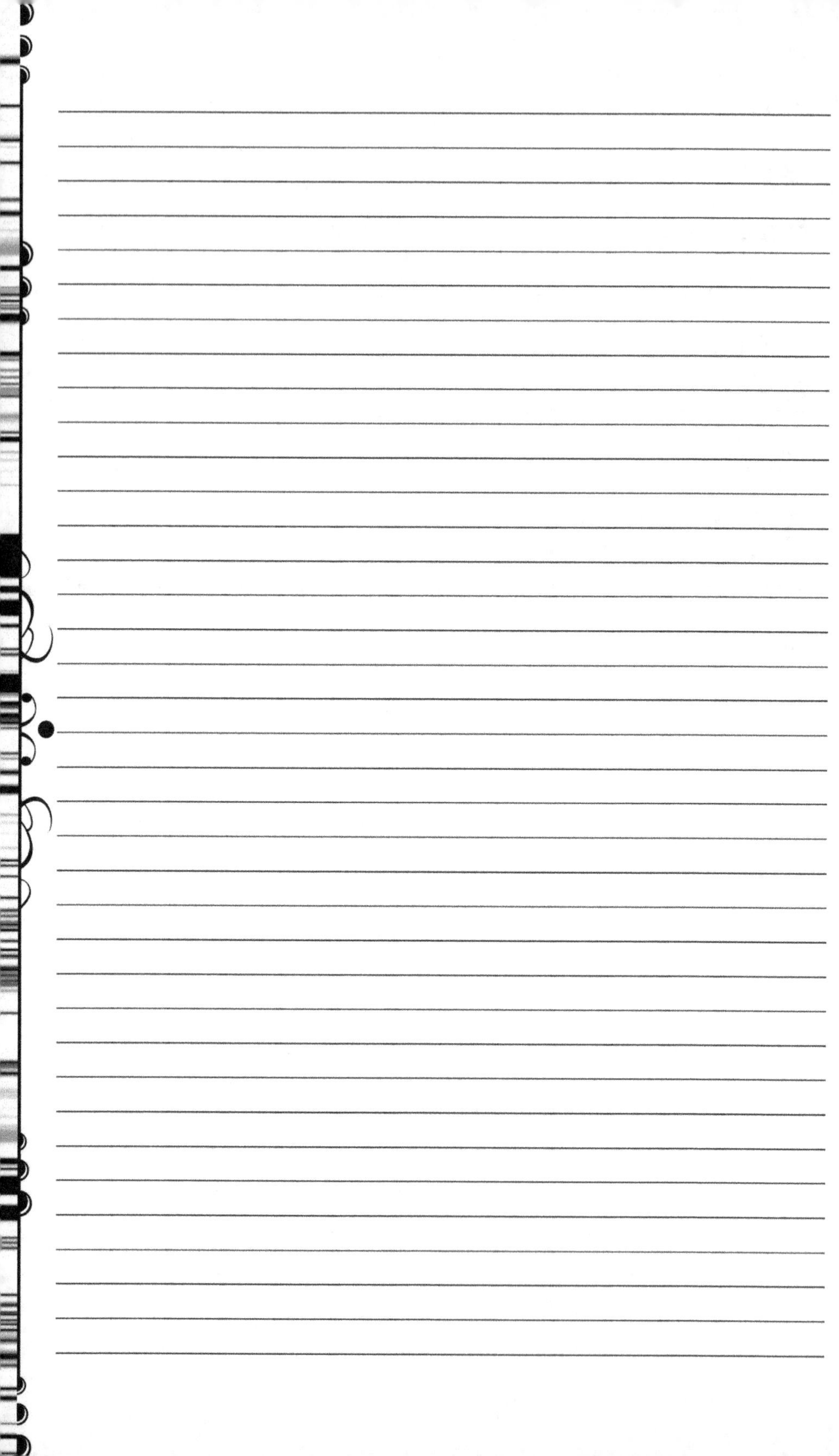

TITLE:

GENRE:

SERIES:

AUTHOR:

PAGES:

STARTED:

FINISHED:

FORMAT READ: EBOOK / PRINT / AUDIOBOOK

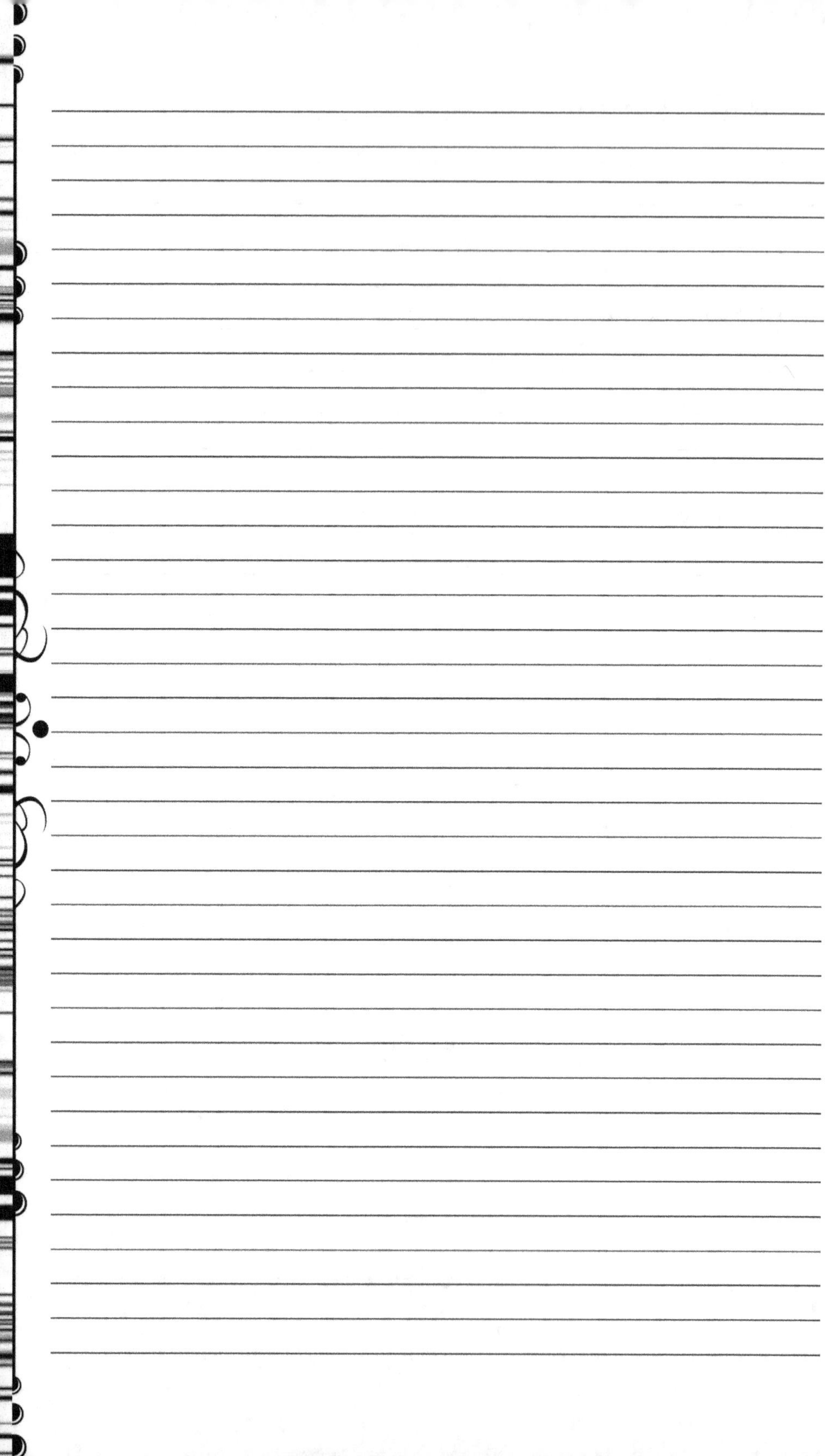

🚫 THINGS I DIDN'T LIKE:

✎ FAVORITE QUOTE(S):

TITLE:

GENRE:

SERIES:

AUTHOR:

PAGES:

STARTED:

FINISHED:

☆ ☆ ☆ ☆ ☆

FORMAT READ: EBOOK / PRINT / AUDIOBOOK

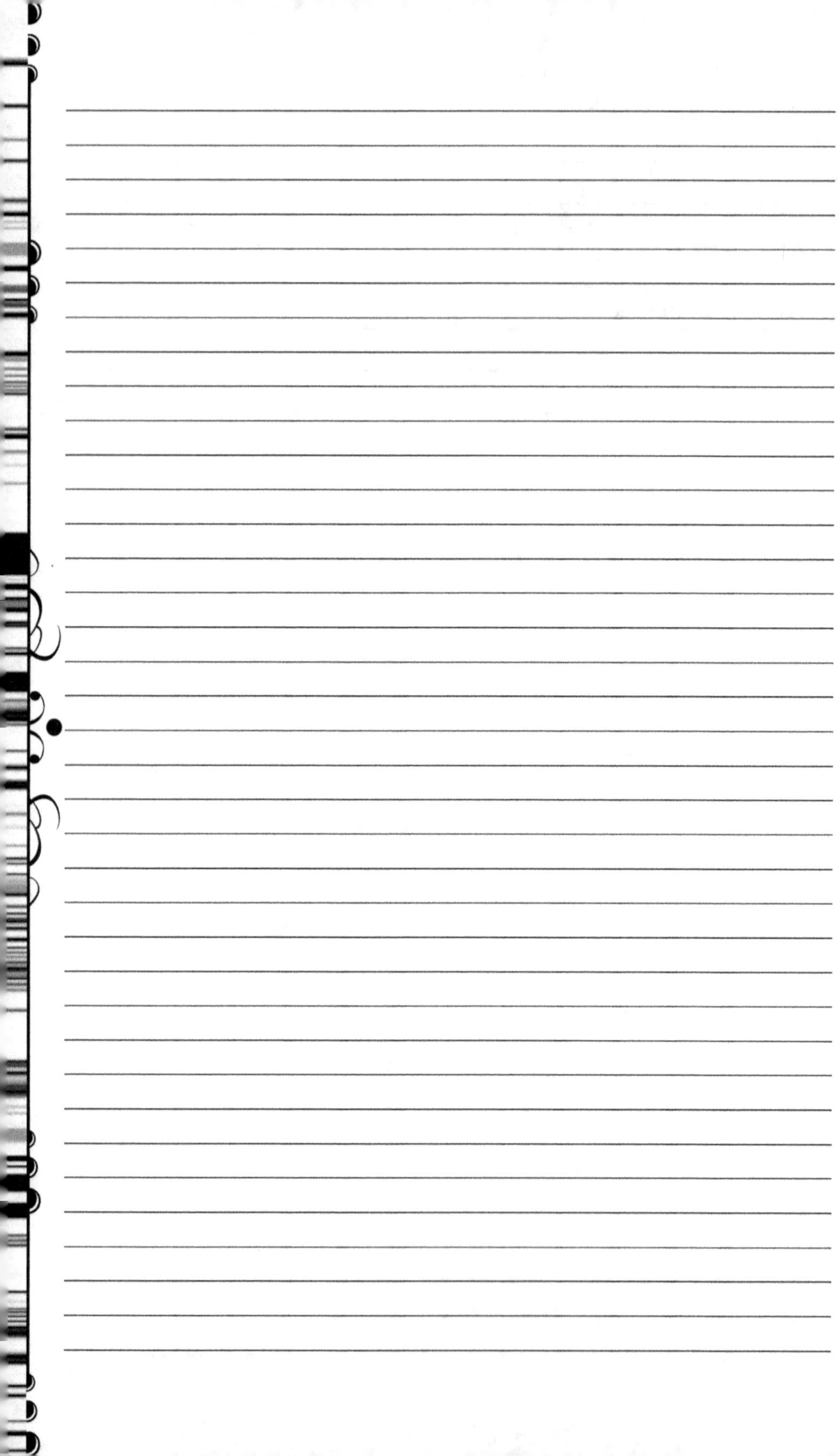

TITLE:

GENRE:

SERIES:

AUTHOR:

PAGES:

STARTED:

FINISHED:

☆ ☆ ☆ ☆ ☆

FORMAT READ: EBOOK / PRINT / AUDIOBOOK

✔ SYNOPSIS/THINGS I LIKED:

🚫 THINGS I DIDN'T LIKE:

✏ FAVORITE QUOTE(S):

TITLE:

GENRE:

SERIES:

AUTHOR:

PAGES:

STARTED:

FINISHED:

FORMAT READ: EBOOK / PRINT / AUDIOBOOK

✓ SYNOPSIS/THINGS I LIKED:

🚫 THINGS I DIDN'T LIKE:

✎ FAVORITE QUOTE(S):

TITLE:

GENRE:

SERIES:

AUTHOR:

PAGES:

STARTED:

FINISHED:

FORMAT READ: EBOOK / PRINT / AUDIOBOOK

TITLE:

GENRE:

SERIES:

AUTHOR:

PAGES:

STARTED:

FINISHED:

FORMAT READ: EBOOK / PRINT / AUDIOBOOK

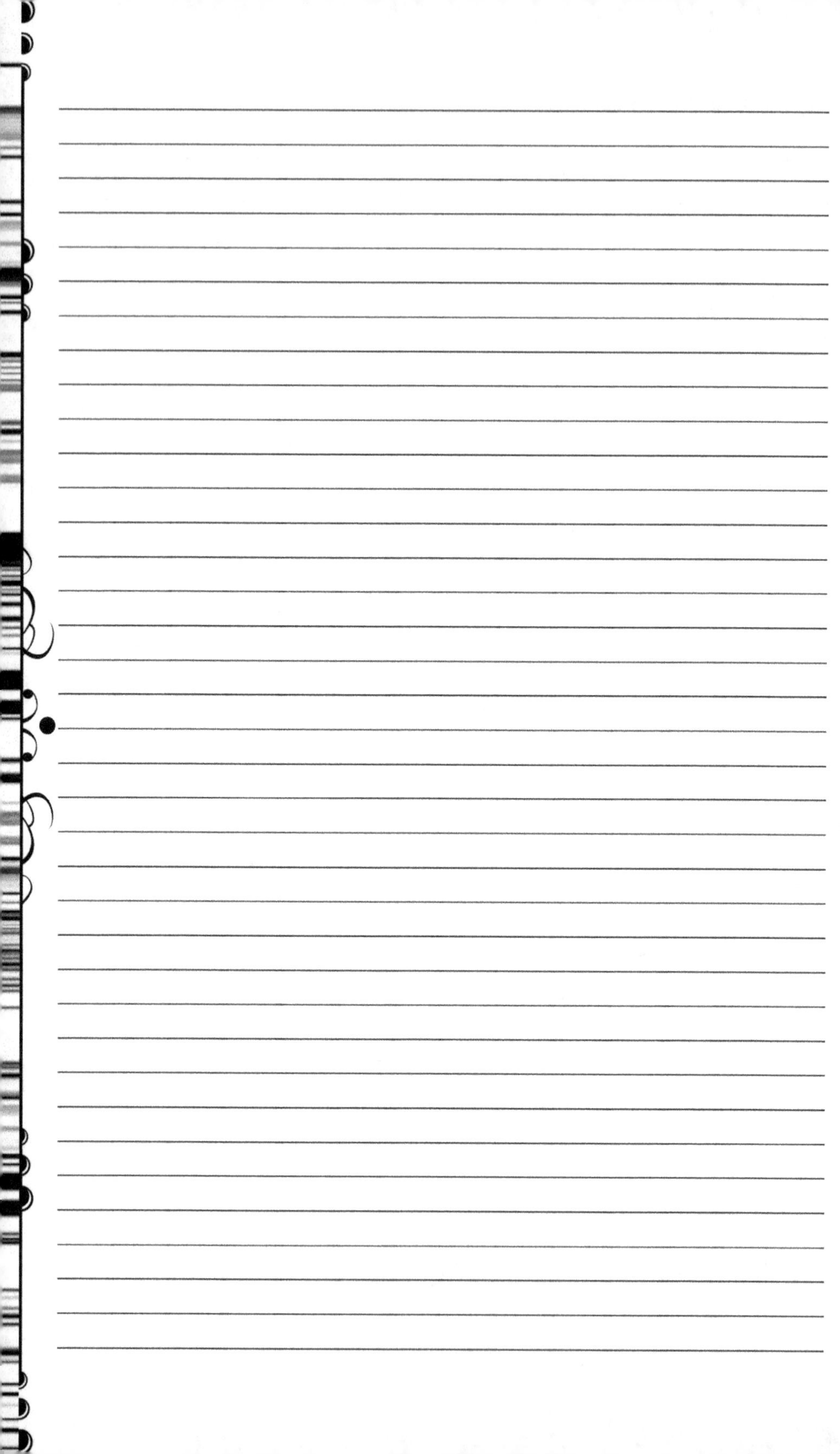

TITLE:

GENRE:

SERIES:

AUTHOR:

PAGES:

STARTED:

FINISHED:

FORMAT READ: EBOOK / PRINT / AUDIOBOOK

SYNOPSIS/THINGS I LIKED:

THINGS I DIDN'T LIKE:

FAVORITE QUOTE(S):

TITLE:

GENRE:

SERIES:

AUTHOR:

PAGES:

STARTED:

FINISHED:

☆ ☆ ☆ ☆ ☆

FORMAT READ: EBOOK / PRINT / AUDIOBOOK

✔ **SYNOPSIS/THINGS I LIKED:**

🚫 **THINGS I DIDN'T LIKE:**

✎ **FAVORITE QUOTE(S):**

TITLE:

GENRE:

SERIES:

AUTHOR:

PAGES:

STARTED:

FINISHED:

FORMAT READ: EBOOK / PRINT / AUDIOBOOK

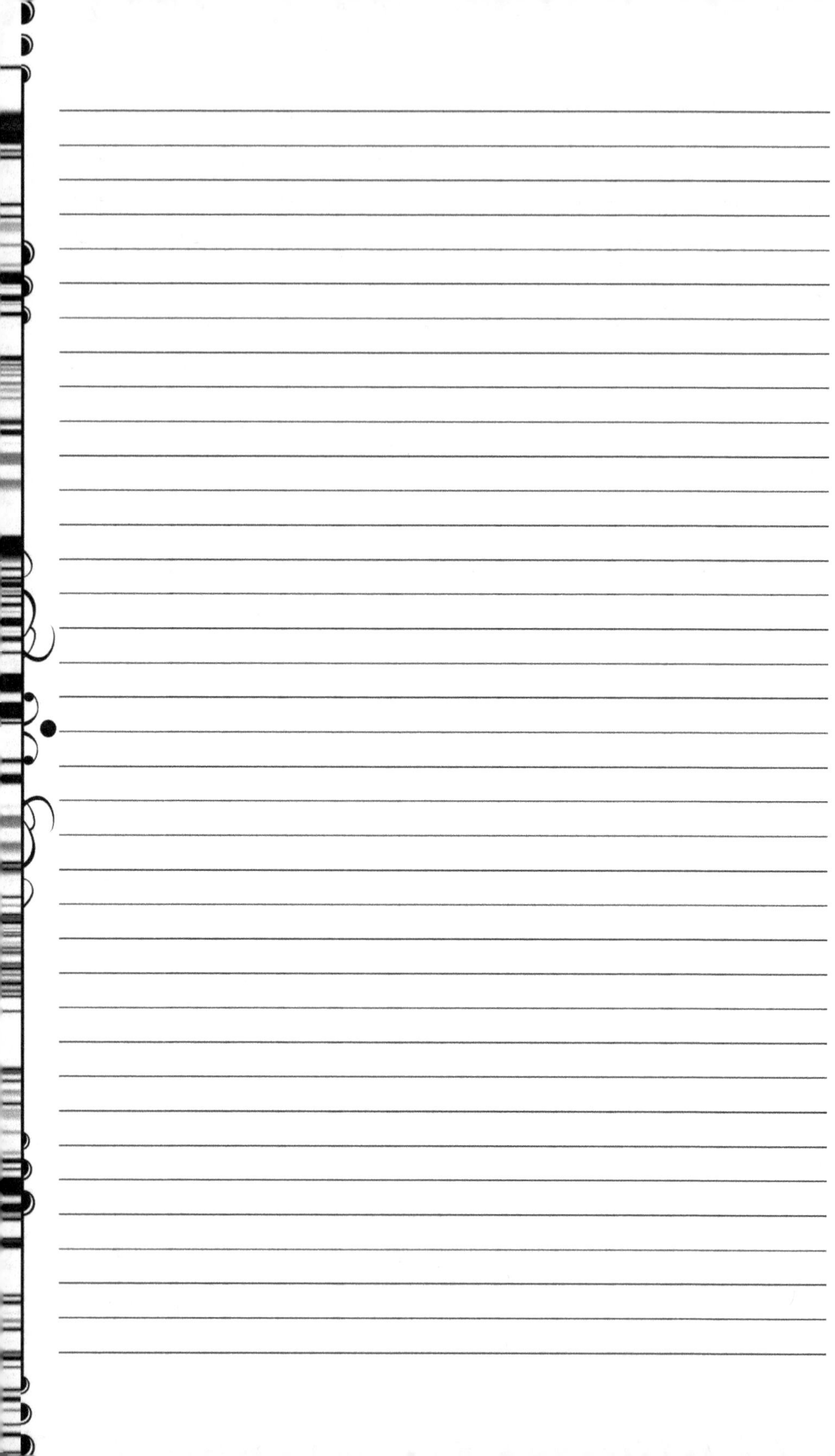

TITLE:

GENRE:

SERIES:

AUTHOR:

PAGES:

STARTED:

FINISHED:

FORMAT READ: EBOOK / PRINT / AUDIOBOOK

TITLE:

GENRE:

SERIES:

AUTHOR:

PAGES:

STARTED:

FINISHED:

FORMAT READ: EBOOK / PRINT / AUDIOBOOK

SYNOPSIS/THINGS I LIKED:

THINGS I DIDN'T LIKE:

FAVORITE QUOTE(S):

TITLE:

GENRE:

SERIES:

AUTHOR:

PAGES:

STARTED:

FINISHED:

☆☆☆☆☆

FORMAT READ: EBOOK / PRINT / AUDIOBOOK

✓ SYNOPSIS/THINGS I LIKED:

🚫 THINGS I DIDN'T LIKE:

✏️ FAVORITE QUOTE(S):

SYNOPSIS/THINGS I LIKED:

THINGS I DIDN'T LIKE:

FAVORITE QUOTE(S):

TITLE:
GENRE:
SERIES:
AUTHOR:
PAGES:
STARTED:
FINISHED:
FORMAT READ: EBOOK / PRINT / AUDIOBOOK

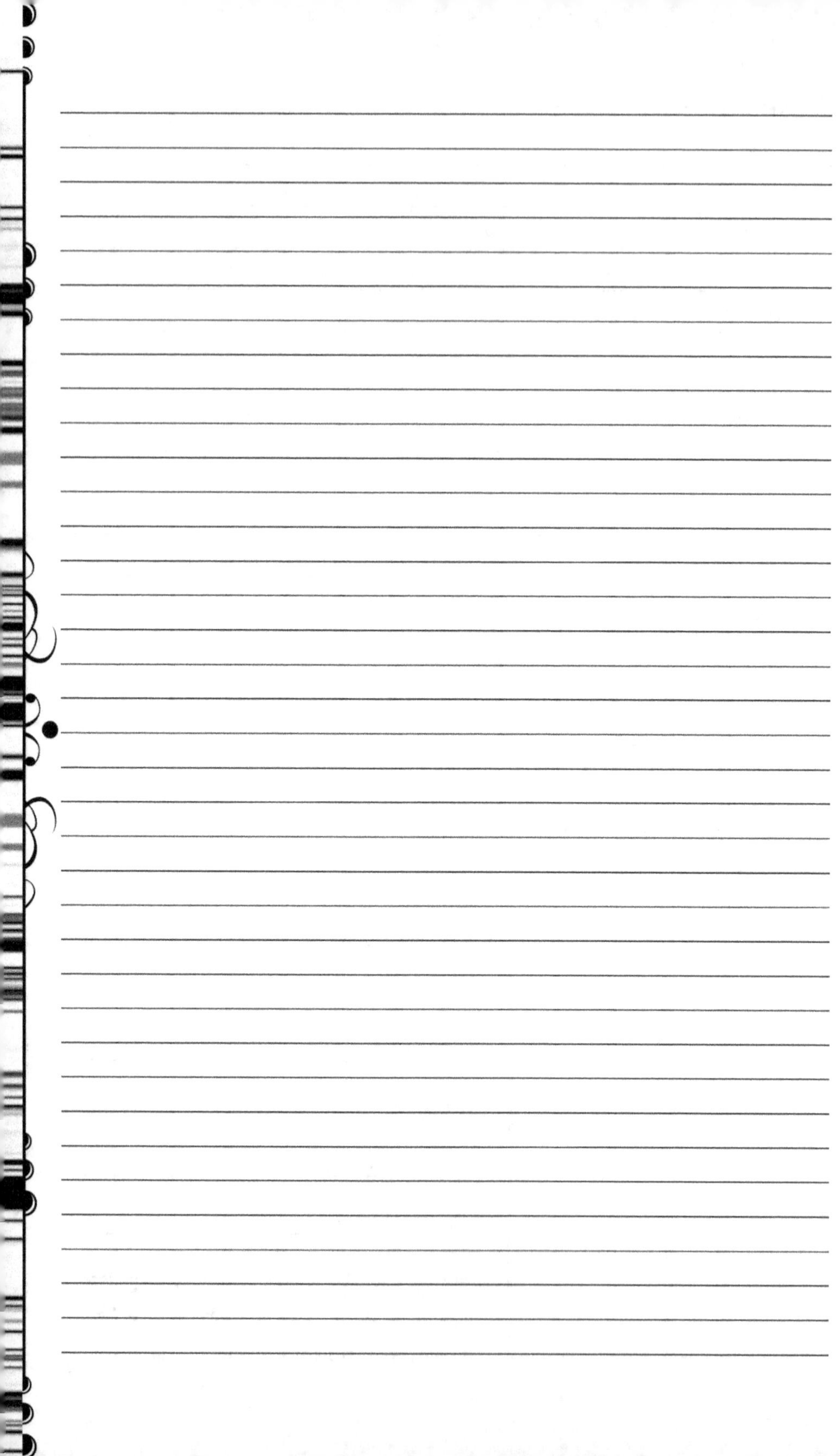

TITLE:

GENRE:

SERIES:

AUTHOR:

PAGES:

STARTED:

FINISHED:

FORMAT READ: EBOOK / PRINT / AUDIOBOOK

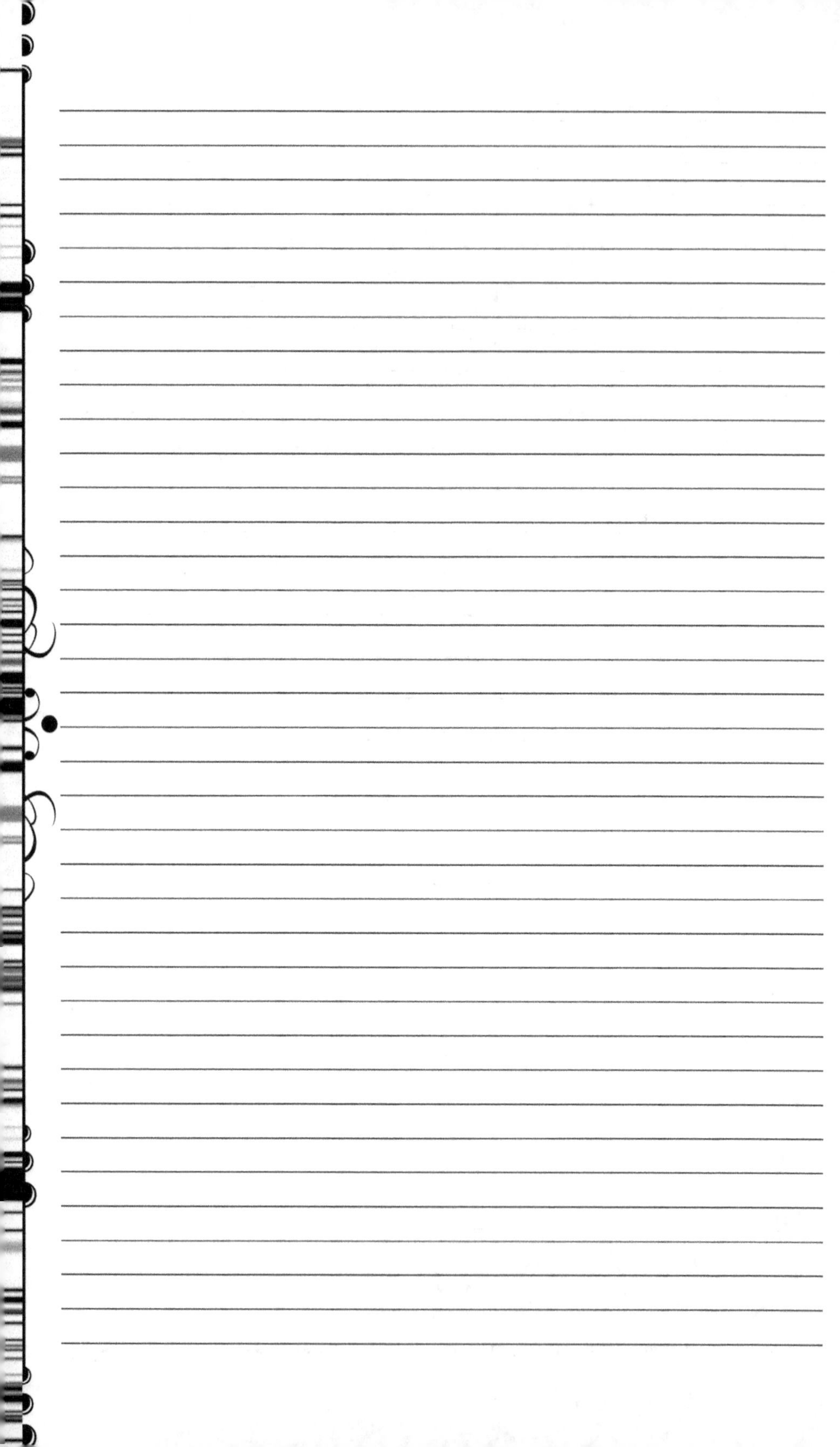

TITLE:

GENRE:

SERIES:

AUTHOR:

PAGES:

STARTED:

FINISHED:

FORMAT READ: EBOOK / PRINT / AUDIOBOOK

SYNOPSIS/THINGS I LIKED:

THINGS I DIDN'T LIKE:

FAVORITE QUOTE(S):

TITLE: ___________________________

GENRE: ___________________________

SERIES: ___________________________

AUTHOR: ___________________________

PAGES: ___________________________

STARTED: ___________________________

FINISHED: ___________________________

☆ ☆ ☆ ☆ ☆

FORMAT READ: EBOOK / PRINT / AUDIOBOOK

✔ **SYNOPSIS/THINGS I LIKED:**

____

____

____

____

🚫 **THINGS I DIDN'T LIKE:**

____

____

____

____

✎ **FAVORITE QUOTE(S):**

____

____

____

____

____

____

____

TITLE:

GENRE:

SERIES:

AUTHOR:

PAGES:

STARTED:

FINISHED:

FORMAT READ: EBOOK / PRINT / AUDIOBOOK

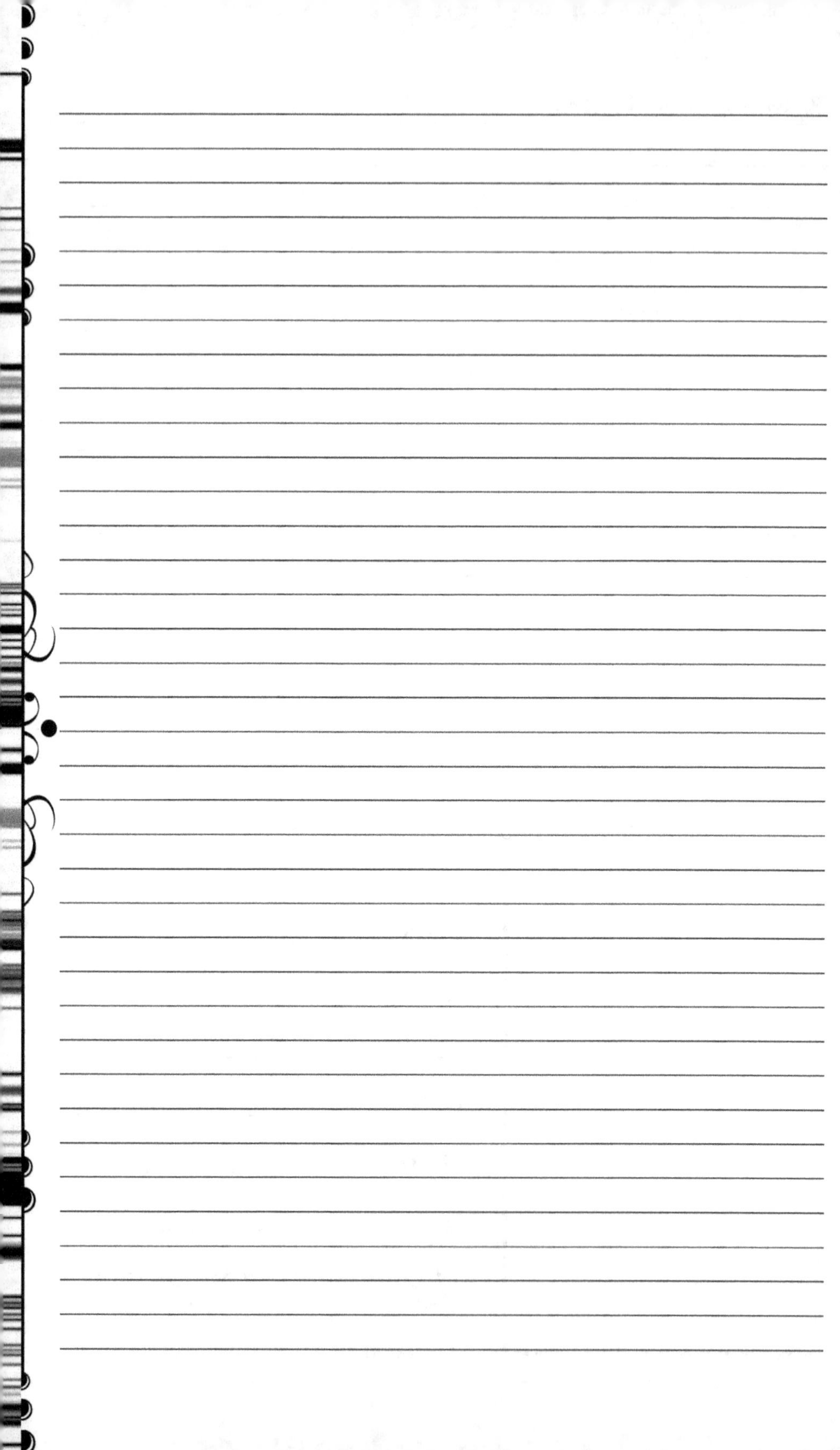

SYNOPSIS/THINGS I LIKED:

THINGS I DIDN'T LIKE:

FAVORITE QUOTE(S):

TITLE:

GENRE:

SERIES:

AUTHOR:

PAGES:

STARTED:

FINISHED:

FORMAT READ: EBOOK / PRINT / AUDIOBOOK

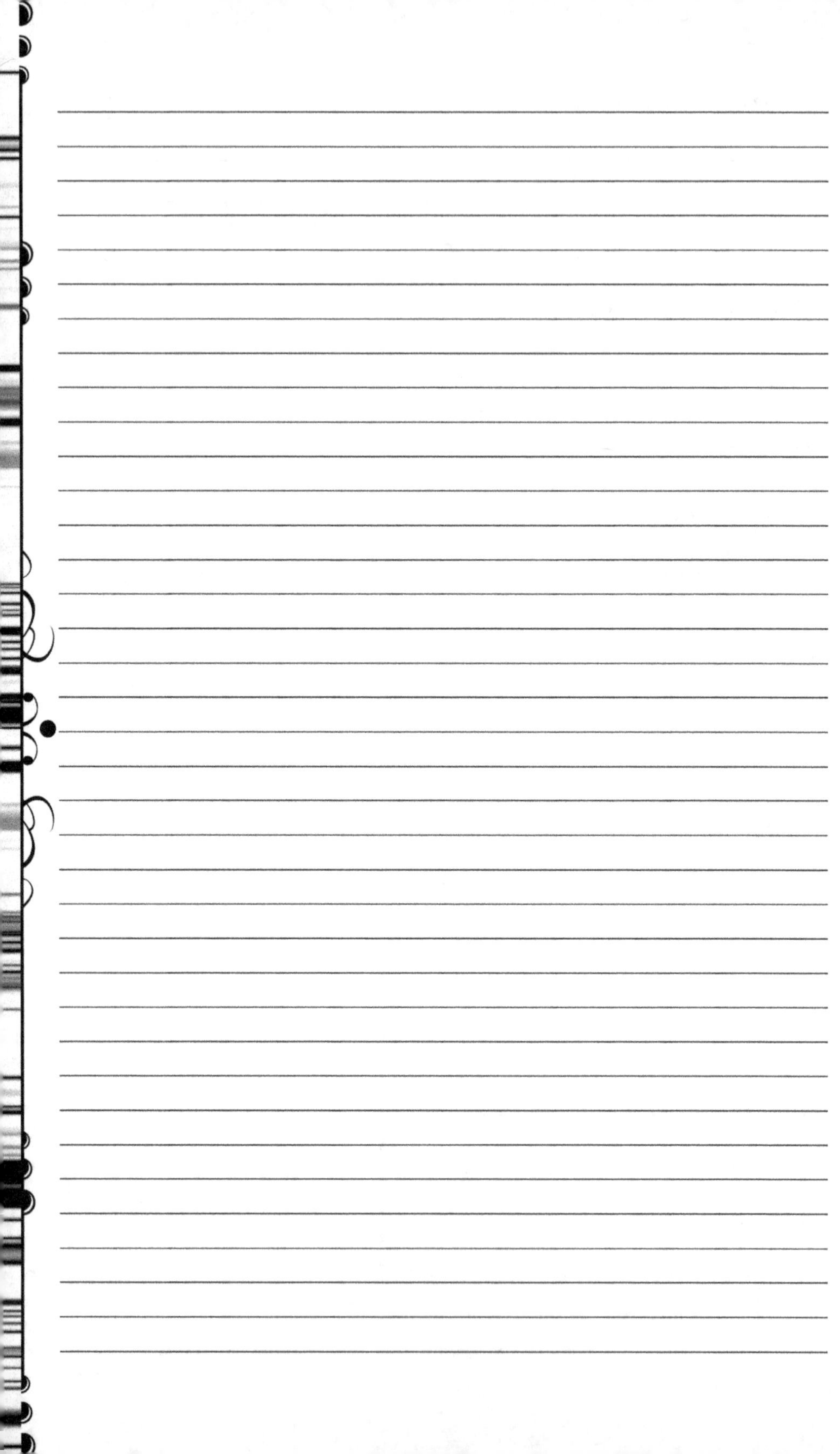

TITLE:

GENRE:

SERIES:

AUTHOR:

PAGES:

STARTED:

FINISHED:

FORMAT READ: EBOOK / PRINT / AUDIOBOOK

SYNOPSIS/THINGS I LIKED:

THINGS I DIDN'T LIKE:

FAVORITE QUOTE(S):

161

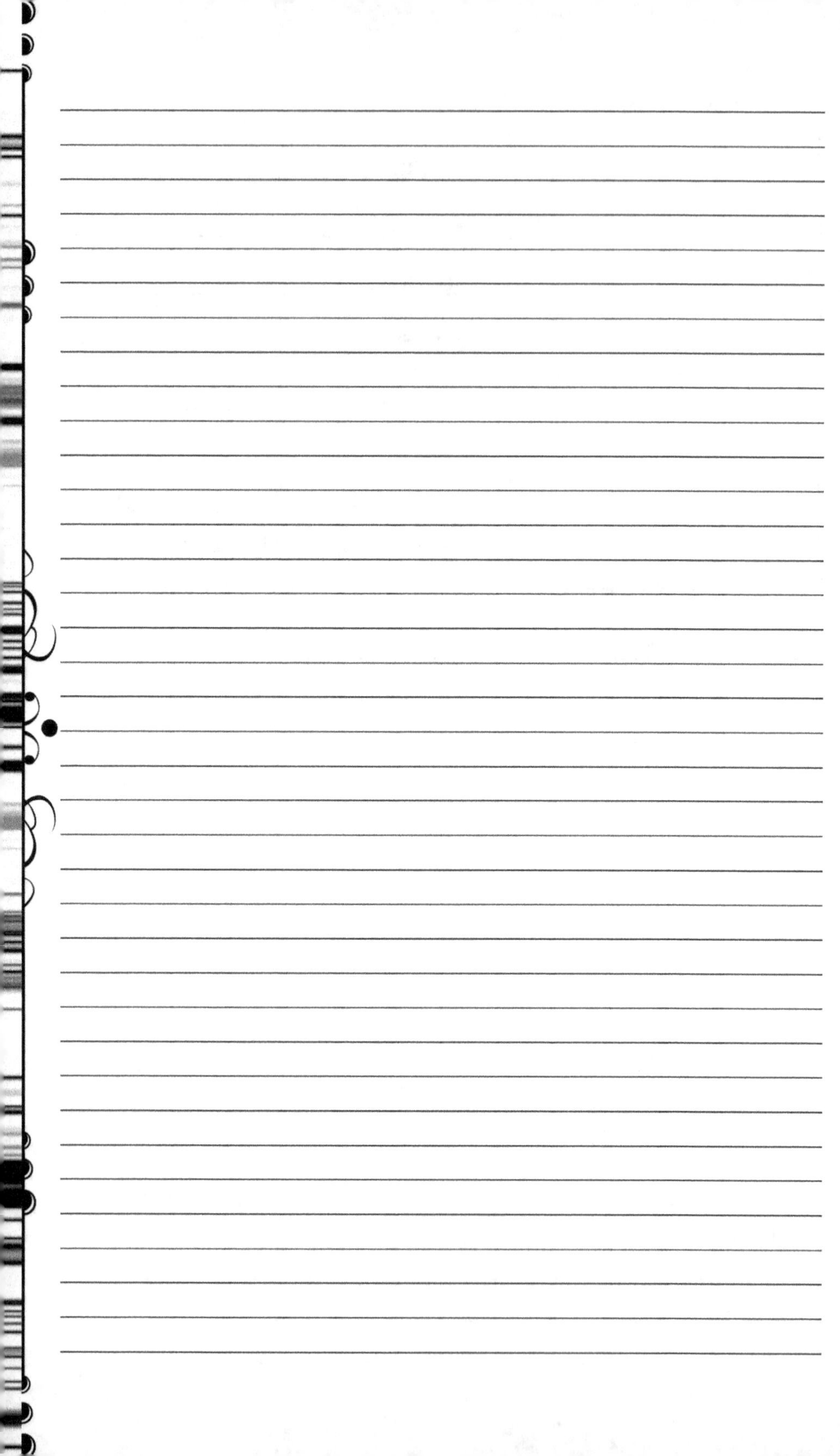

TITLE: ______________________

GENRE: ______________________

SERIES: ______________________

AUTHOR: ______________________

PAGES: ______________________

STARTED: ______________________

FINISHED: ______________________

☆☆☆☆☆

FORMAT READ: EBOOK / PRINT / AUDIOBOOK

✓ SYNOPSIS/THINGS I LIKED:

🚫 THINGS I DIDN'T LIKE:

✎ FAVORITE QUOTE(S):

🚫 THINGS I DIDN'T LIKE:

✎ FAVORITE QUOTE(S):

TITLE:

GENRE:

SERIES:

AUTHOR:

PAGES:

STARTED:

FINISHED:

☆ ☆ ☆ ☆ ☆

FORMAT READ: EBOOK / PRINT / AUDIOBOOK

🚫 **THINGS I DIDN'T LIKE:**

✎ **FAVORITE QUOTE(S):**

TITLE:

GENRE:

SERIES:

AUTHOR:

PAGES:

STARTED:

FINISHED:

☆ ☆ ☆ ☆ ☆

FORMAT READ: EBOOK / PRINT / AUDIOBOOK

TITLE:

GENRE:

SERIES:

AUTHOR:

PAGES:

STARTED:

FINISHED:

FORMAT READ: EBOOK / PRINT / AUDIOBOOK

SYNOPSIS/THINGS I LIKED:

THINGS I DIDN'T LIKE:

FAVORITE QUOTE(S):

TITLE:

GENRE:

SERIES:

AUTHOR:

PAGES:

STARTED:

FINISHED:

FORMAT READ: EBOOK / PRINT / AUDIOBOOK

SYNOPSIS/THINGS I LIKED:

THINGS I DIDN'T LIKE:

FAVORITE QUOTE(S):

✔ **Synopsis/Things I liked:**

⊘ **Things I didn't like:**

✎ **Favorite quote(s):**

Title:

Genre:

Series:

Author:

Pages:

Started:

Finished:

☆ ☆ ☆ ☆ ☆

Format read: Ebook / Print / Audiobook

TITLE:

GENRE:

SERIES:

AUTHOR:

PAGES:

STARTED:

FINISHED:

FORMAT READ: EBOOK / PRINT / AUDIOBOOK

SYNOPSIS/THINGS I LIKED:

THINGS I DIDN'T LIKE:

FAVORITE QUOTE(S):

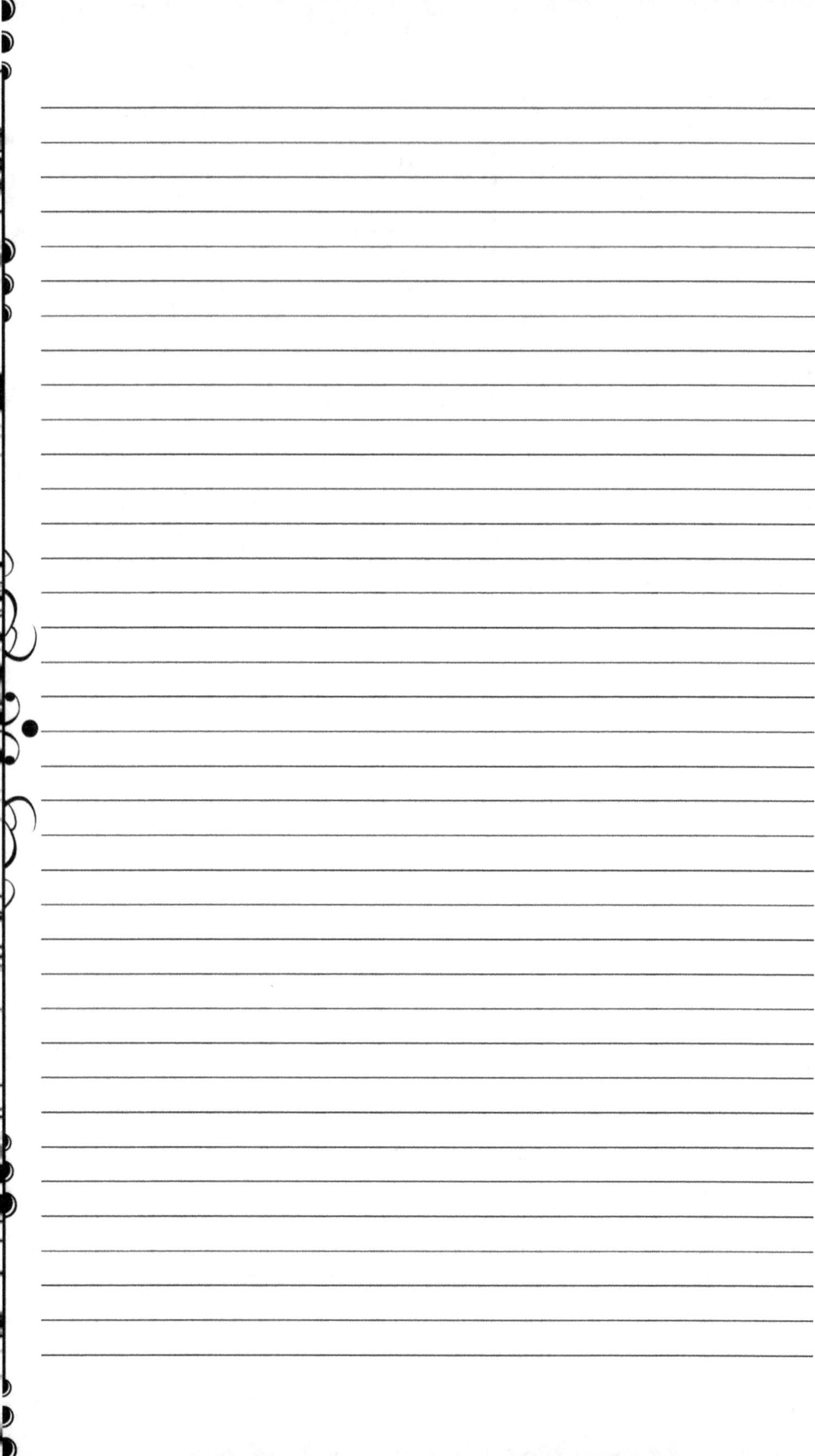

TITLE: _______________

GENRE: _______________

SERIES: _______________

AUTHOR: _______________

PAGES: _______________

STARTED: _______________

FINISHED: _______________

☆ ☆ ☆ ☆ ☆

FORMAT READ: EBOOK / PRINT / AUDIOBOOK

✓ **SYNOPSIS/THINGS I LIKED:**

____
____
____

🚫 **THINGS I DIDN'T LIKE:**

____
____
____

✎ **FAVORITE QUOTE(S):**

____
____
____
____
____

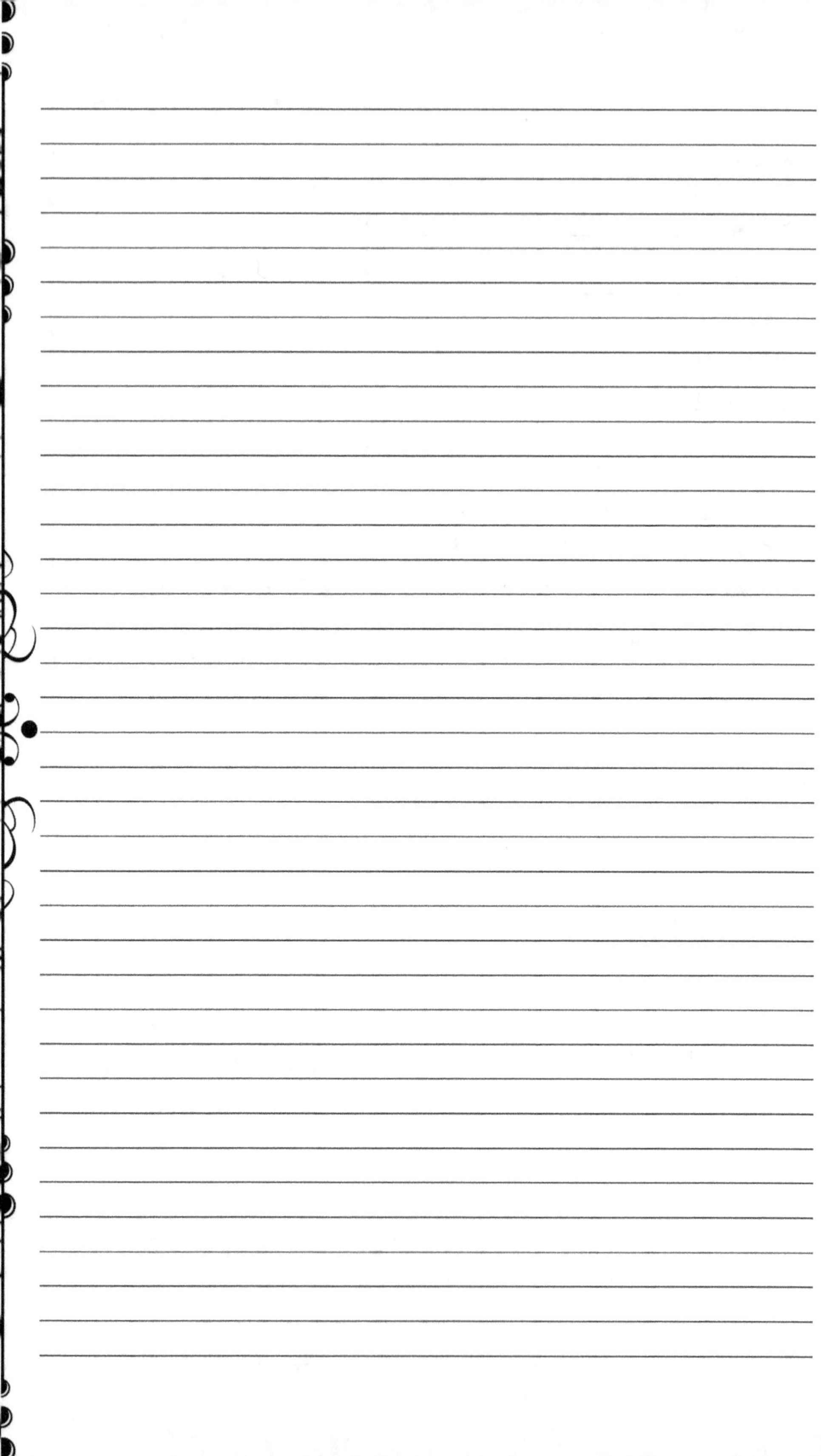

☑ **SYNOPSIS/THINGS I LIKED:**

🚫 **THINGS I DIDN'T LIKE:**

✏️ **FAVORITE QUOTE(S):**

TITLE:

GENRE:

SERIES:

AUTHOR:

PAGES:

STARTED:

FINISHED:

☆ ☆ ☆ ☆ ☆

FORMAT READ: EBOOK / PRINT / AUDIOBOOK

TITLE:

GENRE:

SERIES:

AUTHOR:

PAGES:

STARTED:

FINISHED:

FORMAT READ: EBOOK / PRINT / AUDIOBOOK

TITLE: ______________________

GENRE: ______________________

SERIES: ______________________

AUTHOR: ______________________

PAGES: ______________________

STARTED: ______________________

FINISHED: ______________________

☆ ☆ ☆ ☆ ☆

FORMAT READ: EBOOK / PRINT / AUDIOBOOK

☑ SYNOPSIS/THINGS I LIKED:

____
____
____
____

🚫 THINGS I DIDN'T LIKE:

____
____
____
____

✏ FAVORITE QUOTE(S):

____
____
____
____
____
____

TITLE:

GENRE:

SERIES:

AUTHOR:

PAGES:

STARTED:

FINISHED:

☆☆☆☆☆

FORMAT READ: EBOOK / PRINT / AUDIOBOOK

✔ **SYNOPSIS/THINGS I LIKED:**

🚫 **THINGS I DIDN'T LIKE:**

✏ **FAVORITE QUOTE(S):**

175

TITLE:

GENRE:

SERIES:

AUTHOR:

PAGES:

STARTED:

FINISHED:

FORMAT READ: EBOOK / PRINT / AUDIOBOOK

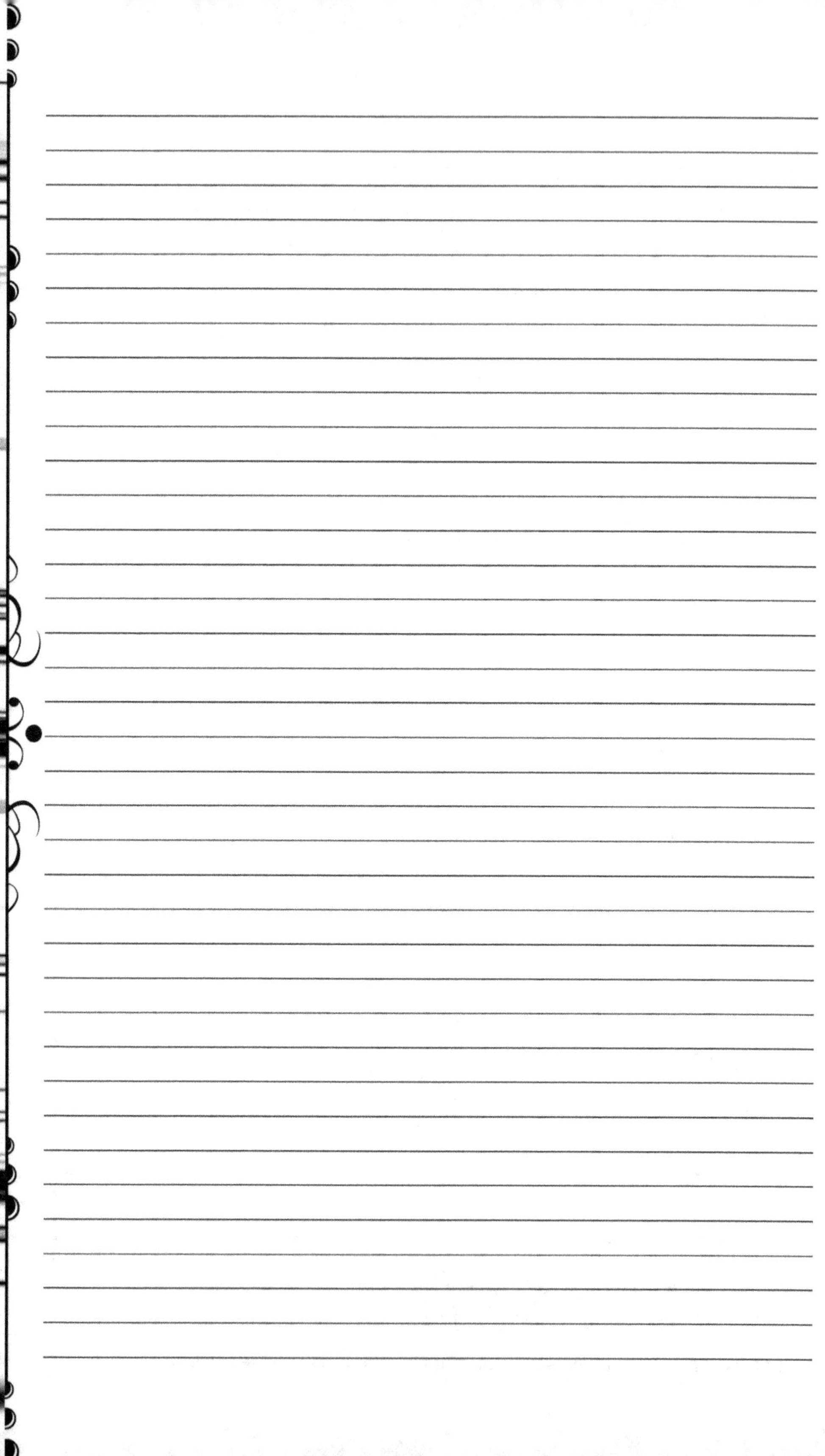

	Title: ______________________
	Genre: ______________________
	Series: ______________________
	Author: ______________________
	Pages: ______________________
	Started: ______________________
	Finished: ______________________

☆☆☆☆☆

FORMAT READ: Ebook / Print / Audiobook

☑ Synopsis/Things I liked:

____

____

____

____

🚫 Things I didn't like:

____

____

____

____

✎ Favorite quote(s):

____

____

____

____

____

____

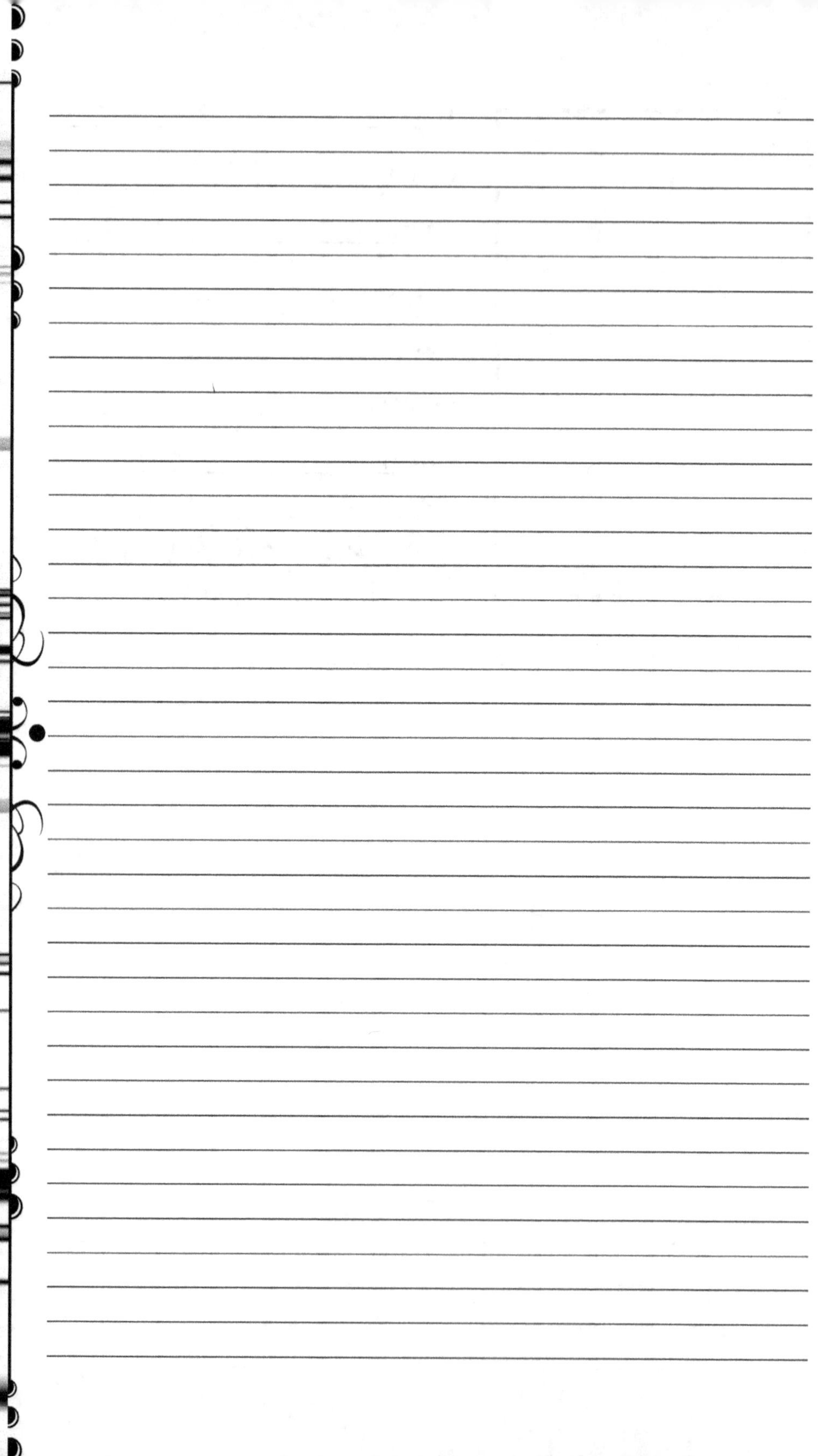

TITLE: _______________

GENRE: _______________

SERIES: _______________

AUTHOR: _______________

PAGES: _______________

STARTED: _______________

FINISHED: _______________

☆☆☆☆☆

FORMAT READ: EBOOK / PRINT / AUDIOBOOK

☑ **SYNOPSIS/THINGS I LIKED:**

🚫 **THINGS I DIDN'T LIKE:**

FAVORITE QUOTE(S):

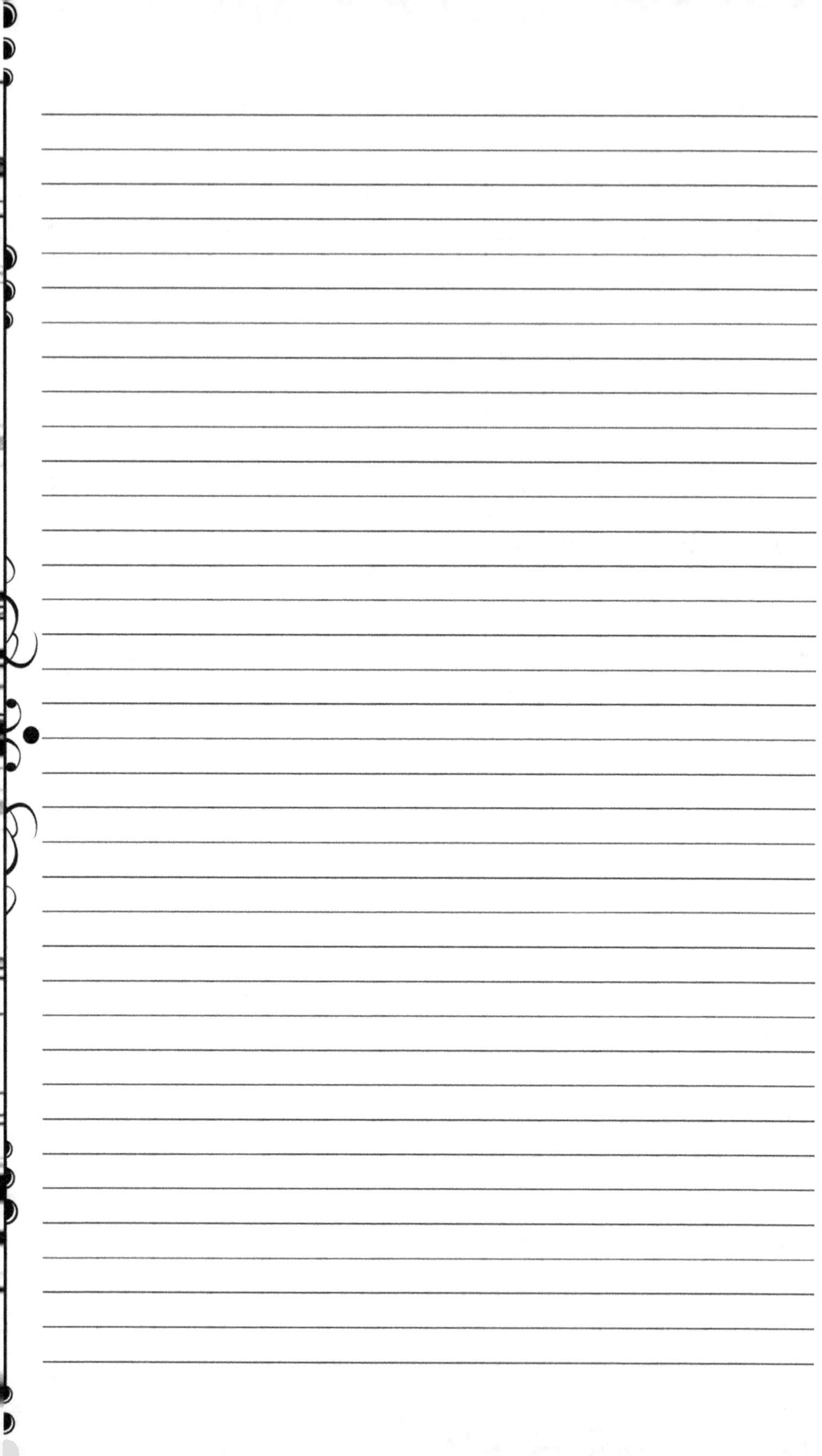

☑ **SYNOPSIS/THINGS I LIKED:**

🚫 **THINGS I DIDN'T LIKE:**

✏ **FAVORITE QUOTE(S):**

TITLE:

GENRE:

SERIES:

AUTHOR:

PAGES:

STARTED:

FINISHED:

☆ ☆ ☆ ☆ ☆

FORMAT READ: EBOOK / PRINT / AUDIOBOOK

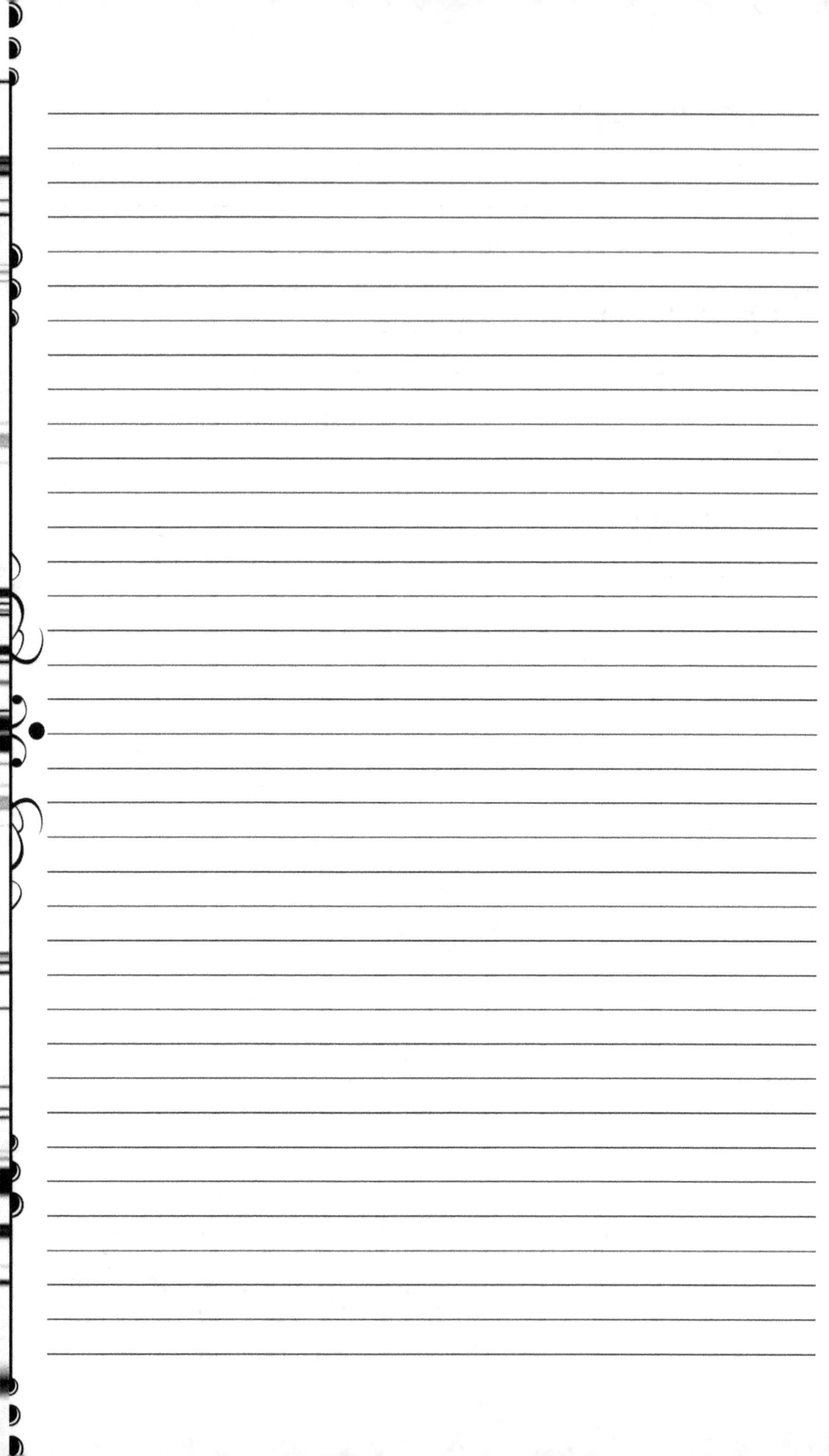

TITLE:

GENRE:

SERIES:

AUTHOR:

PAGES:

STARTED:

FINISHED:

FORMAT READ: EBOOK / PRINT / AUDIOBOOK

TITLE: ______________________

GENRE: ______________________

SERIES: ______________________

AUTHOR: ______________________

PAGES: ______________________

STARTED: ______________________

FINISHED: ______________________

☆ ☆ ☆ ☆ ☆

FORMAT READ: EBOOK / PRINT / AUDIOBOOK

✔ **SYNOPSIS/THINGS I LIKED:**

____
____
____
____

🚫 **THINGS I DIDN'T LIKE:**

____
____
____
____

✎ **FAVORITE QUOTE(S):**

____
____
____
____
____
____
____

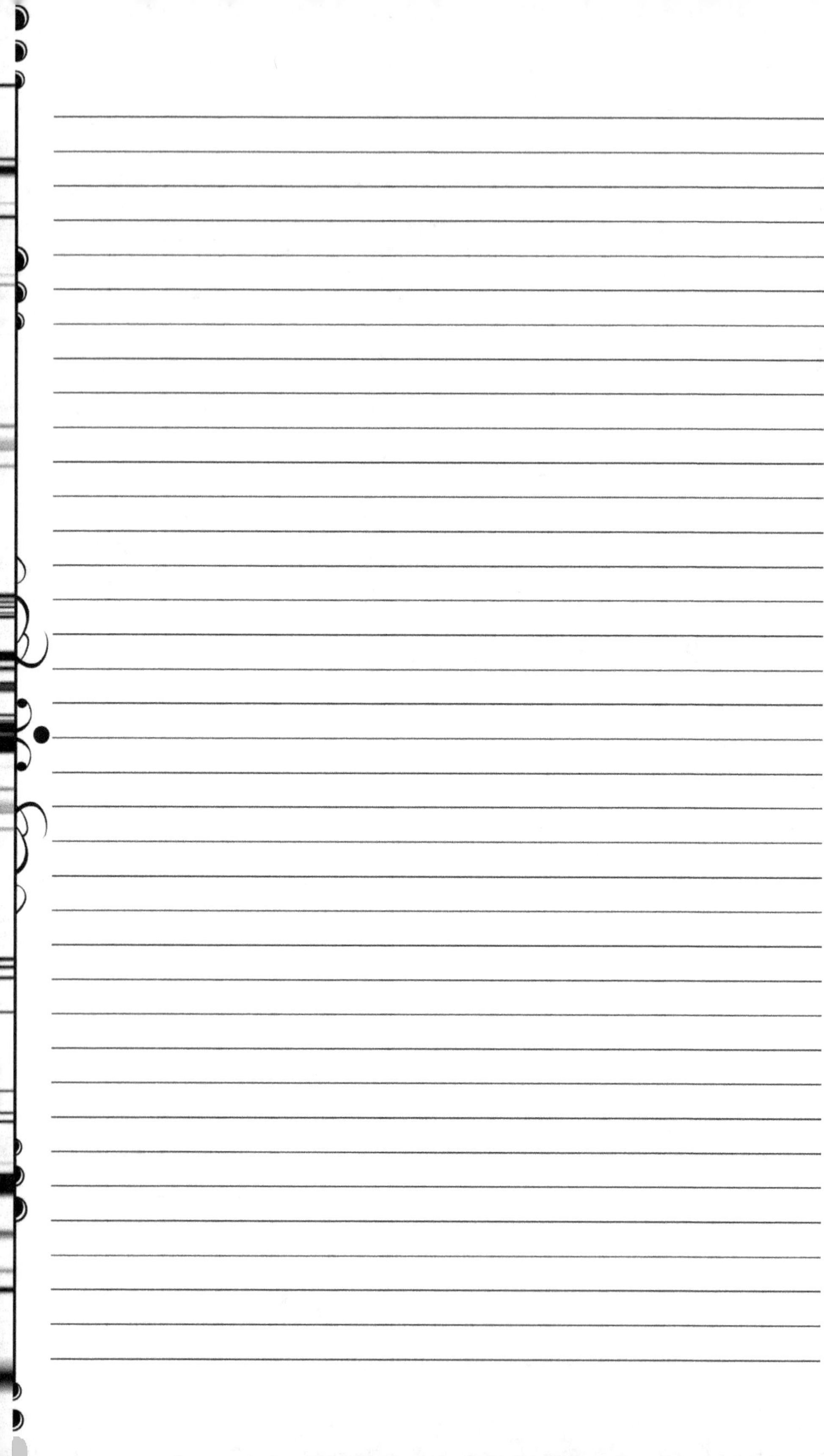

TITLE: _______________________

GENRE: _______________________

SERIES: _______________________

AUTHOR: _______________________

PAGES: _______________________

STARTED: _______________________

FINISHED: _______________________

☆☆☆☆☆

FORMAT READ: EBOOK / PRINT / AUDIOBOOK

✔ **SYNOPSIS/THINGS I LIKED:**

____
____
____
____

🚫 **THINGS I DIDN'T LIKE:**

____
____
____
____

✏ **FAVORITE QUOTE(S):**

____
____
____
____
____
____
____

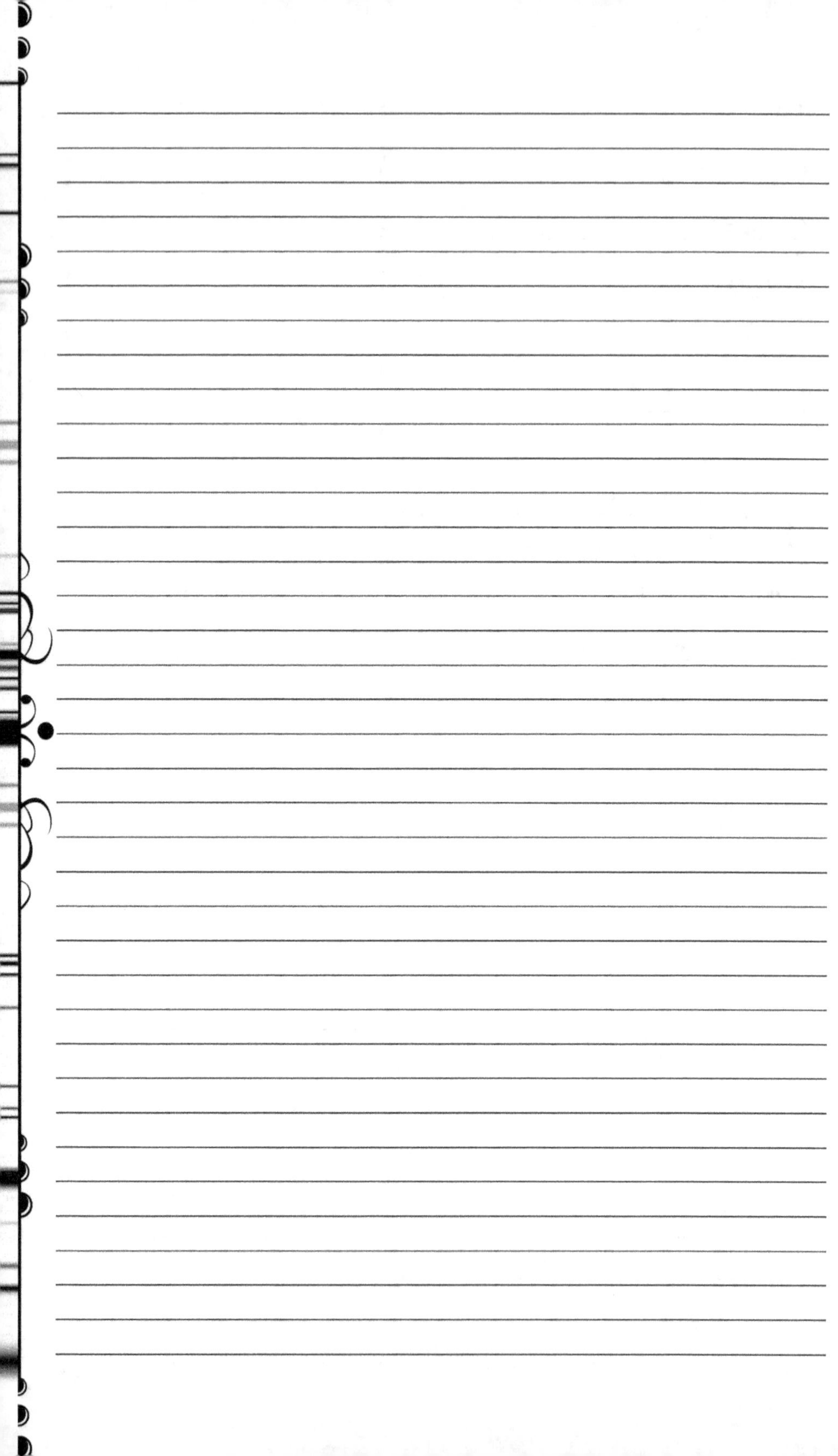

SYNOPSIS/THINGS I LIKED:

THINGS I DIDN'T LIKE:

FAVORITE QUOTE(S):

TITLE:

GENRE:

SERIES:

AUTHOR:

PAGES:

STARTED:

FINISHED:

FORMAT READ: EBOOK / PRINT / AUDIOBOOK

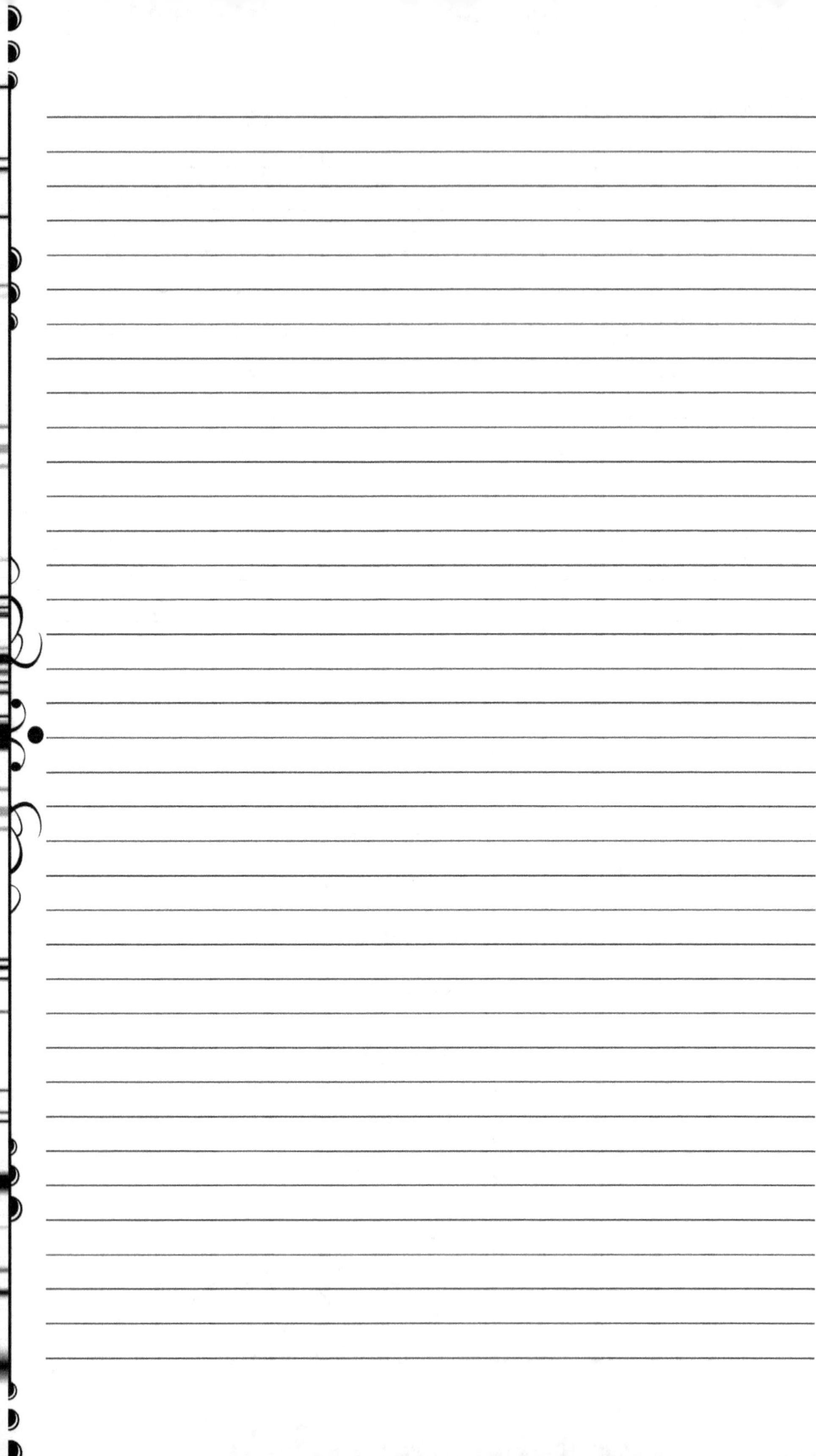

TITLE:

GENRE:

SERIES:

AUTHOR:

PAGES:

STARTED:

FINISHED:

FORMAT READ: EBOOK / PRINT / AUDIOBOOK

TITLE:

GENRE:

SERIES:

AUTHOR:

PAGES:

STARTED:

FINISHED:

FORMAT READ: EBOOK / PRINT / AUDIOBOOK

SYNOPSIS/THINGS I LIKED:

THINGS I DIDN'T LIKE:

FAVORITE QUOTE(S):

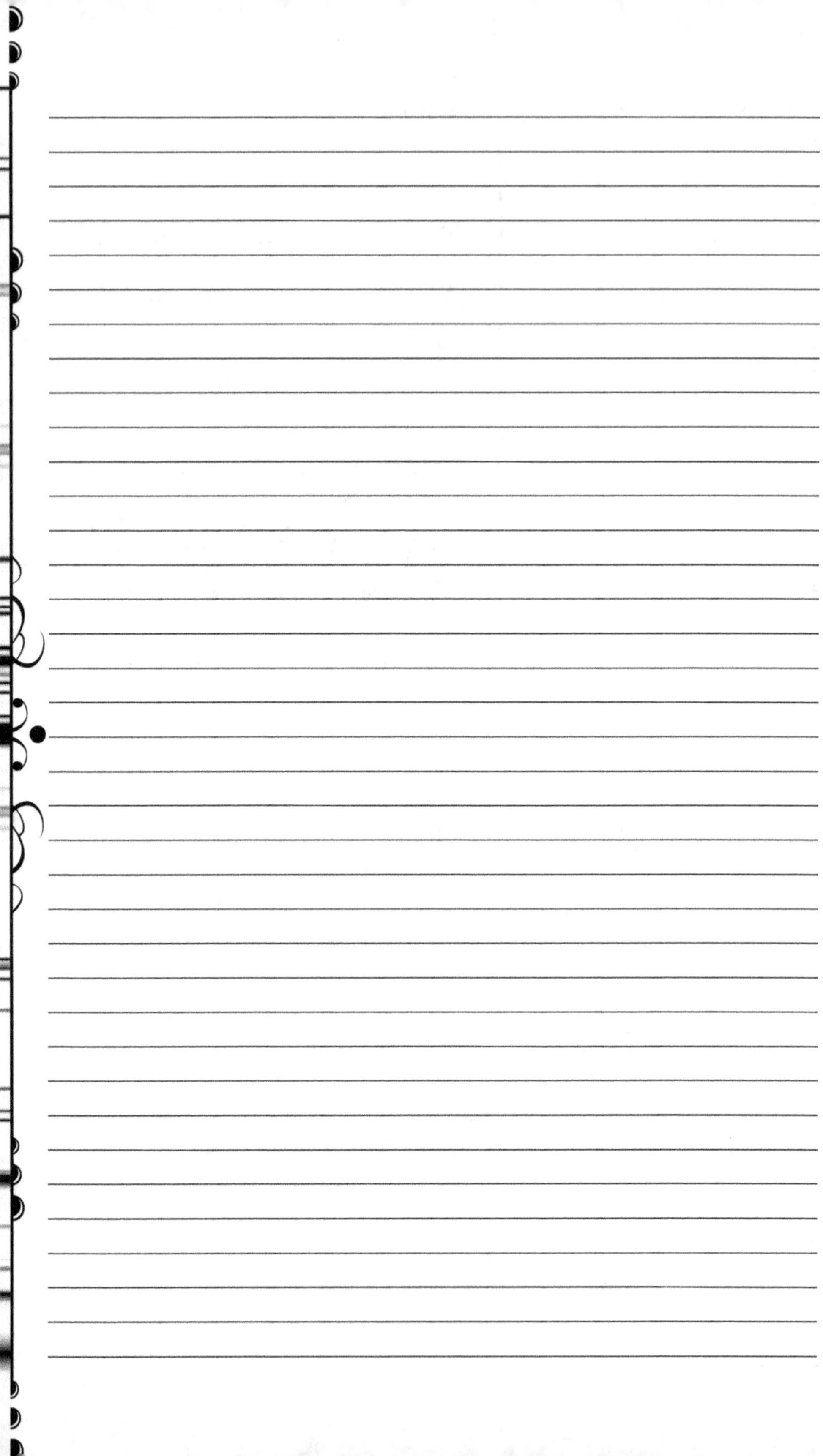

TITLE: ___________________________

GENRE: ___________________________

SERIES: ___________________________

AUTHOR: ___________________________

PAGES: ___________________________

STARTED: ___________________________

FINISHED: ___________________________

☆☆☆☆☆

FORMAT READ: EBOOK / PRINT / AUDIOBOOK

✔ **SYNOPSIS/THINGS I LIKED:**

____
____
____

🚫 **THINGS I DIDN'T LIKE:**

____
____
____

✏ **FAVORITE QUOTE(S):**

____
____
____
____
____

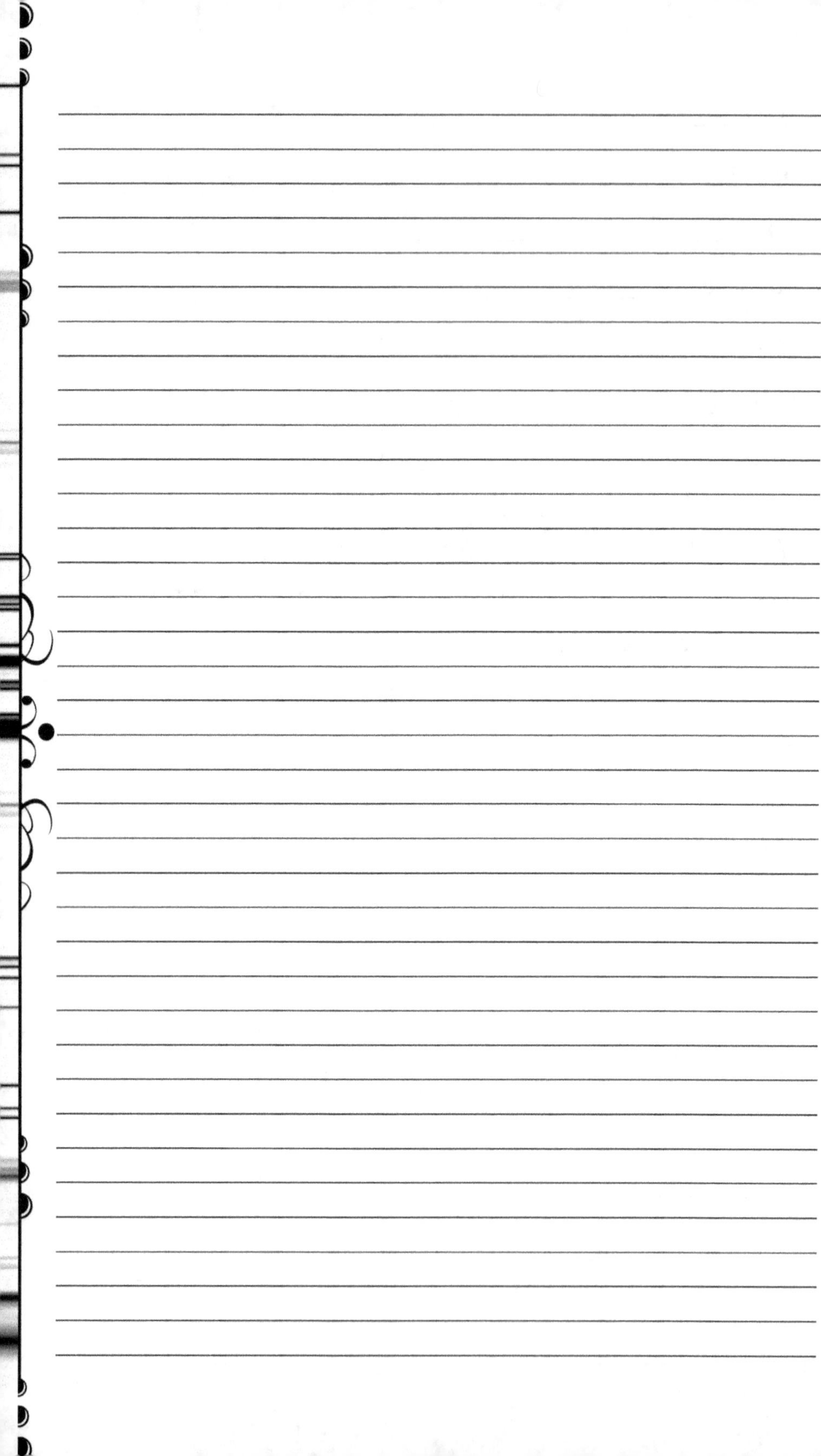

🚫 THINGS I DIDN'T LIKE:

✎ FAVORITE QUOTE(S):

TITLE:

GENRE:

SERIES:

AUTHOR:

PAGES:

STARTED:

FINISHED:

☆ ☆ ☆ ☆ ☆

FORMAT READ: EBOOK / PRINT / AUDIOBOOK

TITLE:

GENRE:

SERIES:

AUTHOR:

PAGES:

STARTED:

FINISHED:

FORMAT READ: EBOOK / PRINT / AUDIOBOOK

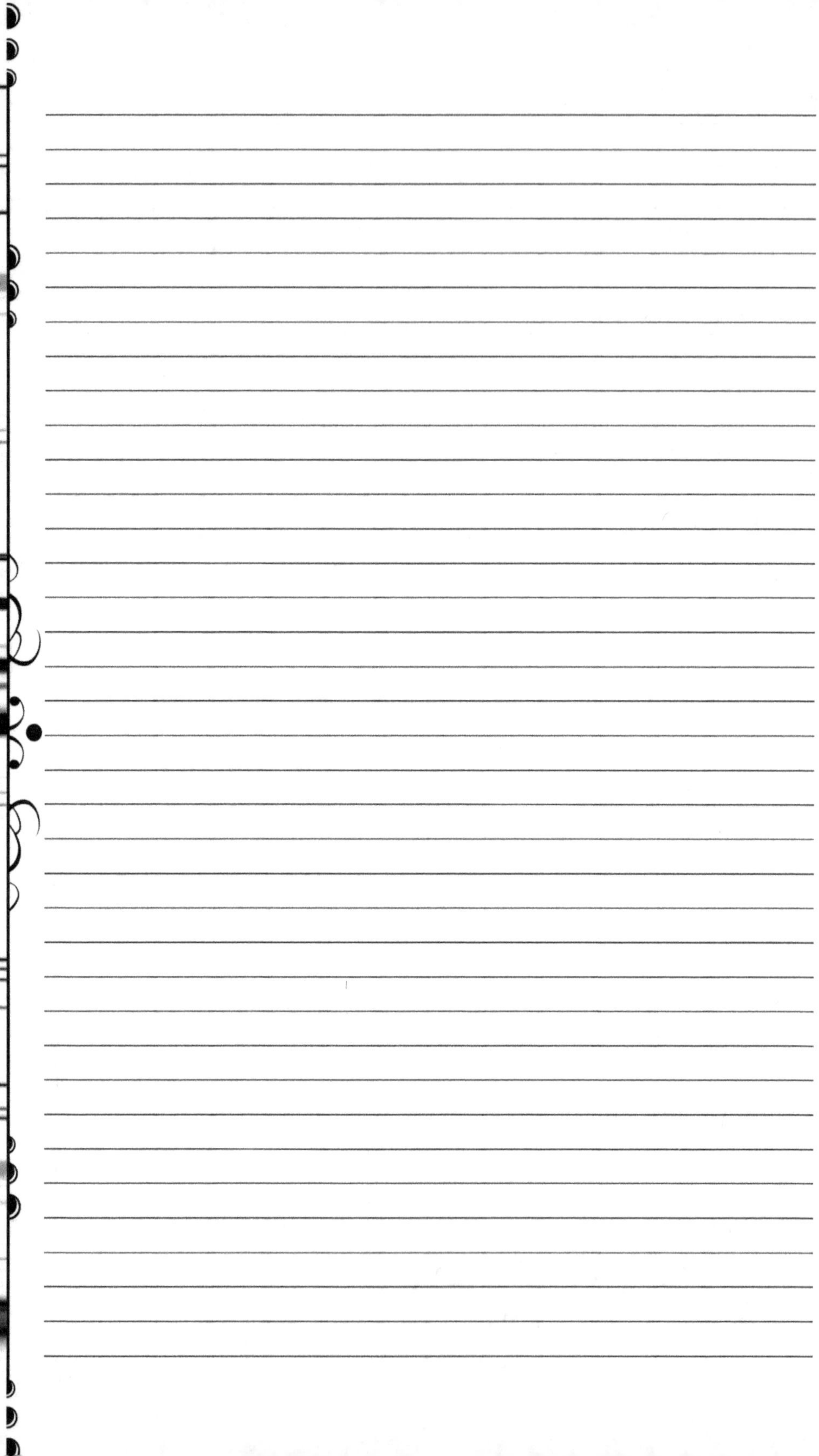

TITLE:

GENRE:

SERIES:

AUTHOR:

PAGES:

STARTED:

FINISHED:

FORMAT READ: EBOOK / PRINT / AUDIOBOOK

✓ **SYNOPSIS/THINGS I LIKED:**

🚫 **THINGS I DIDN'T LIKE:**

✏️ **FAVORITE QUOTE(S):**

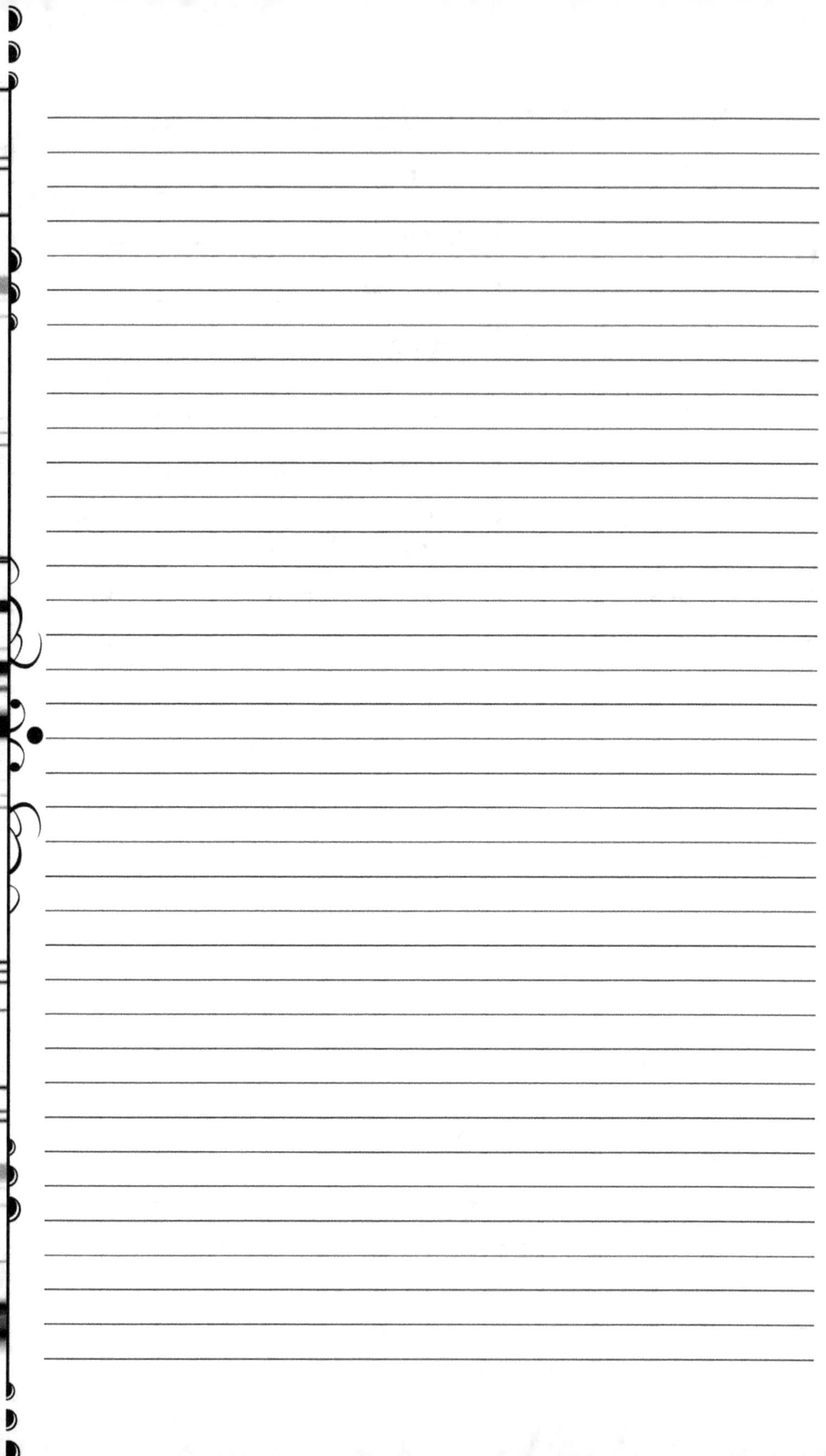

TITLE: _______________________

GENRE: _______________________

SERIES: _______________________

AUTHOR: _______________________

PAGES: _______________________

STARTED: _______________________

FINISHED: _______________________

☆☆☆☆☆

FORMAT READ: EBOOK / PRINT / AUDIOBOOK

✔ **SYNOPSIS/THINGS I LIKED:**

🚫 **THINGS I DIDN'T LIKE:**

✐ **FAVORITE QUOTE(S):**

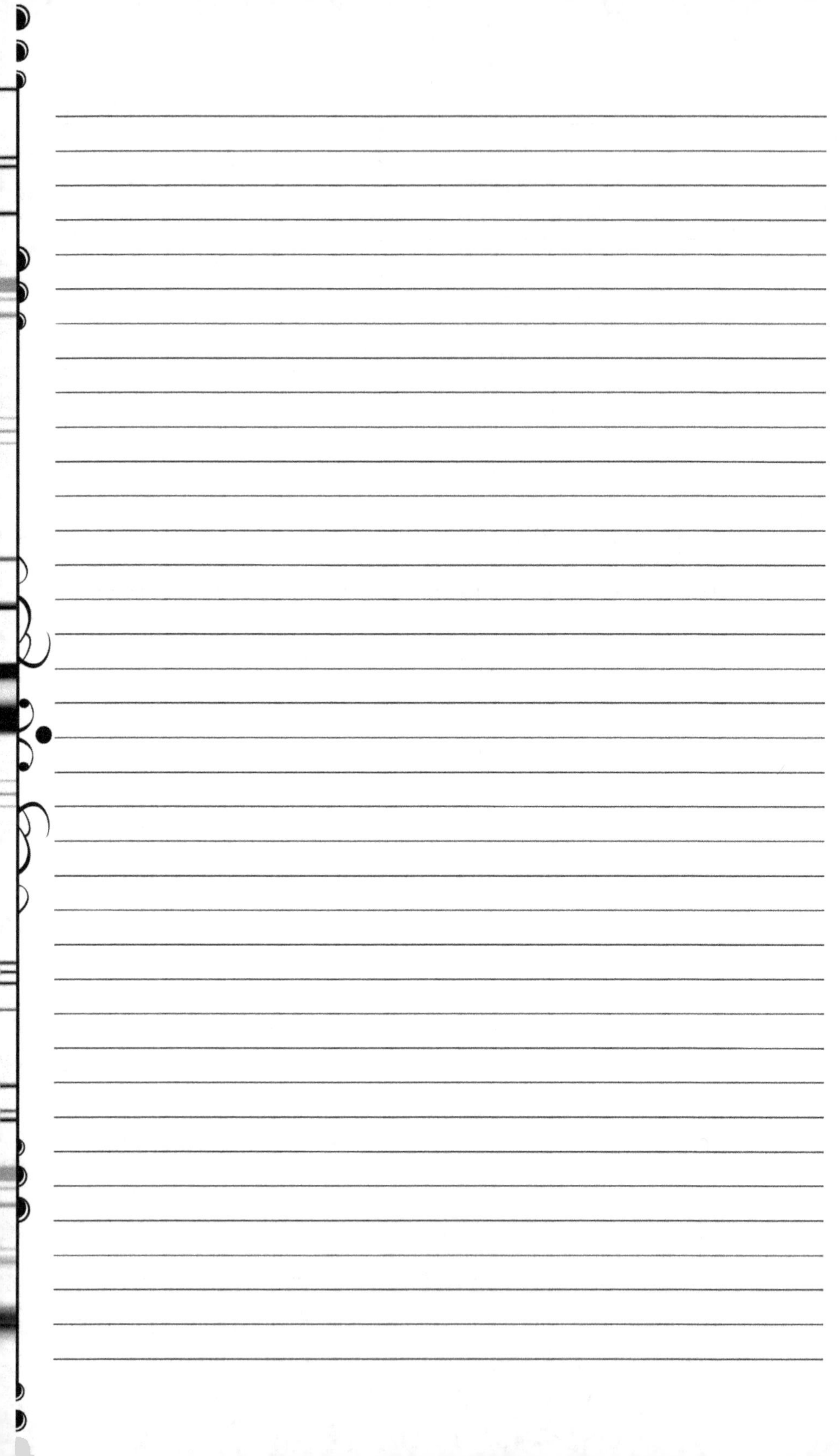

TITLE:

GENRE:

SERIES:

AUTHOR:

PAGES:

STARTED:

FINISHED:

FORMAT READ: EBOOK / PRINT / AUDIOBOOK

191

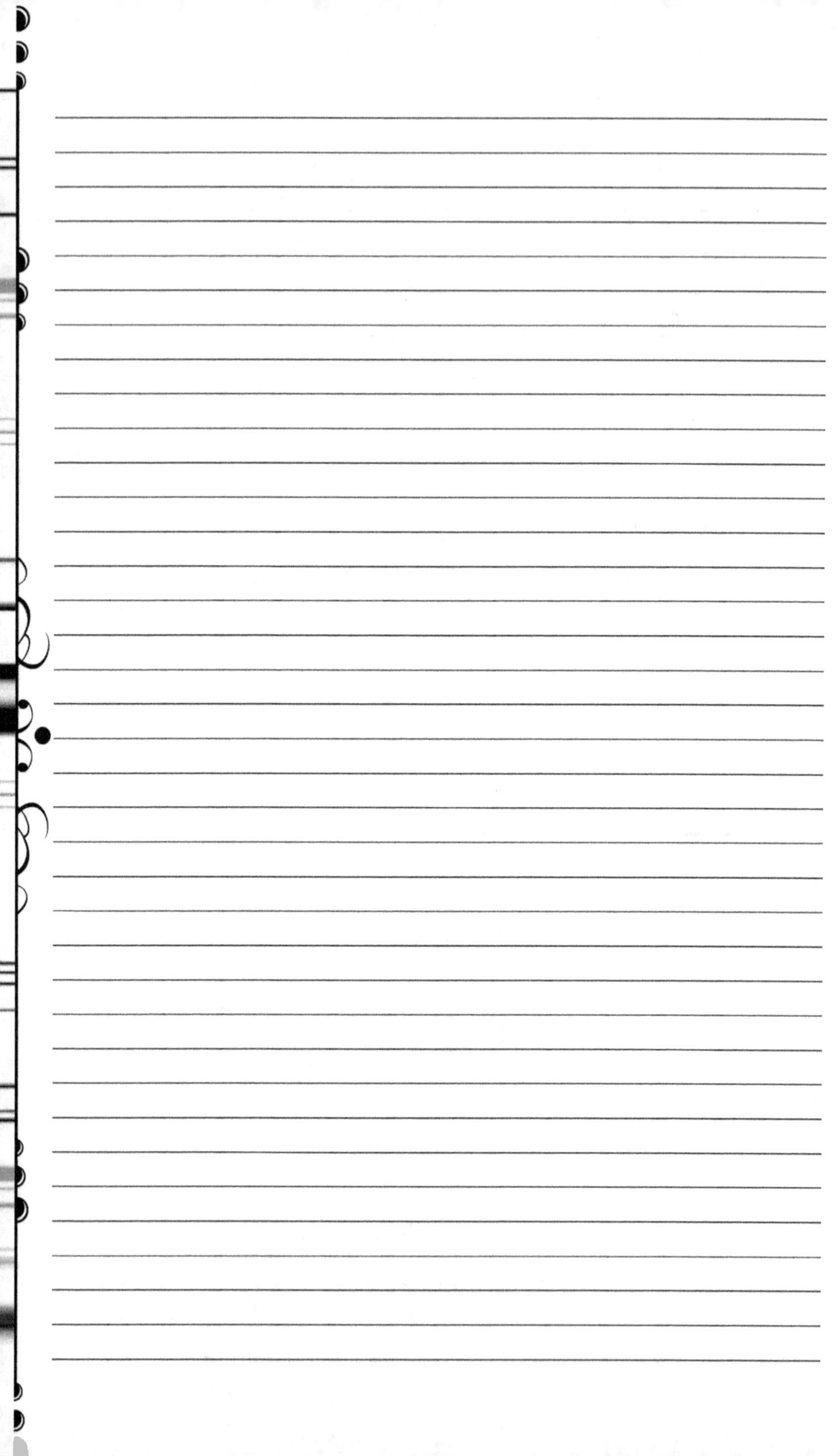

SYNOPSIS/THINGS I LIKED:

THINGS I DIDN'T LIKE:

FAVORITE QUOTE(S):

TITLE:

GENRE:

SERIES:

AUTHOR:

PAGES:

STARTED:

FINISHED:

FORMAT READ: EBOOK / PRINT / AUDIOBOOK

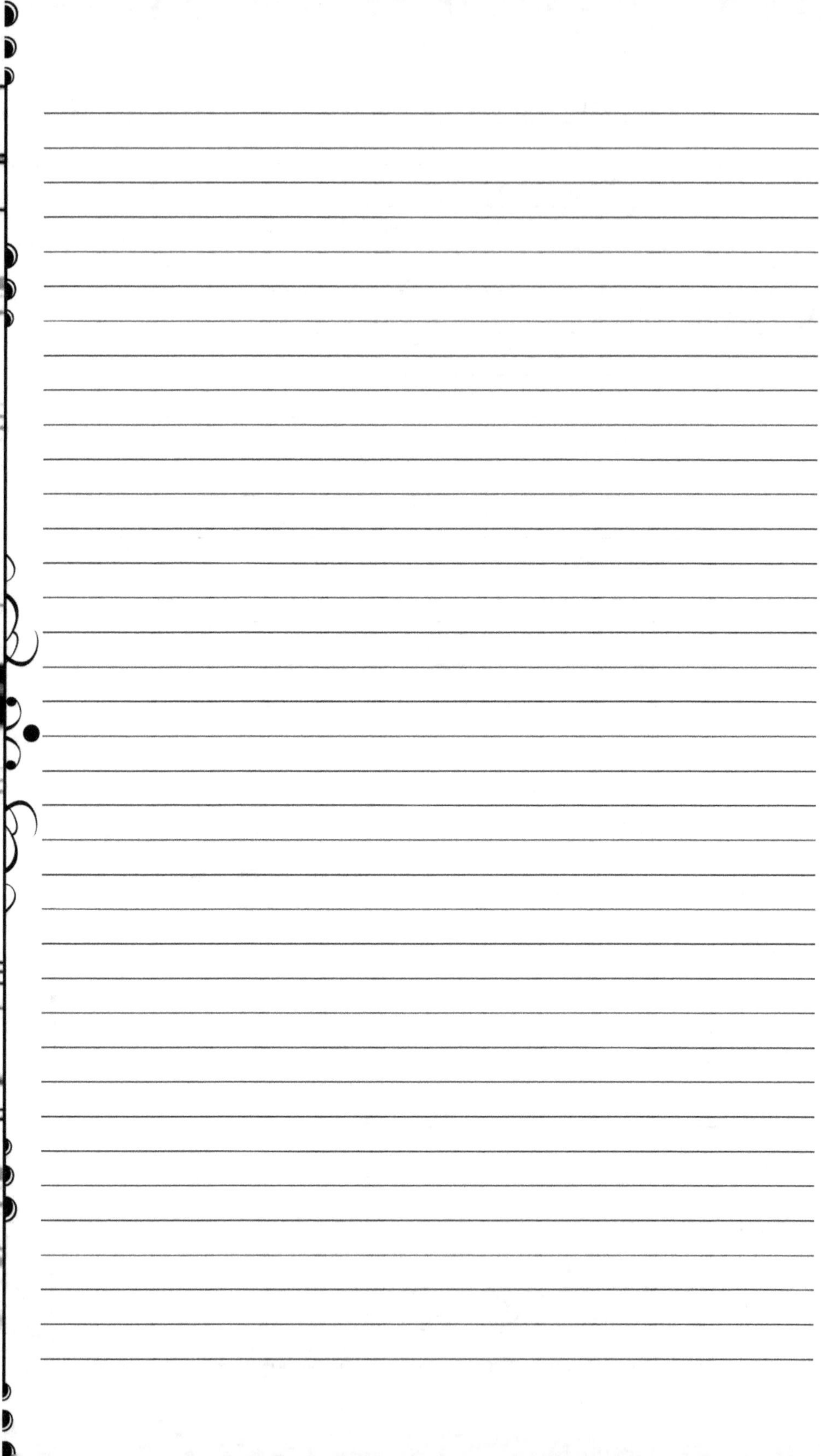

TITLE:

GENRE:

SERIES:

AUTHOR:

PAGES:

STARTED:

FINISHED:

FORMAT READ: EBOOK / PRINT / AUDIOBOOK

✓ SYNOPSIS/THINGS I LIKED:

🚫 THINGS I DIDN'T LIKE:

✏️ FAVORITE QUOTE(S):

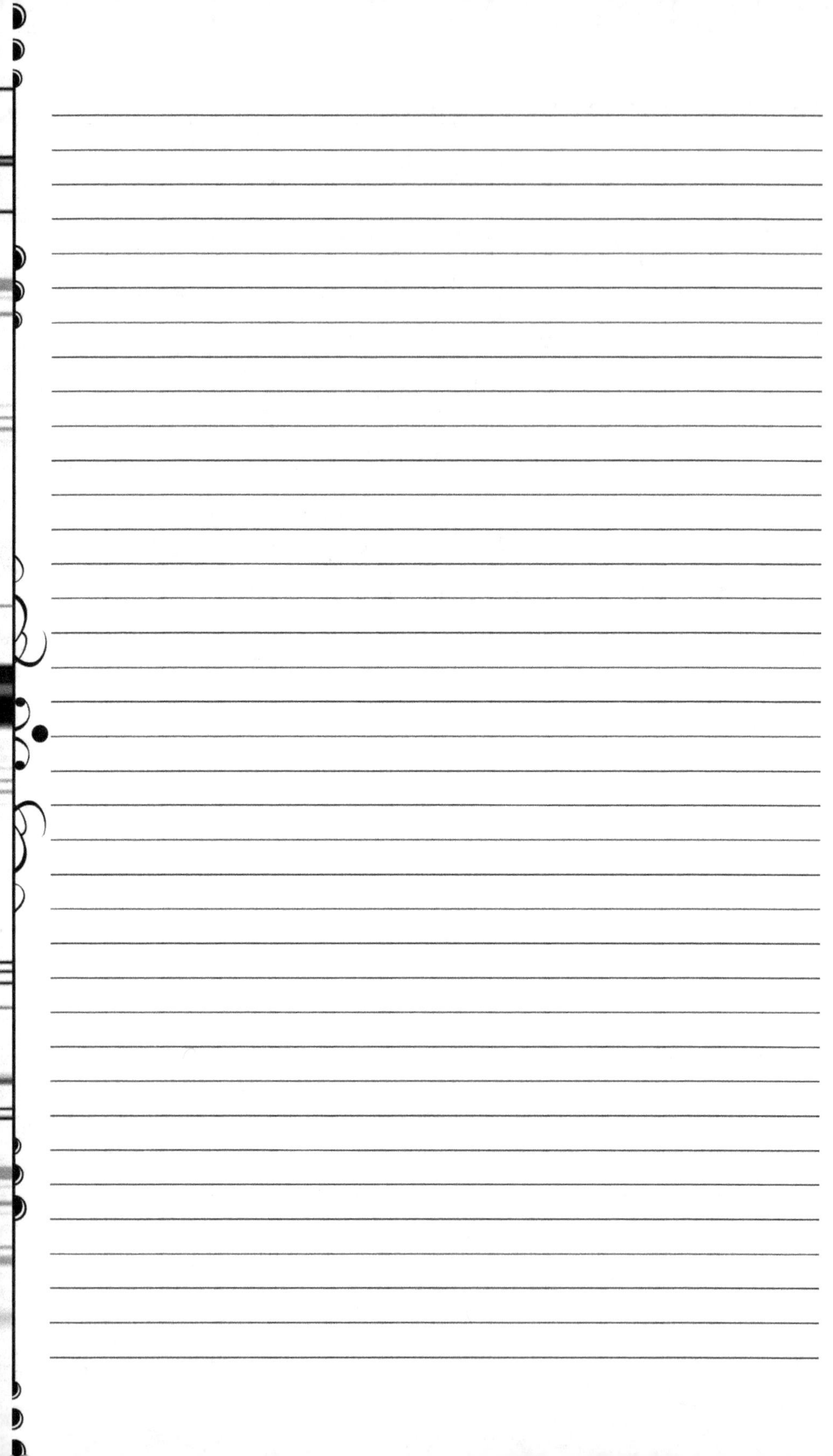

TITLE: _______________________

GENRE: _______________________

SERIES: _______________________

AUTHOR: _______________________

PAGES: _______________________

STARTED: _______________________

FINISHED: _______________________

☆☆☆☆☆

FORMAT READ: EBOOK / PRINT / AUDIOBOOK

✔ SYNOPSIS/THINGS I LIKED:

____
____
____
____

🚫 THINGS I DIDN'T LIKE:

____
____
____
____

✎ FAVORITE QUOTE(S):

____
____
____
____
____
____
____

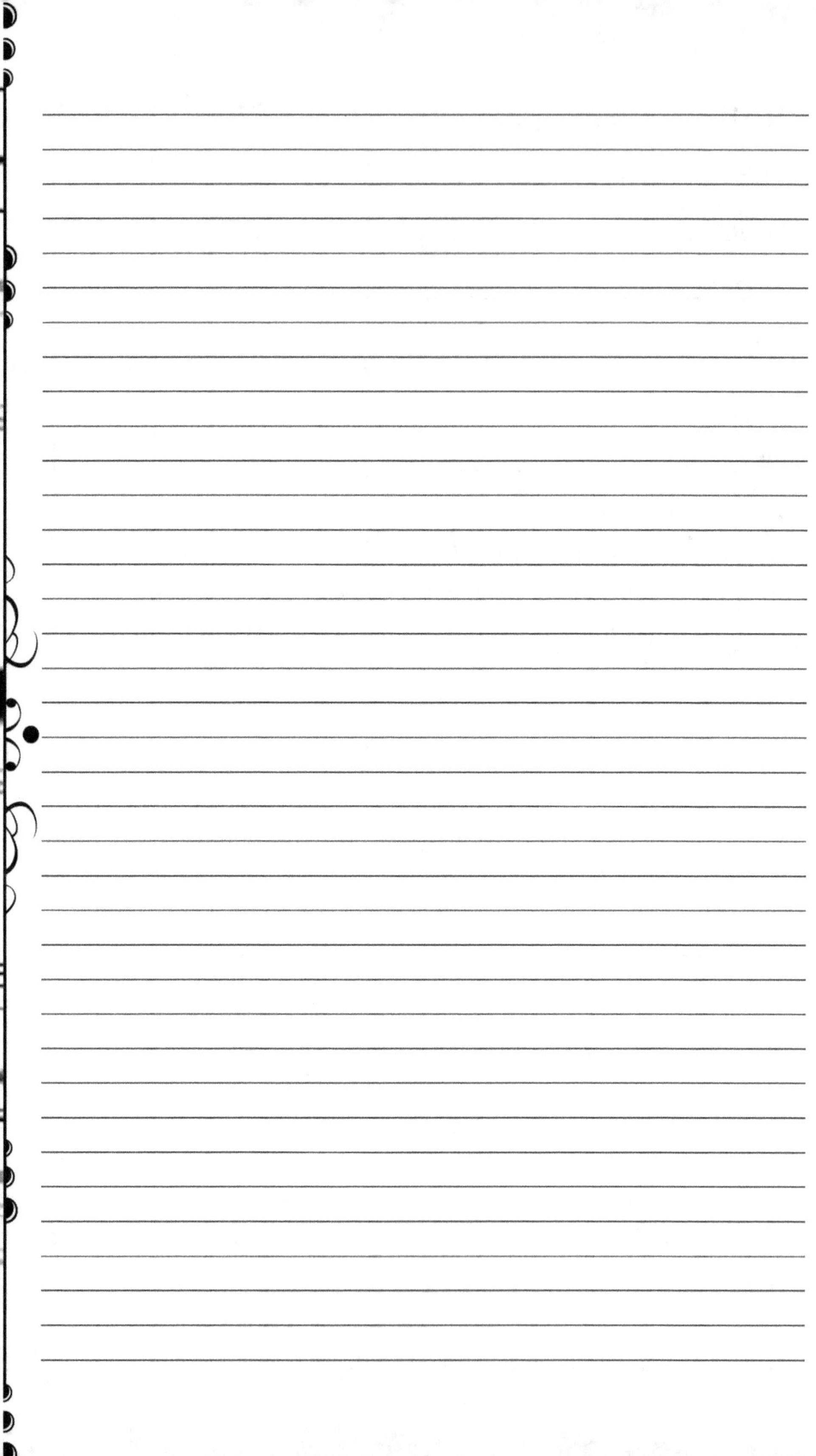

SYNOPSIS/THINGS I LIKED:

THINGS I DIDN'T LIKE:

FAVORITE QUOTE(S):

TITLE:

GENRE:

SERIES:

AUTHOR:

PAGES:

STARTED:

FINISHED:

FORMAT READ: EBOOK / PRINT / AUDIOBOOK

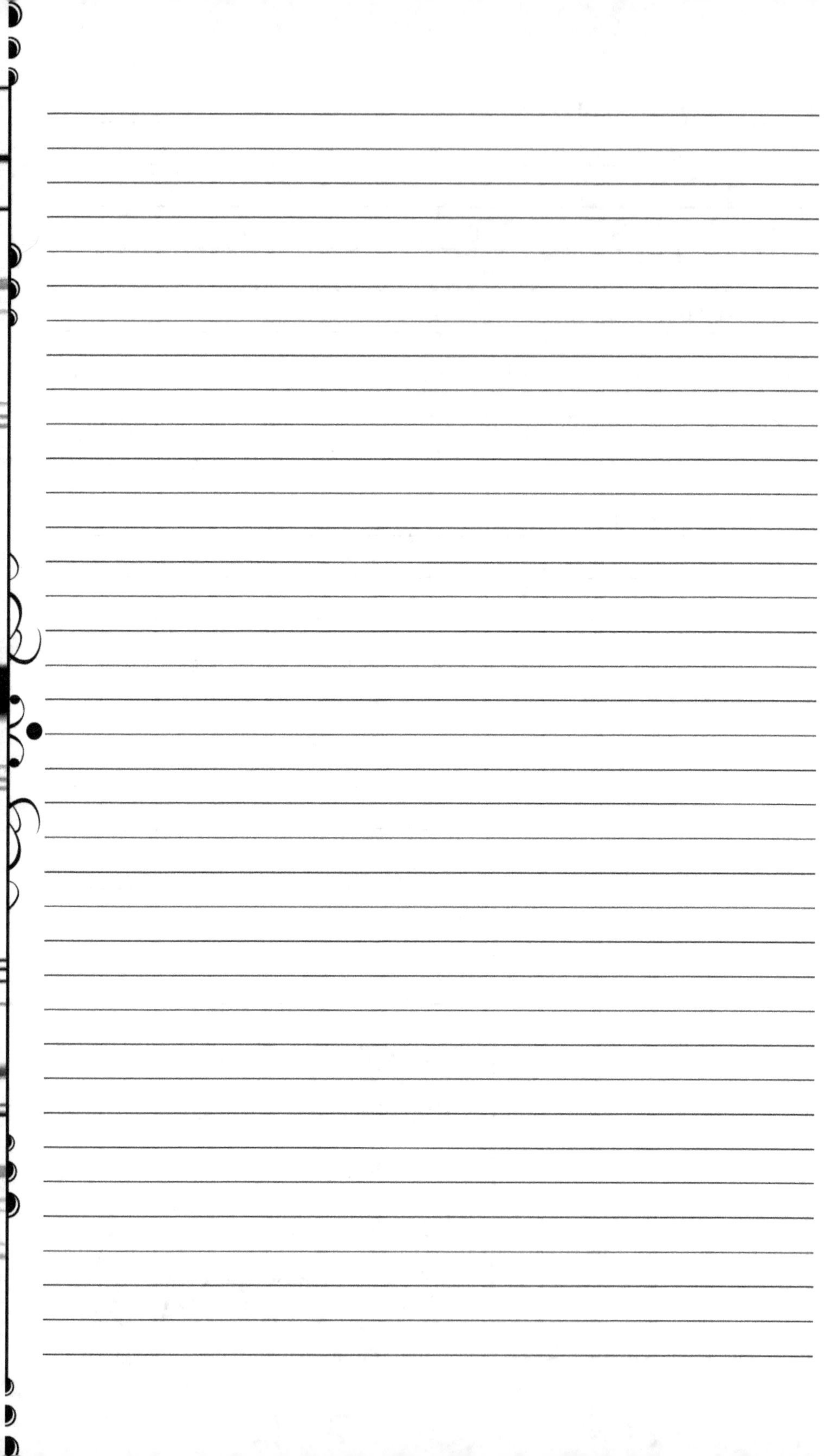

TITLE:

GENRE:

SERIES:

AUTHOR:

PAGES:

STARTED:

FINISHED:

FORMAT READ: EBOOK / PRINT / AUDIOBOOK

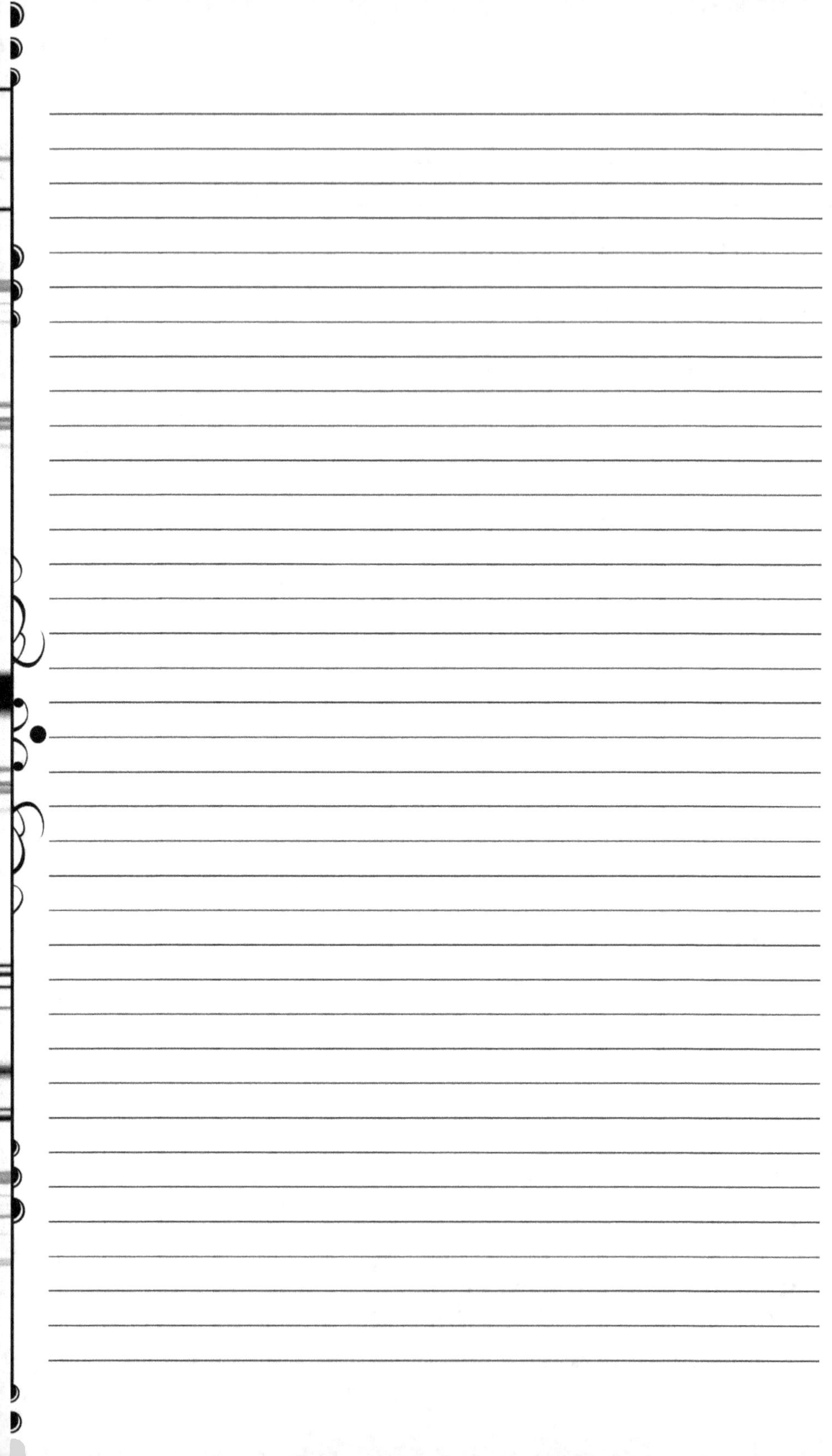

TITLE:

GENRE:

SERIES:

AUTHOR:

PAGES:

STARTED:

FINISHED:

FORMAT READ: EBOOK / PRINT / AUDIOBOOK

✓ **SYNOPSIS/THINGS I LIKED:**

🚫 **THINGS I DIDN'T LIKE:**

✏️ **FAVORITE QUOTE(S):**

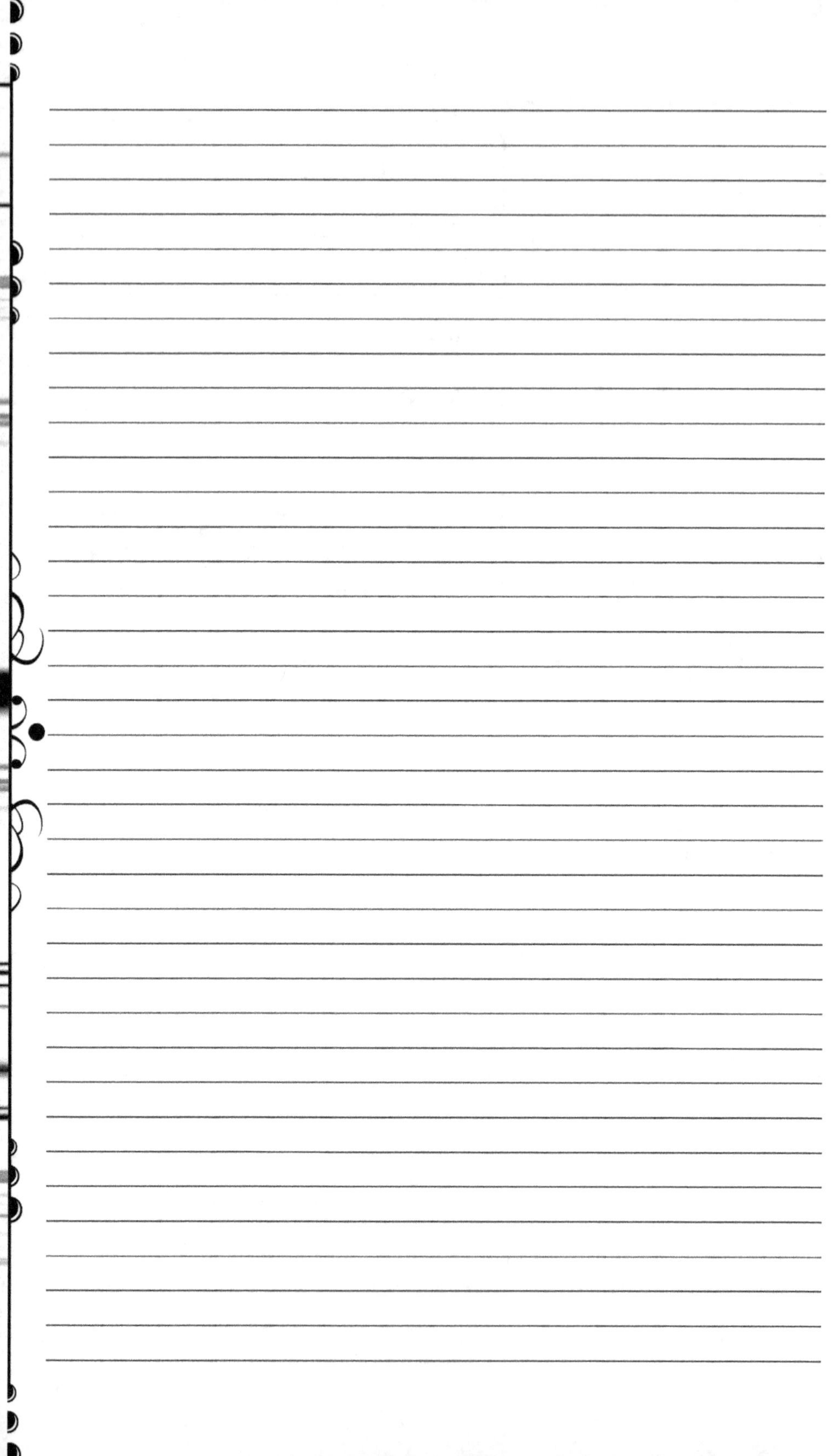

TITLE: ______________________

GENRE: ______________________

SERIES: ______________________

AUTHOR: ______________________

PAGES: ______________________

STARTED: ______________________

FINISHED: ______________________

☆ ☆ ☆ ☆ ☆

FORMAT READ: EBOOK / PRINT / AUDIOBOOK

✔ **SYNOPSIS/THINGS I LIKED:**

____
____
____
____

🚫 **THINGS I DIDN'T LIKE:**

____
____
____
____

✎ **FAVORITE QUOTE(S):**

____
____
____
____
____
____
____

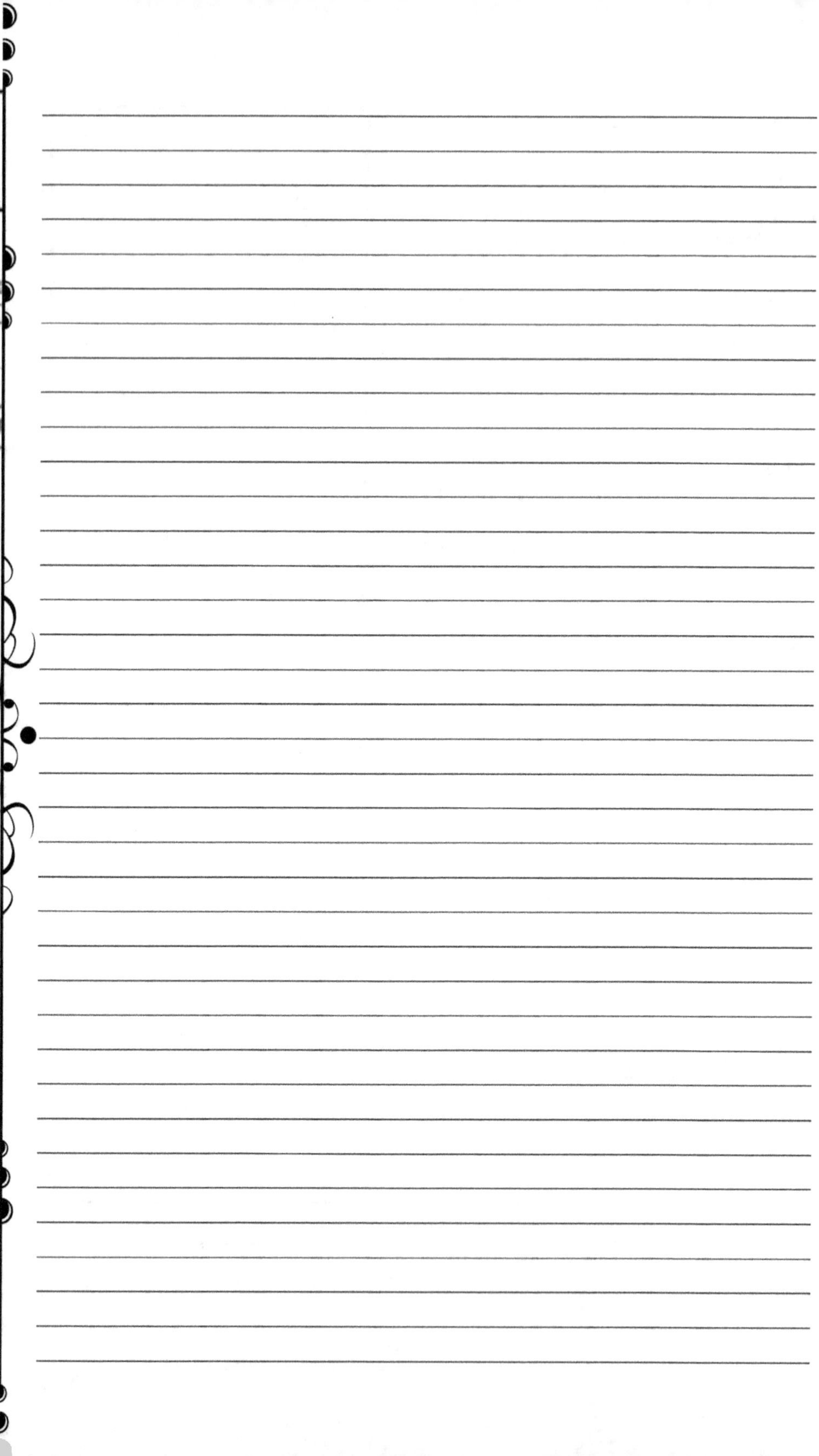

✓ **Synopsis/Things I liked:**

🚫 **Things I didn't like:**

✏ **Favorite quote(s):**

Title:

Genre:

Series:

Author:

Pages:

Started:

Finished:

☆ ☆ ☆ ☆ ☆

Format read: Ebook / Print / Audiobook

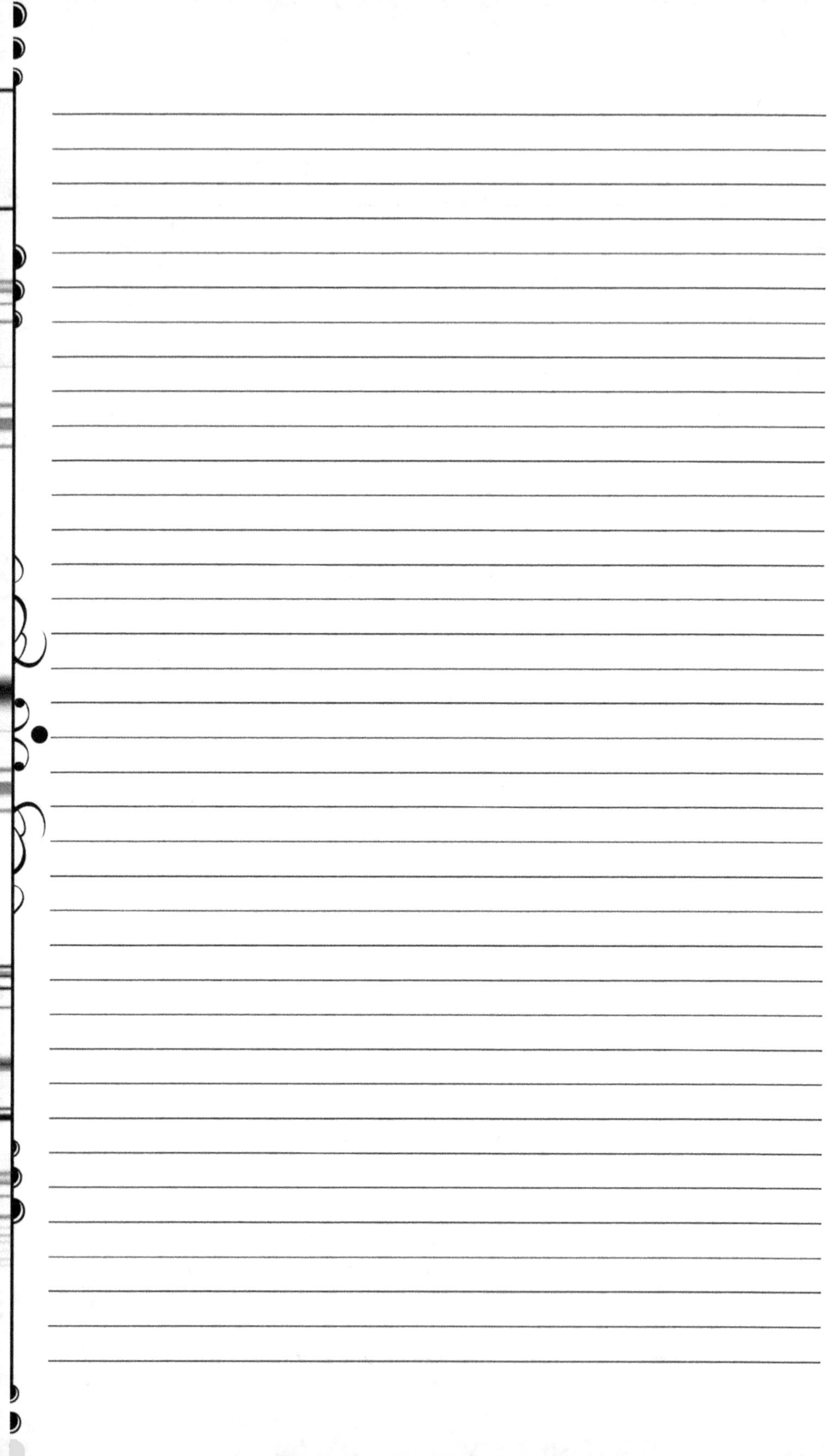

TITLE:

GENRE:

SERIES:

AUTHOR:

PAGES:

STARTED:

FINISHED:

FORMAT READ: EBOOK / PRINT / AUDIOBOOK

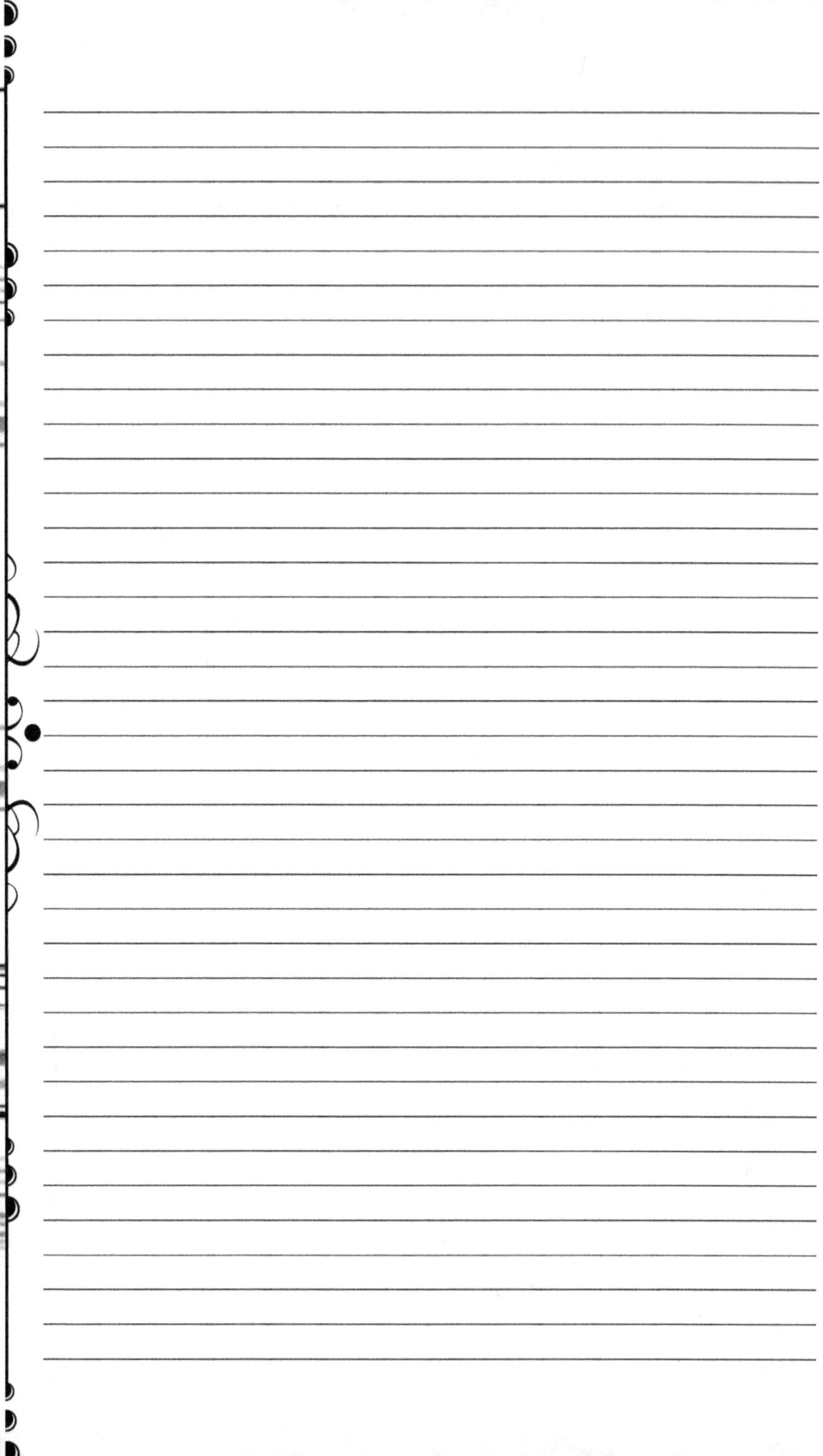

TITLE: ___________________

GENRE: ___________________

SERIES: ___________________

AUTHOR: ___________________

PAGES: ___________________

STARTED: ___________________

FINISHED: ___________________

FORMAT READ: EBOOK / PRINT / AUDIOBOOK

☑ SYNOPSIS/THINGS I LIKED: ___________________

🚫 THINGS I DIDN'T LIKE: ___________________

✎ FAVORITE QUOTE(S): ___________________

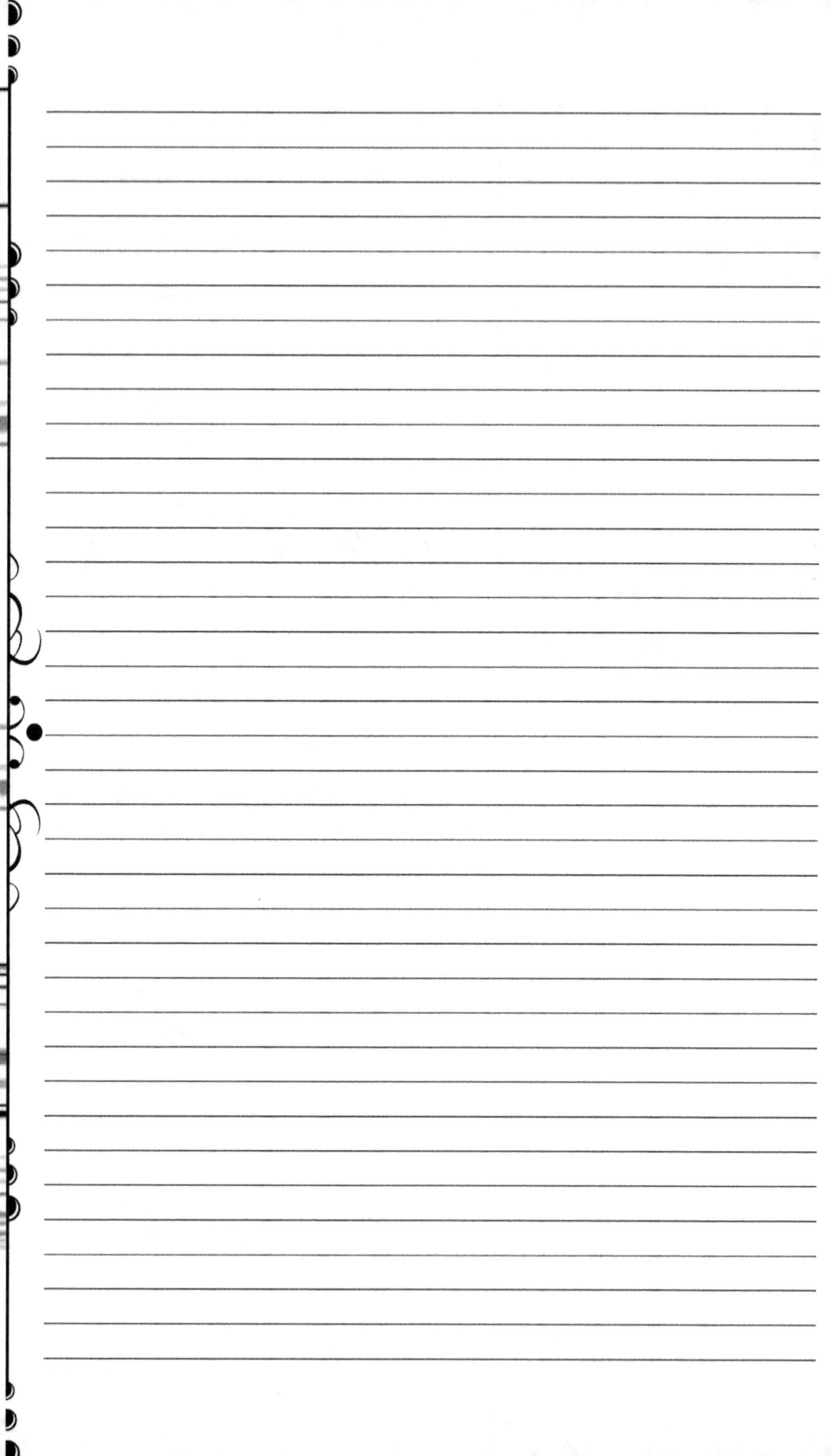

TITLE:

GENRE:

SERIES:

AUTHOR:

PAGES:

STARTED:

FINISHED:

FORMAT READ: EBOOK / PRINT / AUDIOBOOK

✔ **SYNOPSIS/THINGS I LIKED:**

🚫 **THINGS I DIDN'T LIKE:**

✎ **FAVORITE QUOTE(S):**

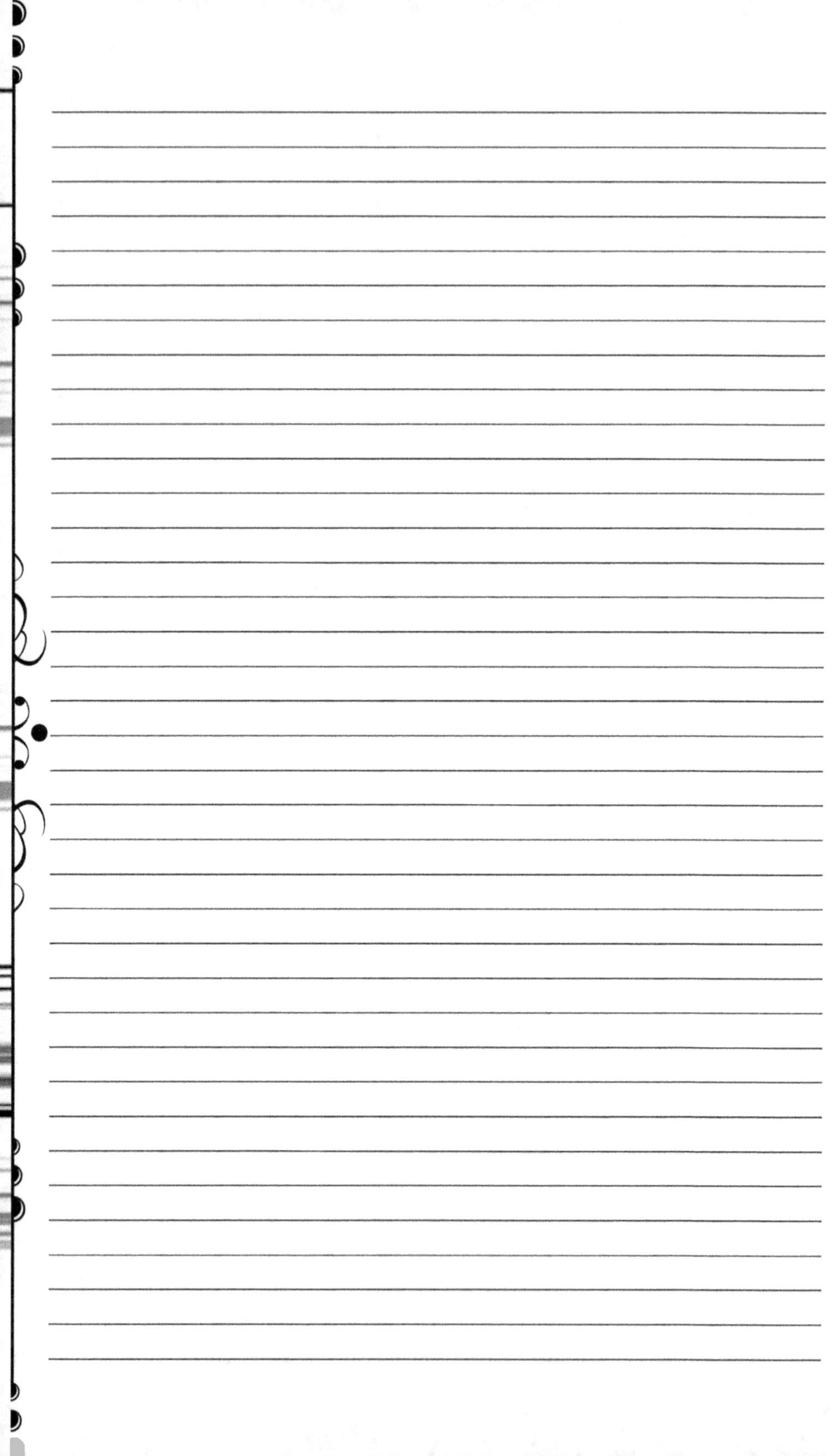

SYNOPSIS/THINGS I LIKED:

THINGS I DIDN'T LIKE:

FAVORITE QUOTE(S):

TITLE:
GENRE:
SERIES:
AUTHOR:
PAGES:
STARTED:
FINISHED:
FORMAT READ: EBOOK / PRINT / AUDIOBOOK

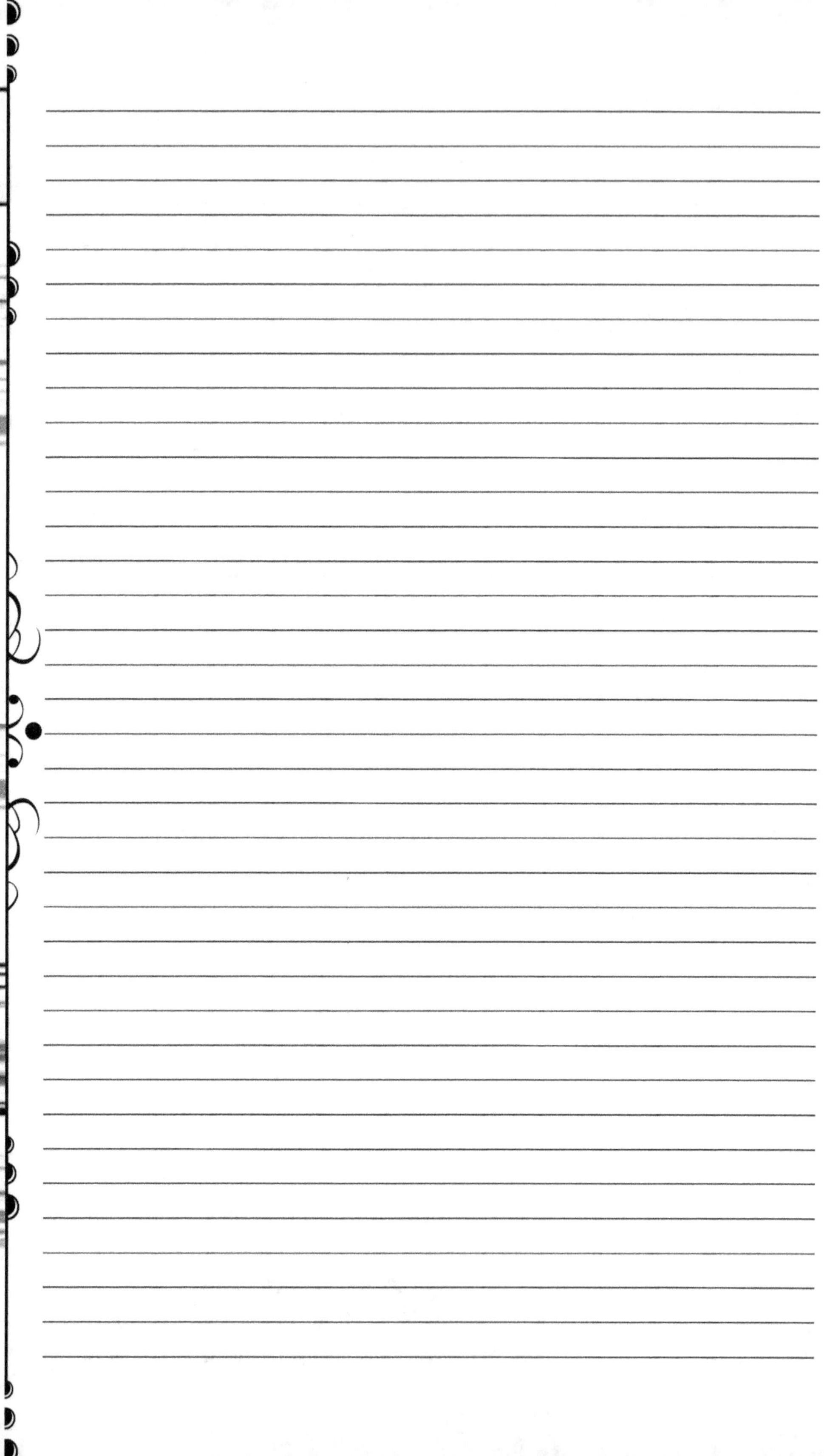

✓ **SYNOPSIS/THINGS I LIKED:**

⊘ **THINGS I DIDN'T LIKE:**

FAVORITE QUOTE(S):

TITLE:

GENRE:

SERIES:

AUTHOR:

PAGES:

STARTED:

FINISHED:

☆ ☆ ☆ ☆ ☆

FORMAT READ: EBOOK / PRINT / AUDIOBOOK

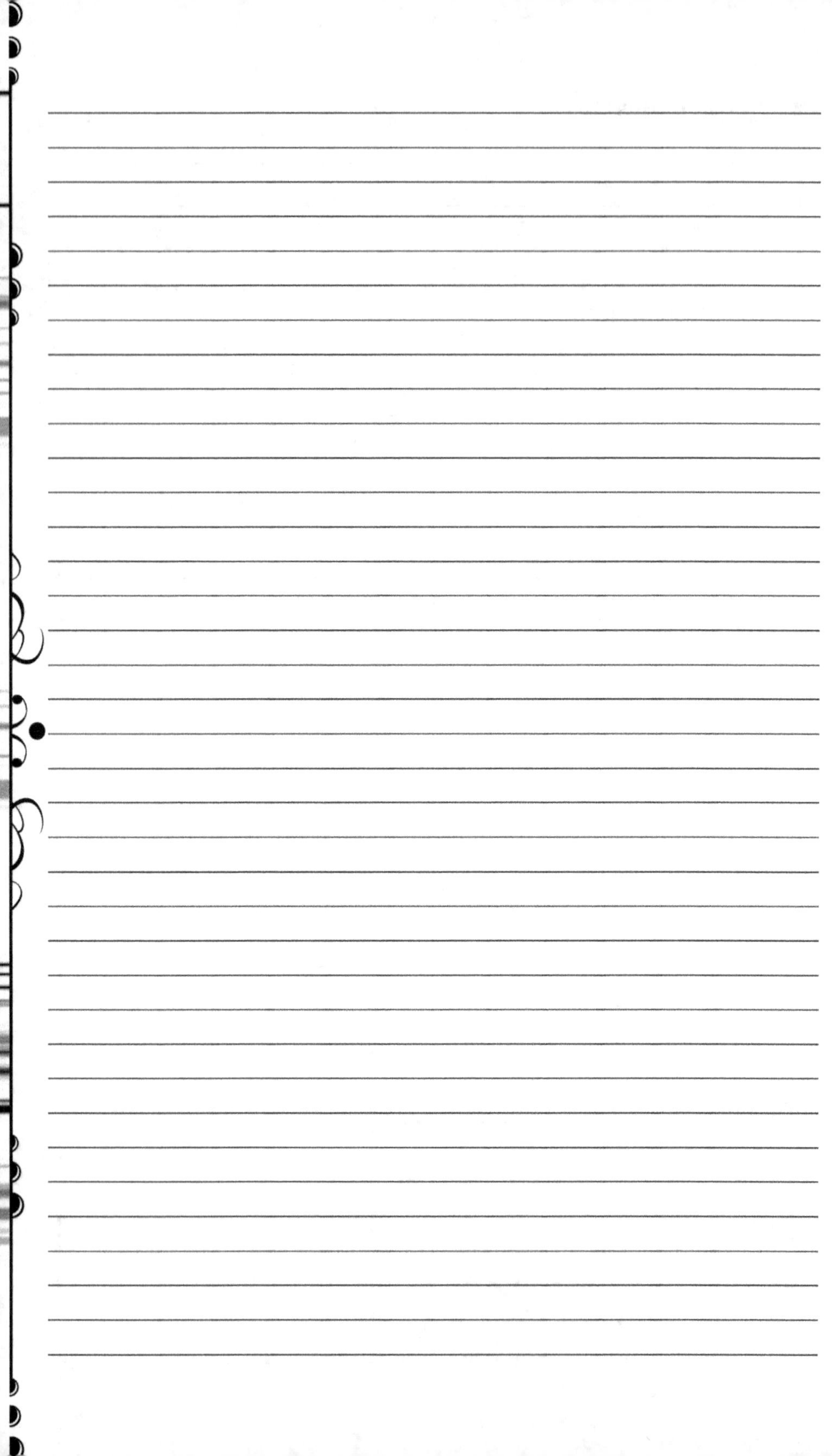

TITLE:

GENRE:

SERIES:

AUTHOR:

PAGES:

STARTED:

FINISHED:

FORMAT READ: EBOOK / PRINT / AUDIOBOOK

✔ SYNOPSIS/THINGS I LIKED:

🚫 THINGS I DIDN'T LIKE:

✏ FAVORITE QUOTE(S):

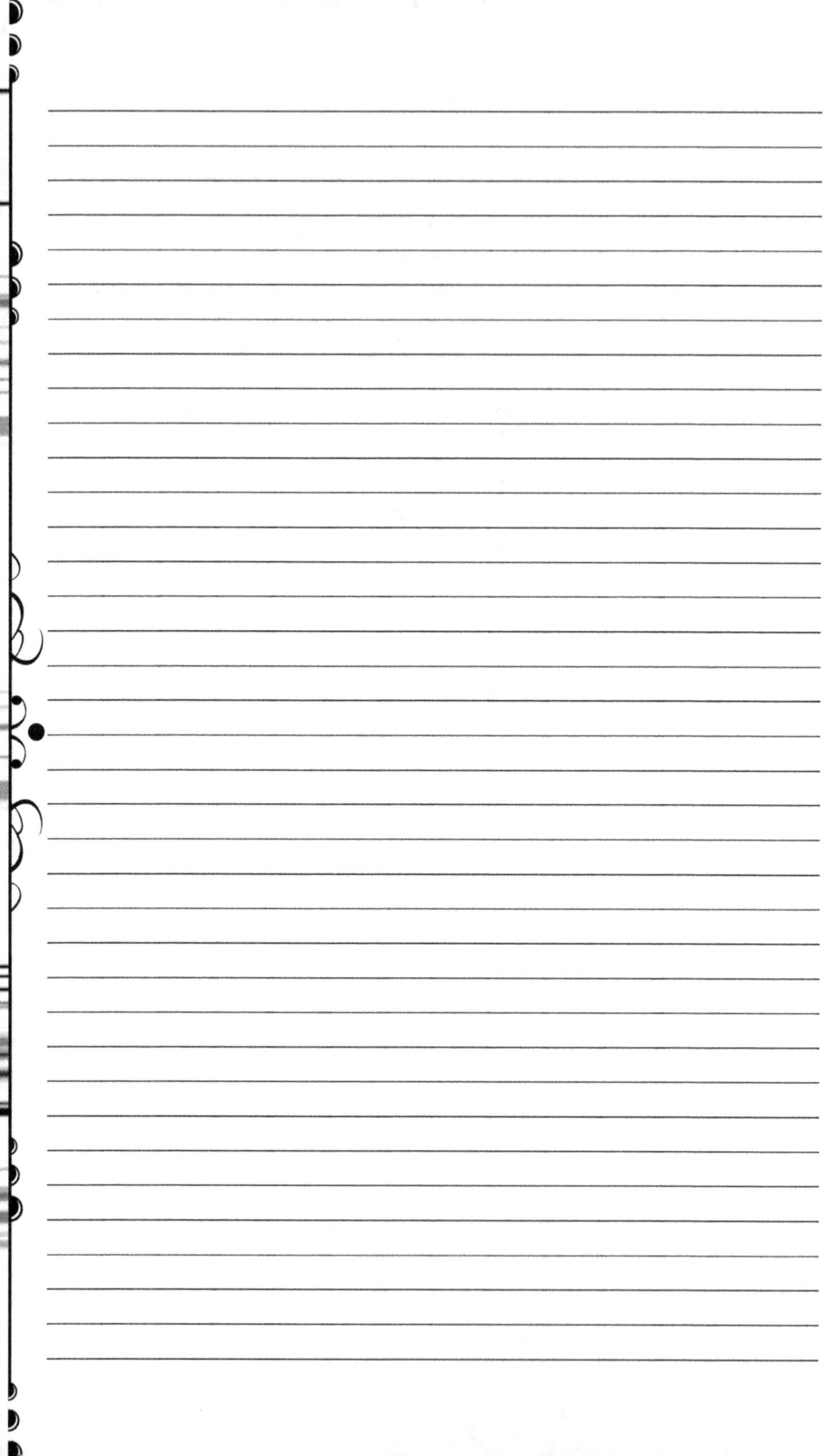

TITLE:

GENRE:

SERIES:

AUTHOR:

PAGES:

STARTED:

FINISHED:

FORMAT READ: EBOOK / PRINT / AUDIOBOOK

SYNOPSIS/THINGS I LIKED:

THINGS I DIDN'T LIKE:

FAVORITE QUOTE(S):

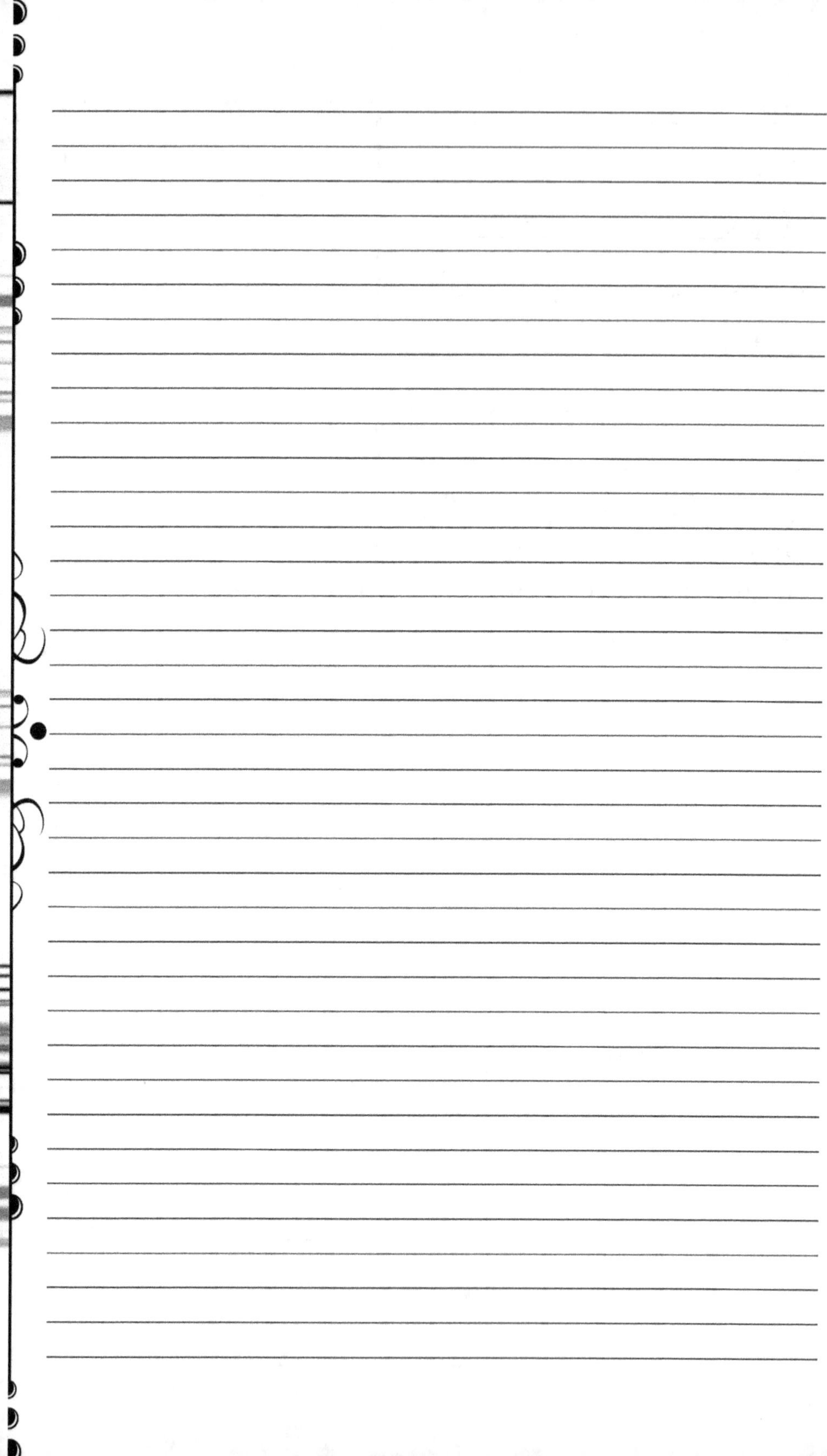

☑ **Synopsis/Things I liked:**

🚫 **Things I didn't like:**

✏ **Favorite quote(s):**

Title:

Genre:

Series:

Author:

Pages:

Started:

Finished:

☆ ☆ ☆ ☆ ☆

Format read: Ebook / Print / Audiobook

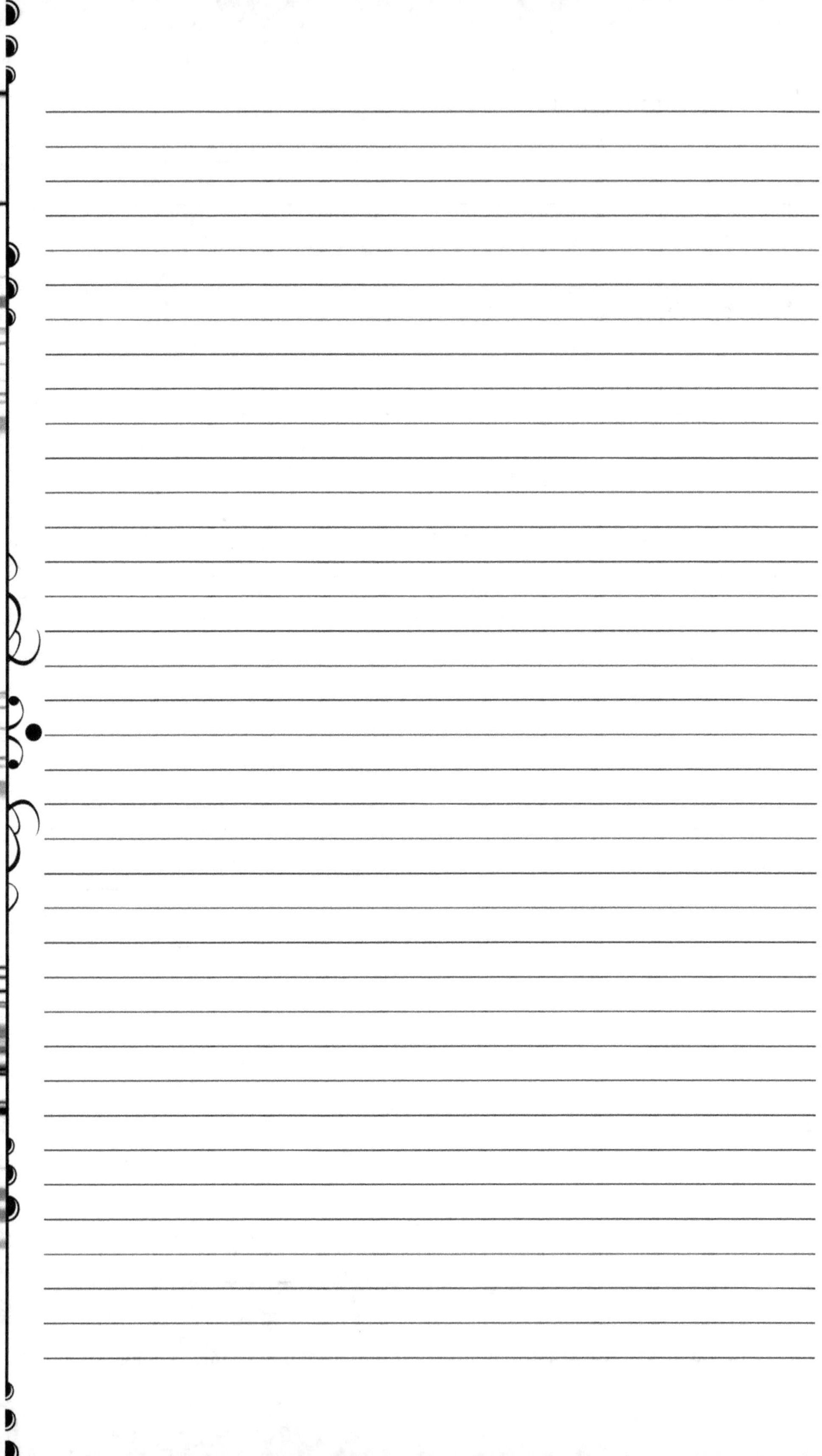

TITLE:

GENRE:

SERIES:

AUTHOR:

PAGES:

STARTED:

FINISHED:

FORMAT READ: EBOOK / PRINT / AUDIOBOOK

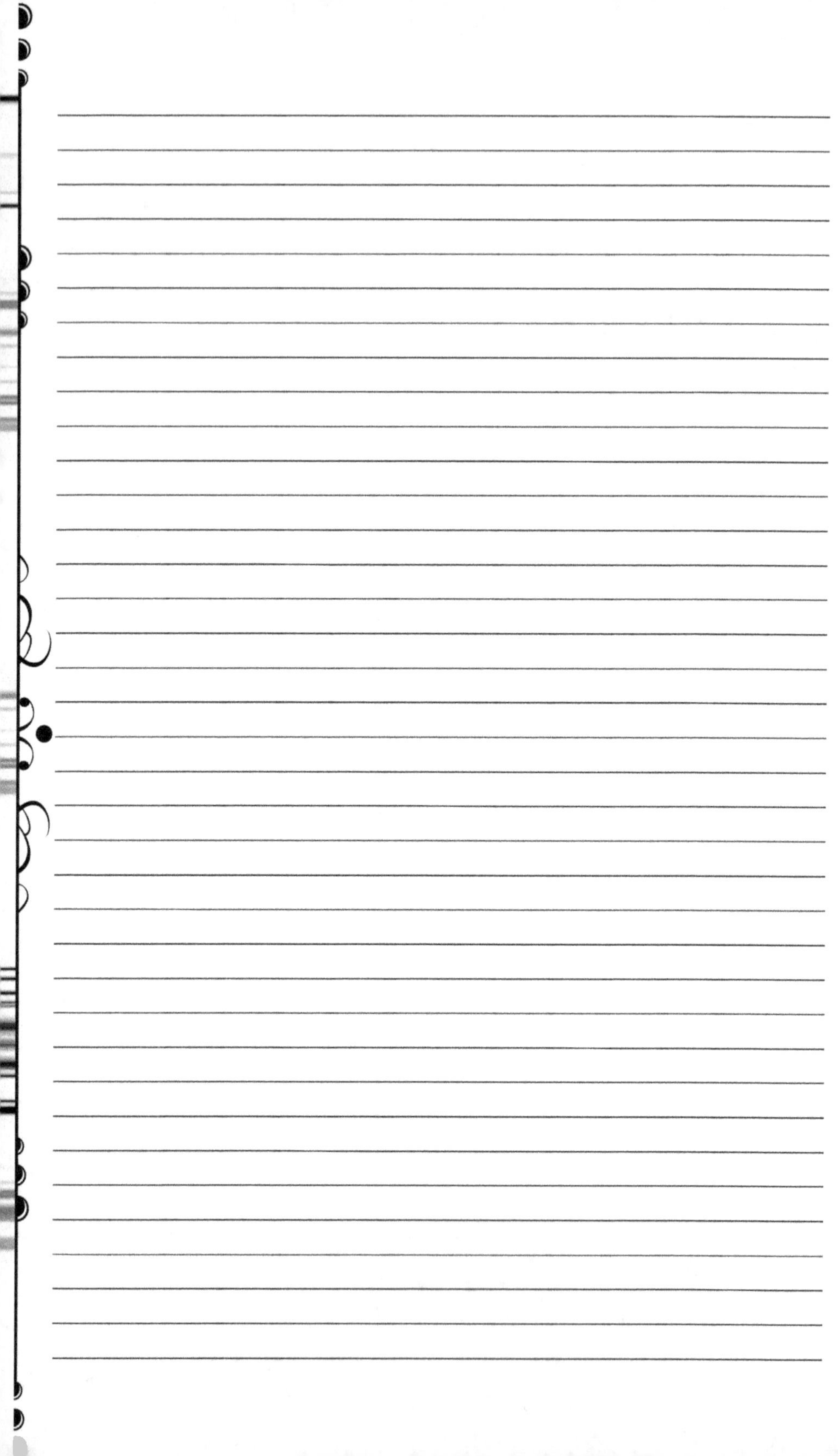

TITLE:

GENRE:

SERIES:

AUTHOR:

PAGES:

STARTED:

FINISHED:

FORMAT READ: EBOOK / PRINT / AUDIOBOOK

☑ SYNOPSIS/THINGS I LIKED:

🚫 THINGS I DIDN'T LIKE:

✏ FAVORITE QUOTE(S):

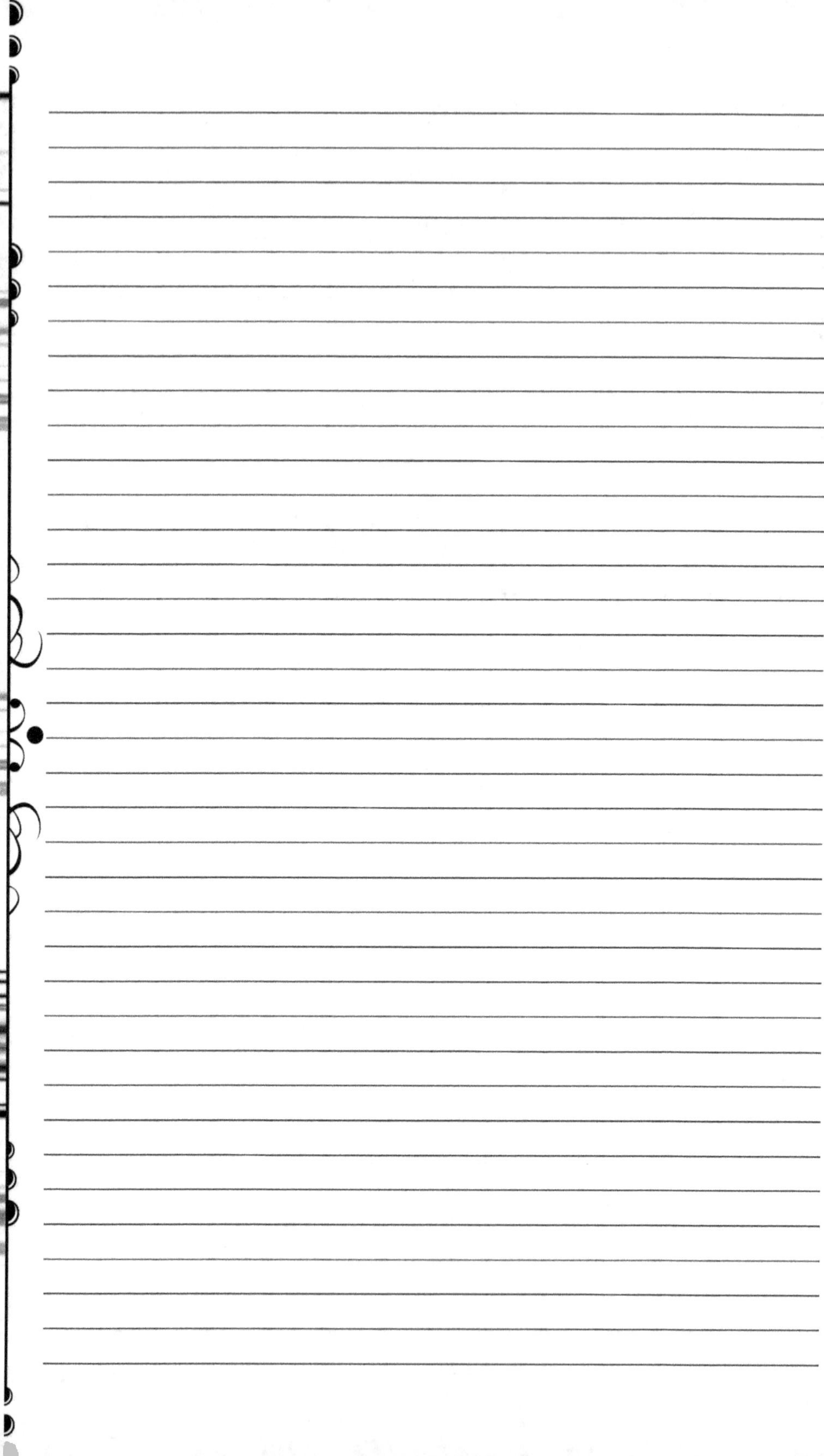

TITLE:

GENRE:

SERIES:

AUTHOR:

PAGES:

STARTED:

FINISHED:

☆ ☆ ☆ ☆ ☆

FORMAT READ: EBOOK / PRINT / AUDIOBOOK

✓ **SYNOPSIS/THINGS I LIKED:**

🚫 **THINGS I DIDN'T LIKE:**

✏ **FAVORITE QUOTE(S):**

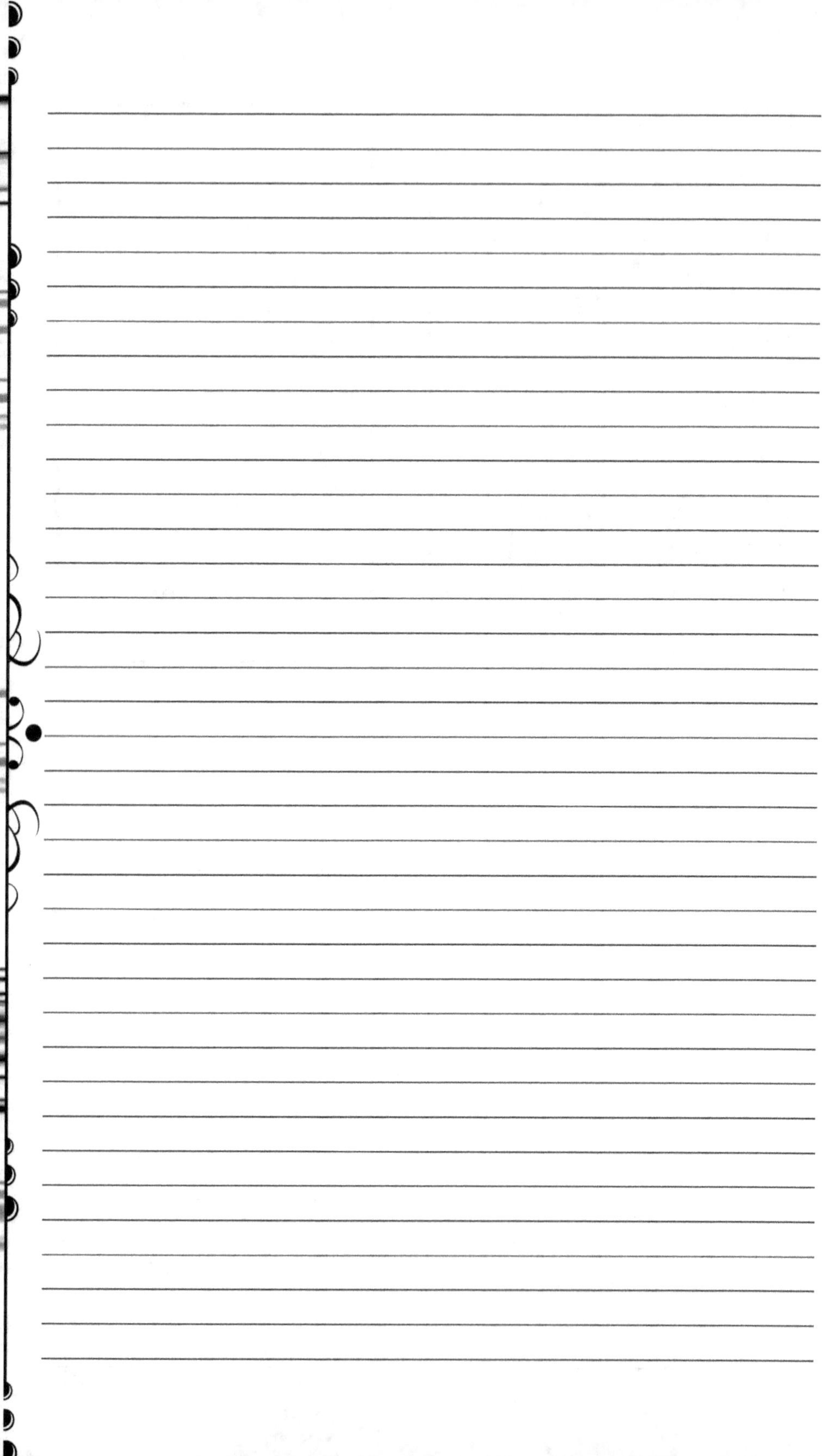

SYNOPSIS/THINGS I LIKED:

THINGS I DIDN'T LIKE:

FAVORITE QUOTE(S):

TITLE:
GENRE:
SERIES:
AUTHOR:
PAGES:
STARTED:
FINISHED:
FORMAT READ: EBOOK / PRINT / AUDIOBOOK

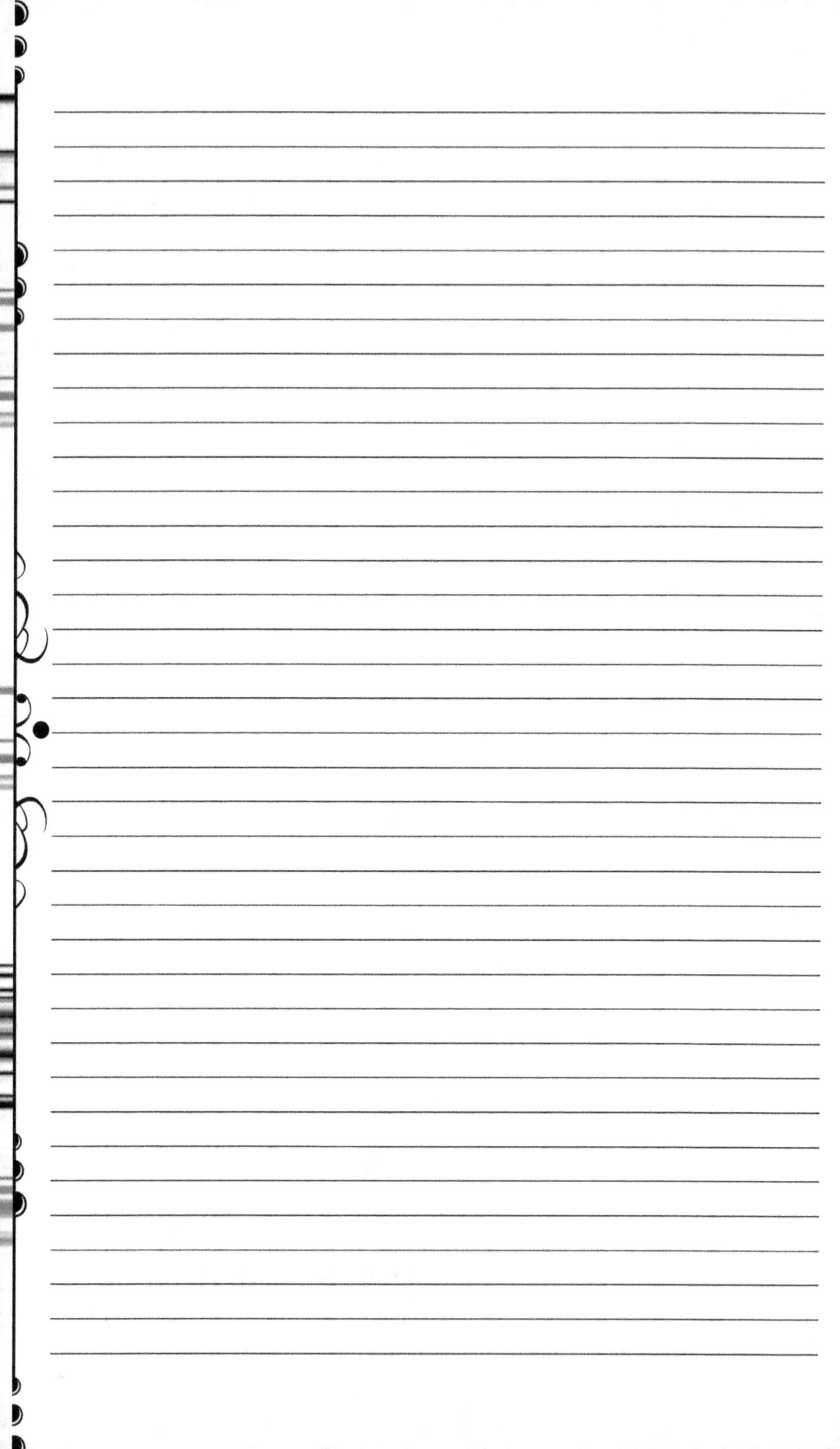

✔ **SYNOPSIS/THINGS I LIKED:**

⊘ **THINGS I DIDN'T LIKE:**

✎ **FAVORITE QUOTE(S):**

TITLE:

GENRE:

SERIES:

AUTHOR:

PAGES:

STARTED:

FINISHED:

☆ ☆ ☆ ☆ ☆

FORMAT READ: EBOOK / PRINT / AUDIOBOOK

212

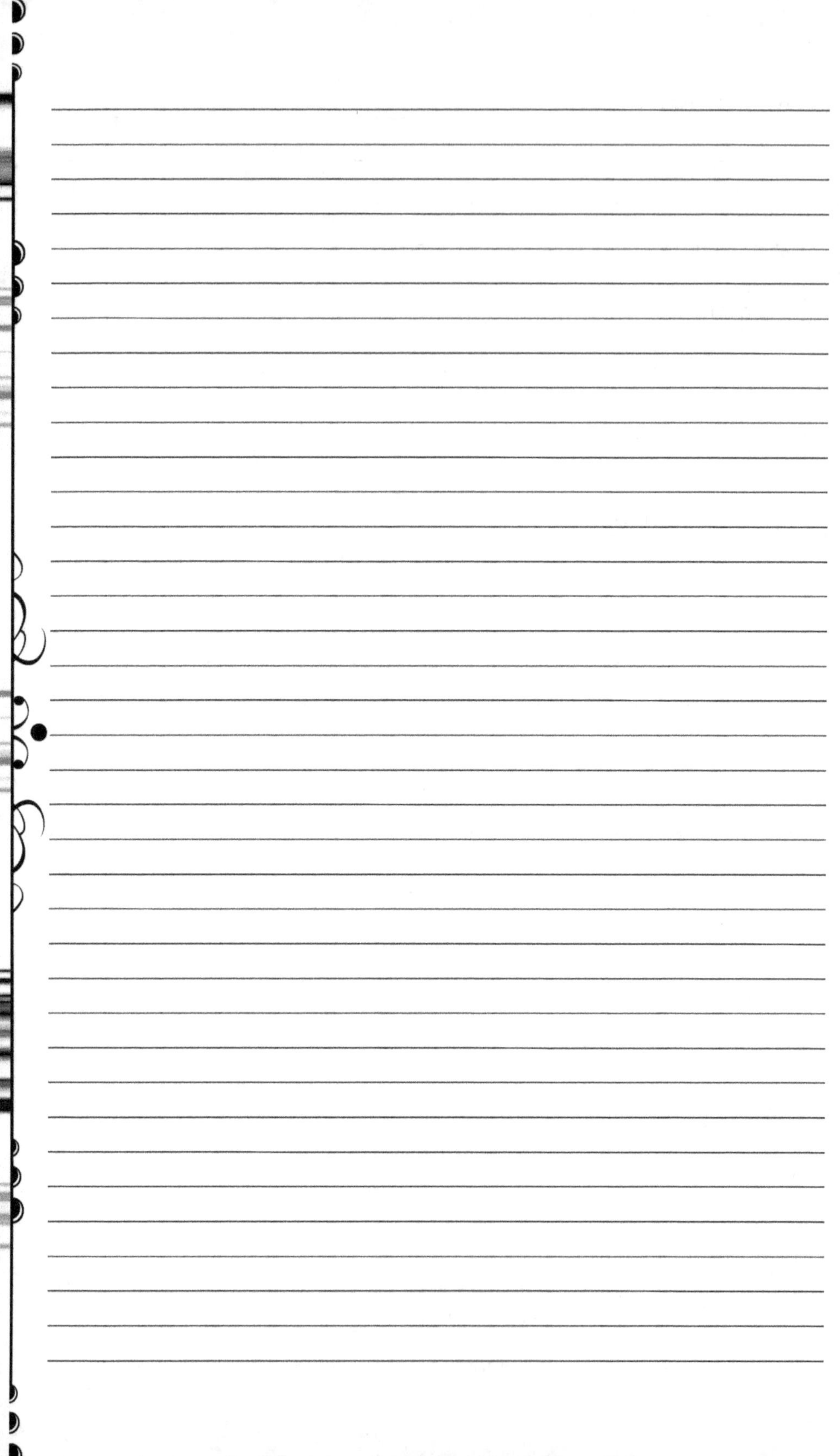

✅ **SYNOPSIS/THINGS I LIKED:**

🚫 **THINGS I DIDN'T LIKE:**

✏️ **FAVORITE QUOTE(S):**

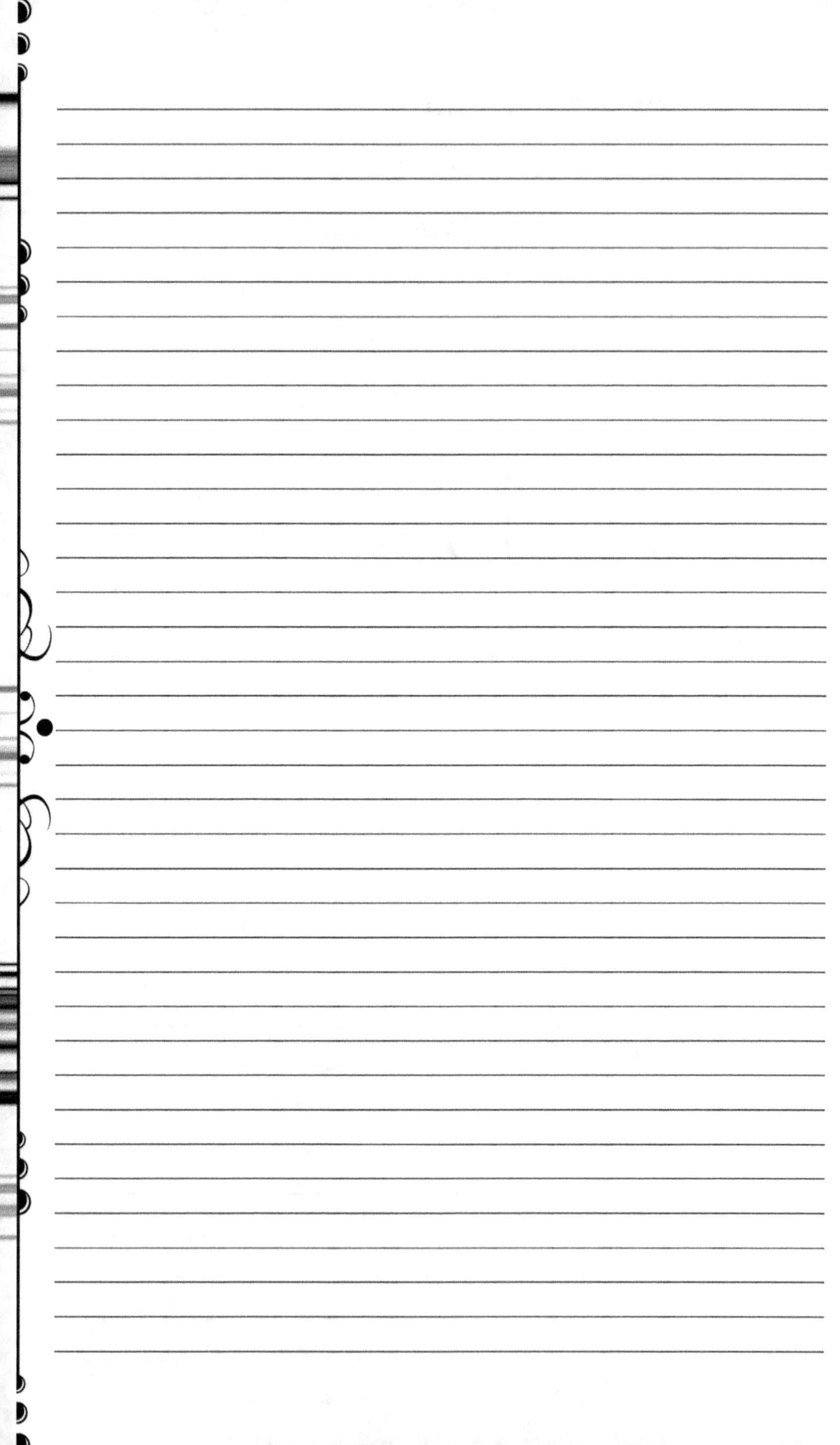

TITLE:

GENRE:

SERIES:

AUTHOR:

PAGES:

STARTED:

FINISHED:

☆☆☆☆☆

FORMAT READ: EBOOK / PRINT / AUDIOBOOK

☑ **SYNOPSIS/THINGS I LIKED:**

🚫 **THINGS I DIDN'T LIKE:**

✎ **FAVORITE QUOTE(S):**

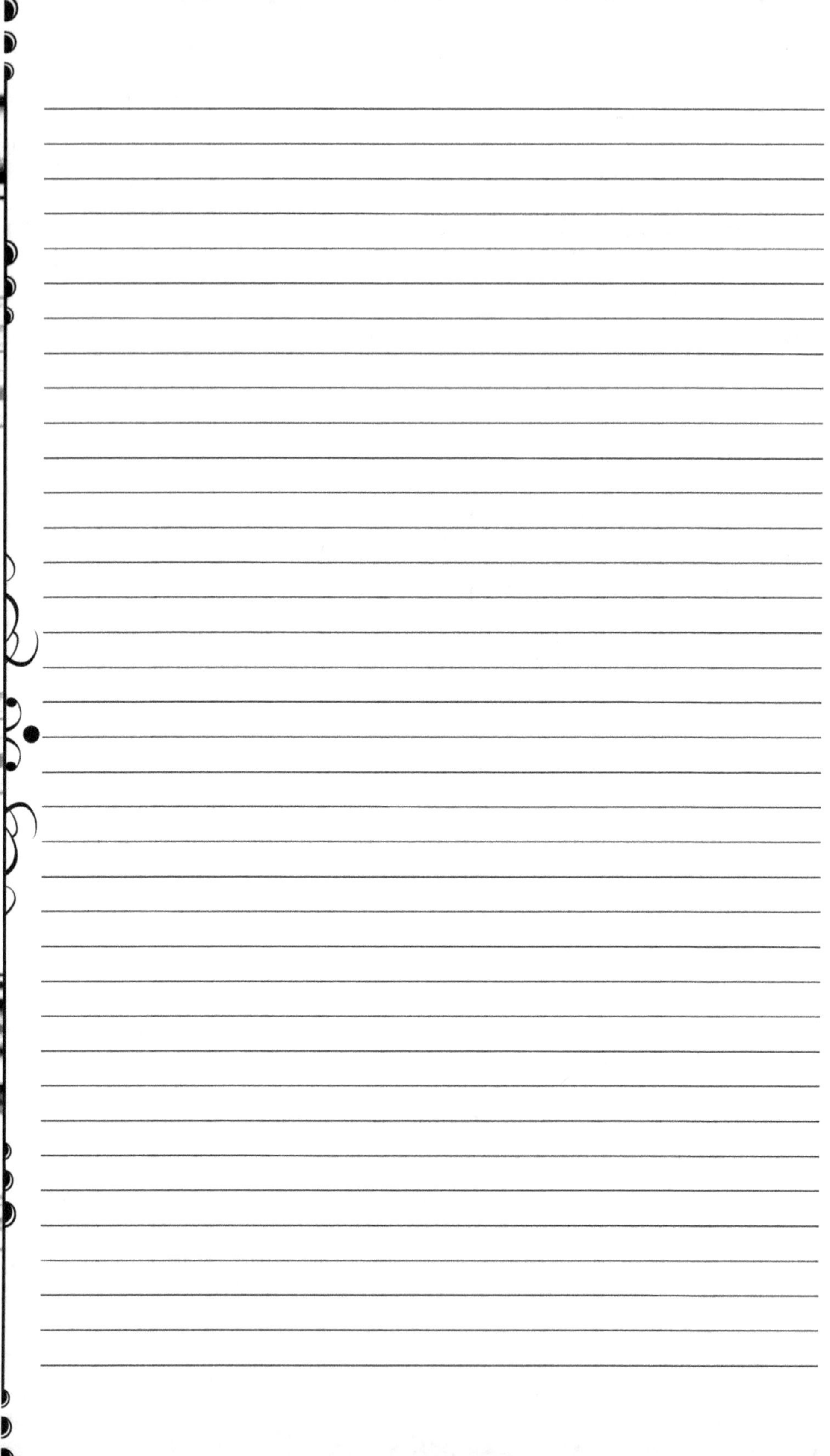

SYNOPSIS/THINGS I LIKED:

THINGS I DIDN'T LIKE:

FAVORITE QUOTE(S):

TITLE:
GENRE:
SERIES:
AUTHOR:
PAGES:
STARTED:
FINISHED:
FORMAT READ: EBOOK / PRINT / AUDIOBOOK

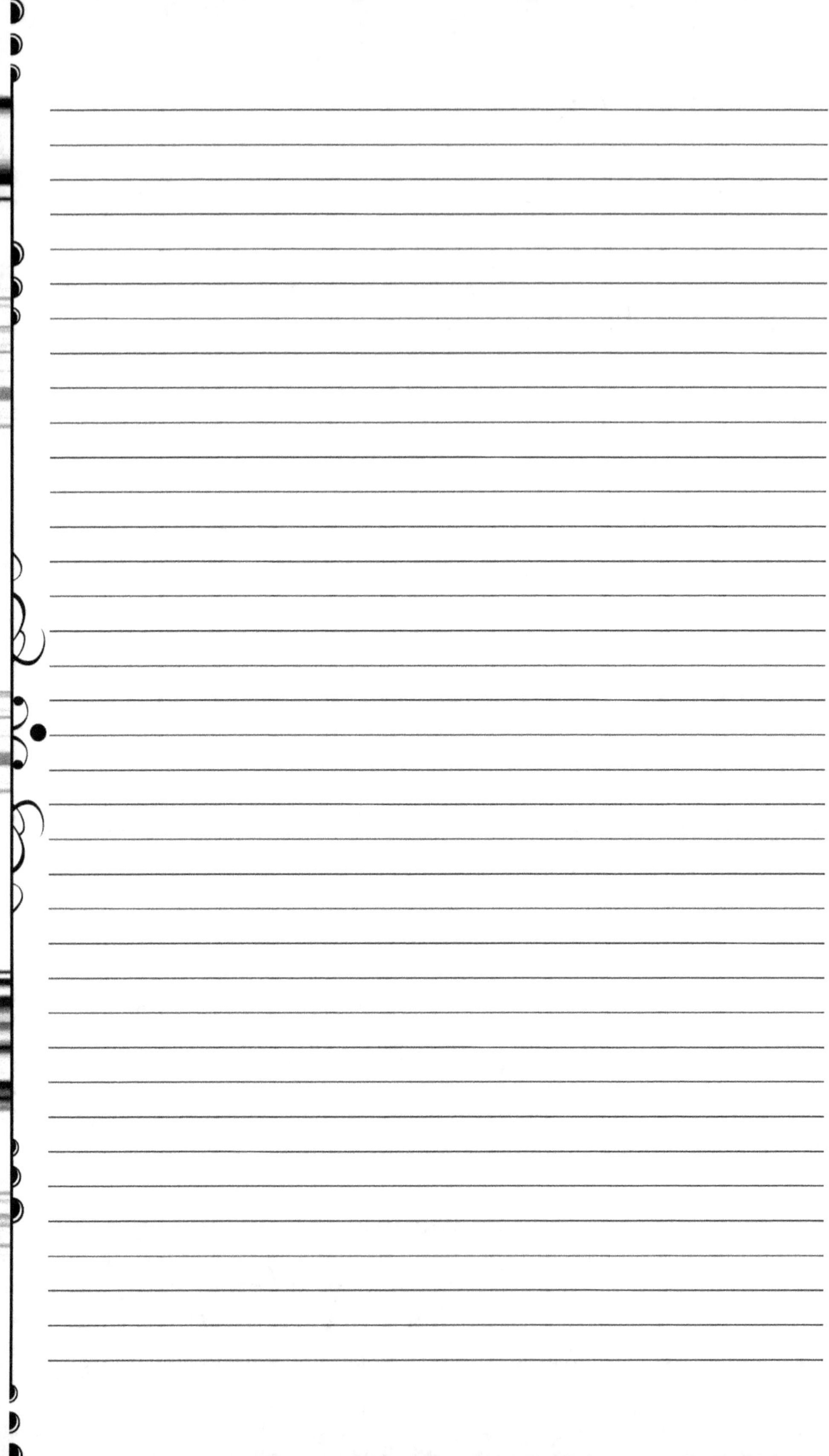

✅ **Synopsis/Things I liked:**

🚫 **Things I didn't like:**

✏️ **Favorite quote(s):**

Title:

Genre:

Series:

Author:

Pages:

Started:

Finished:

☆ ☆ ☆ ☆ ☆

Format read: Ebook / Print / Audiobook

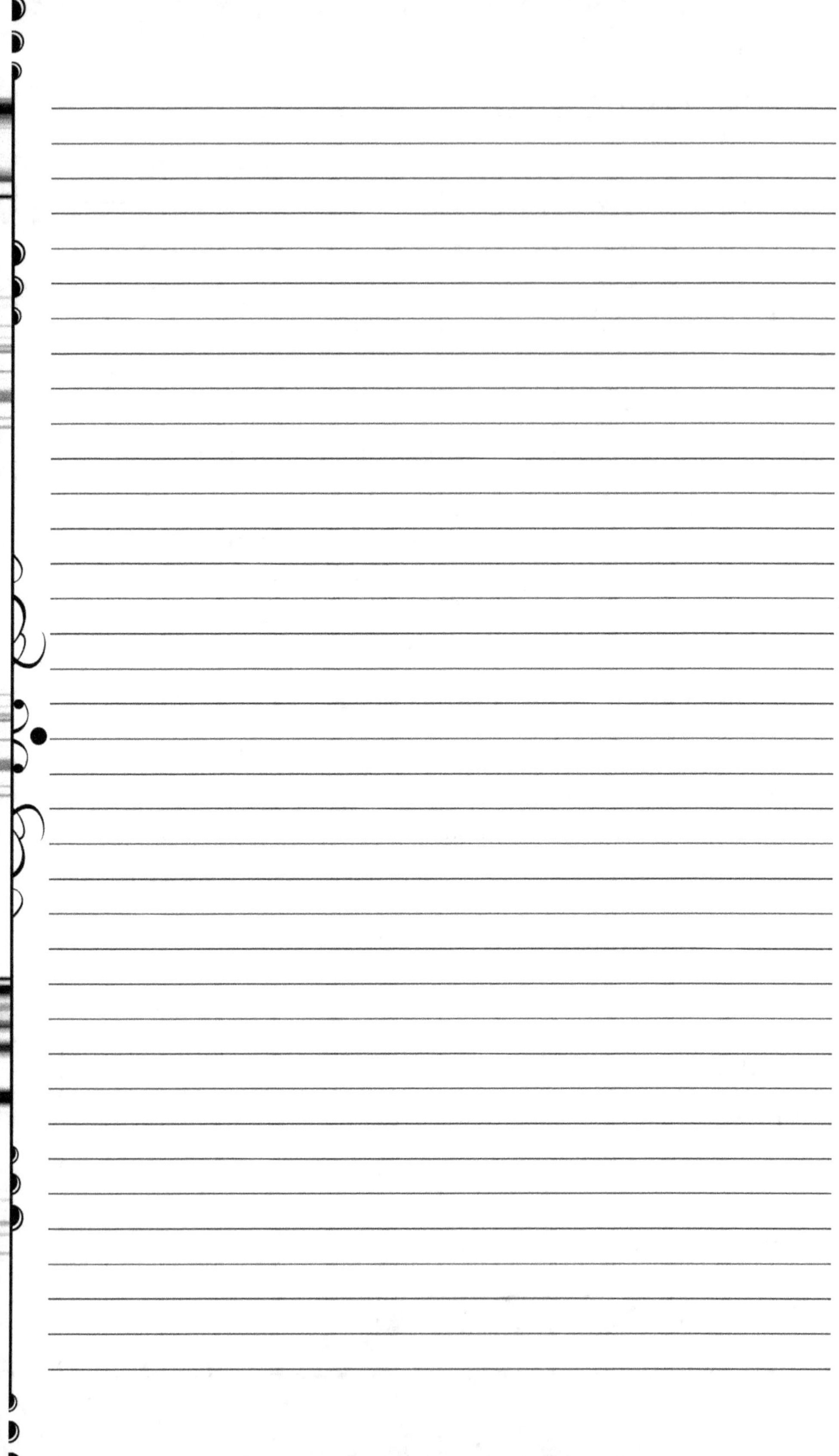

TITLE:

GENRE:

SERIES:

AUTHOR:

PAGES:

STARTED:

FINISHED:

FORMAT READ: EBOOK / PRINT / AUDIOBOOK

✓ SYNOPSIS/THINGS I LIKED:

🚫 THINGS I DIDN'T LIKE:

✏️ FAVORITE QUOTE(S):

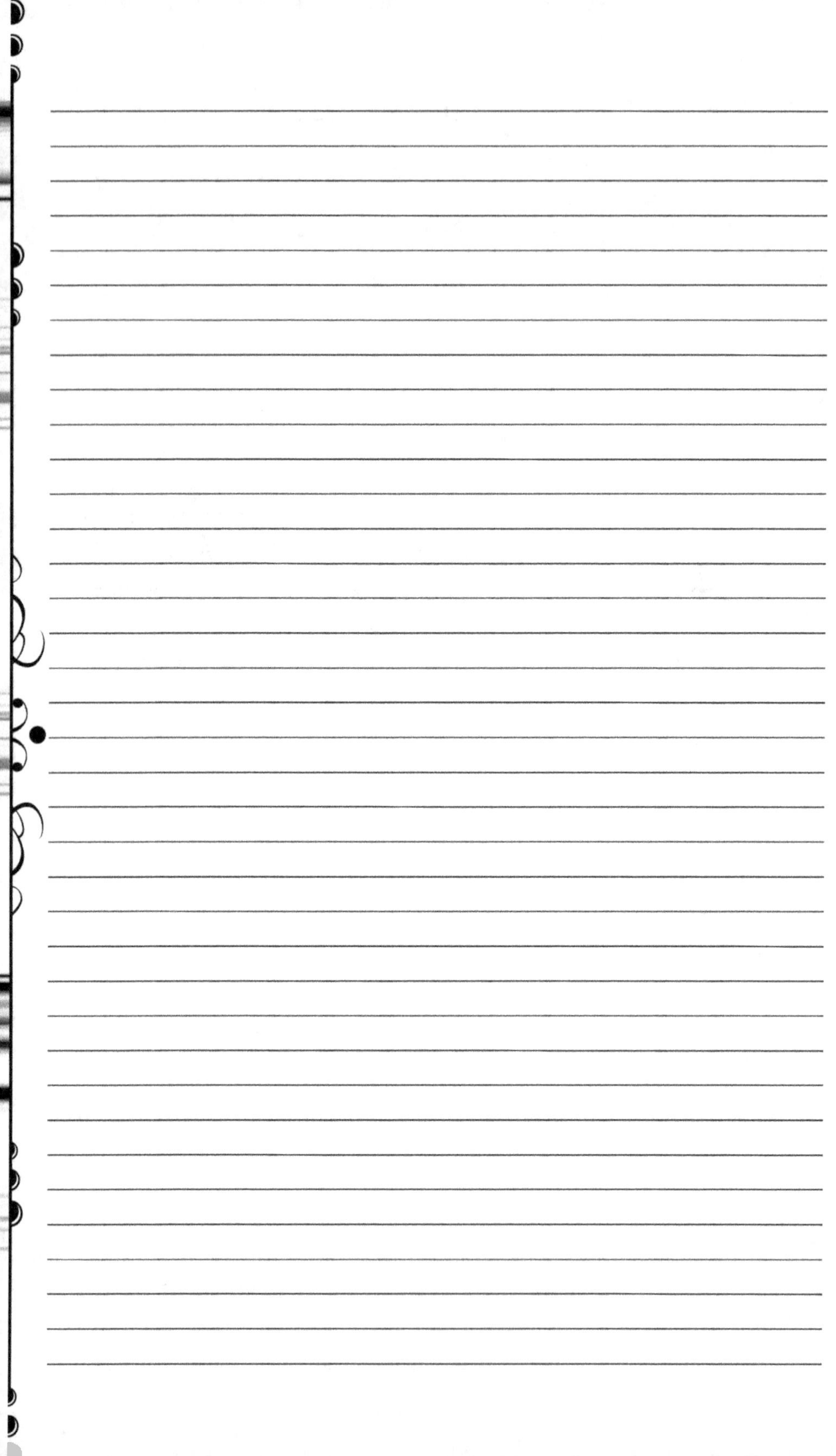

TITLE:

GENRE:

SERIES:

AUTHOR:

PAGES:

STARTED:

FINISHED:

FORMAT READ: EBOOK / PRINT / AUDIOBOOK

SYNOPSIS/THINGS I LIKED:

THINGS I DIDN'T LIKE:

FAVORITE QUOTE(S):

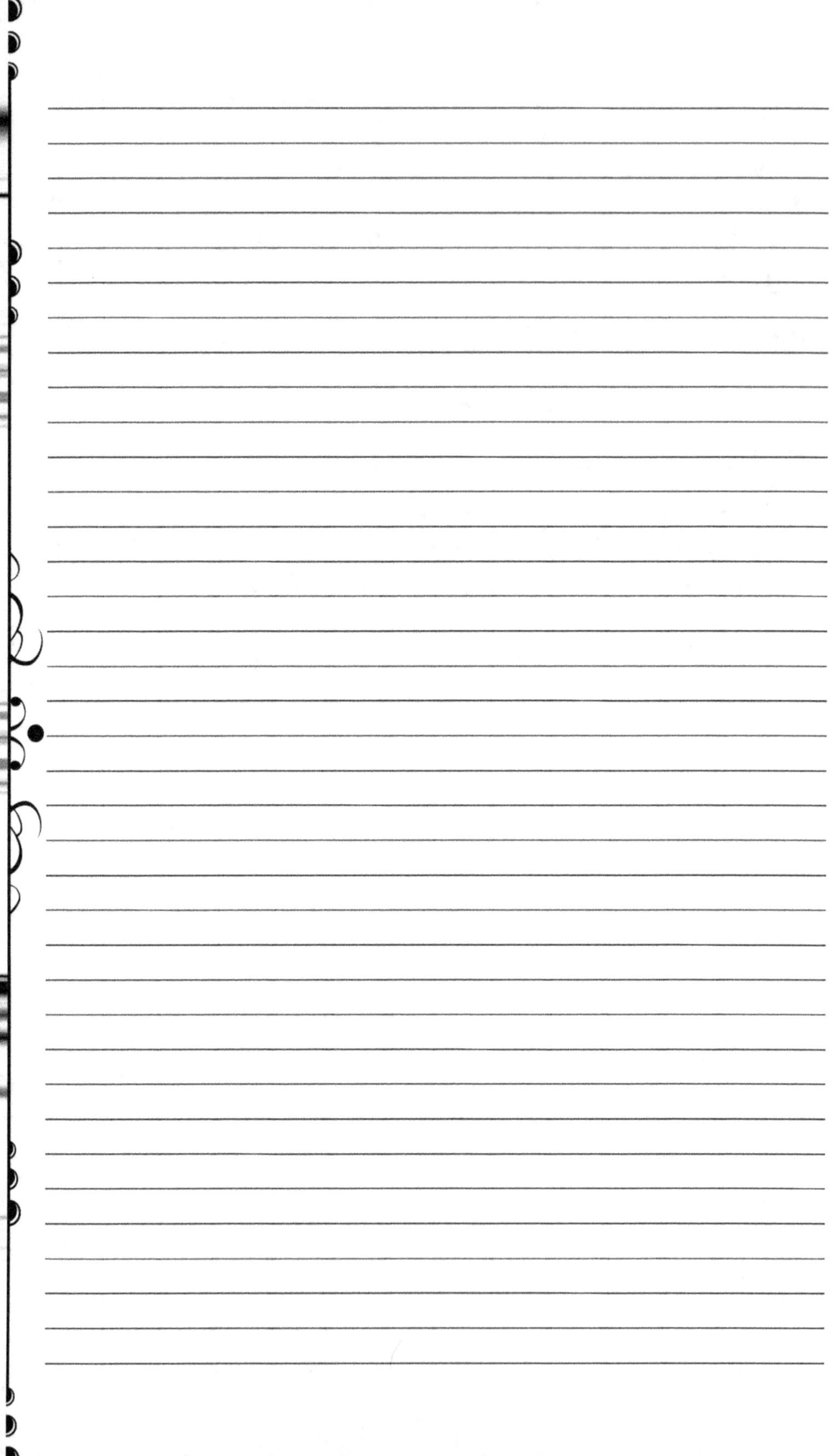

SYNOPSIS/THINGS I LIKED:

THINGS I DIDN'T LIKE:

FAVORITE QUOTE(S):

TITLE:
GENRE:
SERIES:
AUTHOR:
PAGES:
STARTED:
FINISHED:
FORMAT READ: EBOOK / PRINT / AUDIOBOOK

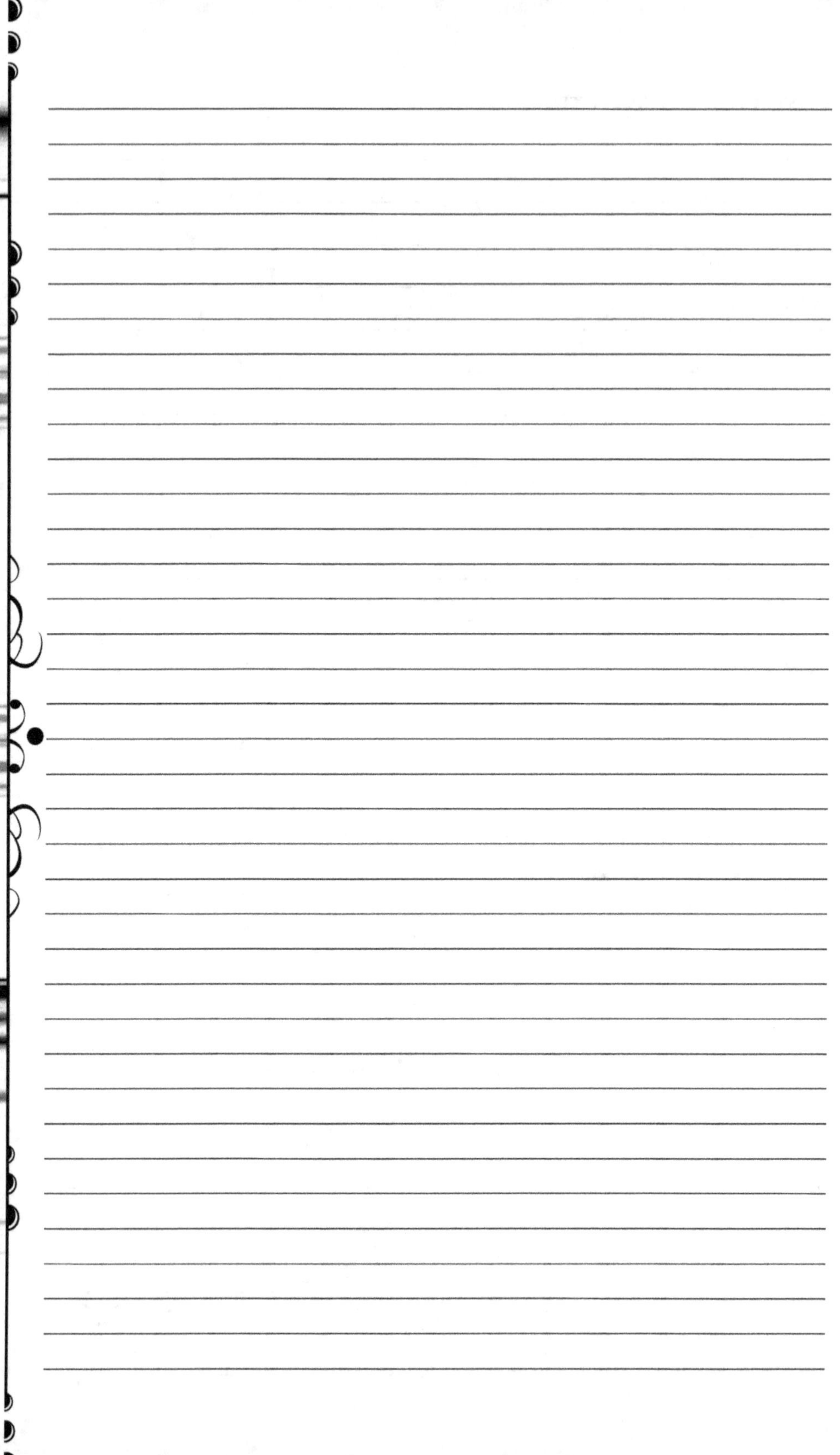

TITLE:

GENRE:

SERIES:

AUTHOR:

PAGES:

STARTED:

FINISHED:

FORMAT READ: EBOOK / PRINT / AUDIOBOOK

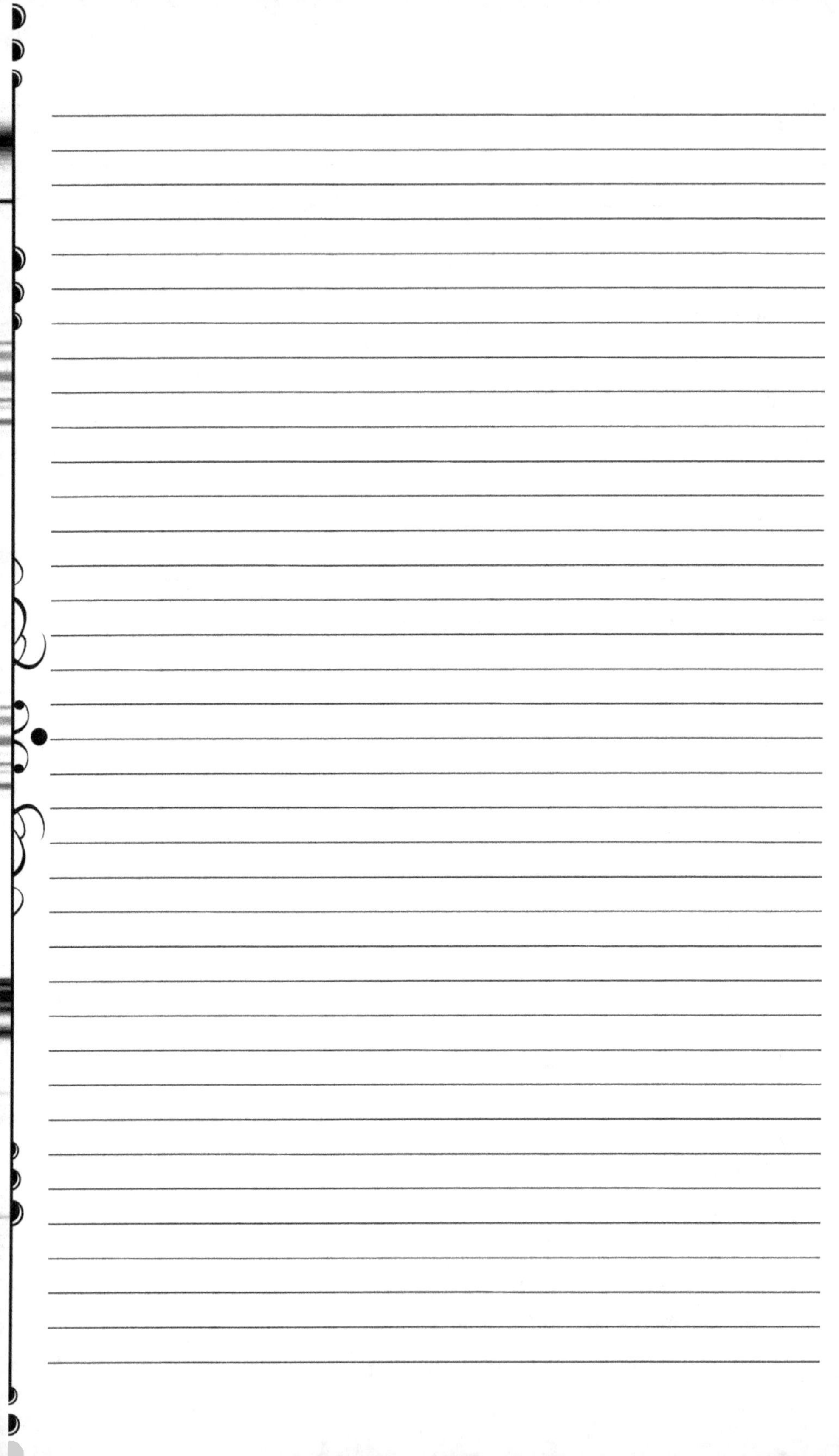

TITLE:

GENRE:

SERIES:

AUTHOR:

PAGES:

STARTED:

FINISHED:

FORMAT READ: EBOOK / PRINT / AUDIOBOOK

☑ SYNOPSIS/THINGS I LIKED:

🚫 THINGS I DIDN'T LIKE:

✎ FAVORITE QUOTE(S):

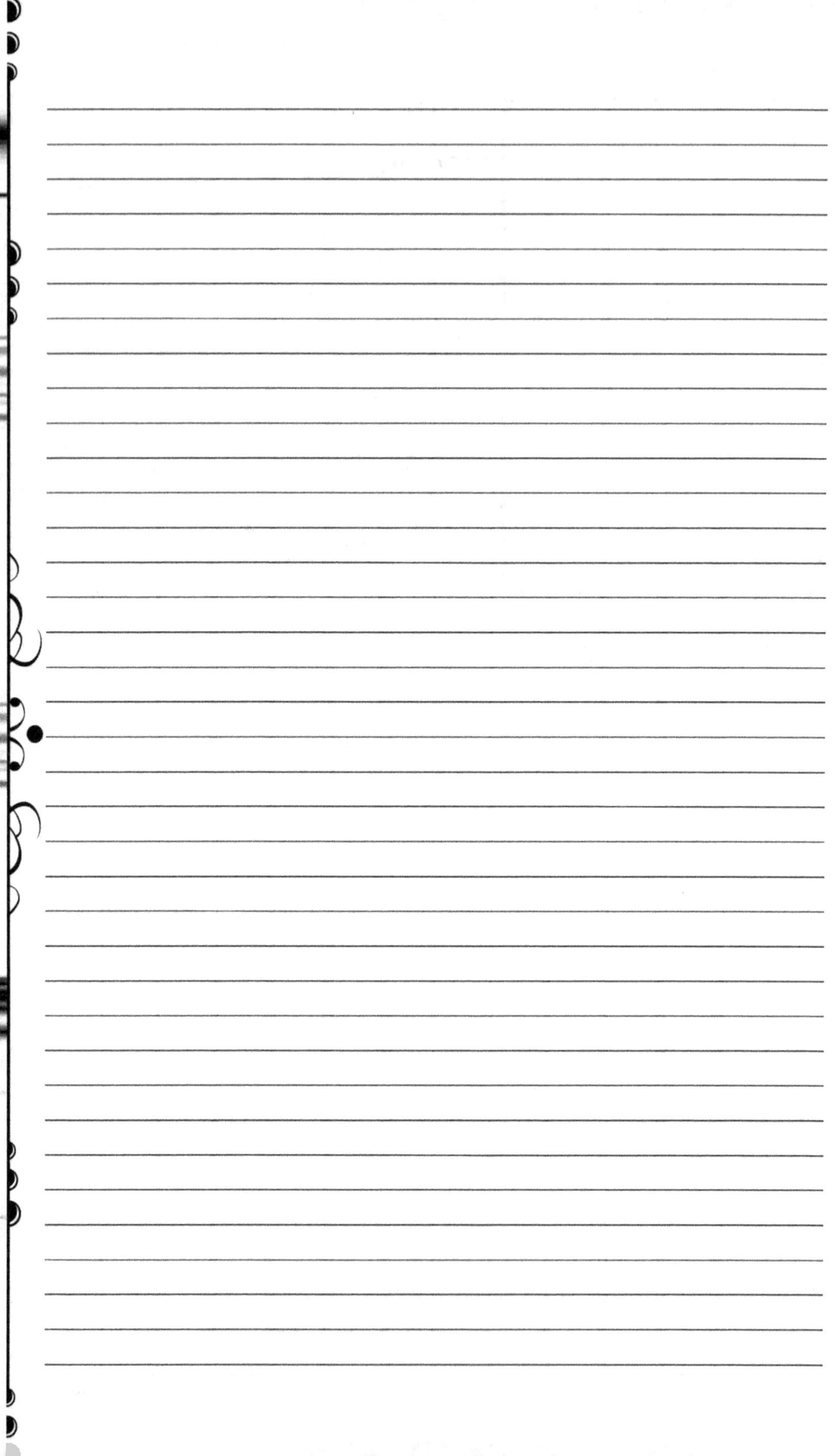

TITLE: _______________

GENRE: _______________

SERIES: _______________

AUTHOR: _______________

PAGES: _______________

STARTED: _______________

FINISHED: _______________

☆☆☆☆☆

FORMAT READ: EBOOK / PRINT / AUDIOBOOK

☑ **SYNOPSIS/THINGS I LIKED:**

____
____
____
____

🚫 **THINGS I DIDN'T LIKE:**

____
____
____
____

✎ **FAVORITE QUOTE(S):**

____
____
____
____
____
____
____

223

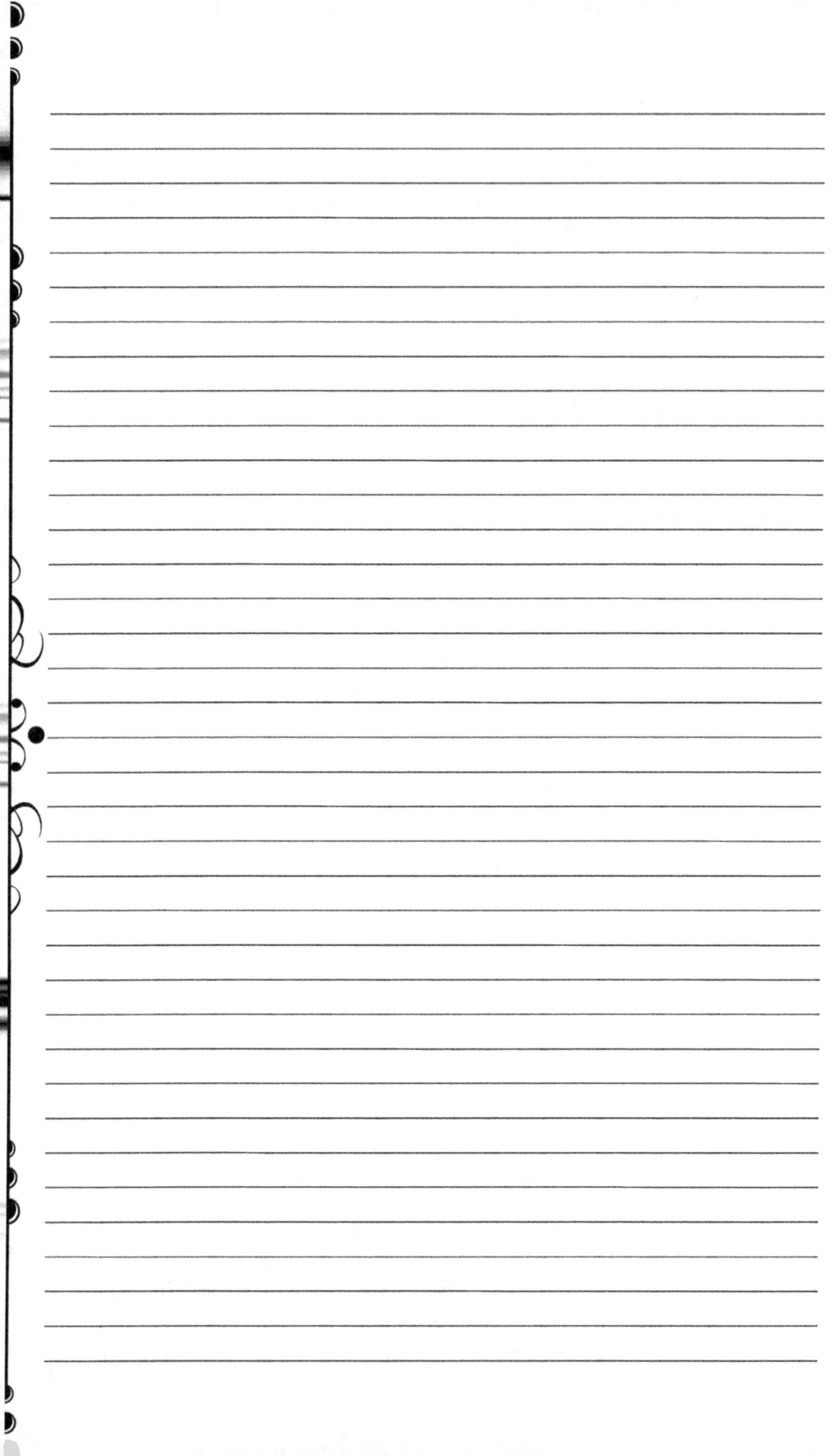

TITLE:

GENRE:

SERIES:

AUTHOR:

PAGES:

STARTED:

FINISHED:

FORMAT READ: EBOOK / PRINT / AUDIOBOOK

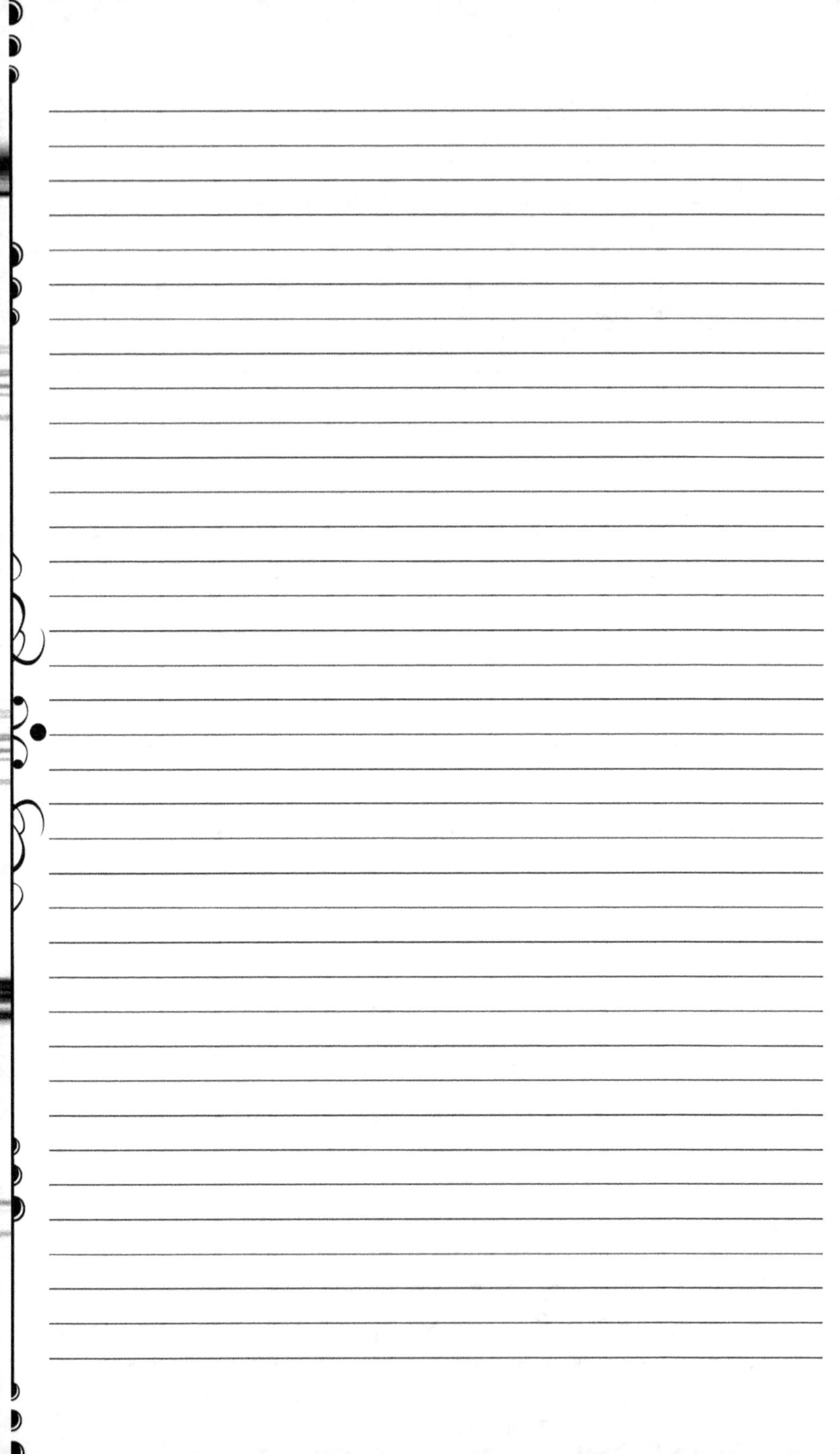

TITLE: _______________

GENRE: _______________

SERIES: _______________

AUTHOR: _______________

PAGES: _______________

STARTED: _______________

FINISHED: _______________

☆ ☆ ☆ ☆ ☆

FORMAT READ: EBOOK / PRINT / AUDIOBOOK

✓ SYNOPSIS/THINGS I LIKED:

____
____
____
____

🚫 THINGS I DIDN'T LIKE:

____
____
____
____

✏ FAVORITE QUOTE(S):

____
____
____
____
____
____
____

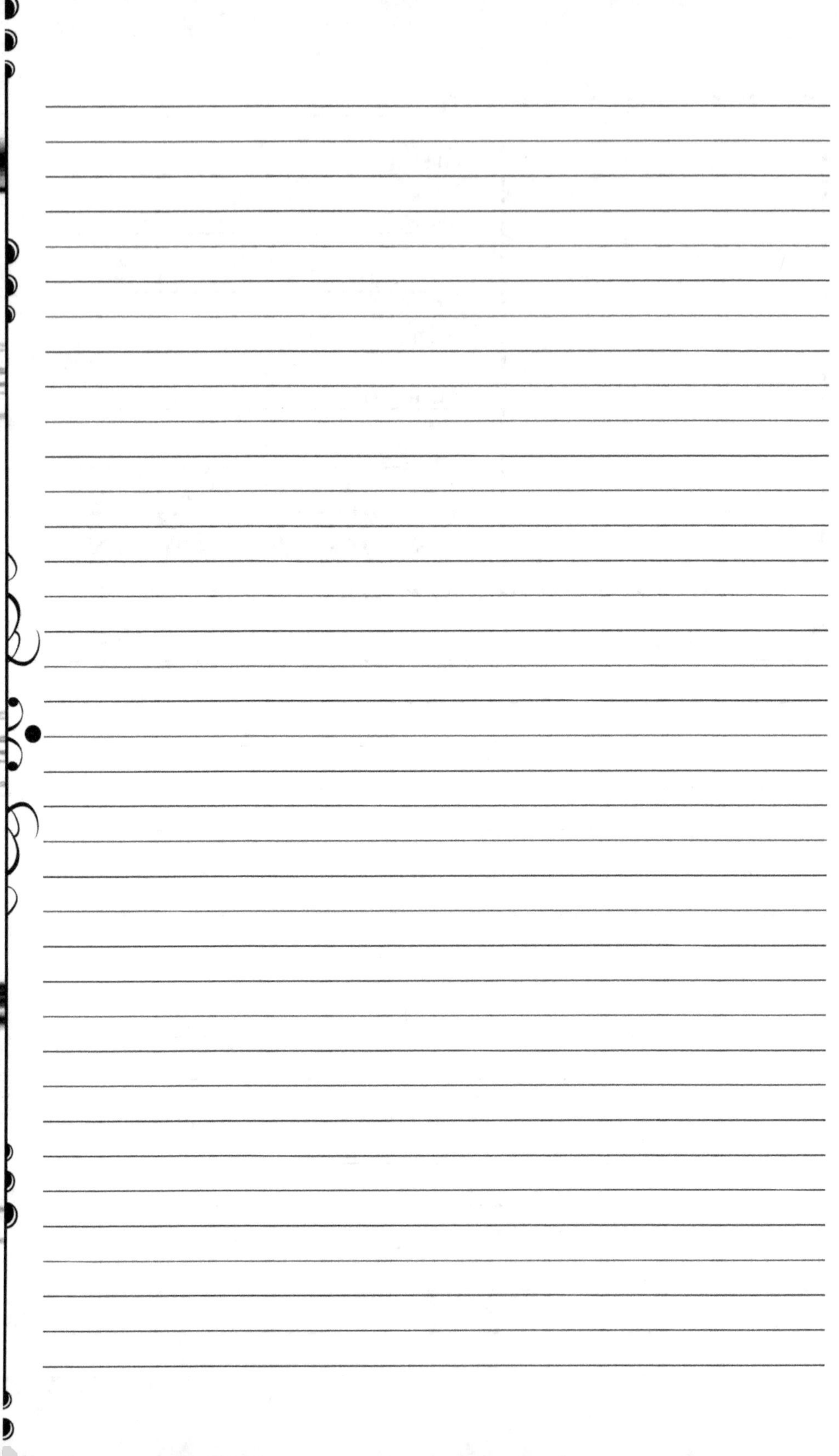

TITLE:

GENRE:

SERIES:

AUTHOR:

PAGES:

STARTED:

FINISHED:

FORMAT READ: EBOOK / PRINT / AUDIOBOOK

SYNOPSIS/THINGS I LIKED:

THINGS I DIDN'T LIKE:

FAVORITE QUOTE(S):

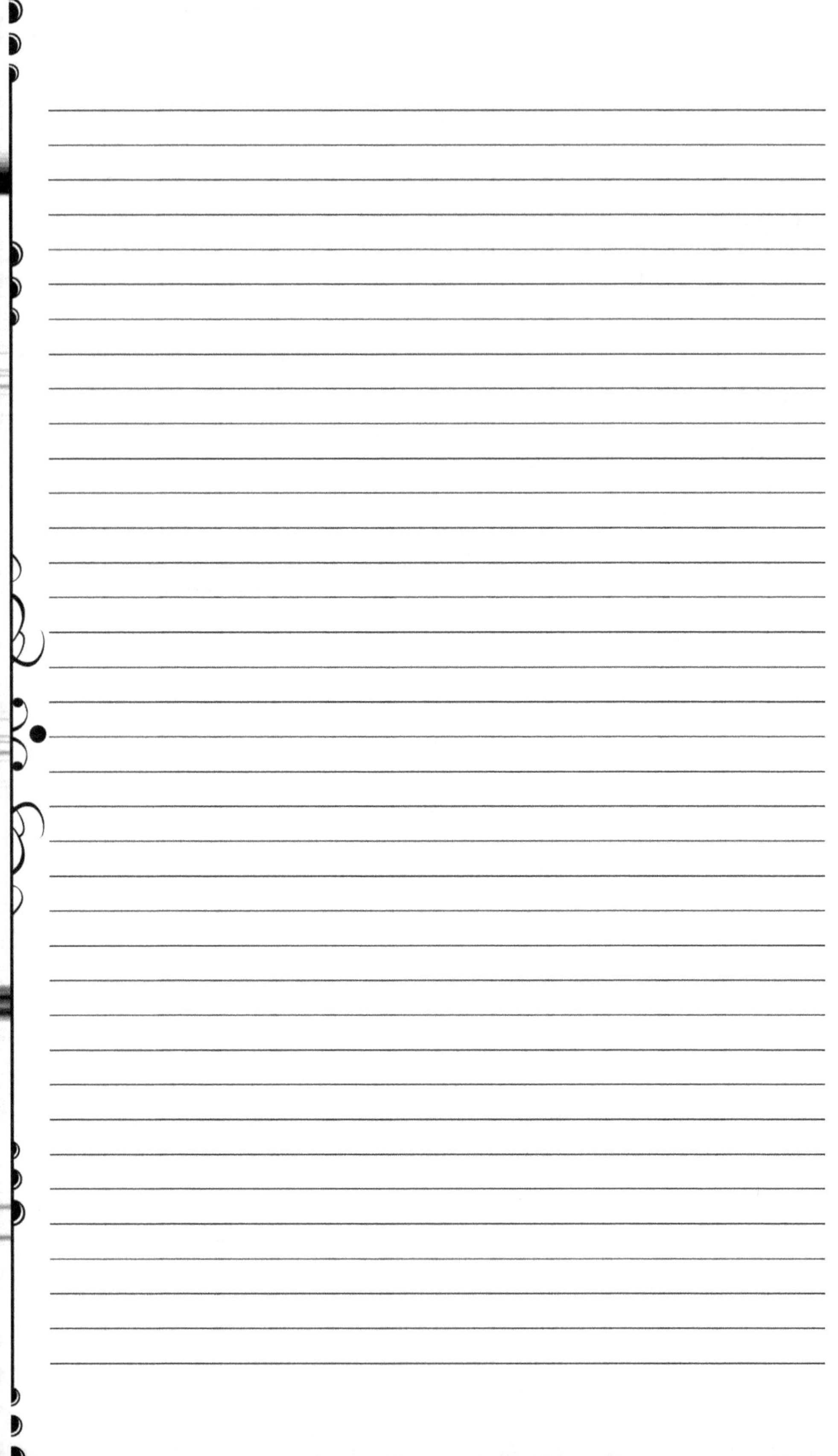

SYNOPSIS/THINGS I LIKED:

THINGS I DIDN'T LIKE:

FAVORITE QUOTE(S):

TITLE:

GENRE:

SERIES:

AUTHOR:

PAGES:

STARTED:

FINISHED:

FORMAT READ: EBOOK / PRINT / AUDIOBOOK

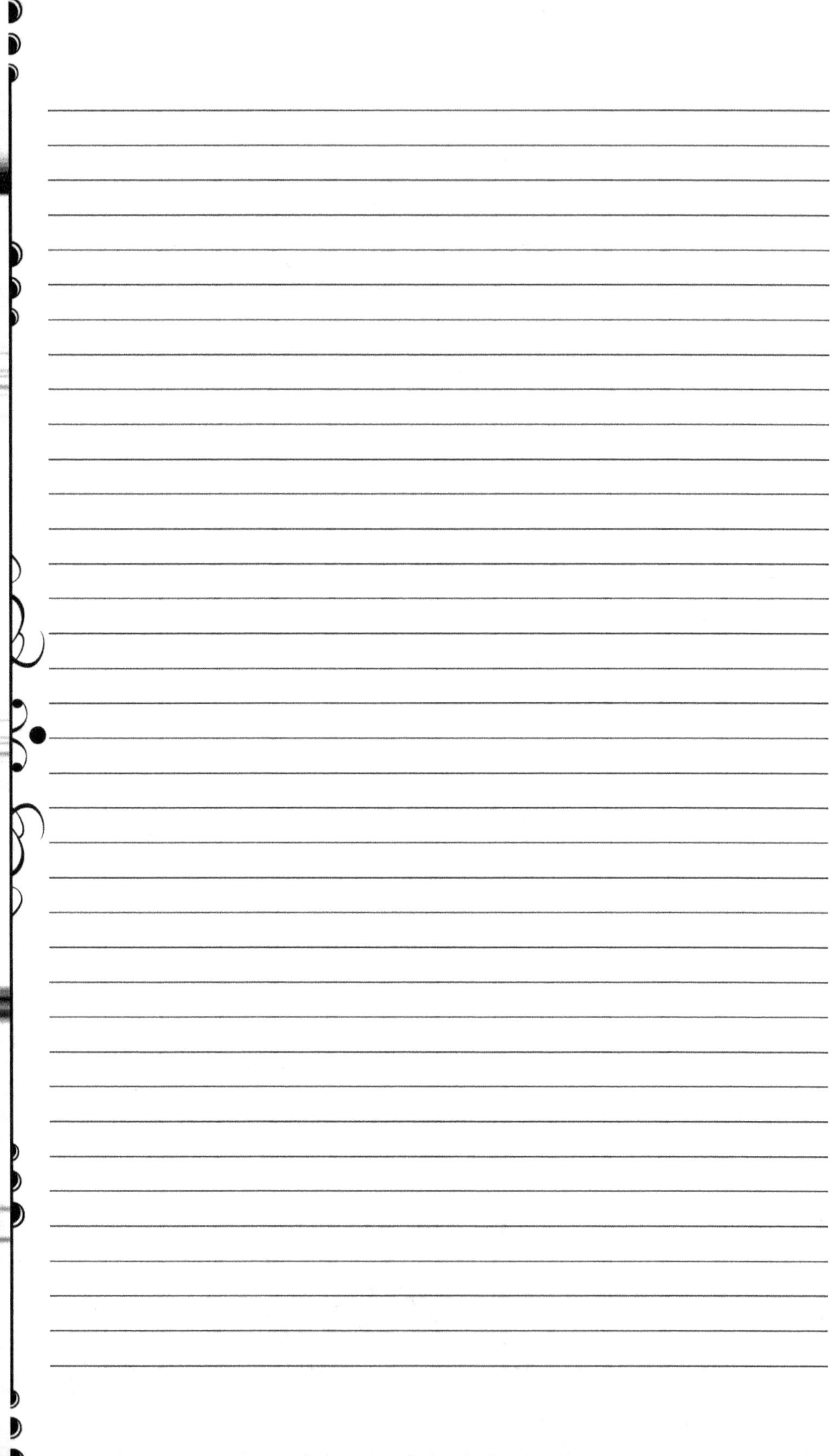

TITLE:

GENRE:

SERIES:

AUTHOR:

PAGES:

STARTED:

FINISHED:

FORMAT READ: EBOOK / PRINT / AUDIOBOOK

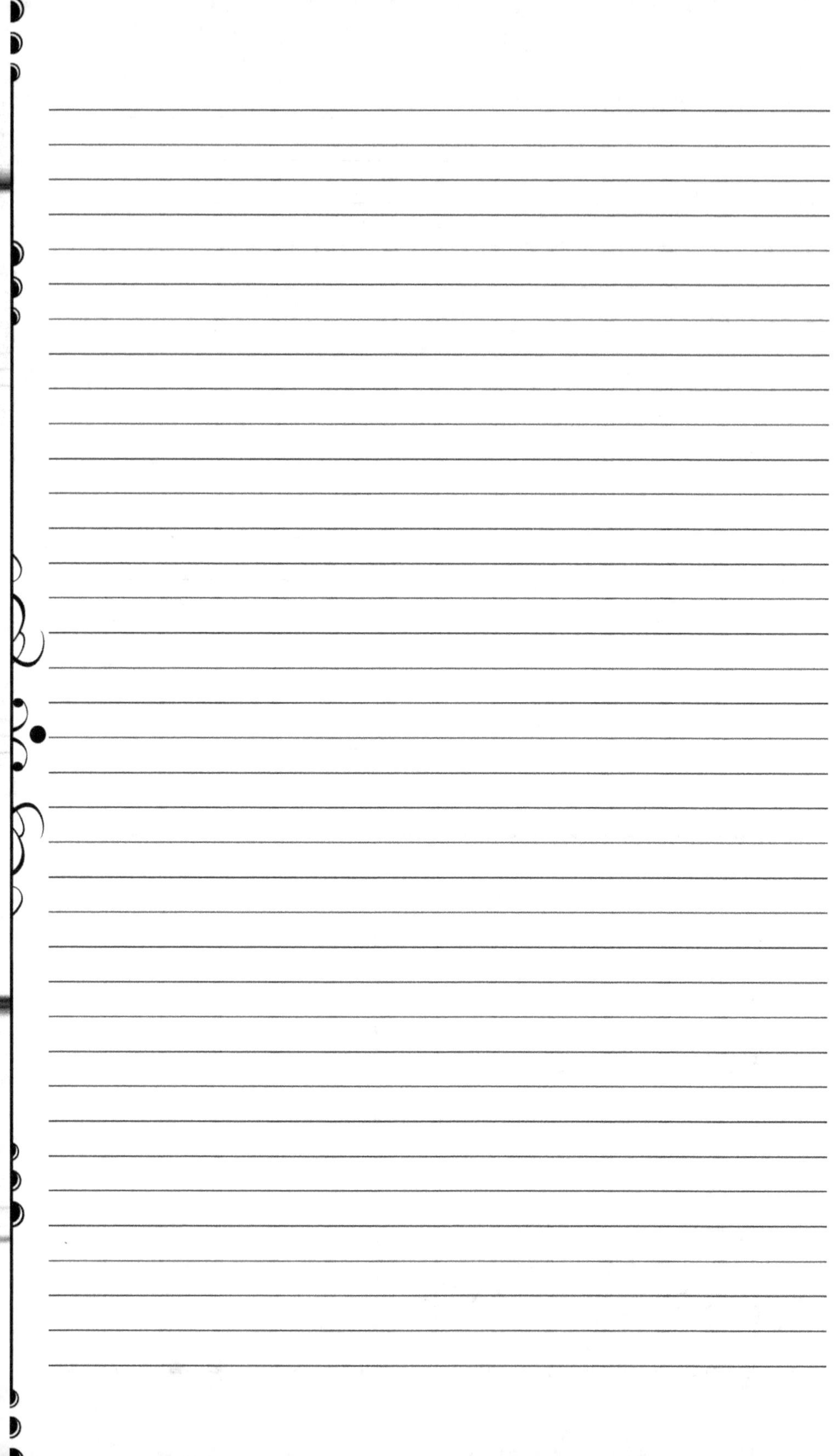

TITLE:

GENRE:

SERIES:

AUTHOR:

PAGES:

STARTED:

FINISHED:

FORMAT READ: EBOOK / PRINT / AUDIOBOOK

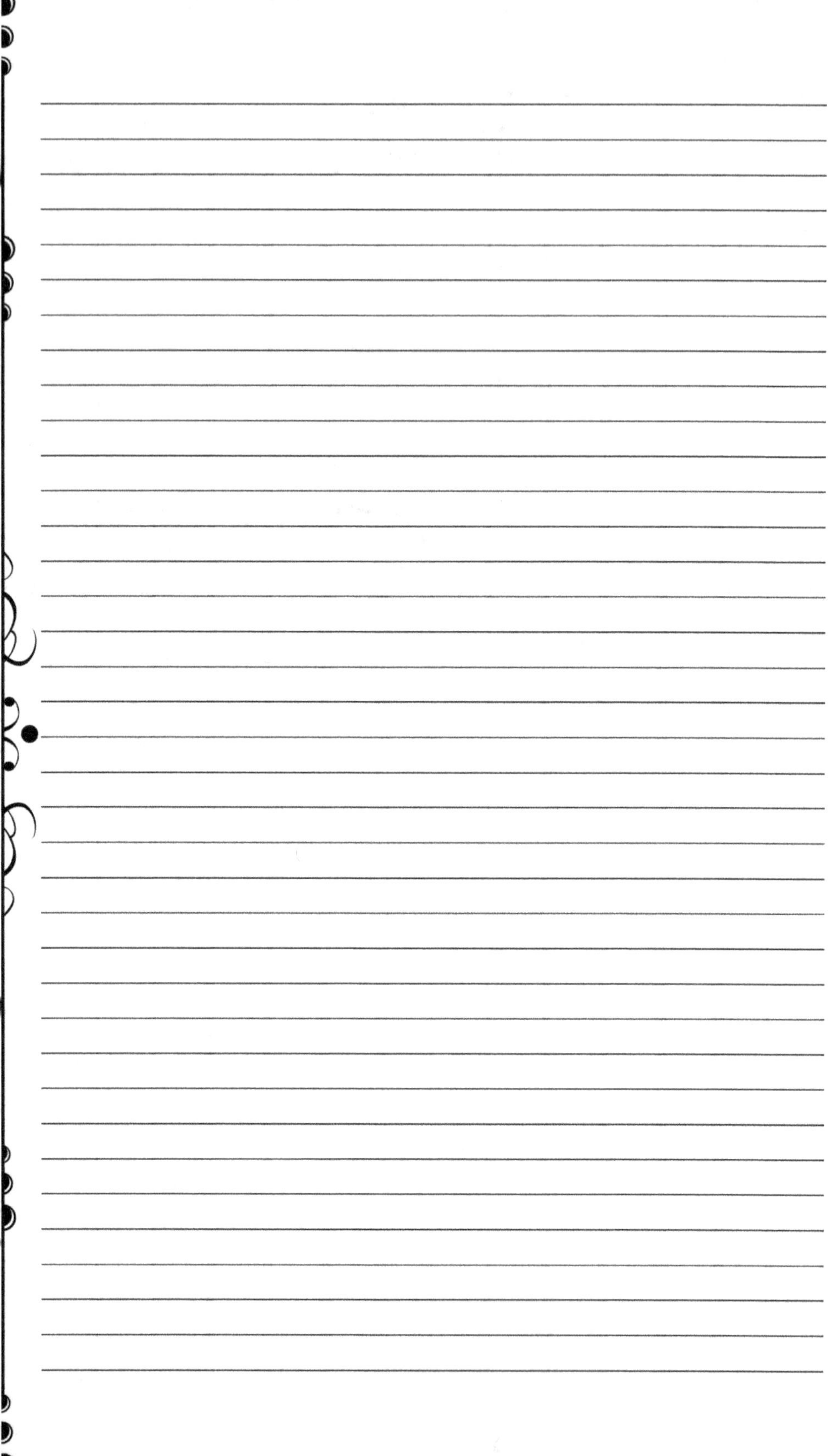

TITLE:

GENRE:

SERIES:

AUTHOR:

PAGES:

STARTED:

FINISHED:

☆ ☆ ☆ ☆ ☆

FORMAT READ: EBOOK / PRINT / AUDIOBOOK

✓ **SYNOPSIS/THINGS I LIKED:**

🚫 **THINGS I DIDN'T LIKE:**

✏️ **FAVORITE QUOTE(S):**

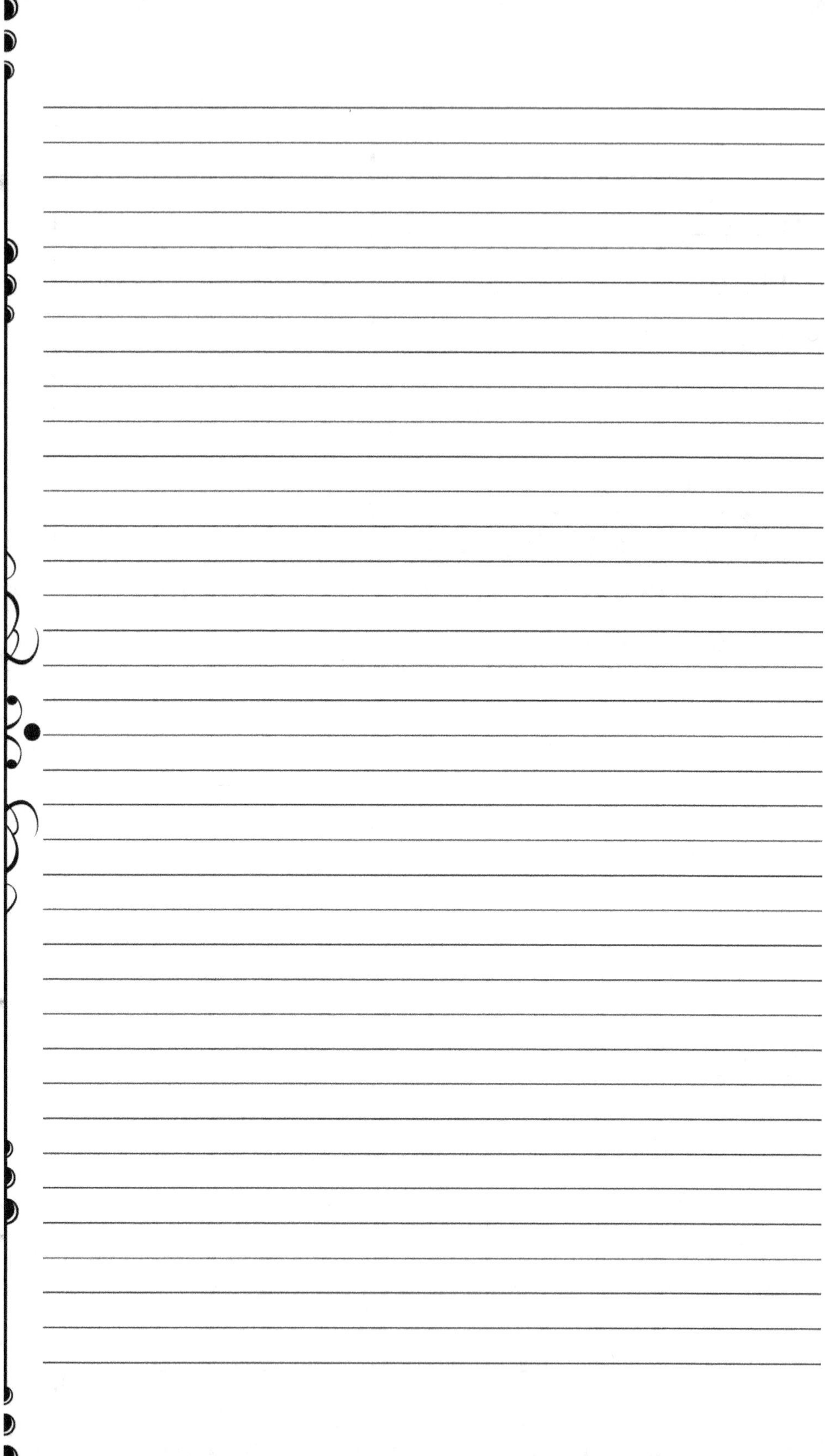

TITLE:

GENRE:

SERIES:

AUTHOR:

PAGES:

STARTED:

FINISHED:

FORMAT READ: EBOOK / PRINT / AUDIOBOOK

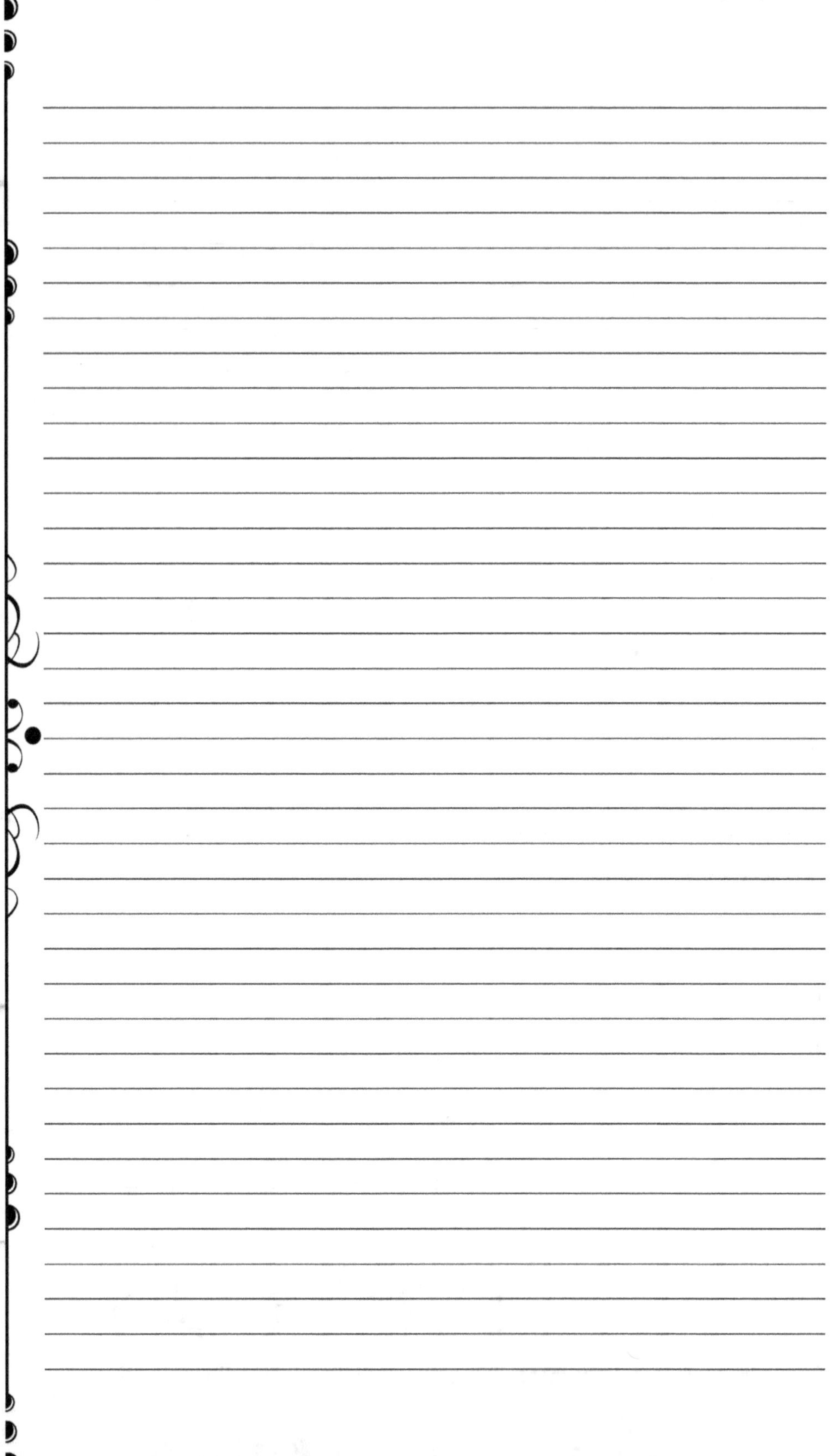

✓ **SYNOPSIS/THINGS I LIKED:**

🚫 **THINGS I DIDN'T LIKE:**

✎ **FAVORITE QUOTE(S):**

TITLE:

GENRE:

SERIES:

AUTHOR:

PAGES:

STARTED:

FINISHED:

☆ ☆ ☆ ☆ ☆

FORMAT READ: EBOOK / PRINT / AUDIOBOOK

TITLE:

GENRE:

SERIES:

AUTHOR:

PAGES:

STARTED:

FINISHED:

☆☆☆☆☆

FORMAT READ: EBOOK / PRINT / AUDIOBOOK

✔ SYNOPSIS/THINGS I LIKED:

🚫 THINGS I DIDN'T LIKE:

✎ FAVORITE QUOTE(S):

TITLE: ______________________

GENRE: ______________________

SERIES: ______________________

AUTHOR: ______________________

PAGES: ______________________

STARTED: ______________________

FINISHED: ______________________

☆☆☆☆☆

FORMAT READ: EBOOK / PRINT / AUDIOBOOK

✅ **SYNOPSIS/THINGS I LIKED:**

____
____
____
____

🚫 **THINGS I DIDN'T LIKE:**

____
____
____
____

✏️ **FAVORITE QUOTE(S):**

____
____
____
____
____
____

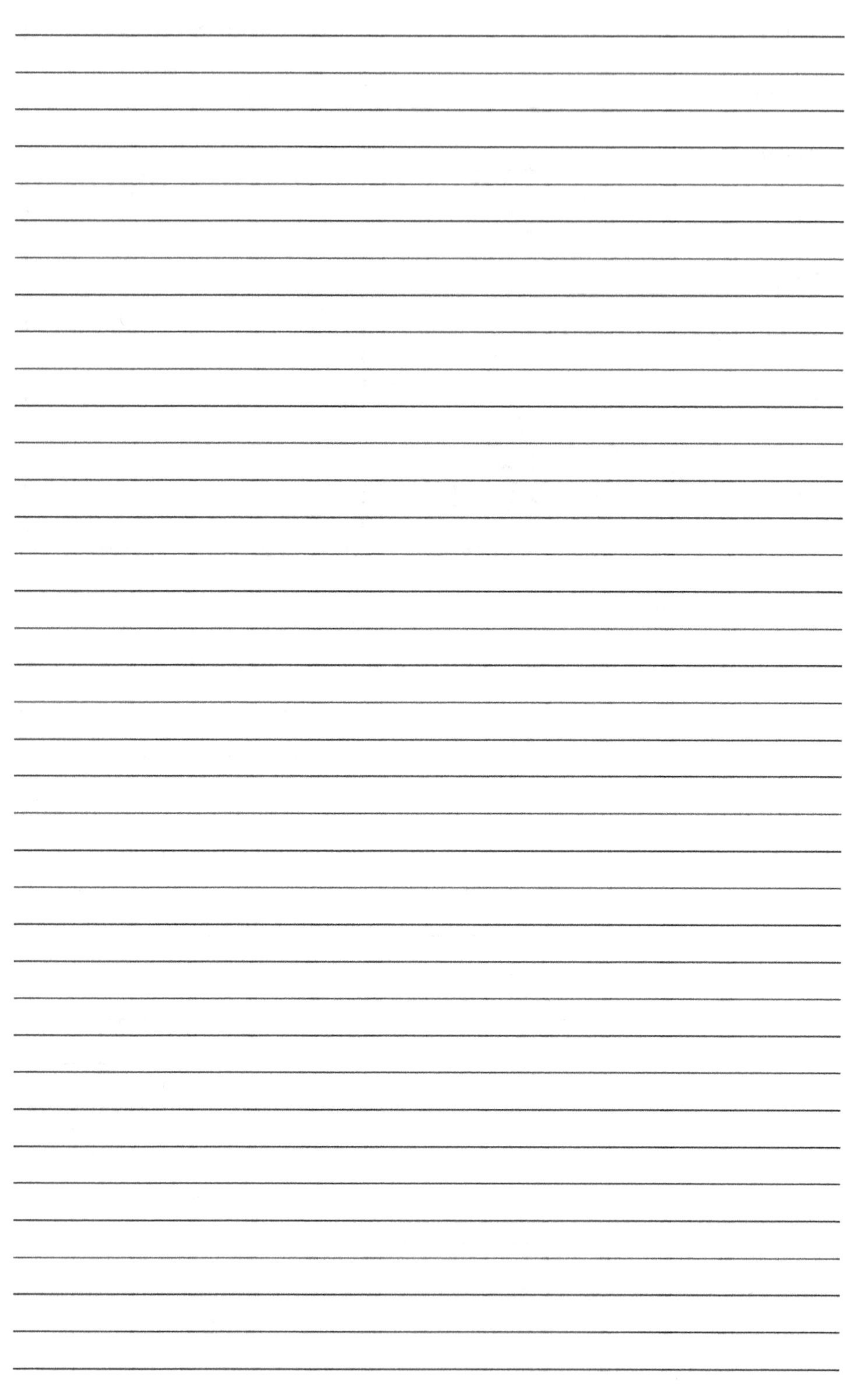

TITLE:

GENRE:

SERIES:

AUTHOR:

PAGES:

STARTED:

FINISHED:

FORMAT READ: EBOOK / PRINT / AUDIOBOOK

TITLE:

GENRE:

SERIES:

AUTHOR:

PAGES:

STARTED:

FINISHED:

FORMAT READ: EBOOK / PRINT / AUDIOBOOK

236

TITLE:

GENRE:

SERIES:

AUTHOR:

PAGES:

STARTED:

FINISHED:

☆ ☆ ☆ ☆ ☆

FORMAT READ: EBOOK / PRINT / AUDIOBOOK

✅ SYNOPSIS/THINGS I LIKED:

🚫 THINGS I DIDN'T LIKE:

✏️ FAVORITE QUOTE(S):

TITLE:

GENRE:

SERIES:

AUTHOR:

PAGES:

STARTED:

FINISHED:

FORMAT READ: EBOOK / PRINT / AUDIOBOOK

SYNOPSIS/THINGS I LIKED:

THINGS I DIDN'T LIKE:

FAVORITE QUOTE(S):

239

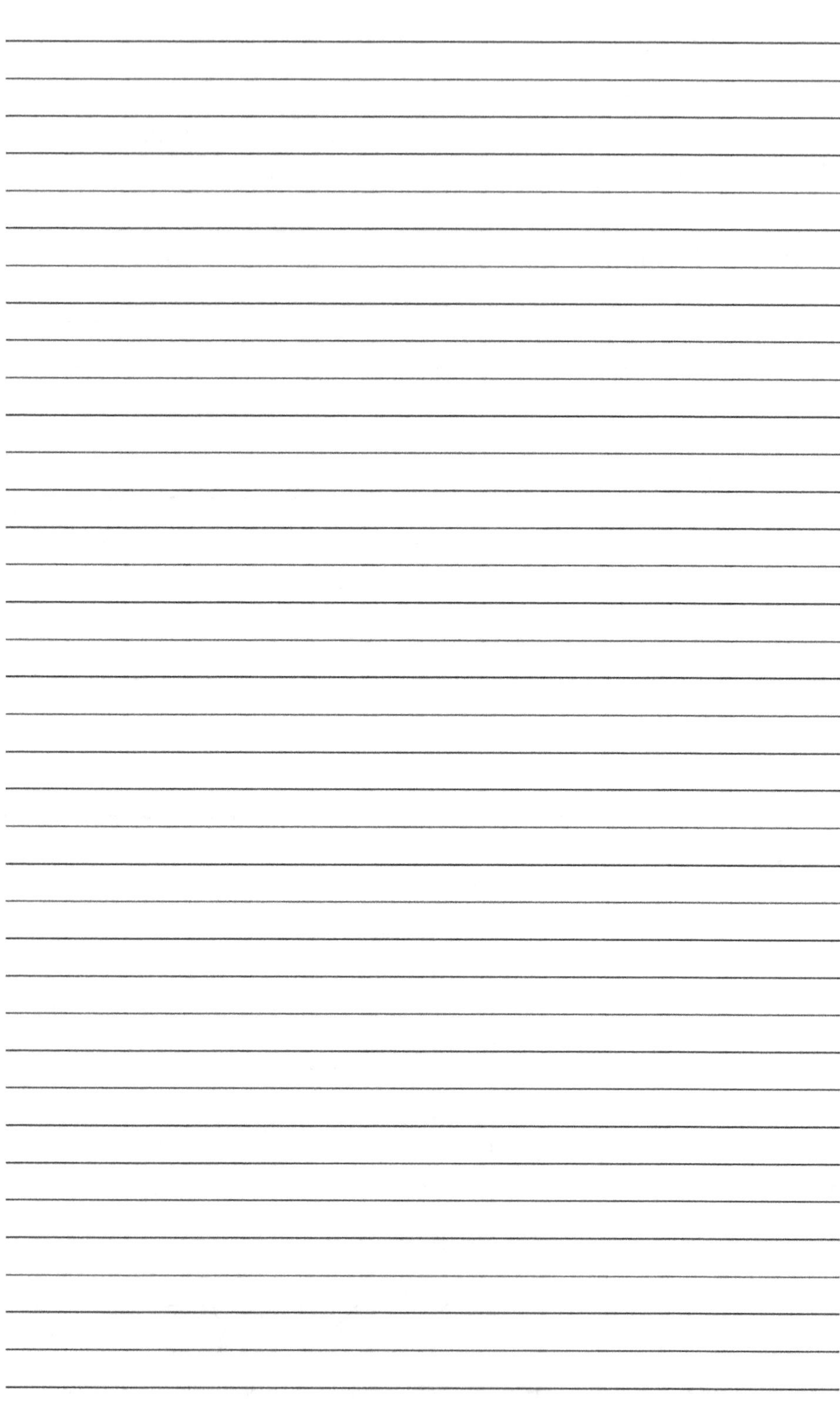

TITLE:

GENRE:

SERIES:

AUTHOR:

PAGES:

STARTED:

FINISHED:

FORMAT READ: EBOOK / PRINT / AUDIOBOOK

TITLE:

GENRE:

SERIES:

AUTHOR:

PAGES:

STARTED:

FINISHED:

FORMAT READ: EBOOK / PRINT / AUDIOBOOK

✓ **SYNOPSIS/THINGS I LIKED:**

🚫 **THINGS I DIDN'T LIKE:**

✎ **FAVORITE QUOTE(S):**

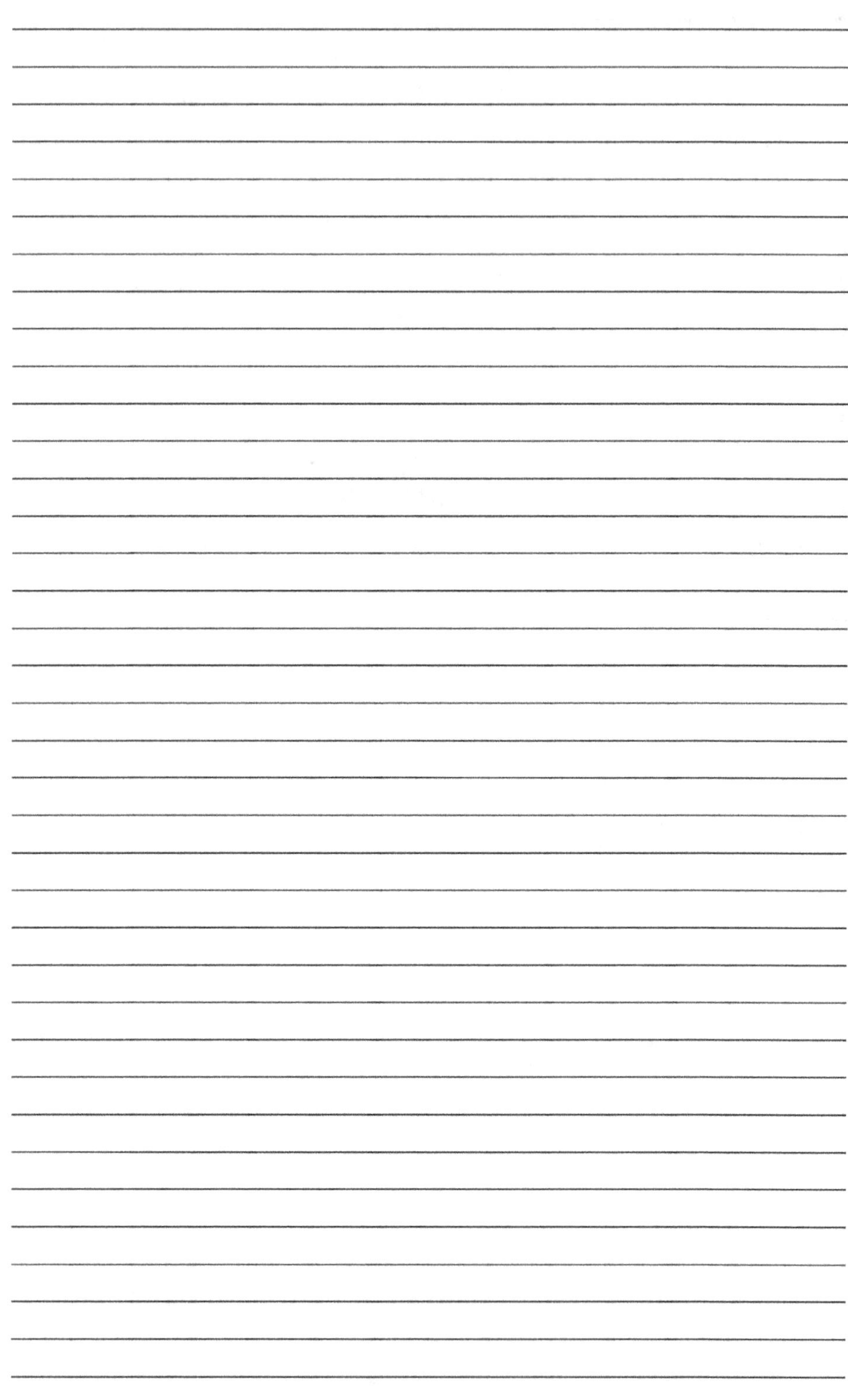

TITLE:

GENRE:

SERIES:

AUTHOR:

PAGES:

STARTED:

FINISHED:

FORMAT READ: EBOOK / PRINT / AUDIOBOOK

SYNOPSIS/THINGS I LIKED:

THINGS I DIDN'T LIKE:

FAVORITE QUOTE(S):

✔️ **Synopsis/Things I liked:**

🚫 **Things I didn't like:**

✏️ **Favorite quote(s):**

Title:

Genre:

Series:

Author:

Pages:

Started:

Finished:

☆☆☆☆☆

Format read: Ebook / Print / Audiobook

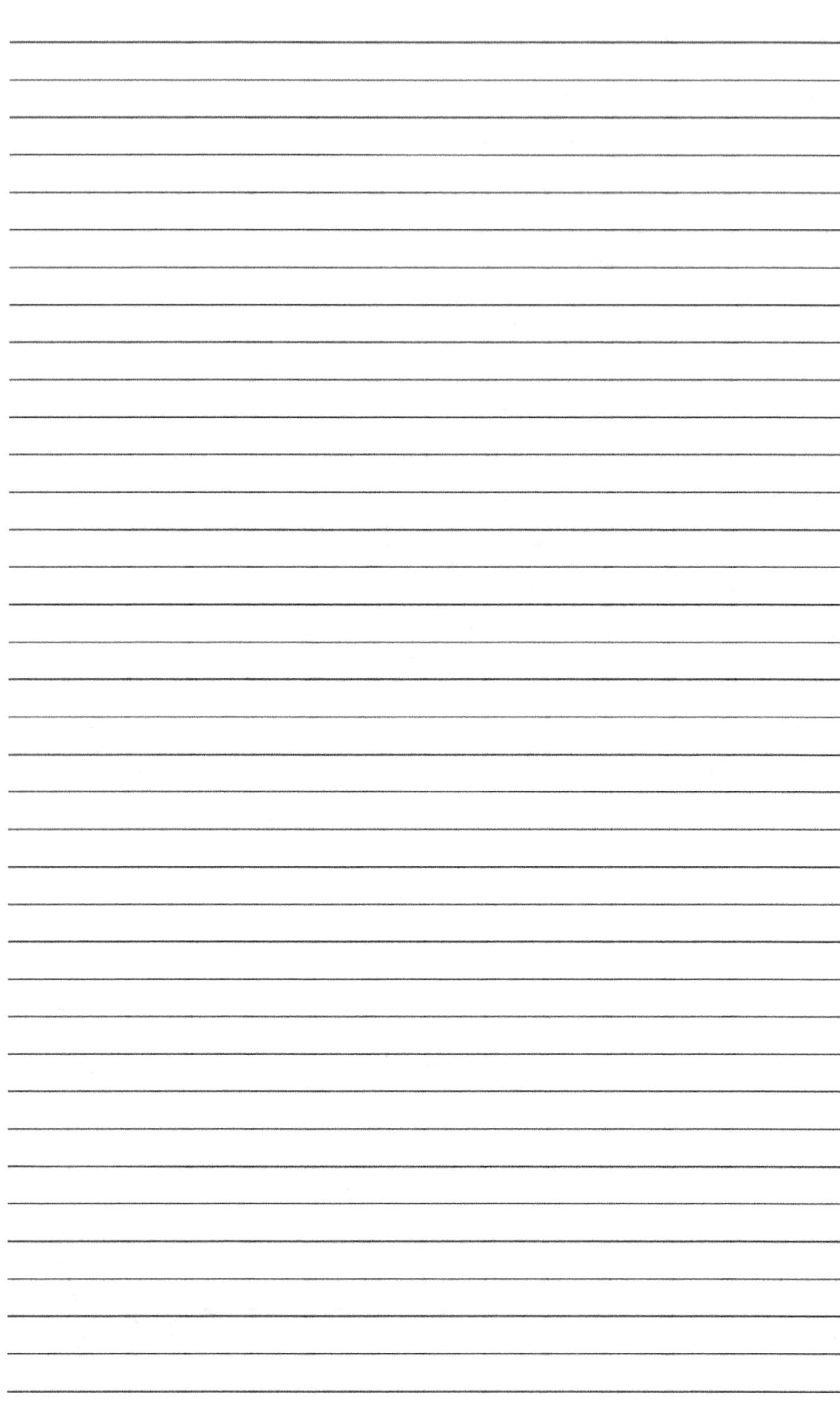

TITLE:

GENRE:

SERIES:

AUTHOR:

PAGES:

STARTED:

FINISHED:

FORMAT READ: EBOOK / PRINT / AUDIOBOOK

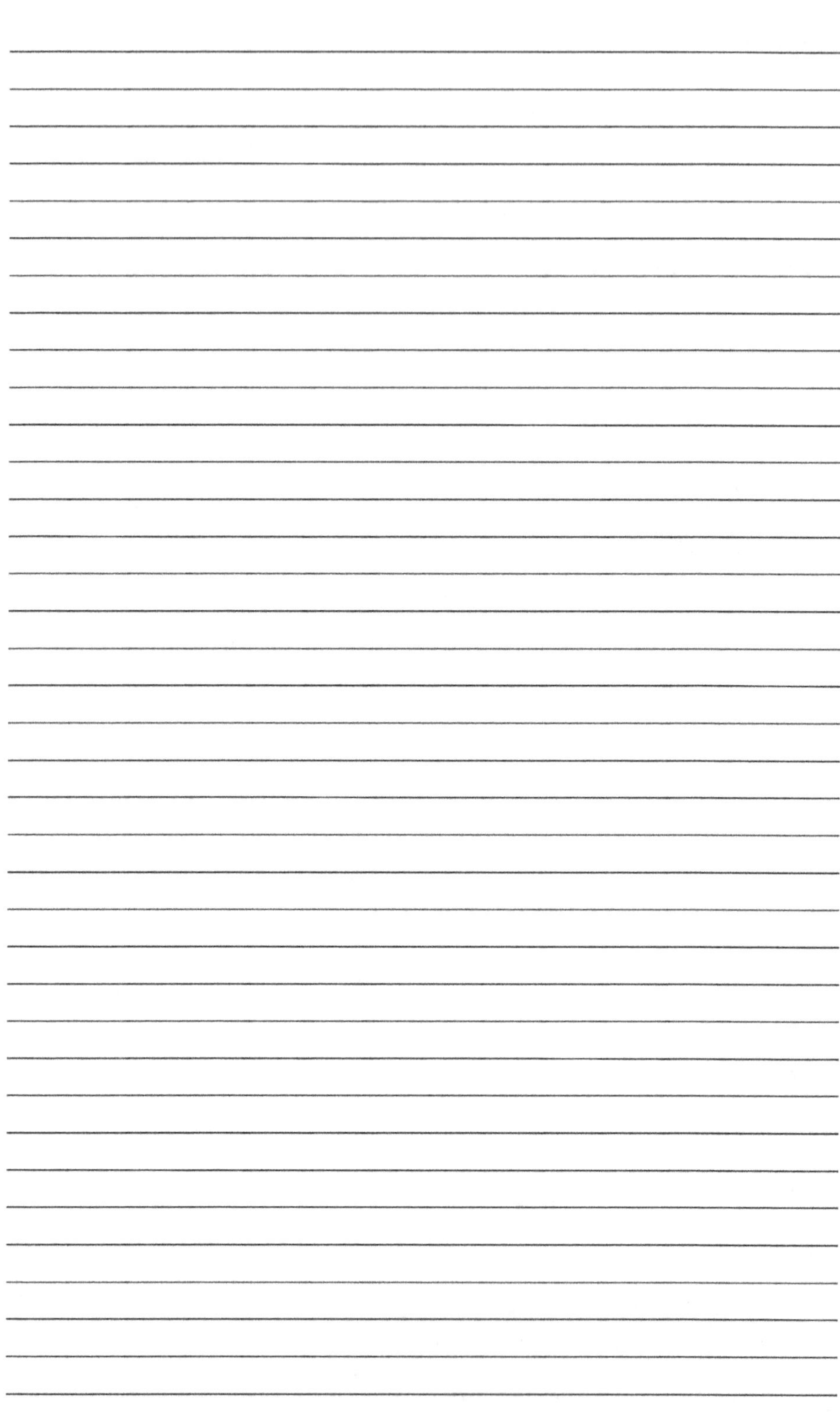

TITLE:

GENRE:

SERIES:

AUTHOR:

PAGES:

STARTED:

FINISHED:

FORMAT READ: EBOOK / PRINT / AUDIOBOOK

✓ SYNOPSIS/THINGS I LIKED:

🚫 THINGS I DIDN'T LIKE:

✏️ FAVORITE QUOTE(S):

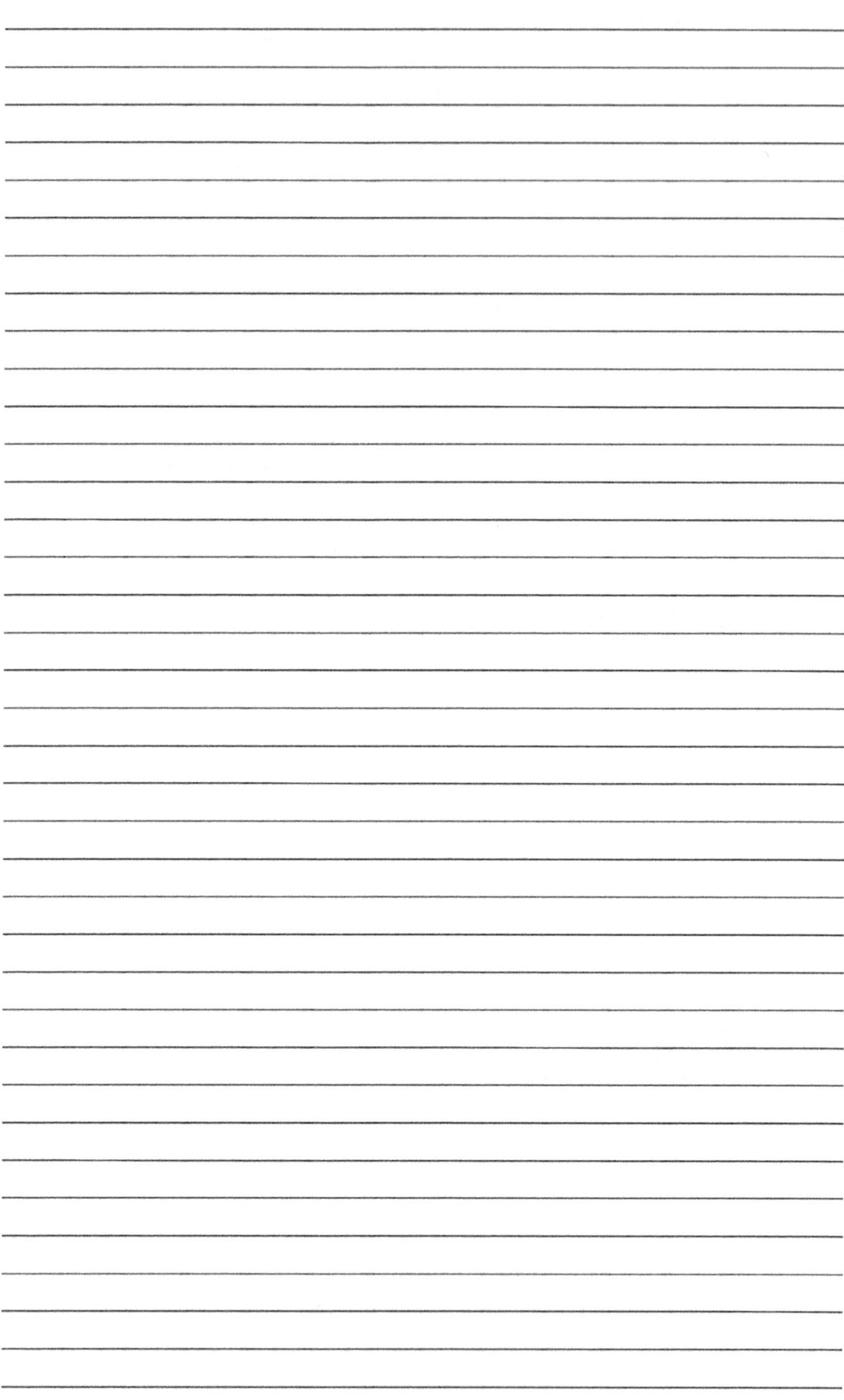

TITLE:

GENRE:

SERIES:

AUTHOR:

PAGES:

STARTED:

FINISHED:

☆ ☆ ☆ ☆ ☆

FORMAT READ: EBOOK / PRINT / AUDIOBOOK

✅ **SYNOPSIS/THINGS I LIKED:**

🚫 **THINGS I DIDN'T LIKE:**

✏️ **FAVORITE QUOTE(S):**

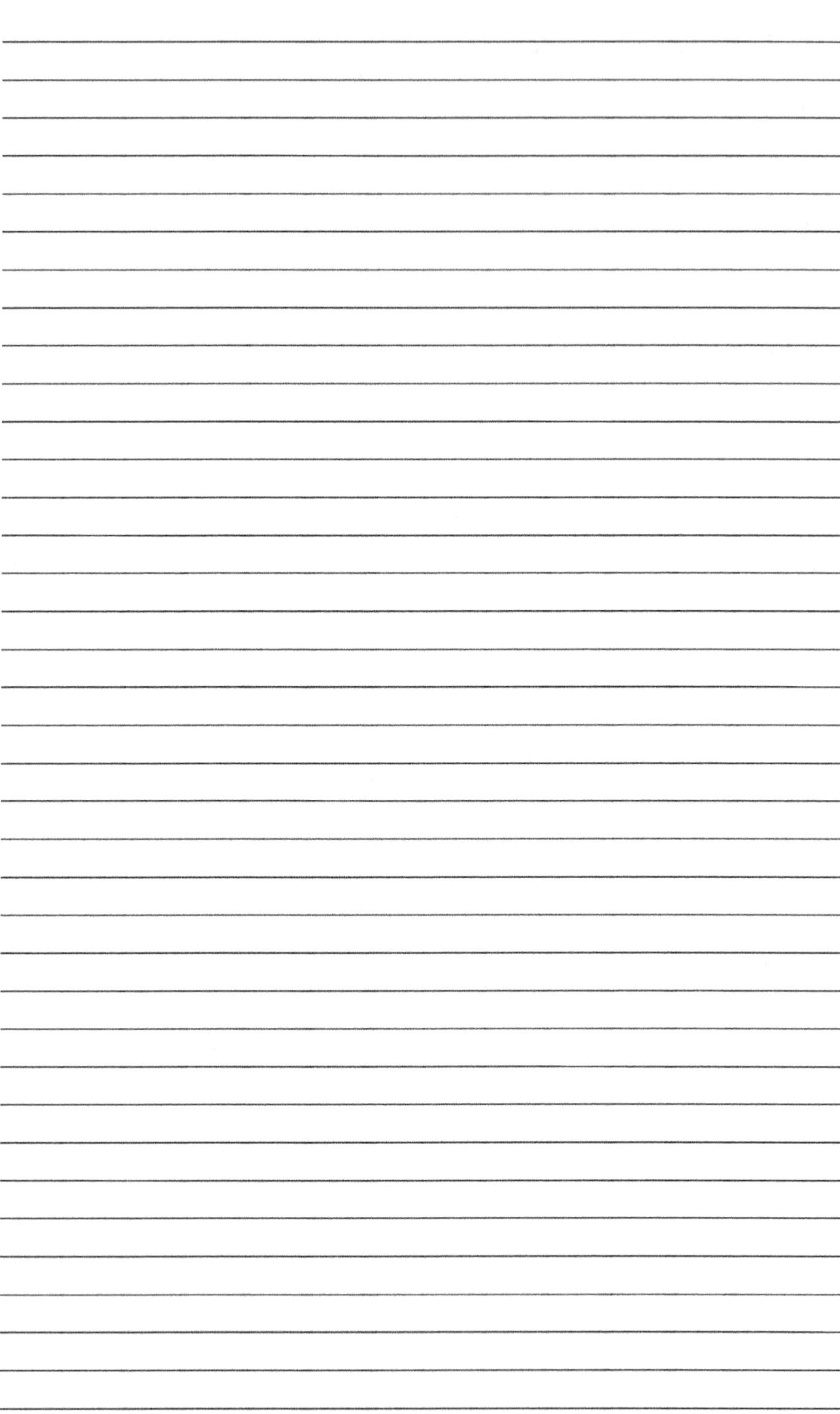

TITLE:

GENRE:

SERIES:

AUTHOR:

PAGES:

STARTED:

FINISHED:

FORMAT READ: EBOOK / PRINT / AUDIOBOOK

SYNOPSIS/THINGS I LIKED:

THINGS I DIDN'T LIKE:

FAVORITE QUOTE(S):

TITLE:

GENRE:

SERIES:

AUTHOR:

PAGES:

STARTED:

FINISHED:

FORMAT READ: EBOOK / PRINT / AUDIOBOOK

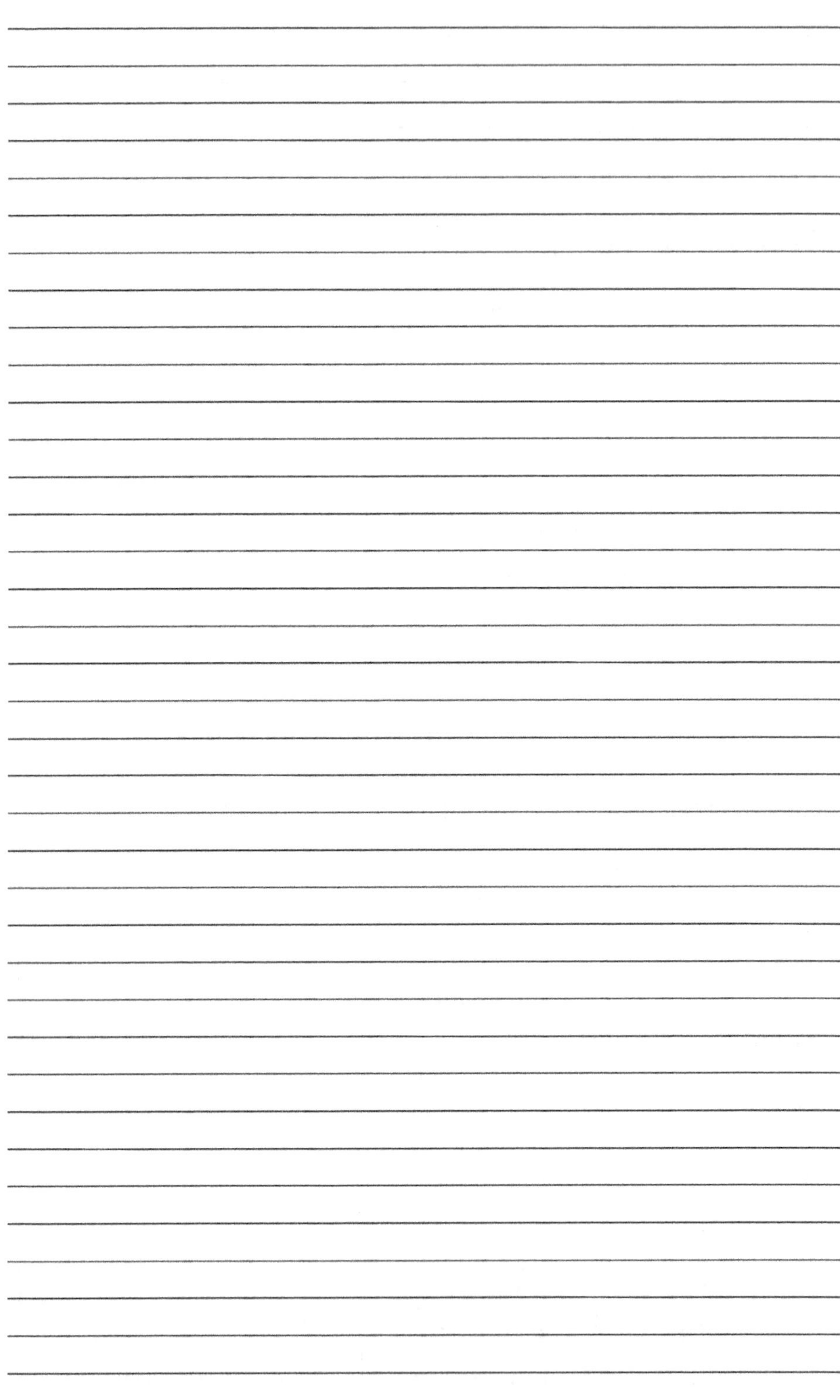

SYNOPSIS/THINGS I LIKED:

THINGS I DIDN'T LIKE:

FAVORITE QUOTE(S):

TITLE:

GENRE:

SERIES:

AUTHOR:

PAGES:

STARTED:

FINISHED:

☆☆☆☆☆

FORMAT READ: EBOOK / PRINT / AUDIOBOOK

✓ SYNOPSIS/THINGS I LIKED:

🚫 THINGS I DIDN'T LIKE:

✎ FAVORITE QUOTE(S):

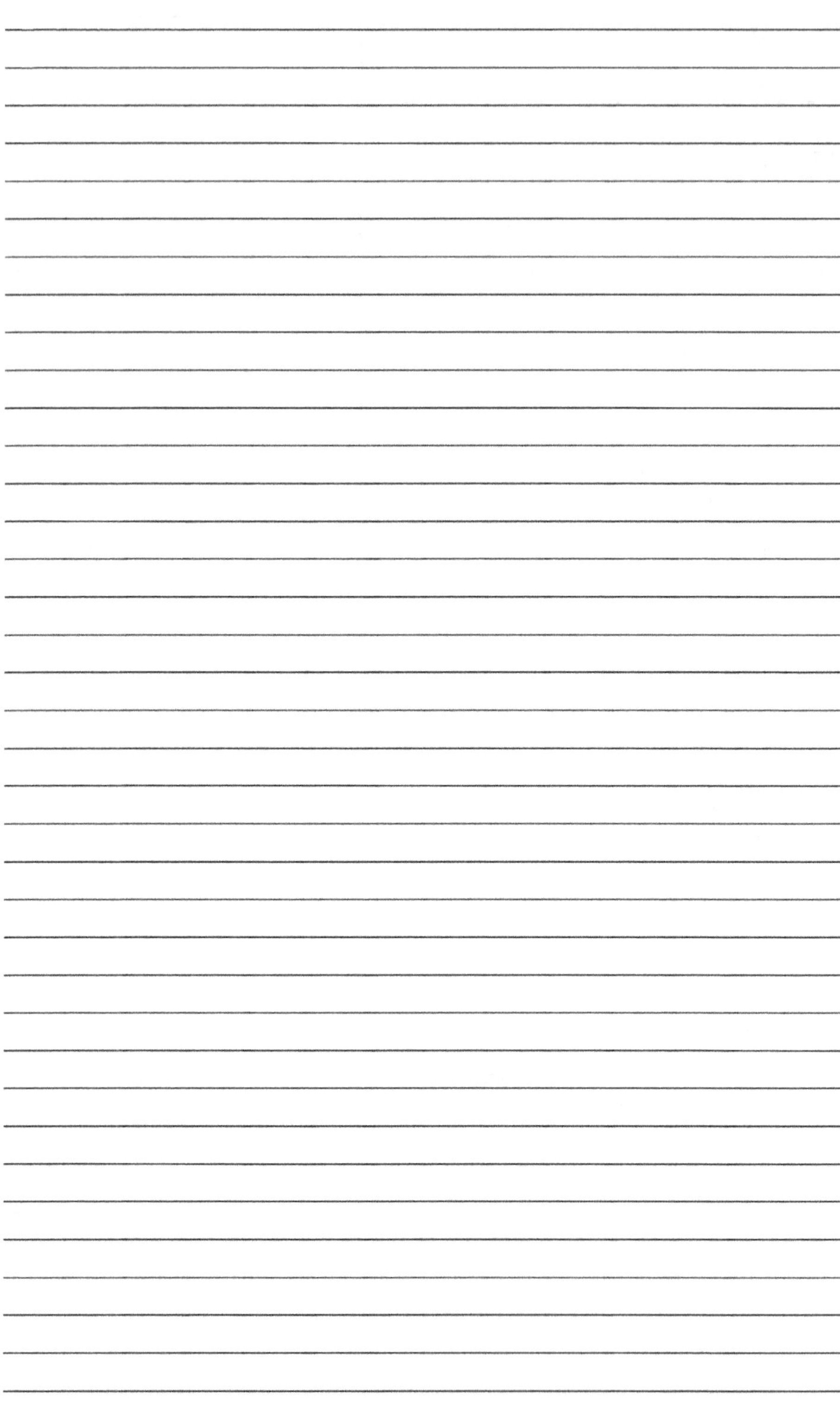

The Dusty DNFs (Did Not Finish)

Title/Progress:

Commentary:

Title/Progress:

Commentary:

Title/Progress:

Commentary:

Title/Progress:

Commentary:

Title/Progress:

Commentary:

Title/Progress:

Commentary:

Title/Progress:

Commentary:

Title/Progress:

Commentary:

Title/Progress:

Commentary:

Title/Progress:

Commentary:

Title/Progress:

Commentary:

Title/Progress:

Commentary:

The Dusty DNFs
(Did Not Finish)

Title/Progress:

Commentary:

Title/Progress:

Commentary:

Title/Progress:

Commentary:

Title/Progress:

Commentary:

Title/Progress:

Commentary:

Title/Progress:

Commentary:

Title/Progress:

Commentary:

Title/Progress:

Commentary:

Title/Progress:

Commentary:

Title/Progress:

Commentary:

Title/Progress:

Commentary:

Title/Progress:

Commentary:

The Dusty DNFs (Did Not Finish)

Title/Progress:

Commentary:

Title/Progress:

Commentary:

Title/Progress:

Commentary:

Title/Progress:

Commentary:

Title/Progress:

Commentary:

Title/Progress:

Commentary:

Title/Progress:

Commentary:

Title/Progress:

Commentary:

Title/Progress:

Commentary:

Title/Progress:

Commentary:

Title/Progress:

Commentary:

The Dusty DNFs (Did Not Finish)

Title/Progress: _______________________________

Commentary: _______________________________

Title/Progress: _______________________________

Commentary: _______________________________

Title/Progress: _______________________________

Commentary: _______________________________

Title/Progress: _______________________________

Commentary: _______________________________

Title/Progress: _______________________________

Commentary: _______________________________

Title/Progress: _______________________________

Commentary: _______________________________

Title/Progress: _______________________________

Commentary: _______________________________

Title/Progress: _______________________________

Commentary: _______________________________

Title/Progress: _______________________________

Commentary: _______________________________

Title/Progress: _______________________________

Commentary: _______________________________

Title/Progress: _______________________________

Commentary: _______________________________

Title/Progress: _______________________________

Commentary: _______________________________

The Dusty DNFs (Did Not Finish)

Title/Progress:

Commentary:

Title/Progress:

Commentary:

Title/Progress:

Commentary:

Title/Progress:

Commentary:

Title/Progress:

Commentary:

Title/Progress:

Commentary:

Title/Progress:

Commentary:

Title/Progress:

Commentary:

Title/Progress:

Commentary:

Title/Progress:

Commentary:

Title/Progress:

Commentary:

Title/Progress:

Commentary:

THE DUSTY DNFS (DID NOT FINISH)

TITLE/PROGRESS:

COMMENTARY:

TITLE/PROGRESS:

COMMENTARY:

TITLE/PROGRESS:

COMMENTARY:

TITLE/PROGRESS:

COMMENTARY:

TITLE/PROGRESS:

COMMENTARY:

TITLE/PROGRESS:

COMMENTARY:

TITLE/PROGRESS:

COMMENTARY:

TITLE/PROGRESS:

COMMENTARY:

TITLE/PROGRESS:

COMMENTARY:

TITLE/PROGRESS:

COMMENTARY:

TITLE/PROGRESS:

COMMENTARY:

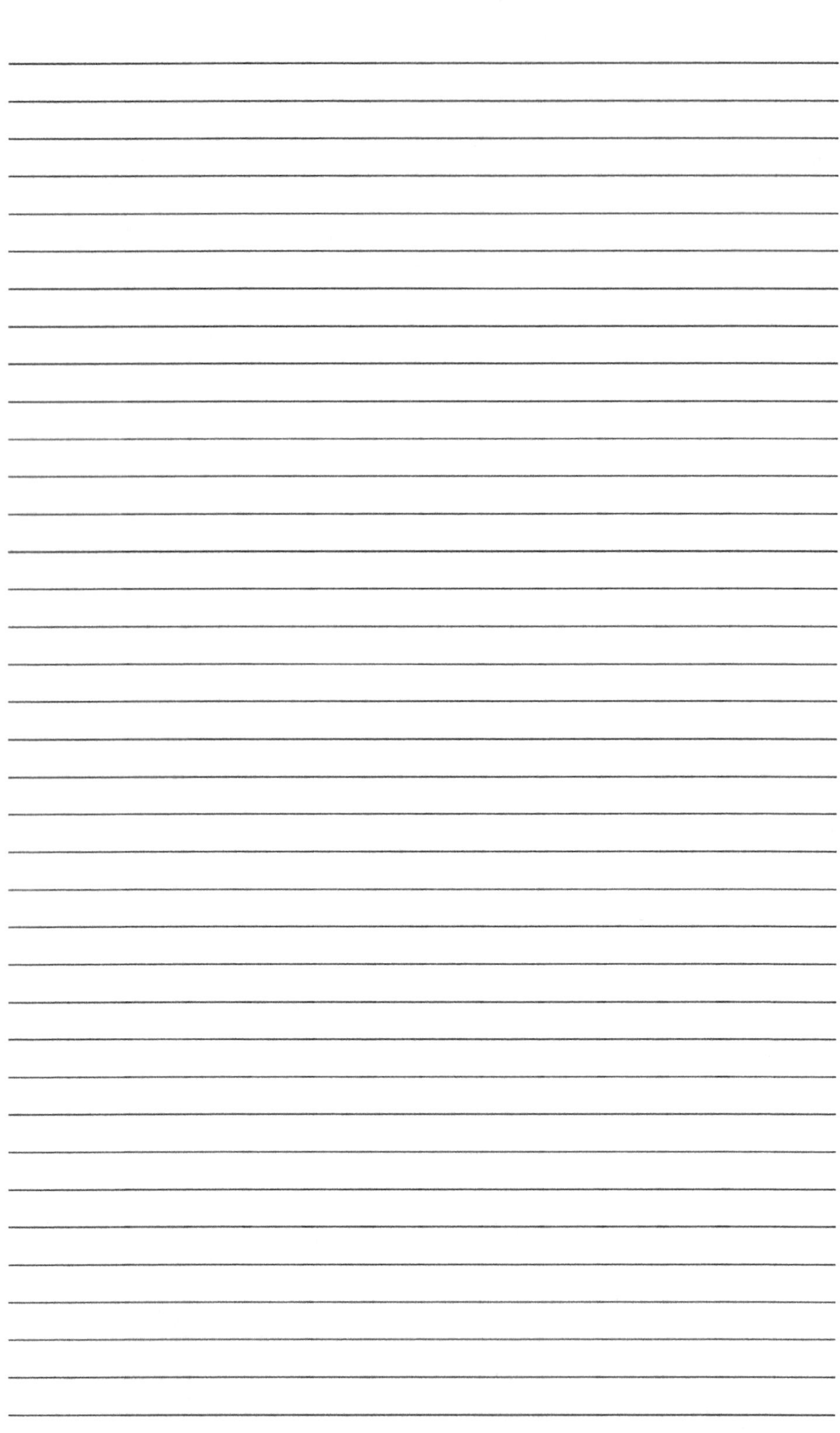

Refills & Book Recommendations

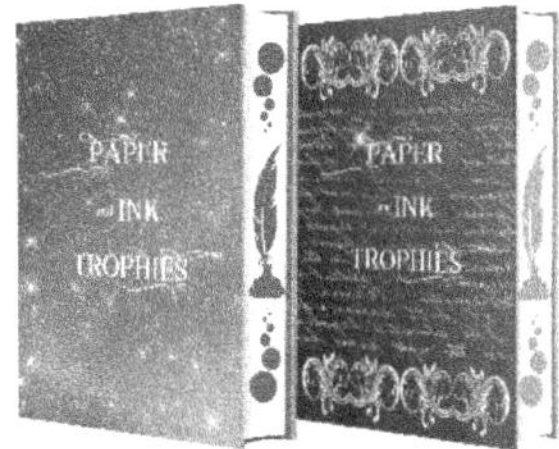

Pick up your next volume now!

Paper and Ink Trophies, *Gems & Genres*. & *Titles & Treasures* are similar premium book journals also offered by Painted Wings Publishing. They each accommodate entries for 250 books and have individual aesthetic touches.

THE SEEDER WARS TRILOGY

THE HEIR'S DUOLOGY

Seeder Wars is a Young Adult Contemporary Romantic Fantasy series featuring unique magic, botanical beings, spies, & assassins. The series starts with a central trilogy and expands to a spin-off duology (& more on the way!)

Magic in the Match is a series of standalone Adult Fairy Tale Sweet Romances.

Magic in the Match
Fairy Tale Romances

For more information, go to
JHouserWrites.com!